DEADLY ECHOES

Also by Philip Donlay

The Donovan Nash Series

Pegasus Down
Aftershock
Zero Separation
Code Black
Category Five

DEADLY ECHOES

A Novel

Philip Donlay

Oceanview Publishing

LONGBOAT KEY, FLORIDA

ISBN: 978-1-60809-182-9

Published in the United States of America by Oceanview Publishing, Longboat Key, Florida

www.oceanviewpub.com

10 9 8 7 6 5 4 3 2

PRINTED IN THE UNITED STATES OF AMERICA

For Kerry
You inspire me—

Acknowledgments

This book would not have been possible without the skilled law enforcement professionals around the world whose tireless work and dedication help keep our nation safe. Special thanks goes out to the United States Coast Guard, as well as the Federal Bureau of Investigation.

For their patience, friendship, and insight, I offer a heartfelt thanks to Rebecca Norgaard Peterson, Scott Erickson, Bo Lewis, Gary Kaelson, and Brian Bellmont. You've played a bigger part in all of this than you'll ever know. For always giving me the unvarnished truth in a way that inevitably makes the stories better, Glenna Rossiter, Jonathan Mischkot, Kimberley Cameron, my brother, Chris; my parents, Cliff and Janet; and my son, Patrick. You're an indispensible group of gifted people, thank you for keeping me on course.

A special thanks goes out to Dr. Philip Sidell, Dr. D. P. Lyle, and Dr. Paul F. Bruer for their remarkable medical expertise. As always, I'm most appreciative on many levels. A very special thanks goes to fellow creative souls, Richard S. Drury and Pamela Sue Martin. You encourage me to keep the faith, continue writing, and along the way always manage to teach me something.

I'd also like to thank dear friends and experts of all things nautical, Amanda and Joseph Dayton. For specialized knowledge about a myriad of subjects, thanks go to Margaret Buchanan, Laurie Savage, Arlene Chafe, and Braden Lusk. I'm the first to admit that I couldn't have written this story without you. All of you have my eternal gratitude.

Finally, to the people who turn words into books. Thank you to my literary agency, Kimberley Cameron & Associates, you're the best. Utmost praise also goes to my publisher: Patricia and Bob Gussin, Frank Troncale, David Ivester, Emily Baar, and Susan Hayes. You believed in this project, brought it life, and along the way, made it a better book. Thank you, Oceanview Publishing, there isn't a better team anywhere.

DEADLY ECHOES

PROLOGUE

The Zodiac maneuvered quietly in the darkness, riding the mild swells of the Pacific Ocean. The sky was moonless, a perfect night for killing. The man in charge watched the *Kaiyo Maru #7* through binoculars. The garish lights from the fishing vessel lit up the ocean, illuminating the screeching, circling ocean birds that wheeled above the carnage. The six-person team was dressed in black, each carrying an assortment of weapons. They motored confidently toward the larger ship, the stench of dead fish stronger as they drew near. The sound of the powerful winch hauling the ship's catch helped mask the Zodiac's approach. The leader focused his binoculars on the fisherman tending the long-line. The main cable ran for miles with monofilament line tied to a razor-sharp hook at one-hundred-foot intervals.

He watched with growing revulsion as each hook was stripped of its prize. The line had been set to run shallow, which also allowed for the indiscriminate catch of diving birds and sea turtles, their lifeless carcasses tossed back into the ocean. But most of the hooks held the fishermen's target catch: sharks. They ranged from four to seven feet in length. Each shark was hauled aboard where every fin was expertly sliced off. Spewing blood, the shark was then thrown back into the water, still alive. The sharks could no longer swim so they sank. The lucky ones would quickly bleed to death, or drown, since sharks need to stay in constant forward motion for water to flow over their gills. Others would linger for days as they died of starvation. He'd seen footage of the butchery before, they

all had, but to see it firsthand was like touching a match to the dry
tinder of his outrage.

Using hand signals, he instructed his man to bring the Zodiac
around, careful not to create a telltale wake. They motored in a
slow arc until they were directly in the path of the *Kaiyo Maru #7*
then waited. As the one-hundred-sixty-foot vessel drew close, they
matched the Zodiac to the speed of the ship and using rubberized
grappling hooks, looped lines over the forward section of the hull.
Once secured, five members of the team quietly boarded the ship
leaving one man behind with the Zodiac.

Two of them hurried through a watertight hatch and disappeared into the superstructure; their job was to go below decks, secure the engine room, and then round up the crew below. Guns at
the ready, the leader, flanked on either side by the remaining two
members of his team, moved undetected toward the bridge. The
captain was alone at the helm, leaning over a chart. At the popping
sound of gunshots coming from below, he turned his attention to
the instruments, as if searching for a mechanical reason for the unexpected noises. The three intruders burst through the hatch, guns
raised. The man on the left spoke Japanese and ordered the captain
to put his hands on his head. He emphasized his words by jamming
the barrel of his machine gun into the soft skin under the captain's
chin. The captain immediately complied.

The leader gestured for the prisoner to step away from the controls. He knew that the fishermen would be no match for his skilled
team. One by one, the reports from below confirmed that the crew
had been rounded up and that the captured sailors were secured at
gunpoint on the main deck. The leader glanced at his watch. Less
than fifteen minutes after boarding, the ship and crew were his.

The leader pulled off his ski mask and ran his hand through
his longish gray hair. He was tall, over six feet, but alarmingly thin.
He may have been handsome once, but deep scarring marred his
face and neck. It looked as if the skin around his eyes had been
melted, and when he blinked, it appeared to take a great deal of effort. The person on his right followed suit, and the mask slipped

off, revealing perfect olive skin accented by short spiky black hair. The woman was more striking than beautiful, green eyes radiated both self-assurance and intelligence. She was five foot seven, muscular like an athlete, yet slender. She smiled in a subtle way that implied that she was in control of her surroundings, confident that no matter the conflict, victory would be hers.

"Ask them how many in his crew." The leader ordered his translator, who had elected to keep his mask on.

A flurry of Japanese was initiated by the man who still held his gun to the captain's chin. The captain grunted a reply, his eyes wide with fear.

"He says there are twenty-one men plus himself."

The leader raised the walkie-talkie to his mouth. "How many prisoners do you have?"

"We've got nineteen on deck. Two were killed and left below."

"That's everyone. Start filming. Make the crew finish reeling in the line, only be sure to release each fish. Pay particular attention to anything that comes up dead. Get it all."

"Yes, sir."

He turned to his translator. "Take the captain down on deck. We'll be there in a minute."

Once the bridge was theirs, he set down his machine gun and began to punch buttons on the navigation unit. It took him several minutes, but he finally programmed the autopilot to guide the ship on the course he'd chosen. After he double-checked the plot, he adjusted the ship's speed and then made a discreet radio call to his own vessel to come and retrieve the team. The one-hundred-sixty-foot megayacht *Triton* was standing by just out of radar range and would be alongside in less than thirty minutes.

"How long will it take them to find this boat once we leave?" the woman asked.

"I set their speed for ten knots. Left undisturbed, they should arrive near land in a little over two days. We'll be long gone before anything we've done is discovered."

The walkie-talkie sprang to life, and his men down on the main deck reported that the last of the long line had been reeled in and all the fish released.

"We're on our way down," the leader replied, pulling his mask back over his head and carefully adjusting the material until the slits fit perfectly around his damaged eyes.

The woman replaced her mask then removed a small handheld video camera from her rucksack.

They both hurried down the gangway to the killing floor of the fishing vessel. The leader knelt down and picked up one of the knives the fishermen had been using to fin the sharks. It was a simple knife with an unremarkable wooden handle, but it would do the job. He glanced at the woman, she nodded and began recording. Two of his men grabbed the captain, the third man held an automatic weapon on the frightened crew. With a man on each side, the captain's arms were stretched away from his body. Despite his violent struggles, the leader used the knife to cut away the captain's shirt until the man was naked from the waist up. An expression of horror mixed with disbelief contorted his face. He began to moan and shake his head back and forth as they pulled a plastic wrap snug around his ankles.

This night had been twenty years in the making, and though it only represented the beginning, the leader knew he was about to taste the sweetness of revenge. He made a show of testing the sharpness of the blade on his thumb and then smiled as he moved toward the sobbing fisherman. As the knife parted flesh, he ignored the screams and felt an upwelling of elation. Everything was now set in motion.

CHAPTER ONE

At the sound of his phone, Donovan Nash was instantly awake. The caller ID told him the number was restricted and that it was 3:42 in the morning. He braced himself; nothing good ever came of a call at this hour. "Donovan Nash."

"Donovan Nash," a strained, raspy voice repeated. "I was hoping to speak to Robert Huntington."

Donovan sat up in bed. *Robert Huntington* was a name he hadn't used in over twenty years. A name only a handful of people knew—the man on the phone wasn't one of them. "Who is this?"

"All you need to understand is that I know who and what you are. This is your wake-up call to let you know I'm going to destroy everything that's important to you."

"Don't threaten me." Donovan threw off his covers and launched himself out of bed, adrenaline pumping. He opened the drawer to the bedside table and grabbed his gun, went to the bedroom window, and peered at the street and driveway below. He saw no vehicles outside. Everything looked normal.

"Think of it as less of a threat and more of a promise. I can also assure you it will be a slow and painful destruction. Go to YouTube and find: *shark payback*. I'll be in touch, Robert."

Donovan could hear the deathly silence as the call ended. *I'm going to destroy everything that's important to you.* The words replayed over and over in his head, and he appreciated the weight of the pistol in his hand.

He threw on pants and a sweatshirt but not before his eyes shot to the ugly scar that ran across his right thigh and the matching one on his right wrist. All products of a murderer armed with a knife. It had been seven months since he'd been attacked. The physical wounds of that night had mostly healed, but the scars were a constant reminder of what could happen if he let his guard down. With the pistol in hand, he slipped downstairs.

The house was nearly silent, only the soft hum from the refrigerator reached his ears. He thought of his wife and young daughter and for once was happy they weren't here. Seven months ago Lauren had packed up Abigail and moved to Europe to get away from him. He'd tried to spin it any number of ways, but in the end it always came back to the simple truth. Lauren didn't want to be with him—in fact she needed to be on another continent to feel comfortable. He missed his daughter terribly. They spoke often, and video-chatted nearly every day. He was thankful that his absence hadn't seemed to dampen Abigail's enthusiasm for life. He knew Lauren still loved him, but she didn't want to live with him, nor did she want to be entirely without him. They were at an impasse, and he'd reached a sort of uneasy peace with the situation.

Donovan double-checked the alarm system and then went into the study, closed the drapes, and sat down at the computer. It didn't take long to find the *shark payback* video. He clicked on the play icon and noted that it had already been viewed one hundred eighty-three times. He could tell at once this was an amateur video shot at night on a ship. The handheld image jumped and swayed, but the subject was unmistakable. Men wearing masks were pulling in a long line, except they were releasing the fish impaled on each hook instead of keeping them. Occasionally a dead turtle or ocean bird was hauled in and tossed onto the deck where it was closely photographed. A man dressed in black, holding a machine gun walked into view, and it was then Donovan understood. Someone had boarded a fishing vessel and stopped the fishing. The camera did a long, slow shot of the bloodstained deck, the plastic tubs filled with severed shark fins. Next, a container of fish that were still alive, gills opening and closing, straining, bodies flopping helplessly. Donovan knew this was what the industry called by-catch, fish that were cut into pieces to bait the thousands of hooks.

The homemade video panned upward and then zoomed in and focused on a lone fisherman. Shirtless, he was held so that his arms were outstretched, his ankles bound together. Moaning, and clearly terrified, he struggled in vain to get free. A single man came into the field of view and with little fanfare raised his knife and then the picture went black, but the audio recorded screams of agony. A simple web address flashed on the screen. Donovan quickly typed it into his browser and started the separate video. Without the constraints of YouTube, every horrific detail filled the screen.

Donovan watched as the fisherman's detached arms were thrown into a plastic tub with the shark fins, and still alive and screaming, he was tossed overboard. The camera followed the doomed fisherman as he tried desperately to remain afloat but slowly sank from view. Still trained on the ocean, a Zodiac flashed past the camera. Shocked, Donovan instantly backed up the image and then froze the playback. Painted on the side of the rigid inflatable boat was the unmistakable gold logo and blue letters of Eco-Watch, the scientific research organization that Donovan had founded ten years ago.

Donovan let the video play to the end, to a message in bold print that nearly forty million sharks are killed each year to feed Asia's market for shark fin soup. The view counter showed that over two thousand people had watched already. Donovan jumped back to YouTube and glanced at the early postings. The first two were riddled with poor grammar and typos; they congratulated Eco-Watch on killing the bastards. Then there were four more that labeled Eco-Watch a band of assassins and called for the arrest and immediate execution of every member of Eco-Watch responsible.

The shrill sound from the telephone on the desk startled him. It was a secure line installed by the Defense Intelligence Agency. Before she'd left, Lauren had worked part time for the DIA. She'd graduated with a Ph.D. from MIT in Earth Science and had gone to work for the government. In all the months since she'd left, that phone hadn't rung once.

"Donovan Nash."

"Donovan, it's William. Sorry to wake you, but we need to talk."

William VanGelder had raised him since he was fourteen years old. William had made a fortune in the oil business with Donovan's late father, and in turn had amassed a vast fortune in both money and power since then. Nearing seventy-five years of age, William showed no signs of slowing down. He was still an active member of Washington's political elite, a behind-the-scenes power broker with a long-held position within the State Department as an ambassador at large.

"You didn't wake me," Donovan replied. "Why are you calling on this phone?"

"We have a problem and we need to make some decisions."

"I'm listening."

"I just got a phone call from a nearly hysterical Beverly Stratton."

"Wait. John's wife?"

"Yes. She'd just been informed that her husband's yacht had run aground in Hawaii. All aboard had been murdered, including John."

"Oh, no." Donovan felt all the air leave his body. John Stratton had been one of William's closest friends, and by default, one of Donovan's. John and William had gone to Harvard Law together. John had built a conglomerate of companies through a successful career as a venture capitalist. Always a major supporter of environmental groups, including Eco-Watch, John's kindness and enthusiasm had a great deal to do with turning Eco-Watch into one of the premier privately funded scientific organizations in the world. Donovan owed the savvy venture capitalist a great deal. John's megayacht, christened *Triton*, was his passion, and he and his crew were experienced and cautious seaman. Nothing about this made any sense.

"We don't know much, but Beverly gave me a heads-up on one development. It's the reason I called on the secure line." William stopped as if collecting himself for a moment. "There's a closed-circuit camera system on his boat, you know how John loved his gadgets. The Coast Guard played back the last images stored on the hard drive and found that whoever boarded the *Triton* were welcomed with open arms because they arrived in an Eco-Watch Zodiac."

"Did they get a good look at them?"

"Not really. The FBI is investigating, but the security system was disabled shortly afterward."

"I got a phone call this morning too," Donovan said. "It's why I was already up. Someone, a man I didn't recognize, called and asked for Robert Huntington. He told me he knew who I was and that he was going to destroy everything that was important to me."

"Do you think it's connected to what happened to John?"

"Absolutely. Go to YouTube and search for *shark payback*. You'll see what I mean. After you do that, pack a bag and get to the Eco-Watch hangar. We're going to Hawaii. What island did John's ship run aground?"

"Kauai."

"Okay, we'll fly to Lihue Airport. Do we need to swing by John Wayne Airport and pick up Beverly?"

"She told me she was making arrangements to use one of her husband's company aircraft."

"If that's the case, then she'll get there before we do." Donovan felt the adrenaline rush of starting things in motion. "I'll make all the arrangements. Let's try and be wheels up no later than zero six thirty."

"I'll see you at the hangar."

Donovan hung up, snatched his pistol, and hurried into the kitchen to make coffee, taking care to close all of the drapes and curtains in the house. Before the phone call this morning only seven people in the world knew that Robert Huntington was still alive. It was a secret that had remained hidden from the public for over twenty years, and Donovan would go to almost any length to make sure it remained that way. Failure would result in the whole-sale destruction of everything he'd built. Eco-Watch might survive at this point, but it would have to go on without him. There were treasured friendships he'd forged under false pretenses that would immediately alter and more than likely end badly. It was a lie he owned, and it, in turn, owned him. Everything he held dear was dependent on the perpetuation of the lie. Exposed, he became Robert Huntington, one of the most despised men in the world. He poured a cup of coffee and speed-dialed his assistant, Peggy, on his cell phone.

"Peggy. It's Donovan. Sorry for the early hour, but there's an emergency."

"I'm awake," she said in a sleep-filled voice that didn't match her words. "What can I do?"

"John Stratton has been murdered. I need the *da Vinci* readied for a trip to Kauai." Donovan had named all of Eco-Watch's aircraft after famous men in the history of science. "Call Michael and Buck, I want to be wheels up by zero six thirty."

"That's awful news. I always liked John." Peggy sounded gen-uinely upset. "I'll make the calls and get everything moving."

"There's also a YouTube video called *shark payback* you need to watch. Once you do, pull the file for the public relations firm we have on retainer as well as our attorneys. This could get ugly in a hurry."

"Got it," Peggy replied, now fully awake. "I'll see you at the hangar."

He topped off his coffee, snatched the pistol, and hurried back to the study. He refreshed the *shark payback* web page and saw that there were now 4,317 hits. He scrolled forward until the Eco-Watch Zodiac came into view. He froze the image and stared. John was dead, which combined with the phone call, meant that whoever was after him knew a great deal about Eco-Watch and had already killed John Stratton, which meant everyone in his world was at risk. Lauren was in France with their daughter. A similar situation seven months ago had driven her off in the first place, and he had to warn her now. It was nine thirty in the morning there. He picked up his phone and dialed, and as it rang, he looked at the pistol he'd carefully laid on the desk and wondered if the day would ever come where he didn't feel the need to be armed.

CHAPTER TWO

Dr. Lauren McKenna recognized the number on her phone and frowned. She was on the balcony having a quiet morning tea with Stephanie VanGelder, a dear friend visiting from London. Lauren's daughter, Abigail, was at the park with the nanny and Henri, her head of security. She and Stephanie were in the process of planning their day.

Stephanie reacted to Lauren's expression. "Who's calling?"

"It's Donovan calling from a secure phone. This can't be good."

Stephanie looked at her watch and frowned. "It's four thirty in the morning there."

Lauren, too, had done the math. She braced herself and put the phone to her ear. "Hello."

"Hey, it's me," Donovan said.

"I'm here with Stephanie." Lauren didn't want to have a prolonged conversation in front of Stephanie. As the niece of William VanGelder, Stephanie had known Donovan since he was a boy. She knew the truth about all of the secrets, making her one of the few people that Lauren could confide in totally. Over the years the two women had grown into close friends, and Stephanie had supported her decision to leave Donovan. Deep down, Lauren understood Stephanie loved them both, but if she had to choose, she'd pick Donovan.

"Stephanie's there?"

"She came in from London for a few days. Can I can call you later?"

"I'm sorry to bother you, but we might have a problem. This involves her too," Donovan said. "Some unknown person called me this morning and referred to me as Robert Huntington. He said he knew the truth and was going to destroy everything important to me. It's not a bluff, it's already started."

"What do you mean?" Lauren felt the first tingle of impending danger gnaw at her nerves.

"Do you remember John and Beverly Stratton? They're old friends of William. They live in Laguna Beach."

"I remember the Strattons. They were at our wedding." Lauren saw Stephanie nod that she knew them. "Stephanie remembers them as well. What's happened?"

"John's boat ran aground in Hawaii. He and his crew were found murdered."

"That's terrible. How is that even possible? Was his wife with him?"

"No. She's in California. Security tape showed the killers boarded John's yacht by using an Eco-Watch Zodiac. The guy that called this morning with the threat told me about a YouTube video entitled *shark payback*. I'll warn you, it's gruesome, and it, too, involves an Eco-Watch Zodiac."

"So you think we're in some kind of danger?"

"We have no idea who these people are, but they've already killed. I think we're all at risk, Stephanie included, and we should act accordingly."

"I already have around-the-clock security, so I think we're safe for the time being."

"I understand. But I needed to pass along the information, to be on the safe side. Please, just be alert."

"We'll be careful."

"Tell Stephanie hello and be sure and tell Abigail I called. I'll keep you posted."

Lauren severed the connection and set the phone down. She noticed that her hands were shaking and folded them in her lap.

"Start from the beginning," Stephanie demanded. "There was more to that call than John Stratton being murdered."

"Let's go inside," Lauren said, gathering up the tray and carrying it inside the luxurious apartment. Located near the center of Paris, the flat had been her refuge since she'd left Donovan. The residence was courtesy of Aaron Keller, a senior official at Mossad, Israel's equivalent to the United States Central Intelligence Agency. The security protection was payment for Lauren's unofficial help in finding and stopping a terrorist who was deemed a major threat to both Israel and the United States. The group behind the attempted attack was eliminated, but Mossad wasn't 100 percent certain that the threat to Lauren had died with those men. At times Lauren hated the presence of bodyguards, but now it seemed even more necessary than ever.

"What's happened?" Stephanie asked.

"First, we need to get to a computer and watch a video," Lauren said "Then I'll tell you everything I know."

Lauren led Stephanie to the spacious master suite where Lauren's laptop was set up on a desk. Both women huddled close as Lauren's fingers flew over her keyboard to bring up YouTube. They stood in silence as the video began. When the link to the other website was established, they both flinched at the graphic images and then watched the appearance of the Eco-Watch Zodiac. When it was over, the scientist in Lauren replayed the video while Stephanie turned away.

"That was awful, how can you watch it again?" Stephanie said.

"Scientific observation is rarely accomplished by looking at something once." Lauren sat and watched the video three more times before she leaned in and froze one of the images. She opened the search engine, and brought up a page of various images of actual Eco-Watch Zodiacs. She arranged them on the screen next to the Zodiac in the shark video. "Like this."

Stephanie turned to look at the screen. "What am I looking for?"

"Look at the outboard motors," Lauren said. "Donovan likes Mercury Marine. Every Zodiac in the Eco-Watch fleet is equipped with twin Mercury outboards. Now, I don't know Mercury from any other outboard, but the motors in these two pictures look different."

"You're right. They're not the same. The Eco-Watch engine is taller and thinner. The other one is counterfeit. But we knew that already."

"We did," Lauren refreshed the YouTube page. "But the 245,852 people who've watched this video have no idea. They think Eco-Watch did this."

Lauren clicked away from YouTube. "I need to forward this information to Peggy at Eco-Watch. It's something the lawyers and the public relations people need to see."

"What about the other things Donovan told you?" Stephanie asked then looked around the room. "You don't think the apartment is bugged, do you? We can talk about anything, right?"

"We're good. Officially, I'm still an analyst for the Defense Intelligence Agency so my friends at the CIA drop by and sweep the place regularly."

"The CIA? You're a meteorological analyst for the DIA—you predict weather."

"From time to time I do a little more than that," Lauren replied. "Anyway, this morning a man Donovan didn't recognize called and asked for Robert Huntington. He said he knew who Donovan was and that he was going to destroy everything that was important to him. Then the caller told him where to find the YouTube video."

"And John Stratton's death is a part of this?"

"The killers used an Eco-Watch Zodiac to gain access to John's yacht. They waited until the yacht had been found to post the video and call Donovan. Everything's got to be connected."

"Their first mistake was warning him they were coming for him," Stephanie said. "We both know how he is right now. He's going after these people, right?"

Lauren nodded. "When does all of this stop? I want things to even out, so he and I can maybe find some firmer ground. Death threats and bodyguards is no way to live."

"Maybe this is exactly what he needs in terms of finding some focus."

"What do you mean?" Lauren was taken aback. Stephanie wasn't usually so direct. Her upbringing was such that she defaulted to diplomacy and tact, like her uncle.

"I'm saying that Donovan has been more than a little lost since you left. He recovered from his physical injuries, but emotionally he was pretty messed up before you left, and he's not any better now—how could he be?"

"He seems better," Lauren said, but she knew the words sounded hollow.

"It's okay. I'm not trying to make you feel bad. We both know that Donovan eventually does something with his turmoil and anger. He channels it into something useful. I mean, look at everything he's accomplished in his life. After his parents died, he made Huntington Oil into a global force from what had been a regional family-owned company. Then he lost Meredith and fell apart. From that despair sprang the idea of faking his own death, changing his entire life, including his appearance, and then using his fortune to help others. He built Eco-Watch into a first-class nonprofit scientific research foundation, one of the best in the world. That's what he needs right now—to feel that need for focus, for action. Once he does, things usually start happening."

Lauren admired the passion Stephanie had displayed, and loved her for it, even though she remained skeptical of her husband's ability to deal with even more stress. "I know he's done those things. He's one of the most capable men I've ever met. That's the problem. He does *things* instead of dealing with *issues*. It's why we're not together. He hides from his past, from everything really, including me."

"I understand why you feel the way you do, and I'm not choosing sides. You know I love you both. I've been around Donovan since he was a kid, seen what he's been through, and at times I've wondered how he can function at all. Let him do what he does, but please, whatever you do, don't give up on him—it would be the worst thing possible. He's about to get back into a game he does better than anyone, and it's going to do wonders for his state of mind. He'll fix this. All I ask is for you to hang in there until this is over."

"I hope you're right, but I'm afraid for him. He doesn't need this right now. We both know that when he's threatened, he's reckless. If something happens to him, then all of our waiting and trying to figure out who we are to each other is gone—lost forever."

CHAPTER THREE

The Eco-Watch Gulfstream 500 had already covered four thousand miles, and Donovan and his team were about to start their initial descent into the Lihue Airport on the island of Kauai. The nine-hour-and-fifteen-minute flight from Eco-Watch's headquarters at Washington's Dulles Airport had been a blur of activity.

The Gulfstream 500 was only two months old. Donovan had christened the aircraft *The Spirit of da Vinci*, after its predecessor. In the cockpit was Michael Ross, Donovan's closest friend and Eco-Watch chief pilot. Michael was captain for this flight, and Donovan acted as co-captain, splitting his time between his flying duties and the activity in the back of the plane.

"Michael," Donovan poked his head into the cockpit, "I need a little more time back here, are you still good?"

"Yeah, we've got another twenty minutes before we start down."

"Thanks, I'll be back in fifteen." Donovan turned and headed back to the cabin. The passenger section of the *da Vinci* was anything but plush. Instead of an opulent boardroom, there were a series of modular workstations. Stacks of computer equipment and monitors were linked between stations by thick conduits. The flying science platform could be modified to perform any number of high-altitude missions from hurricane surveillance, atmospheric sample recovery, to a myriad of imaging capabilities through a purpose-built camera and antenna array blended into the belly of the 85,000-pound jet. Capable of altitudes up to 51,000 feet, a top speed of 575 mph, and a maximum range of 5,800 nautical miles, the Gulfstream 500 was a highly mission-capable aircraft. *The Spirit of da Vinci* was just one of the many reasons Eco-Watch was considered one of the top-tier organizations in the scientific community.

Today's mission was less about science and more about damage control. Seated in the back was William VanGelder, as well as Eco-Watch's director of security, Howard "Buck" Buckley. Buck was the newest member of the veteran group, a former Navy SEAL who had been assigned to Eco-Watch on a temporary basis on two previous occasions. Now in his mid-thirties, Buck was still in shape, his features were open, friendly, and his demeanor easygoing. But just under the surface was an understated lethality that commanded respect. Seven months ago, Donovan had been so impressed with the man's performance that he made him a job offer that was impossible to turn down. The mission statement of Buck's newly formed department was to oversee the far-flung activities of the organization and protect the people and assets within Eco-Watch. In the interview process, Donovan quietly explained that Buck had an unlimited budget, but with that came the expectation of a zero margin for error. This crisis was the first test of that agreement.

Via satellite, they'd just watched the statement released by Eco-Watch denying any involvement in the attack on the Japanese fishing vessel. The information about the outboard motors that Lauren had discovered had been forwarded to both the FBI and Coast Guard. That the Zodiac was counterfeit was verified. The YouTube video was now at 1,194,997 views and climbing. Every news outlet was showing an edited version of the clip on television, and Eco-Watch headquarters, which was located at Dulles International Airport, just outside Washington D.C., was being besieged by a crowd of reporters, as well as groups of protesters and a far smaller collection of supporters. So far, the Fairfax County Sheriff personnel were keeping the peace. Inside the locked-down building, a handful of staff were manning the phones, carefully taking each call, recording anything that could be construed as a threat.

"I just got the latest operational list from Peggy." Buck held up several sheets of paper he'd lifted from one of the printers. "She's contacted every member of Eco-Watch's board and put them on alert as well as our twenty-five largest donors. Most are foundations and trusts, but she's reaching out to anyone who may be at risk. I've also directed that any potential threat, no matter how small, be immediately routed to me so that appropriate action can be taken."

"This is a nightmare." William rubbed his temples. Despite the long flight, he was, as always, still dressed in his suit, tie snug at his neck. "Is it possible that John was simply in the wrong place at the wrong time?"

"Anything's possible," Buck replied. "But I think it's highly improbable. With two counterfeit Zodiacs in play, it's a coincidence of the highest order."

"I agree with Buck," Donovan added.

"If that's a given," William continued. "How on earth can we realistically expect to protect everyone connected to Eco-Watch?"

"We have to." Buck replied. "But I also think that this group is fairly small, which limits their geographical reach. If John Stratton's yacht was the base they used to attack the fishing vessel, then they're probably still somewhere in Hawaii. If they've left the islands, there are only so many places to go. I think with the FBI's help, we'll be able to narrow the search pretty quickly."

"Buck, what about our people? Where is everyone and how can we best protect them?" Donovan asked. As director of operations he had a running idea of what projects were currently in progress, but it didn't include specific knowledge of each employee or exactly where they might be.

"Okay, *The Spirit of Galileo* is currently on the ground at the Keflavik Airport in Iceland. The flight crew and the Austrian scientists are at the hotel. Security is now in place for the clients, crew, and airplane."

"Good. What about the ships?" Donovan asked. "Have they confirmed their new orders?"

"Yes, the *Atlantic Titan* is on full alert off the coast of West

Africa. Twenty-four-hour security measures are in effect as well as fifteen-minute reporting intervals to headquarters. If something happens, we'll know in a hurry. The *Pacific Titan* is in port in Seward, Alaska. They should be underway by this evening. There have been some scattered protests from local fisherman, but it's under control. The U.S. Navy and Coast Guard have been apprised of the situation and know the position of our vessels and have stepped up their vigilance of ships in the area."

"What about our people not attached to Eco-Watch ships or planes?" Donovan asked.

"They're easier to camouflage and protect. There are our liaison people working with NASA, JPL, Woods Hole, and the Scripps Institute, but by their very nature, those facilities are secure. Then there are the people working in conjunction with several universities and corporations on various research and development projects. Those in remote locations are probably the safest due to their minimal contact with the outside world. Regardless, I've directed all of our people to break up their routine, switch hotels if possible, and avoid wearing anything that might identify them as being connected with Eco-Watch. If they suspect anything suspicious or out of the ordinary, they're to contact local law enforcement and then call me. The airplanes and ships, the high-value targets, are at the highest risk and, of course, headquarters and senior management."

"What are our immediate plans once we land?" William asked. "The State Department has informed me that the Coast Guard is in charge of the vessel while the FBI is investigating the murders. We can pull on assets of both services."

"Since I believe we're at the greatest risk, I took the liberty of calling ahead to some connections I have in the Navy." Buck handed around sheets of paper that listed eight men's names. "There will be a small group of former SEAL team members meeting us when we land, men I know. Their job is to protect the airplane, as well as us, and act as backup for anything we do. They'll also be doing advance security sweeps at the hotel and any other destinations we travel without law enforcement on hand. I've arranged for a helicopter to be standing by to fly out to Stratton's yacht. I'm not sure if it's still on the beach or if high tide has allowed them to pull it off the sand. We'll know when we land."

"Where's Beverly?" Donovan asked, looking at William, as he knew the elder statesman had been in touch with her.

"She's with the FBI. She identified the bodies of her husband and their crew. There was a captain, two engineers, three stewards, and the chef. All told, there were eight fatalities—all died by a single bullet wound to the head. All Beverly could tell me before she broke down was that John had been tortured before he was killed. They weren't going to release the bodies anytime soon, so her intention was to turn around and go back to California."

"I can't say I blame her. I'm sure you've told her that if there's anything we can do to just ask." William nodded and Donovan continued, "What else do we need to cover before we land?"

Both Buck and William shook their heads.

"Okay, keep working, and I want us to all be vigilant. To the FBI and Coast Guard, these are crimes to be solved. To us, it's personal. We need to figure out who's doing this to us and stop them—no matter what."

Donovan made his way up past a small seating area and galley, slipped into the cockpit, and eased himself down in the copilot's seat. He fastened his harness and took in the panoramic view only visible from 48,000 feet. Out ahead, the vast blue Pacific Ocean spread out and merged with the sky, creating the illusion of infinity. Off to the left were a smattering of low clouds and underneath was the faint outline of an island. The big island was the easiest to spot, a smooth trail of steam drifting from the top of a volcano. The islands seemed small compared to the size of the ocean, until Donovan pictured each as the peak of an enormous underwater mountain range with only the tops breaking the surface of the water. Measured from the ocean floor, the highest peak of the Hawaiian Islands reached up over 33,000 feet, which was four thousand feet higher than Everest. As he scanned westward, he found Maui, Lanai, Molokai, Oahu, and then finally their destination, Kauai.

"You get everything squared away?" Michael asked as Donovan settled in for the final phase of the flight.

"I think so. Security has been arranged for you and the airplane. Are you sure you don't want to come with us?"

"I'll pass. As fluid as this situation is, at least one of us should get some rest. You go, I'll take care of the airplane and get it ready to go back out. I'm assuming we have no idea when or where that might be."

"No clue." Donovan shrugged. "Like I told William and Buck, this is personal, and we need to be flexible."

"I know. How are you holding up?"

Donovan knew the question probed at several different levels. He and Michael were close friends, so it was no secret that his split with Lauren had been difficult, as was the separation from his daughter. There were also his recent injuries. His leg still throbbed if he overtaxed it, and his injured hand would stiffen and hurt for no reason. The adversary with the knife would have killed him if he could have, so, overall, he was lucky. "If you're asking about my physical well-being, thank you. I'm fine."

"That was one of my questions. This is the longest flight you've taken since you were hurt. You seem okay, but I wanted to ask."

"I'm good, thanks."

"And you?" Donovan returned the question. Michael, too, had suffered at the hands of the same attacker—only Michael had been shot.

"I couldn't be better." Michael nodded as if to emphasize that this conversation wasn't about him. "How are you doing otherwise? Susan will never let up on me until she knows how you're getting along. Have you talked to Lauren lately?"

"I talked to her this morning," Donovan replied. Susan, Michael's wife, worried about him and had since the day Donovan had met her. Michael and Susan, as well as their two boys, were his closest friends, almost like family, and Donovan knew it was pointless to be evasive when it came to his relationship with Lauren. "I called to brief her on what was happening, but she was with a friend, so we didn't really get a chance to talk."

"So everything is still status quo?"

Donovan nodded. "She doesn't want to live with me or without me, or something to that effect. I'm pretty sure my phone call this morning informing her that Eco-Watch, and so by default, she and Abigail were under attack, didn't sit all that well."

"Don't worry about it, this is going to be a nonevent. Some whack jobs are trying to deflect their agenda onto us. I think you're exactly right to react by arriving at the scene of the crime in Eco-Watch's flagship. It's the perfect response. We're cooperating with the FBI and the Coast Guard. What better public relations move is there?"

"Unless it's exactly what these so-called whack jobs want, and one of us gets hurt."

"If you think about it, who could possibly hate us? I mean, we save people and do scientific stuff—been doing it for years. We are without a doubt the good guys and since you brought up the possibility of great personal risk, I think this would be an excellent time for a raise, maybe some additional vacation days. The guys wearing the white hats who take big risks always deserve the best."

Despite his mood, Donovan managed a smile. Michael was never happy until he made someone laugh. It was one of the things about his friend that Donovan counted on the most. They'd been friends and colleagues for over ten years now. In fact, Michael had been the first employee of the then newly formed Eco-Watch. There was no one Donovan trusted more, in or out of the cockpit, than Michael. As much as he treasured their friendship, Donovan suspected that it would vanish in a storm of betrayal if Michael ever found out who Donovan had once been. Over the years, conversations about the late Robert Huntington and the billionaire's involvement with Meredith Barnes had been the topic of discussion more than once. Michael held the view that most of the world shared. Robert Huntington was most certainly the instrument in the death of the beloved Meredith Barnes. Meredith had been part environmental activist, part celebrity, and she was loved worldwide for her work on behalf of the planet. She took on global corporations as well as tyrannical governments and would take the fight anywhere. Her followers were in the millions; her book, *One Earth,* was still in print after twenty-five years, and her television series, as well as numerous award-winning documentaries, could still be found on television on any given night. In short, Meredith Barnes was an angelic soul sent to save us from ourselves, and billionaire oilman Robert Huntington had murdered her.

The reality was that he'd been deeply in love with Meredith, and there wasn't a day that went by Donovan didn't miss her. His guilt and sense of failed responsibility was with him always. That was the core reason Lauren had left him. She'd felt second best and decided she wasn't going to compete with a dead woman for the love of her husband. Lauren was right, but she was also wrong, and Donovan wasn't sure where the lines actually were anymore. The bottom line was he didn't know what to do to fix his marriage. Lauren deserved better than she got, and the end result of any contemplation on the matter always ended with the same stalemate. Through the tempest of this undercurrent of self-recrimination, Donovan heard the tail end of an Air Traffic Control clearance meant for them.

"I missed that." Donovan said to Michael as he reached for the microphone. "What was the clearance?"

"They cleared us down to flight level two four zero," Michael said as he tightened his harness and adjusted the autopilot to begin their descent.

Donovan read back the clearance and spun 24,000 feet into the altitude alerter.

"You sure you're okay?" Michael asked. "You looked a million miles away for a moment."

"Not a million," Donovan lied and pointed to their mileage to the Kauai airport. "One hundred and twenty."

CHAPTER FOUR

Michael lined up the *da Vinci* for final approach to runway three-five at the Lihue Airport. Below and to the east was only ocean; to the north and west, mountains. It was a spectacular approach, and Michael flew the Gulfstream perfectly until the wheels gently kissed the pavement. Once they'd slowed, Michael swung off the runway, and ground control directed them toward the executive terminal. The airport wasn't large, two commercial jets were huddled close to the terminal, and a smattering of smaller airplanes dotted the ramp. Up ahead, a lineman with red batons directed them to their stand on the ramp. Donovan could see the helicopter Buck had arranged parked off to the side. There were three official-looking vehicles, a fuel truck, and two police cars with lights flashing; the gathering created a sense of urgency.

Not far away, behind a chain-link fence, was a cluster of media vehicles, cameras no doubt rolling, shooting the arrival of Eco-Watch. Farther away, a crowd of people was cordoned off by barricades and uniformed officials. Donovan was too far away to make out the signs they held.

"I'm sure those signs are all about how much they love us," Michael said as he swung the Gulfstream in a wide arc and eased forward until the lineman crossed his batons as a signal to stop.

"Yeah, and the armed guards are all about containing the love." Donovan threw off his harness and went back to the cabin door only to find Buck already standing there, a handheld radio to his mouth as he put out his hand to keep Donovan from opening the door.

"What's the hold up?" Donovan asked.

"One final sweep of the area, and we'll be clear."

A voice crackled from the radio, and Buck nodded they were good. As the air-stair unfolded and stretched to the tarmac, Buck placed himself in front of Donovan and descended to the ramp. With William behind him, Donovan joined the group awaiting their arrival. He, William, and Buck met a Mr. Erickson, the governor's envoy, and the local chief of police who pledged his department's full cooperation and protection. Donovan shook everyone's hand, thanked them, then turned and found himself face-to-face with a man who radiated quiet authority. Despite the heat, he wore a black suit with a dark tie. The crew cut head hinted at his being former military, and steel-gray eyes gave the impression he didn't miss much.

"Mr. Nash, I'm FBI Special Agent Christopher Hudson. Welcome to Kauai."

"Agent Hudson," Donovan returned the firm handshake. "Nice to meet you. The quicker we're out of here, the happier I'm going to be."

"You'll be on your way in a minute. I'm assuming the helicopter is your doing."

Donovan nodded, then turned and helped William politely extract himself from the governor's man. Buck signaled toward a white Suburban, and two men in dark pants and sports jackets appeared from open doors. They collected the luggage Michael handed out of the rear compartment and then quickly took up positions that created a perimeter between the *da Vinci* and the distant crowd of protesters.

Agent Hudson looked at Donovan and then at Buck. "Are your men armed?"

Buck nodded that they were.

"I'll allow your private security, but if they get in my way, they're done. Are we clear?"

"Perfectly."

"Gentlemen, while I have everyone here, I'll quickly bring you up to date on what the FBI has so far," Hudson said. "We processed the *Triton's* onboard navigation logs and now know where the vessel has been for the last week. It was maneuvering approximately eight hundred nautical miles west of the Hawaiian Islands until two days ago, when it turned and set a constant course for Kauai. As we already know, the ship ran aground on a sandy beach, which as it turned out, did very little damage to the hull. We combed the area and found no evidence that anyone was onboard at the time. Our speculation is that the people responsible abandoned ship well before it reached shore. The *Triton* is still there waiting for a tug and the next high tide to pull it off the beach."

"Did you find the Zodiac?" Donovan asked.

"No, we believe they either used it to escape before the *Triton* ran aground or it was sunk far out at sea. We received the photo analysis of the Zodiac in the video, versus the actual Zodiacs used by Eco-Watch. It seems to support the theory that Eco-Watch was set up."

"Does that mean that you actually entertained the theory that Eco-Watch was somehow involved?" Donovan asked without bothering to disguise this irritation.

"We look at all the evidence, Mr. Nash," Hudson replied evenly. "And then go where it leads."

"So where is it leading you now?" Donovan asked. "Any sign of the fishing vessel?"

"The Coast Guard diverted one of their cutters to patrol the area where the *Triton* turned and set course for Kauai. So far, no one has identified the fishing ship in the video." Hudson continued, "We're looking at everything we can find, starting the day the *Triton* set sail from Southern California. They arrived in Oahu a week ago, where they took on fuel, water, and stores for an extended cruise and then sailed from Oahu four days ago with an itinerary that was eventually designed to put them in New Zealand, where Mrs. Stratton had planned to join her husband."

"Is Beverly, Mrs. Stratton, still on the island?" William asked.

"I don't believe so. She identified her husband and the crew. When she learned that we weren't ready to release the bodies, she seemed a little lost. We tried to explain that in the course of a criminal investigation it could be days or perhaps even weeks before the medical examiner releases the remains to the family. She was upset by that information, and I overheard her make a phone call telling someone that she was going home."

"When I spoke to her earlier," William said, "she told me that her husband was tortured before he was killed. Can you shed more light on that aspect of the investigation?"

"The preliminary report is that everyone died by a single gunshot wound to the head. Mr. Stratton died that way as well, but I can confirm that he was tortured first. He has marks on his body indicative of someone trying to extract information—or induce pain. The medical examiner is working on the details."

"What kind of marks?"

"It's a key part of the ongoing investigation and a detail we're keeping to ourselves."

"We know they were hijacked at sea," Donovan said. "Any luck with the images from the *Triton* security cameras?"

"We're running what little we have through our database. It may take a while."

"I want to see them," Donovan said.

"Just so we're clear, this is the FBI's investigation. For the record, the only reason you're here is because Eco-Watch has some political influence, and I was ordered to read you in, but the second you become a hindrance, or start playing vigilante, you'll be arrested. Off the record, the word I got from the top is that you and your group are reckless. I hate reckless, and as far as evidence, including images from an active crime scene, it will be shared when it's deemed appropriate by the FBI."

"We're here to cooperate," William said. "But we do expect to be kept in the loop and we'd appreciate that at your earliest convenience you'd issue a statement to the press that the *evidence* points toward the fact that Eco-Watch is in no way involved with recent events and is cooperating fully with the investigation."

Donovan smiled inwardly at how William slowly and succinctly pronounced the word evidence, as if it were a sharp stick used to prod Agent Hudson. From past experience, Donovan could have easily predicted that both sides would stake out their territory early. At least that part was out of the way.

"A press release to that effect is in the works and will be released from FBI Headquarters within the hour."

"I'd like to go out to where the ship ran aground," Donovan asked. "Is that possible?"

"As far as the FBI is concerned, we're done processing the scene. The salvage team is on site preparing to pull the boat off the beach at high tide so I'm not sure how much you'll actually see."

"Just the same," William said, "it's where I'd like to go as well."

"It'll be good to have eyes on what's going on out there," Buck said and motioned for the helicopter pilot to spool up the engine. "Agent Hudson, are there still police out at the *Triton*?"

"Yes, they were going to maintain a presence until the ship is off the beach and back out to sea."

"Good, can you let them know that Mr. Nash and Mr. Van-Gelder are en route via helicopter and ask them if they'd provide security for my people?"

"I can do that, but the beach is pretty secluded. I wouldn't think there's any risk," Hudson replied.

"I'll help Michael finish up here and then he and I will go to the hotel so he can get some rest," Buck said. "You two call me when you're coming back in, and I'll pick you up."

Donovan nodded, and then he and William headed toward the helicopter. With William leading the way, Donovan put his head down against the rotor wash as they walked toward the idling machine. The Hughes 500D was a compact machine, sleek and fast, the single distinguishing feature of this particular helicopter was the fact that all of its doors had been removed. The pilot introduced himself as Glen, handed them each a headset, and asked them to take their seats. Donovan and William strapped in behind the pilot. The helicopter lifted off, flying low toward the west.

Donovan wasn't particularly fond of helicopters, too many

moving parts for his taste. The lack of doors only added to his dislike. At least the *Triton* wasn't out at sea. It was a poorly kept secret that the director of operations of Eco-Watch was terrified of being in the ocean. When he was fourteen years old, he'd been involved in a boating disaster. The sights and sounds of that day as the boat sank were imprinted into his brain, and anytime he was even close to being on a ship, the flashbacks would begin, the fear would grip him, and he couldn't convince himself that the sea, if given a second chance, would not finish the job it started all those years ago.

As they passed over the group of protesters, Donovan saw the smattering of signs, all condemning Eco-Watch for the cold-blooded murder of helpless fisherman. As they swept past, he also spotted a biblical reference: *Thou shall not kill*. Donovan momentarily contemplated the commandment, but it did nothing to alter his intentions toward the people who'd threatened him.

CHAPTER FIVE

As the helicopter topped the lush hills and banked out over the water, Donovan could see the rakish dark-blue hull and the white superstructure of the *Triton*. The yacht looked distinctly forlorn perched on the white sand beach that seemed to stretch endlessly in both directions.

"Dead ahead is Polihale State Park," Glen said over the intercom. "It's one of the most remote beaches on this side of the island. Only four-wheel-drive vehicles will get you in and out."

Donovan spotted the road, set well back from the high-tide mark. As low as they were flying, he couldn't see a single structure along the entire beach. Rising above the sand, the *Triton* was tilted twenty degrees to port. The sleek, pristine, one-hundred-sixty-foot megayacht soared above the official vehicles parked nearby in the sand. Including its mast, which held numerous antennas and radar domes, the *Triton* reached nearly six stories into the air and dwarfed the small collection of boats that had gathered offshore to take in the scene. Donovan had been on the vessel once, several years ago when it was moored in San Diego. He remembered John explaining that he could invite a maximum of twelve guests with a staff-to-guest ratio of one-to-one. A huge salon with a full bar, a library, hot tub, a gym, a theatre, elevators to take passengers from below decks up to the flybridge where one could enjoy all the creature comforts. The vessel was powered by twin one-thousand-horsepower Caterpillar diesel engines. She held over 16,000 gallons of fuel and could generate up to sixteen knots and had a range of 6,000 nautical miles. Donovan was happy the ship was intact; a fuel spill in these waters would be catastrophic to the fragile ecosystem.

They passed over the *Triton*, slowed, and circled in preparation to land.

"Hudson didn't mention John's helicopter?" Donovan said as he twisted in his seat and found the light gray *H* within a circle painted on the aft quarterdeck. "Where'd it go?"

"Good question," William replied.

"Mr. Nash," Glen's voice sounded over the intercom, "I'm listening to a report that a fishing vessel has been spotted about twenty-five miles west of here by a Coast Guard C-130 transport. The ship nearly collided with a sightseeing boat. So far, they haven't responded to any transmissions or altered course."

"Can we get out there and take a look?" Donovan said without hesitation.

William shot Donovan a worried glance as the chopper abruptly climbed away from the beach to race out over the water.

"It's only three miles offshore of Niihau," Glen said. "The C-130 crew reports the ship's speed is at least ten knots with no sign of slowing."

"That means we've got less than twenty minutes before it comes ashore," Donovan said as the ocean flashed past at 175 mph. They crossed the seventeen-mile strait between Kauai and the far smaller island of Niihau, then skirted the north side of Niihau between the main archipelago and a small island. Once clear of the rocky cliffs, they raced out over open ocean, and Donovan saw that the waves below had grown considerably bigger. A minute later, Glen spotted the ship.

Donovan found the vessel. His first thought was that the ship had once been white, that heavy use was evident by the dark streaks that trailed from her scuppers and the reddish tinge of rust on the superstructure. The hull was patched and faded, in need of more than fresh paint. The vessel was slightly longer than the *Triton* but nowhere near as modern. Her aft deck bristled with masts and lines used to haul in the miles of long cables. As the bow rose and fell in the swells, each downward plunge displaced tons of water and exploded it upward, drenching the forward deck. Donovan figured it was going faster than ten knots.

"I'm talking to the Coast Guard C-130," Glen reported. "They've initially identified the ship as the Japanese registered vessel *Kaiyo Maru #7*. Repeated hails have gone unanswered."

Several minutes later, the helicopter made a steep turn over the Japanese vessel, and Donovan got a look at the ship, immediately recognizing the deck setup. "I guarantee you that's the ship from the video."

The helicopter began a gradual descent and hovered above the white superstructure of the *Kaiyo Maru #7*. To Donovan, it felt as if the helicopter was hanging motionless in space, which was a most uncomfortable aspect for an airplane pilot. Locked into position level with the bridge, it was obvious there was no one at the helm, and the shoreline of Niihau was alarmingly close. The *Kaiyo Maru #7* wasn't headed for a soft sandy beach, but massive reefs that jutted up from the surface of the ocean.

"Damn it!" Donovan said. "We're going to lose any evidence that might be onboard."

"There's nothing anyone can do," William replied.

Donovan knew if he thought about it any longer, he'd do nothing. His every rational thought screamed for him to sit down and shut up, to think about getting solid ground beneath his feet. "Glen, can you bring us down close enough for me to get onboard?"

"What are you thinking?" William asked.

"Glen, is there a spot that would work?"

"Yeah," Glen replied. "The bow area is clear enough. I can't land, you'd have to drop maybe four, five feet, but it'll work. It's a one-way trip—I don't see any way to get you back aboard the chopper."

"Get me as close as you can." Donovan said.

"Even if you make it down to the deck, do you know what to do?" William asked.

"Turn the ship—how hard can it be?"

"I'm moving in," Glen said. "Unbuckle and sit on the ledge, ease your legs down to the skids, but hang on to something. Once you go, if you've ever skydived, try and land the same way, knees flexed, and plan to go down and roll with the impact as soon as you hit."

Donovan had, in fact, skydived once, years before. He removed his headset, slid out of his seat, gave William a reassuring squeeze on the shoulder, and then carefully perched himself on the edge of the cabin, his legs dangling out into the rotor wash. Glen matched the rising and falling of the ship's bow with the helicopter as he eased closer. When Glen gave him the nod, Donovan pushed himself off into space. He favored his good leg as he hit the deck, rolled to his side to dissipate the impact, then lay there for a moment to make sure he'd survived the jump unscathed.

Above him, the helicopter climbed and pulled away. Donovan was instantly aware of the pitching deck beneath him, and there was nothing he could do to quell the fear that rose up inside him. He hated ships, petrified they would sink. For once his fear was based in truth, this one was definitely going to sink unless he acted fast.

Galvanized by adrenaline, he climbed down the foredeck and ran across the open deck toward a covered passageway where he hoped stairs would lead him up to the bridge. As he ran, he saw a steel stairway and took the steps two at a time, his wounded thigh burning, but he ignored the pain and burst onto the empty bridge.

Donovan went to the wheel and began spinning it all the way starboard. The beach was close, and the ship was responding far too slow to avert running aground. Everything was written in Japanese, but he yanked back on two levers that had to be the throttles. He pulled the starboard lever to the center detent, waited a beat, and then eased it all the way back into reverse. Somewhere below his feet he felt a subtle clank of machinery that told him something had happened. He could hear the growl and feel the vibration of a diesel engine begin to roar from the bowels of the ship.

He grabbed the port throttle and pushed it all the way forward. Differential thrust from the props would help increase the rate of turn. It was an old trick from flying twin-engine propeller airplanes. Dead ahead, the water went from azure blue to greenish brown. A reef was directly in their path, and he had no way of knowing the draft of the ship or the depth of the water.

He scanned the panel and found a much-used lever with arrows pointing left and right. Underneath was a rocker switch. Donovan threw the switch and then held the lever all the way to the right. Below the waterline, the bow thruster powered to life and began to swing the ship even faster to starboard.

Donovan gripped the wheel and waited as the bow merged with the far shallower water. He held his breath at the sound of steel scraping rock. The jolt rocked the ship, and the vessel shuddered and groaned. The shriek of rock grinding metal sounded cataclysmic, but the ship kept moving, its momentum never wavering. Gradually, the horrible sounds of the collision eased. The ship, now paralleling the shore, moved once again toward blue water. Straight ahead was another reef. He stood and measured the distance to the rocks against the turning radius of the hull. His eyes darted back and forth, processing each degree of movement until he decided he might actually make it into deeper water.

He kept the wheel hard in the turn until he was pointed forty-five degrees away from the shore. He eased both engines into forward and set the throttles slightly above idle. They wouldn't go very fast, but with the props turning they'd stay headed away from the beach. When the ship was out of immediate danger, he grabbed a flashlight and headed below. He had no idea if the ship was taking on water.

He went through a rusty hatch, down a flight of stairs badly in need of a paint job, and came out into what he thought looked like a processing room. The stench of rotted fish mixed with something else, something sweeter, hit him like a solid wave. Even breathing through his mouth, it was hard not to gag. The room was fairly dark, but he could see gray plastic tubs used to hold fish and what appeared

to be conveyer belts, that while silent, seemed to lead into the bowels
of the ship. It took him a moment for his eyes to adjust to the dim-
mer light before he realized that they weren't holding fish.

Donovan's stomach lurched. He fought the urge to be violently
sick as he recognized human arms and hands, all cleanly severed
and arranged within the dimensions of the tubs as though about
to be frozen and packed for market. Judging by the number of tubs,
there were body parts that would account for at least a dozen of
the ship's crew, maybe more. He pictured the video and what they'd
done to that poor soul, then he understood, they'd butchered the
entire crew the same way.

He clicked on the flashlight and continued deeper into the ship.
The metal deck was dirty and faded, rust eating away at the edges.
He searched several rooms, finding the sleeping quarters, a mess
hall, a couple of mechanical rooms, and, finally, he threw open the
hatch for the engine room. The noise from the two diesels was
deafening, but he needed to search for anyone left alive and for
any water coming in through a breach in the hull. Donovan found
no water, no sign that the hull had been compromised. More than
anything, he yearned to be back up in the sunshine.

He burst out onto the main deck and hurried up the stairs toward the bridge. The ship had put more distance from the beach.
Glen was orbiting overhead, and in the distance, he spotted a second helicopter off the stern and coming fast.

Donovan returned to the bridge and looked around the clut-
tered compartment. An ashtray overflowing with filterless cigarette butts was affixed to the edge of the captain's chair. The chart
table was strewn with papers. The windows were filthy, spotted,
and streaked with salt spray on the outside and years of cigarette
smoke on the inside. Everything looked tired and weathered, but
Donovan's eye caught something that seemed out of place. Near
the top of the console was a single photograph thumbtacked to the
faded wooden trim, a girl. As Donovan leaned in, he realized she
wasn't Asian, but Caucasian. He pulled the photograph from under
the tack to get a closer look. After several seconds, the reality of

the image clicked into place, and when it did, he closed his eyes as memories of Meredith began to pound at his internal armor. In the photograph, Meredith couldn't have been much older than eighteen, her first year in college. The long, auburn hair and impossibly green eyes were the same as he remembered, as was her smile. She had more freckles in this picture than when he'd met her years later. An immense sadness began to well up from inside. Any rekindled memory of her was always the same, the flashbacks always ended the same. They were both in a muddy field in Costa Rica. He was alive and she wasn't. Her pale, broken body splayed on the ground, her sightless eyes pleading at him to save her, but the bullet hole in her forehead clear evidence that he'd been too late.

Donovan's thoughts were broken by the sound of a helicopter. He closed himself down and the image dissolved, but he knew he would pay later for indulging in the memory. He carefully slid the photo into his pocket and moved closer to the window. Looking up, he saw the second helicopter hovering overhead, a red-and-white Coast Guard HH-65. A crewman was being lowered to the deck. Donovan confirmed that the ship was still on a course for the open ocean and then left the bridge. He'd been in such a rush to get to the bridge when he'd first arrived, he didn't notice the details, the main working deck with wood deeply stained from years of fishing and exposed to the elements. Turning, he looked up at the bridge, then out at the ocean. He realized he was standing in the exact place where the man's arms were severed in the video. Upon closer inspection, Donovan spotted dozens of spent shell casings scattered amongst the equipment. He hoped for the crew's sake they were shot before being cut apart.

"Are you injured?" The Coast Guard crewman yelled as he came closer.

"No, I'm fine." Donovan said.

"Sir, follow me. Let's get you off this boat."

CHAPTER SIX

The Coast Guard helicopter gently touched down near the *da Vinci* at the Lihue airport. Donovan was relieved to see that the media horde and protesters were gone. The Eco-Watch Gulfstream was buttoned up and under guard. Buck was waiting for him. The chartered helicopter was nowhere in sight, which meant William was already at the hotel.

Donovan shook hands with the flight crew, then stepped out and moved clear. The pilot lifted back up into the sky, tilting east toward their base on Oahu.

Buck held the passenger door open for Donovan. "Welcome back," he said before wrinkling his nose and powering down his side window. "What's that smell?"

"You don't want to know."

"William filled me in on today's events. You are not trained to be part of a boarding party. What in the hell were you thinking?"

"Thinking about saving evidence." Donovan knew Buck was angry, as he should be, but what happened couldn't be undone. "We also know the *Triton's* helicopter is missing."

"I've already spoken with Special Agent Hudson about John's helicopter. They're searching. What kind of range does his chopper have?" Buck asked.

"With full tanks it could easily fly three hundred miles."

"So if they waited until they were, say, fifty miles off the coast of Kauai, they could have flown off of the *Triton* and made it to any one of the islands."

"Yeah," Donovan said. "And land anywhere. What have I missed at this end?"

"So far there haven't been any direct threats phoned into Eco-Watch. The FBI is trying to trace who actually posted the video, and they're also running any of the online comments that seem even remotely suspicious. All of our assets are in full defensive posture, but besides some name calling, we're fine."

Donovan nodded. "Where are we staying?"

"The Kauai Beach Resort. It's only a few miles north of the airport. Nice place, full of honeymooners, makes it hard for anyone trying to harm us to blend in. The head of security is an old Navy guy out of Pearl Harbor. He's giving us whatever we need, which right now is access to a freight elevator so we can get you up to your room. I suggest burning those clothes."

They drove into the lush surroundings and parked near a loading dock. Buck walked Donovan onto the elevator, and they went up to the fifth floor. After checking the hallway, Buck escorted him to his room at the end of the hall.

Donovan closed the door and welcomed the silence. He emptied his pockets, being especially careful with the photograph. He set it facedown on the table then stripped off his clothes and stuffed everything but his shoes and belt into a plastic laundry bag before wrapping them in a trash bag and tying off the opening. Buck was right—his clothes were history. While the water in the shower heated up, Donovan ripped the paper off all the soaps he could find and put them in the shower stall. He stood in front of the mirror, recognizing the signs of fatigue on his face, the lines around his eyes looked deeper, the circles underneath darker, more pronounced. His short-cropped brown hair was dashed with a bit of gray, as was the hair on his chest, but that was from being forty-nine years old. With all of the reconstructive facial surgery he'd undergone, he didn't look his age. His eyes were still the same vivid blue they'd been when he was a kid, but everything else was different. He wondered what he'd look like if he was still Robert Huntington, and the answer was usually the same—Robert Huntington wasn't on a path that promised any kind of longevity and probably would have died years ago.

The math told him he was pushing fifty, but he still imagined he could do everything he could do in his thirties, though his body was telling him otherwise. He'd lost weight since Lauren had left and was leaner than he'd been in a decade, but his body had taken a beating in the last year. The eight-inch scar on his thigh was crimson red and throbbing from today's activities, as was the almost identical wound on the inside of his right wrist. A small round scar near his left clavicle marked the entry wound from a nine-millimeter round. Less noticeable was a purplish puncture wound on the back of his right hand. It was round, about the diameter of a pencil with an identical scar on his palm where the screwdriver had passed all the way through. A friend had told him once he was the most scarred man she'd ever met—and she wasn't talking about the visible ones. It was an honest comment and the truth in the words had stuck with him.

Twenty minutes later and an entire bottle of shampoo and three bars of soap, a stench-free Donovan emerged from the bathroom with a towel secured around his waist. He opened the minibar fridge and pulled out a cold beer. He pressed it to his forehead for a moment, extracting its coolness, then found the opener, popped the cap, and took a long pull. He walked to where he'd set his phone and called William.

William picked up immediately.

"I found something today."

"What is it?"

"A picture of Meredith, when she was younger, it was tacked up in the bridge of the fishing boat."

"Any idea what the message is?"

"No, not beyond the obvious. My guess is the picture is a message aimed at me. They want to rattle me, for me to know that they're serious."

"I think the events aboard the fishing boat put a strong emphasis on how serious they are."

"How many views are there now on the video?"

"Last I checked there were 2.8 million and climbing."

"I was afraid of that. Not the kind of publicity I wanted."

"You sound tired. You should get some rest. Remember, you don't have to do this alone. I'll see you at breakfast."

Donovan ended the call, but William's words lingered. Lauren had accused him of operating alone and leaving her on the periphery, and at some level, they were both right, but he wasn't ready to address those issues. He retrieved another beer, and then against his better judgment picked up the picture of Meredith. He sipped his beer and stared into her innocent, yet expectant, eyes. So young and idealistic, with no idea that she was truly going to change the world. She hadn't yet written her wildly bestselling book *One Earth*. She hadn't traveled the world producing and starring in her documentary nature film series. She hadn't become the global ambassador to save our planet, had no idea how loved and famous she was going to be, that her receptions across the globe would rival that of leaders of state, and she'd have the ear of politicians and kings alike.

His cell phone rang and as he picked it up he saw that the area code was 808, which meant the Hawaiian Islands.

"Nash," Donovan answered, expecting it to be the FBI or the Coast Guard.

"Hello, Robert. I'm happy to see you were so quick to arrive in Hawaii."

Donovan stiffened at the raspy voice. Wide awake this time, he caught the faintest hint of an accent. "You have my full attention. You don't need to kill any more people. What is it you want?"

"Oh, I'm just getting started."

"I found the picture you left. Is that how you and I are connected? Through Meredith?"

"You were never connected to her. You used her so you could silence her."

"I didn't kill her."

"That's a lie, and I'm here to punish you for your crimes. It's payback time, Robert. I just sent you an e-mail. You'll find a video I made. It's just between us. I believe the person is important to both you and your friend William. Take note that he died exactly like Meredith. Good-bye, Robert."

The line went dead and Donovan closed his eyes. This call confirmed that Meredith was the common link with this man. Donovan yanked his laptop out of his briefcase and fired it up. He sat down and logged on to the hotel's wireless signal, opened his browser, thumbed through his e-mails, and found the latest message. He opened it and then clicked on an attachment. He was immediately assaulted with the image of a tortured John Stratton. His friend was blindfolded, tied to a chair on the teak deck of the *Triton*. It looked as if the skin on parts of his face had been burned. There didn't seem to be any sound. Then, without warning, a gun went off and a round hole appeared in John's forehead. His head sagged forward and he was still. Moments afterward, the image went black.

Donovan closed his computer. *He died exactly as Meredith had.* Donovan looked at the picture of her as an eighteen-year-old, and all he could think about was the singular event that ended her life. She didn't know that she was going to meet and fall in love with Robert Huntington, the heir to the Huntington Oil Fortune, the man she wanted to marry. She didn't know that despite all of her hopes and plans, the wedding wasn't ever going to take place. She didn't know that when she was twenty-eight years old, she would be kidnapped and murdered.

CHAPTER SEVEN

The phone woke Donovan. He groaned as he pulled his stiff and sore body up from the chair, noting that it was light outside. Reaching for the phone, he saw it was five forty-five in the morning.

"Nash," he said as he rubbed his eyes.

"Mr. Nash. It's Agent Hudson. We found the helicopter."

"Where?" Donovan snapped fully awake.

"In a hangar at Honolulu International airport. Island Aviation is the name of the facility. They're a Bell Helicopter service center."

"When did it arrive? There should be plenty of surveillance of these guys as they passed through an airport facility. Hell, there's probably footage of them going through security at the main terminal. I mean, why else fly to an airport if you're not catching a flight out?"

"We talked to the service manager, and he remembers the pilot. The guy was in a hurry, had passengers, but gave the manager a list of things to do to the helicopter and then used a Stratton Partners credit card to open the work order. The service manager thought nothing of it because a Stratton Partners Falcon 900 was waiting on the ramp. Everyone got aboard, and the plane departed for Orange County."

"Oh, no, not Beverly's plane."

"I'm sorry. She was found in her car at the parking lot at the Orange County airport, the flight crew as well. They're all dead. The people who murdered them are on the loose in California, and they've got a twelve-hour head start."

"You're telling me the bad guys somehow convinced Beverly

to fly from Kauai to Honolulu so they could board there? What kind of leverage did they have that she would leave the company of the FBI, then fly to Honolulu and pick up the people who murdered her husband and fly to the mainland?"

"I don't know," Hudson replied. "But we're going to find out."

Donovan made an instant decision and quickly calculated how soon they could be airborne. "Is there anything else? We're going to leave for Orange County as soon as we can."

"Slow down. I'm on my way to your hotel. There are some pictures I need you to see. I'm about thirty minutes away. Have some coffee ready. It's been a long night."

Donovan called Buck and quickly brought him up to speed on the events surrounding Beverly Stratton.

"We should all meet with Hudson when he arrives, Michael included," Buck said. "Do you want to tell William about Mrs. Stratton or should we let Hudson?"

"I'll do it. Can you make sure Michael is up and that he knows we want to be wheels up for Orange County as soon as possible?"

"He's been up for hours. I ran into him down in the fitness center, but I'll make sure he knows."

"Check in with Peggy. After we finish with Hudson, I'll want a full status report on Eco-Watch's security around the globe, but it's for our ears only. For the moment, I want to leave Hudson out of our internal affairs."

"Yes, sir."

"I'm going to go talk to William. I'll see you shortly." Donovan found Meredith's picture on the floor between the chair and the table, slid it in his briefcase, and headed for the bathroom for a fast shave and shower.

Twenty minutes later, William opened the door and let Donovan into his room.

"Did you get any sleep?" William asked.

"Yeah, I did, a little," Donovan replied. "I got a call from Hudson. He's on the way over to bring us all up to speed on developments."

"What's happened?" William asked, the expression on his face guarded.

"It's Beverly," Donovan said quietly. "She was found murdered."

"Oh, God." William wavered and then sat down on the sofa. "I knew something was wrong and I didn't press. It was as if she wanted to say something, but I let it go, I figured she'd talk when she wanted to. Now that I think about it, everything was off. I spoke with her several times and tried to get her to wait for our arrival, but she said she couldn't. Again, I thought it odd, but she was upset. She'd just lost her husband."

"It's not your fault. Hudson has evidence that points to her being forced to cooperate with the people responsible for John's death. They flew back to California with her and then killed her, as well as her crew. Hudson is bringing us some photos. Maybe we'll know who's behind this."

Donovan heard a knock. William stood and straightened his tie. When Donovan opened the door, he found Buck, along with a steward pushing a meal cart. Behind them were Michael and Special Agent Hudson. The steward quickly set up coffee and Danish. Buck signed for the food and thanked the man.

"I think we should let Special Agent Hudson bring us all up to date," William said as he poured the first cup of coffee and handed it to the FBI agent.

Hudson elected to stand while everyone else took a seat. "As I told Mr. Nash earlier, a few hours ago FBI agents in Honolulu located the *Triton*'s helicopter. It was in a hangar at the Honolulu International Airport. Subsequent investigation led us to believe that Mrs. Beverly Stratton, under duress, was forced to allow the people responsible for her husband's death to board her private jet for the flight back to Orange County. We sent agents to investigate and found Mrs. Stratton and her driver. They were both dead. They never made it out of the parking lot of the airport. The flight crew was also found dead. We have some security camera photographs that were taken in Honolulu, as well as on the executive ramp at

Orange County where Stratton Partners based their jet. None of them are great quality, but I need you to take a look."

Donovan glanced at William who was the first one out of his chair as Hudson retrieved a folder he'd set down earlier. "Oh, before you look at these, I need to show you a photo we found on the bridge of the *Triton*. We can't identify the person in the photo, and we have no idea if it's relevant. It might simply be someone connected to Mr. Stratton or his crew, but we need to ask." Hudson slid a transparent evidence bag from his inside suit pocket and handed it to William.

William shook his head. "I don't recognize her." He then passed it to Donovan.

Meredith. She was younger than in the photograph Donovan had found on the *Kaiyo Maru #7*. She was maybe fourteen or fifteen, standing on the deck of a boat, her hair was short, and she wasn't smiling. Donovan did everything he could to remain passive. "I don't know her either."

Both Michael and Buck shook their heads as the picture of Meredith completed the circle. Hudson slipped it back into his pocket then opened the folder and began to arrange the black-and-white 8 x 10s on a table. "Okay, here are the surveillance photos. We've already got a vague ID on one of them through Interpol, but I want all of you to take a long, hard look."

Donovan, still reeling from the newest image of Meredith, leaned over the grainy images and saw that the first picture was of four men. The tallest, who was the only one even remotely facing the lens, was wearing dark glasses. He had longish dark hair combed straight back until it touched his shoulders. Two of the men were turned away from the camera so Donovan skipped them and studied the fourth person. He was clean shaven and had longish curly dark hair. He too, wore dark glasses.

Donovan glanced at the next several shots finding nothing of significance. He skipped to the photographs taken in Orange County. Donovan counted an extra passenger, a woman with short, spiky hair, though her face was blocked. The man with long curly hair was with Beverly, and it appeared he was helping her into the car, but Donovan could easily imagine he was strong-arming her just before he pulled the trigger.

"We sent these out to all of our allies, and Interpol immediately informed us the taller, long-haired man is a person of interest in several murders in Europe."

"The woman?" Donovan asked. "When did she enter the mix?"

"We're not sure," Hudson replied.

"Were you able to track any of them after they left the airport?" Buck asked.

"We went to the Stratton home and found no signs of illegal entry. I'm afraid we've lost them for now. But I can assure you all levels of law enforcement on the West Coast are on the lookout for these guys."

"Did anyone think to pull up the flight plan information on the Stratton Partners Falcon 900?" Michael asked. "I mean, in terms of the number of people on board each leg of the flight? Was there a bad guy or girl with her on the leg from Kauai to Honolulu, or did they all board her airplane on Oahu?"

"That's a good point," William added. "If Beverly was hijacked from Kauai, it would explain everything."

"I'll get with the FAA, and you'll have that answer the moment I do."

"I'm the executor of the Stratton Estate. There are arrangements to make," William said. "I'll be heading to Los Angeles."

"We're all going. I want to be wheels-up as soon as possible," Donovan added.

"I understand." Hudson nodded. "I'll call ahead and have someone from the bureau meet you. They'll act as your FBI liaison while you're in California. If there's more information to share, you'll have it when you land."

"Thank you," Donovan said, turning to Michael. "How soon can we be airborne?"

"One hour."

"Thank you." William set his cup down as if to signify that the meeting was over.

Moments later the room had emptied except for Donovan and William.

"Did you recognize anyone in those pictures?" William asked.

"No, did you?"

"No. What connection could these people have with you and Meredith's past? We're up against people who are making this personal, and we have no clue who they are. What happens when the FBI figures out who she is? What happens when they start leaving pictures of you and Meredith? We need to figure out if those pictures are part of the public domain or someone's collection."

"He called again last night."

"And you're just now telling me this?"

"It's the same guy, his voice isn't normal. It's altered somehow or damaged. So if it's someone I know, I'd never recognize him. He said that it's payback time. He referenced Meredith for the first time, so it's clear she's the common link."

"What if we ask for some third-party help on this one?" William stroked his chin.

"What are you thinking?"

"We've got Buck, Michael, and the FBI watching our every move. Our hands are a little tied right now. We're slinking around behind our own people's backs. I say we enlist Lauren. She can dig for information. If these people have European backgrounds, maybe she could use her Mossad connections, or her contacts in Washington D.C. Besides, she's got a vested interest in all of this."

"No. It's my baggage that drove her off in the first place. Let's not call her up and dump even more in her lap."

"We have to find who did this," William gripped Donovan by the wrist. "We have to find them and deal with them ourselves."

Donovan looked into the familiar eyes. For nearly thirty-five years William had been Donovan's father figure and mentor. They'd ridden the trials and adversity of what at the time felt like the worst events that life could exact, and they'd both survived.

William represented the moral and intellectual epicenter of Donovan's life, the man had crafted the values that shaped his life, and in all of that time, he'd never seen William as quietly enraged as he was this very moment—nor so resolute about wanting these people to answer for what they'd done.

"We'll find them," Donovan said. "And, I promise you, they'll pay."

CHAPTER EIGHT

"Aaron! What are you doing in Paris?" Lauren was genuinely surprised when Henri, her chief of security, led her benefactor, and senior Mossad agent into the foyer. Her security detail stayed in the apartment across the hall when Lauren was in for the evening. They used cameras to monitor all entry and exit points of the building. This time of the evening all access to this floor of the building was sealed off so any visitor needed an escort.

"Can't I drop in and visit my favorite American in France?" Aaron kissed her on both cheeks.

"This is my friend Stephanie," Lauren said, motioning Aaron into the kitchen. "Stephanie, this is Aaron Keller."

Aaron nodded respectfully. "The niece of William VanGelder, it's an honor to meet you."

"Can I offer you something to drink?" Lauren asked.

Aaron shook his head. "I'm here on business actually. May we sit?"

"I'll give you two some privacy," Stephanie said.

"You can stay." Aaron gestured toward a chair. "This pertains to you as well."

"Aaron, what is it?" Lauren asked, worried.

"There's news from the investigation in Hawaii. We received a bulletin from the FBI about the death of Mrs. Beverly Stratton and her flight crew. They were all found murdered in Southern California."

"Wait, I thought she was in Hawaii," Lauren said.

"First John and now Beverly?" Stephanie's hand shot to her mouth.

"I'm so sorry to have to be the one to tell you." Aaron turned to Lauren. "When did you last speak to your husband?"

Lauren didn't like the question and she felt herself shift into a different mind-set, the one she hated. One that involved lies, half-truths, not trusting anyone. "He called me yesterday morning, when he heard about John Stratton."

Aaron pulled several 5 x 7 photographs from his jacket pocket. "These are some surveillance photos sent by the FBI. Please look at them and tell me if any of these people look familiar."

Lauren studied the pictures. She didn't recognize the men. Stephanie shook her head as well.

"How about this one?" Aaron handed over another photo.

The image showed a woman, Lauren thought maybe in her early thirties with short, dark hair. The woman looked striking, almost beautiful, though something in her eyes seemed dangerous, maybe even reptilian, but Lauren didn't recognize her. Most troubling to Lauren was the fact that Aaron had personally delivered the photographs; he could have simply sent them to Henri to show her. If she had to guess, Aaron was on some kind of fishing expedition.

"Who is she?" Stephanie handed the photo back to Aaron.

"We think she's connected to one of the men photographed in Hawaii, the guy with the dark glasses and curly hair. It's generally thought they're Eastern European and over the last ten years or so, through vague descriptions and grainy images like this, we've linked them to at least a dozen deaths. We're sure they're professional killers, but we don't know if they're backed by some governmental organization or strictly freelance."

"A professional assassin was hired to kill John and Beverly?" Stephanie asked. "Was this woman also involved in the incident aboard the fishing vessel?"

"We don't know how, but we believe the events are somehow related."

"What's Mossad's interest?" Lauren asked.

"We believe the woman played a part in the deaths of staffers who worked at a medical clinic in Dusseldorf, Germany. The doctor there was a friend of Tel Aviv, and at times we called upon him for discreet medical needs. From what we've learned from our friends at the FBI and Interpol, Eco-Watch is being targeted, and if this man and woman are part of that equation—both of you are at risk."

"Is there anything we should be doing?" Lauren asked.

"No, just be vigilant. I've already spoken to Henri. Your protective detail understands the threat." Aaron stood. "I have another pressing engagement and must leave. Again, I apologize for the hour. Good night."

Lauren and Stephanie stood as Aaron bowed and showed himself out. They didn't speak until they heard the front door close.

Stephanie faced Lauren and stood with her hands on her hips. "Now, back to the real question of the evening. Mossad drops in to say hello? What in the hell is going on?"

"I'm not sure. But if Mossad is in the mix, Donovan should be told." Lauren reached for her phone. After trying three numbers, someone picked up. She was greeted by the familiar voice of Howard Buckley.

"Buck, it's Lauren. I'm trying to find Donovan."

"Is everything okay?" Buck asked.

"I'm fine. I just need to pass along some information."

"He's up in the cockpit with Michael. Hang on, I'll go tell him you're on the line."

"Where are they?" Stephanie asked.

"I dialed the satellite link onboard the *da Vinci*. So they're flying somewhere."

"Hello," Donovan said as he came on the line.

"Sorry to intrude while you're working, but I needed to talk to you," Lauren said.

"What's up?" Donovan asked.

"I'm here in the apartment with Stephanie." Lauren chose her words carefully. "I just got a visit from Aaron Keller."

"Oh, really?"

During his one encounter with the Mossad agent, Keller had done nothing but lie and try to maneuver him. Donovan wasn't a big fan.

"What did he have to say?"

"He's very interested and well briefed on finding the people who killed Beverly and John Stratton. Mossad thinks they have knowledge of one of the men in the FBI's pictures. The guy with longish curly hair—he works with a woman. Aaron thinks they're both assassins, and the woman is a person of interest in a case in Dusseldorf, Germany, where workers at a clinic were murdered."

"Really? What kind of clinic?"

"A medical clinic. That's where it gets interesting, Aaron admitted that the doctor there had ties to Israel, and did some work for Mossad. I gathered by his tone that it was all off the books."

"So Keller told you about Beverly?"

"Yes, that's so sad. Tell William that Stephanie and I are really very sorry."

"I'll tell him. I can't help but wonder if we looked at this clinic, we might be able to get a better clue who this woman is, and why she's attacking Eco-Watch. I hate to ask, but it might be really helpful if you could do a little digging. See what you can learn."

"I could do that."

"If you don't want to be involved, I understand."

"I'm already involved," Lauren replied. Donovan was asking her to use her resources in the intelligence community. Something she'd already intended to do. "Where are you, anyway?'

"We're headed to Orange County. William is a trustee for the Stratton estate and needs to be there." Donovan said. "How's Abigail? Is she asleep?"

"Yes, it's late here. It's always a full day when Stephanie is here to spoil her. She's good, I'll tell her you said hello."

"Thanks for the call. I'll be in touch," Donovan said.

"How did he sound?" Stephanie asked as soon as Lauren disconnected the call.

"He sounds tired."

"What next?"

"I need my laptop. I'll meet you in the kitchen; I'm going to need some wine." Lauren went into her bedroom and sat, turning the phone over in her hand several times while she contemplated her next move. When she'd left Washington, her boss within the Defense Intelligence Agency had refused her resignation. Instead, he put her on an indefinite leave of absence. As a DIA analyst living on foreign soil, she'd been given several contact numbers. A man named Fredrick had visited from the embassy. After she'd double-checked his credentials, he'd detailed various ways she could reach him if she needed. He'd given her the code name *Pegasus*.

Fredrick's phone number began with a 703 area code, which was Northern Virginia and was most likely a secure router at Langley that would forward calls. She contemplated her request. Mossad had deemed it important enough to pay her a visit, and if nothing else, the CIA might be interested in that fact. She dialed, and before she could change her mind, a computerized voice asked her to leave a message.

"It's Pegasus. I'm going to follow this up with an e-mail. Talk to you soon."

Laptop in hand, Lauren found Stephanie in the kitchen with a bottle of wine and a corkscrew. Lauren opened her computer and sat down. As the screen blinked to life, Stephanie poured red wine into their glasses.

Lauren typed in a few key words and found what they were looking for, and moments later they were both reading about the arson and multiple murders at the Klasen-Drescher clinic in Dusseldorf, Germany, six months ago. There wasn't much to the report, twelve bodies had been found inside by firefighters, and were so badly burned that the task of identifying the victims was nearly impossible. The police had no leads and had appealed to the public for information. Lauren clicked to pictures of the clinic the day after the fire; not a single wall remained standing.

Lauren composed an e-mail to Fredrick, asking about the clinic and explaining Mossad's interest. She hit send and several minutes later a return e-mail arrived. It was from Fredrick.

That Mossad visit is curious. I'll get back to you.

"What now?" Stephanie said as she sipped her wine.

"We wait."

CHAPTER NINE

Donovan matched the speed of the Gulfstream with the Delta Airlines 757 he was following, knowing there was a Southwest 737 doing the same thing right behind them. The typical arrival sequence for John Wayne Airport. Donovan had lived in Los Angeles for years as a young man, but once he'd left, he'd never missed Southern California, and today was no exception. All that lay in the hills and beaches that stretched out below were the painful memories of Robert Huntington and Meredith Barnes.

For the last hour, Buck had been on the phone between Eco-Watch Headquarters in Virginia and the Eco-Watch ship *Pacific Titan* located in Seward, Alaska. The *Pacific Titan* had been attempting to leave port when several small boats attacked and managed to foul the propellers of the two-hundred-seventy-four-foot vessel. Crippled and dead in the water except for the bow thrusters, the alert crew had immediately dropped anchor and brought the ship to a stop. According to the information coming in to Buck, initial reports were that the attacks were carried out by what was suspected to be local fisherman, protesting Eco-Watch's presumed tactics against their livelihood.

Donovan, wanting to get free from Buck, had suggested Buck get to Alaska to protect the crew of the *Pacific Titan* and oversee the repairs. Buck had agreed. They'd called Peggy to make the airline arrangements, and further communications had resulted in an FBI promise to rush Buck from the *da Vinci* to LAX, so he could catch his flight to Anchorage.

With the FBI waiting, Donovan knew it was going to be hectic once they landed, so he did his best to stay in the moment and do what he loved most, which was to fly. He drank in the late afternoon sun reflecting off the Pacific Ocean as he slid in above and behind the Delta 757 and called for the final landing check.

As soon as the *da Vinci* cleared the active runway, Donovan saw the crowd. It had been no secret they'd departed Kauai bound for John Wayne. In the nearly five hours it had taken them to make the trip, hundreds of people had gathered. It looked as if an entire parking lot south of the main terminal had succumbed to the masses. Donovan spotted the array of antennas snaking upward above the fray, marking the position of the media, poised for their footage and overblown rhetoric. He guided the *da Vinci* toward the spot on the ramp where the FBI would be waiting.

As Donovan eased the Gulfstream to a stop and shut down both engines, he enjoyed the ebb of adrenaline that told him he'd safely arrived after a long flight. Michael was up and out of the cockpit first and stood behind Buck as the former SEAL saw to the task of opening the door and lowering the air-stair to the tarmac. Donovan was thankful that the waiting crowds and media were actually behind the airplane, though off to his left, people lined up along the perimeter fence brandished signs of condemnation. Others were simply taking pictures. As soon as the door was fully opened, three black SUVs pulled up, and men in dark suits wearing communications earpieces piled out of the vehicles and took up positions at the foot of the stairs. Michael and William descended to the tarmac and began shaking hands as the crowd noise rose with protesters' chants.

Donovan slipped out of the cockpit, threw on a light jacket, then knelt, and pulled the carpet up from the corner of the forward closet. He typed in the password for the safe he'd had installed and opened the heavy door. Inside was the exact same model of the forty-caliber Sig Sauer that he kept at home. He slid the pistol under his belt in the small of his back and pulled his jacket down to cover it up. He snapped up two extra clips, closed the compartment, and smoothed the carpet back into place.

Donovan put the clips into his briefcase just moments before

Buck returned. Buck was about to say something when he stopped, furrowed his brow, then nodded toward the small of Donovan's back.

"Where'd you get the gun?"

"I bought it months ago," Donovan replied, impressed that it took Buck all of three seconds to notice.

"We both know it's not legal for you to carry in California. Is it even registered?"

"No," Donovan replied.

"Don't forget to wipe down each shell casing, as well as the clip. People always forget to do that. Use it if you need it, and remember everything I taught you."

"I will."

"Michael wants you outside. He says we have a problem."

Donovan hurried down the steps and the noise from protesters rose yet again. Police were eyeing the crowd, making sure no one decided to try to climb the fence. Donovan turned away and spotted Michael crouched underneath the left main landing gear. As he ducked under the wing, he saw what had caught Michael's eye. A pool of thick reddish fluid had collected on the ground around the tires.

"Hydraulic fluid?" Donovan asked as he knelt next to Michael, dipped a finger into the liquid, and tested the consistency.

"Yeah, it's leaking from up there." Michael pointed up to where the strut slid inside the main gear housing. "We need to get it looked at before we go anywhere."

"I agree."

"You go with William. He needs you more than I do right now," Michael said. "I'll get on the phone with Gulfstream over in Long Beach. They'll get some people over here to fix this."

"Keep me in the loop." Donovan put his hand on Michael's shoulder. "And don't forget to get some rest. Who knows when or where we're headed next."

"You too. I'll call you later when I know more."

Donovan said good-bye to Buck and climbed into the back of

an SUV where William was waiting. From the front passenger's seat, a clean-shaven black man in his early to mid-forties slid off his sunglasses and extended his hand over the seat. "I'm FBI Special Agent Edward Wells."

"This was certainly not the reception we expected," William said.

Wells slid his dark glasses back on. "This is the biggest demonstration we've seen so far."

"Wait," Donovan asked. "There have been other protests here in Southern California?"

"All over the world actually," Wells replied. "Eco-Watch has become a flashpoint for both sides of the environmental debate, but other than a few isolated arrests here in L.A., the protests have been without incident. Before I forget, Hudson sent a picture from a surveillance photo from the airport in Kauai. It's Mrs. Stratton boarding her jet with an unknown female companion. Do either of you recognize the woman?"

Donovan and William shook their heads. The woman was nicely dressed, slender, athletic looking with dark hair. She wore large rimmed sunglasses that obscured most of her face. "Any chance you can get an ID from this?" Donovan asked as he handed the picture back to Wells.

"We're working on it."

His phone rang and Donovan pulled it from his jacket, half hoping it was Lauren. Instead, he discovered a number he didn't recognize. The area code was 714, Southern California. "Nash here."

"Robert, just think, soon you'll be able to drop all the pretense and use your real name," the man said. "I just wanted to call and ask you a question. Do the pictures I've left bother you, seeing the innocent girl you'd later kill? Tomorrow is her birthday. Do you ever light a candle for the woman you murdered?"

"What can I do for you?" Donovan asked, struggling to control his rising anger.

"I do have one question. Does Lauren know about your past?

Does she know about Meredith? How about Abigail? She has a birthday coming up as well, doesn't she? I wonder what she'll think of her father when she's old enough to realize what you've done. I think she'll be horrified, as will the rest of the world. She, too, will grow up an orphan, though I have to believe she'll be relieved by your death. I know I will. Though I'm in no hurry, when I do finally kill you, it'll be up close and personal. You'll be all alone like Meredith was when she died. Scared and alone, a broken man, the world calling for your head. You'll welcome the bullet."

Donovan glanced up and found Wells had turned and was looking at him, as if the phone call might be news that needed to be shared. "Thanks for the update."

"You're with the FBI, aren't you? That's rich, and you can't share, can you? Of course not, how could you? This must be hard for you. You've always hated not being in control. You've been like that ever since your parents drowned and you couldn't do anything to save them."

"Is that all?" Donovan said, his rage boiling up inside at being taunted and threatened at such a personal level.

"Remember what Meredith always told you? How she tried to get you to slow down and enjoy the moment? Well, she was right. Enjoy them; you don't have all that many left. Good-bye, Robert."

"Problem?" Wells asked as soon as Donovan lowered the phone.

"No." Donovan shook his head trying to contain his fury. "Just some Eco-Watch business."

CHAPTER TEN

Donovan leaned against the railing that surrounded John Stratton's deck. He couldn't quit thinking about the earlier call. Meredith *had* always tried to get him to slow down and enjoy the moment. It was a cloudless night, so clear that he could see up the coast to Long Beach, and out to Catalina Island. Boats of all sizes were lit up, coming and going into the city that once had been his home. He had known that tomorrow was Meredith's birthday; she would have been forty-eight. Thinking of all the living she'd missed made him immeasurably sad, both for her and him.

He thought of the few birthdays that they had shared, each one in a different house. Back then he'd had many homes, one of the many privileges of being Robert Huntington. Los Angeles, or more precisely, Malibu and Bel Air had been his playground. Though after he'd met Meredith, everything had changed. They'd left Los Angeles and moved to his house in Monterey, California. The pace was slower and the setting more natural and all of the trappings and distractions of Southern California vanished. The thought of who and what he'd once been now gave him a pang of embarrassment at the excesses of his life. There'd been the houses, the cars, the airplanes, and before Meredith, there'd been many women. That was then, and since, he'd become a completely different man. As he often did, he wondered if she'd be proud of him. The answer was usually yes, and it was what drove him. Tonight, though, he didn't have an answer, or one that he wanted to admit. Right at this moment, he wasn't pleased with what he'd become.

They'd arrived hours ago and William had parked himself at John

Stratton's desk, remaining on the phone and reviewing files since they'd arrived. Donovan, too, had been busy. The *da Vinci* had been moved into a hangar, and Michael was meeting with several technical representatives sent from Gulfstream to assess the problem.

There'd been one visitor. John and Beverly Stratton's attorney delivered a sealed file to William. Though there were plenty of bedrooms in the 7,000 square foot Stratton home, Peggy, on William's suggestion, had booked them rooms at the nearby Montage Hotel.

Donovan's phone rang. Seeing it was Buck, he skipped the greeting and answered, "Where are you?"

"I'm changing planes in Seattle. Any new developments at your end?"

"No, we're at the Stratton house. William is still going through paperwork, but I think we're about to call it a day."

"I already spoke with Peggy, and she's been in touch with the head of security at the Montage Hotel. The property has protocols in place for visiting VIPs with security as a priority. All of that has been implemented, so I'm confident that you should be safe."

"What's the update from Alaska?"

"The *Pacific Titan* has been safely towed back into the Seward harbor and secured at the wharf. A perimeter has been established by a combination of Alaska National Guard troops and the State Police. All non-essential Eco-Watch personnel will be evacuated as soon as I get there. We're being given full support from the military as well as the governor of Alaska. I think we're in good shape."

"What about repairs? Are there facilities there that can handle the ship?"

"Yeah, we're good. Though I don't have any kind of time frame on that yet," Buck said. "Speaking of repairs, have you heard anything about the condition of the *da Vinci*?"

"Michael is working with Gulfstream. If we need to go anywhere, we'll look at chartering an airplane."

"I think that makes sense," Buck replied. "There is one more thing. Peggy sent me a list of phone calls that were logged into the

Eco-Watch main number earlier today. Anything that sounded like a threat was passed on to the FBI. There was one from someone named Erica. Peggy ended up talking to the woman since she expressly asked for you. Peggy said the woman sounded frantic and that she needed to talk with you immediately."

"Did she give a last name?"

"She said she wouldn't give it on an open line. She did leave a number though. It's a 949 area code, which means it's a phone issued from Southern California."

"Sounds like a reporter. Let me know if this woman calls again."

"Will do. I've got to run. My flight is boarding."

"Buck," Donovan said, "nice work. I appreciate all you're doing."

"No problem. Talk to you tomorrow."

Donovan once again surveyed the peaceful ocean, but underneath the placid surface, he knew there was a life-and-death battle being waged, as it had for eons. It occurred to him that his own life wasn't much different. He spotted the red light on his phone that told him he had a message. He saw that it was from Lauren and he quickly opened the e-mail and began to read:

> *Did some digging and this is what turned up. It's classified, so don't share. Not sure what to make of all this, but would be nice to find this woman. Take care of William, Stephanie says he and the Strattons were very close. Call when you get to Laguna.*
>
> *Lauren*
>
> *The October 5th arson and multiple homicides at the Klasen-Drescher medical clinic in Dusseldorf, Germany:*
>
> *All patient files were declared destroyed—no evidence of off-site storage. It was suspected that the records and staff were eliminated to destroy witnesses to criminal activity. By all outward appearances the assailants were professional and effective.*

Bank records of the clinic were intact and nothing out of the ordinary was found, so any off-book payments were handled through different channels, and have so far remained undetected by German police or Interpol.

After your inquiry, we initiated a further sweep and uncovered payroll records for the clinic. They used a small payroll service and we began to compare payroll records with victims and think we found something. There were twelve employees listed as active at the time of the murders. All twelve were killed. We went back a month before the crime and again found the same number of employees, but one of the names was different. A physician's assistant left the clinic a month before the killings; she was replaced two weeks before the attack.

The woman who left is named Erica Covington. (see her attached passport photo) She's thirty-five years old, fluent in both English and German. She has dual citizenship, her mother German and her father American. She graduated six years ago from the University of California Davis with full certification as a physician's assistant. After graduation, she went back to live in Germany and was there until seven months ago. When she returned to the United States, she cleared U.S. Customs at LAX and after that there is no address on record, nor is there a current driver's license issued to her in any state. There's no cell phone in her name and no living relatives. Erica Covington is off the grid. This makes her one of the assassins, or a witness, or deceased.

Identity of dark-haired woman who is wanted for questioning in the clinic murders is still underway. Am looking into this further, but do know she's of the highest priority to Interpol.

Donovan frantically redialed Buck's number. He started pacing as he silently urged the former SEAL to pick up.

"I was just turning this thing off," Buck answered. "What's up?"

"Erica's number. I need it now," Donovan said in a rush.

"Hang on a second. There. I just forwarded it to you. What's up, why the shift?"

"It just started to bother me is all. If she asked for me by name, it could be important."

"Okay. Talk to her, but be careful. Get the FBI involved. This could be anything."

Donovan saw that he had a new message and that the number was there. "I'll be careful. We'll talk in the morning."

Donovan reread the message then clicked on the attachment that would bring up the photograph. Erica Covington's passport picture filled the screen. Donovan's first impression was that she could be a model. Shoulder-length blond hair parted on the side, her complexion was flawless, her eyes were bright blue, and her perfectly proportioned lips hinted at a pretty smile. As he studied the image, he knew that typically there was nothing more unflattering than a passport picture, yet Erica was beautiful. She would be someone easy to spot.

Donovan quickly punched in Erica's number and hoped she would pick up. It rang two times and then a woman answered with a simple hello.

"My name is Donovan Nash. Is this Erica?"

"How do I know it's you?" she asked.

"You don't," Donovan replied. "But you called my office today and spoke with my assistant. Your message was passed along."

"What's the main number of your office?"

Donovan rattled off the number published on the website.

"What's your assistant's name?"

"Eventually you spoke with Peggy. She's in charge when I'm gone. Where are you?"

"No, you tell me where you are."

"I'm in Laguna Beach, California."

"You're close."

"Pick a spot and let's meet."

"There's a Mexican restaurant at the northwest corner of El Toro Road and I-5. It's by the Laguna Hills Mall."

"I know the place. I can be there in twenty minutes." Donovan pictured the location, well lit and busy, with easy access onto the San Diego Freeway. A smart choice. Donovan hurried from the deck and started through the house. He cut through the Strattons' massive formal living room, hurried through the kitchen and down the four steps that led to their garage. He threw open the door. Inside, parked diagonally in two precise rows, were eight cars. In an instant Donovan saw the one he wanted.

"How will I recognize you?" she asked.

He leaned over and spotted the keys in the ignition of the car he'd chosen. "I'll be the one driving a red Porsche 911. It has California vanity plates, 911FLYS."

"Come alone or you'll never see me. And bring me proof you are who you say you are."

"I'm on my way."

Donovan ran back into the kitchen and down the hall to where William was working. He barged in, unzipped his bag, and yanked out the extra clips to his gun.

"What's happened?" William got up from his chair. "What are you doing and why do you need bullets?"

"Hopefully, our first break. Read this. I just got it from Lauren. Remember the clinic in Germany I told you about?" Donovan handed him his phone open to the message. "I just spoke to Erica. We're going to meet."

William was right behind him, reading as they headed toward the garage.

Donovan opened the door to the 911 and slid behind the wheel, then reached down and adjusted his seat and mirrors. Satisfied with his position, he wedged his pistol between the seat and console where it wouldn't slide, but was within easy reach.

"You spoke with her?" William finished reading and handed Donovan his phone. "How did you find her?"

"She found me. Cover for me, I'll call you later."

"Donovan, slow down. For all you know this could be a trap."

"Hence the gun." Donovan pushed the clutch and turned the key. The throaty V-8 filled the garage with an authoritative roar. He switched on the headlights and then found the button for the garage door. He stretched out the seat belt and snapped it into place as William stepped aside.

He let out the clutch and eased the Porsche out of its spot. He threw a parting wave to his longtime friend and wound away from the house toward the exit from the exclusive community.

Donovan gunned the 911 out onto the Pacific Coast Highway and headed north, going as fast as he dared before slowing as he reached downtown Laguna Beach where he turned onto Highway 133 and headed up the canyon. Moments later he was out of town, and he quickly had the German sports car going eighty. His eyes swept the road and the rearview mirror for any sign of a tail, police or otherwise. It was late enough on a weeknight that the road was his. His phone rang and he saw that it was Lauren. He answered and put her on speaker.

"Donovan, did you get my e-mail?"

"Yes. I'm on my way to meet with her now."

"You found her?"

"She called Eco-Watch earlier today. The intelligence you sent me, who's the source?"

"I went through someone I know at the State Department, but if I had to guess, I'd say it came from Langley."

"I was afraid the CIA was involved. Can you wave them off? I don't want them involved."

"Too late, the fact that you've found a certain person of interest has put me in a compromising position. Protocol dictates that I inform my contact."

"Don't do that yet. I'm serious. I'm driving right now, but we have to talk about this. I'll call you back." Donovan hung up and downshifted as he made the right turn onto El Toro Road. He checked the mirror and didn't think he had a tail, but William and

Buck were both right, he could be heading into a trap. The fact that the CIA was involved elevated the risk both he and Erica faced. The only advantage he had was that, thanks to Lauren, he'd seen what Erica Covington looked like. If anyone but her showed up, he'd know immediately.

He swung into the parking lot of the Mexican restaurant and came to a halt. There were cars parked everywhere, and there was no way he wanted to be trapped in a busy parking lot. He put the 911 into a tight right turn, swung through a gas station, and pulled to the side and stopped. He could easily make a fast exit if need be. He held the pistol down low between his legs and waited.

He caught sight of her as she emerged from a row of cars. She was wearing jeans, brown boots, and a leather jacket. Her blond hair was longer than in her picture, and she'd tied it back in a pony-tail. As she neared, he saw the same features he'd seen in the photo. It was her. She was no more than five foot six and on the slender side. She had a black canvas bag looped over her shoulder. Her left hand gripped the bag's strap, her other hand was buried deep in the jacket's pocket. He reached across and threw open the passenger side door. She leaned down and looked at him.

"I have a gun," she said.

"So do I, now get in. We're not safe here."

"Prove to me who you are," Erica said.

Donovan handed her his passport.

She glanced back and forth from the document to his face, then wordlessly tossed her bag on the floor and slid into the seat next to him and handed back his passport. Donovan saw that she was even more attractive than her picture. Despite her obvious stress, she had an effortless beauty that was amplified by vivid blue eyes. Even her facial expression, as wary and nervous as she was, had serious wattage.

"Buckle up." Donovan locked eyes with her as he wedged the Sig beneath his seat then came up and showed her his hands were empty. She reached behind her and pulled the seat belt strap across her chest. The second he heard it click into place, they rocketed out of the parking lot, through a yellow light, and onto the I-5 ramp headed south. He merged into traffic and then eased into the inside lane while memorizing every car he passed. Once he was confident there were no police in sight, he swung into the carpool lane, put his foot into it, and they roared southward at 120 mph.

"Where are we going?" she asked.

"Nowhere yet," Donovan replied. "We're safe for the moment. I think we should cruise around for a bit and once we compare stories, we'll know what to do next."

"Are we being followed?" Erica asked.

"I don't think so." Donovan rechecked the rearview mirror and then glanced over at her. She was looking at him, her hand still in her coat pocket.

"I lived in Germany, the autobahn was very fast. You're a good driver."

Up ahead was an exit that would spill them out in Mission Viejo. Donovan swung to the right and took the ramp at high speed. They slowed and maneuvered the 911 among the sedate suburban drivers. "Why did you call me?"

"You're in charge of Eco-Watch. I watch the news, so I know what these people are doing to you. I've heard your name before, but I had no idea who you were."

"You didn't answer my question."

"I know who's trying to kill you. He wants to kill me too. I'm alone in all of this and you seem to have—resources."

"How do you know all of this?"

"Not so fast. I need some assurances you won't just cut me loose afterward, or simply turn me over to the police. You had no hesitation about coming to find me, so I can only imagine you know something about me. If you won't tell me, then our conversation is over."

Donovan was impressed with her resolve. She was scared, but she was also smart and tough, and she knew he needed her far more than she needed him. Donovan noticed she'd yet to take her hand out of her jacket pocket. "Have you decided if you're going to shoot me or not?"

"I'll let you know. What is it you think you know about me?"

"There are some people who have promised that they're going to destroy Eco-Watch. They've already killed friends of mine. A photograph of an unknown woman led back to a medical clinic in Dusseldorf. From that information I uncovered this."

Erica took the phone from him and as she scrolled through the report Lauren had forwarded, he watched as tears formed, finally spilling from her eyes, and rolling down her cheeks. She handed the phone back, covered her eyes, lowered her head, and silently sobbed.

Donovan made a right turn down a side street, went up a hill, and pulled into the parking lot of a dental office. He backed into a spot away from the overhead lights where he could survey the entire parking lot and then switched off the car. He powered down his window and waited for her to calm herself.

She sniffed and then wiped at her tears with the back of her hand. She fished in her pocket for a tissue and dabbed away the rest. "I'm sorry," she said her voice barely above a whisper.

"Take your time," Donovan said. "You've been on the run for a long time. I know that you're the only survivor of a massacre in Germany. I know you did off-the-books medical work at the clinic and that you're probably a prime suspect in the murders or someone's loose end. I'm not going to tell anyone about you. I promise you're safe."

"Where did that information come from? I saw the name Lauren, who's she?"

"Lauren is my wife. She's in Europe. The information most likely came from the CIA."

"I'll never be safe," she said her voice still thick from crying. "From the moment I heard about what happened in Dusseldorf, I knew it was only a matter of time before everything started to unravel. I'm a dead woman."

"Who's trying to kill you, and how do they connect to the people threatening me?"

"I'll get to that, but if at any point I think you're lying, I won't hesitate to shoot you. Do I have your word that we're in this together?"

"Yes, you have my word. Now, how do you know what's happening to me?"

"I was standing in the room when he vowed to kill you."

CHAPTER ELEVEN

"He gave us a fake name and identification, as did she. It wasn't until near the end that Karl, the doctor at the clinic, found out who he'd been treating. The woman's name is Nikolett Kovarik. Dr. Drescher heard from friends in the Czech Republic that she was an assassin for hire; Hungarian, he thought. The man was an escaped prisoner from Brazil. His name is Garrick Pearce. He was imprisoned over fifteen years ago for—"

"Oh, no," Donovan whispered, cutting her off midsentence.

"What is it? You know him?"

"I do." Donovan nodded. "In the late eighties he formed the One Earth Society, the leader of a militant group of eco-terrorists who fashioned themselves as warriors championing the causes of the book *One Earth*. Have you ever heard of it?"

"By Meredith Barnes, of course. Who hasn't?"

"The story goes that Garrick and Meredith Barnes were more than friends once, but she eventually distanced herself from both Garrick and his group."

"Did you know Meredith?"

"No, I only knew Garrick." Donovan said, careful with what he revealed. "Meredith publically denounced Garrick's tactics when his acts of protest turned violent. Instead of a peaceful revolution to save the planet, Garrick was using bombs and guns, sabotage and blackmail."

"What happened to him?"

"Garrick tried to destroy a mining operation in Brazil after it was determined that the chemical runoff was polluting a huge section of the region's water table. Garrick's raid set off an explosion that killed seven of his own team and fifteen mine employees, most of them local Brazilian workers. During the botched raid on the mining operation, Garrick was blinded and captured. He stood trial and was convicted of murder and sent to some hellhole of a prison for life, and as far as I knew that's where he still was."

"He's not in Brazil anymore," Erica said. "He's out. His eyesight is restored, and he hates you with a rage I've never seen one person have for another."

"I don't doubt that."

"Why?"

Donovan had no intention of explaining that Garrick's rage was personal, that Garrick had been the man in Meredith's life when Robert Huntington had arrived on the scene. Meredith had made the decision that her relationship with Garrick had run its course, but Garrick never saw it that way. He blamed Robert for stealing Meredith and then later blamed Robert for killing Meredith. Garrick was the most vocal of his critics, calling for the deaths of not only Robert but of all of the executives of Huntington Oil. He urged those who loved Meredith to bomb Huntington Oil refineries, ships, and pipelines. Do anything possible to cripple the company and oust its murderous owner. All of that came to an immediate end after Robert Huntington staged his death, and then five years later, ever the eco-terrorist, Garrick ended up in a prison cell in Brazil.

"Why does he want you dead?"

Donovan let go of his memories and quickly came up with a lie that would hopefully placate Erica. "I was part of his circle once myself. But I went another direction long before he became so militant. When he was imprisoned, he reached out to me for help, and I didn't answer. I'm sure he hates me for that. Garrick was always a troubled man with a deep-seated hatred for those he feels have wronged him."

"That's an understatement."

"You said you were there when he vowed to kill me. What happened?"

"It was months ago, before his surgery, so he was still sightless. He liked to listen to the radio, had it on all day, said he hated the silence. One day I was in the room and he was listening to the BBC. It was after the terrorist attack in Washington D.C., last fall. There was a brief segment when you were released from the hospital. You said very little to the reporter, I can't even remember what you said, but it was enough for Garrick to fly into a rage. I clearly remember him ranting that you'd died when your plane crashed. He was livid you were still alive. He kept ranting that *He* was alive. I ended up sedating him, but that was the day I heard him swear to hunt you down and destroy you."

Donovan tried to remain passive. There had in fact been two plane crashes. One was twenty years ago. The other was last summer. He hadn't died in either one. What frightened Donovan was that Garrick had recognized Robert Huntington's voice after all of these years. He wondered if being blind had played a part in the process.

"Did the accident alter Garrick's voice?"

"His vocal cords were damaged after inhaling fumes from the same chemicals that blinded him," Erica replied. "He can talk, just not very loud, and he has a permanent rasp."

"I saw pictures the FBI took of these people leaving Hawaii. None of the men looked like Garrick. He was tall, with a hawklike nose and prominent chin. Was his face altered?"

"If it was, he didn't have the work done at the clinic. As far as I know, he should look exactly the same. There's some scarring around his eyes from the acid that blinded him, and he has a great deal of difficulty blinking. The only other difference from when you knew him is that he won't be able to move his eyeballs in the sockets due to the ocular muscle damage. He's like an owl, in that he has to rotate his head to change his field of vision."

"Okay, then he wasn't in those FBI pictures. I would have recognized him, which means we have no idea where he is right now."

Erica shook her head and then looked away.

Donovan suspected there was something else coming.

"There's one other part of the story you should know. But I don't want it to change our agreement."

"Let's hear it."

"Do I have your word?"

"No, Erica, you don't. I won't agree to something you've obviously withheld. If what you tell me is a deal breaker, then we go our separate ways. I will, however, promise to reward you for what you've told me already—enough to get you on your way to where you can hide again. As soon as Garrick and Nikolett are dealt with, you'll be free."

"No I won't. I'll always have to hide."

"Who else would be trying to kill you if not Garrick?"

"There were two doctors at the clinic. Viktor…Dr. Viktor Klasen, an ophthalmologist, and his business partner Dr. Drescher, who specialized in plastic surgery. We were a research facility for Dr. Klasen's work using stem cells for optical nerve regeneration."

"If you were just a research facility, how did you end up treating Garrick Pearce?"

"There was another facet to the clinic. There would be calls, mainly through Dr. Drescher. We'd treat people off the books, and every once in a while, we'd alter someone's appearance."

"How were these people referred?" Donovan asked.

"I'm not sure, though I did overhear a heated conversation between Dr. Drescher and someone from Tel Aviv."

"Tel Aviv?" Donovan interrupted. "As in Mossad?"

"That was my assumption, though Viktor would never confirm my suspicions."

"What made you finally leave Germany?"

"I was having an affair with Dr. Klasen. He finally admitted to me that he would never leave his wife, though he'd told me a hundred times he didn't love her and wanted to be with me. I was devastated, I felt betrayed, and I made some angry, mindless comments. Dr. Drescher threatened me, promised to destroy my career if I ruined Viktor's marriage, or divulged anything I knew about the clinic. He scared me badly."

"But they're both dead now."

"When I left, I made a file to protect myself. I used Viktor's password and made copies of every patient's record. Each separate procedure, every before-and-after picture, names and dates, payment trails. I have in my possession every incriminating detail about their operation. Besides Garrick and Nikolett, there are exactly seventeen men and five women who have every reason to want me dead."

CHAPTER TWELVE

"I need to know," Erica asked. "Are we still working together?"

"Yeah." Donovan fired up the Porsche. "Let's go back to Laguna Beach. We can check you into a hotel. You'll be safe until we can figure out something longer term."

"I'm not sharing a hotel room with you, and I'm definitely not sitting in some strange hotel that takes cash and fake names. I've been invisible since I came back to the States seven months ago. I lived for three months on a boat in the Pacific Northwest; I bummed around Oregon and Northern California before coming to Orange County. I'm safe where I've been staying. Just get back on the San Diego Freeway."

"I don't like that idea."

"Nothing in the information you showed me mentions where I am. You only found me because I called you. I'll feel safer in familiar surroundings. Don't think for a moment that you have a vote in this. Now drive."

Donovan didn't argue with her. He followed her directions in what seemed like a maze of apartments. He memorized street signs so he could find his way out, only to understand that she was driving him in circles. Finally, she motioned him to pull to the curb.

"This will work. I can walk from here." Erica popped open the door and jumped out with her bag. "Drive two blocks up this street and then turn left. You'll figure out how to get back to the highway from there."

"Be careful. I'll be in touch tomorrow. Call if you change your mind."

"Go." Erica closed the door.

Donovan sped off. In the mirror, he saw her stand her ground, watching him leave. She was still standing there when he made his left turn. He'd traveled three more blocks when his phone rang. He glanced down and saw that it was Erica calling.

"That was quick," he said as he answered.

"Someone was waiting for me. I'm running west of where you dropped me off. Oh, shit, he's coming, hurry!"

Donovan put the phone on speaker, hit the brakes, and cranked the steering wheel hard to the left. The car spun one hundred and eighty degrees. He downshifted and mashed the gas pedal to the floor. In seconds he flew through sixty miles per hour, reached the corner, switched off his headlights, and slammed on the brakes. He made the turn, downshifted, and accelerated, searching the street ahead for Erica or her pursuers.

When he calculated she couldn't have gone much farther on foot, he slowed dramatically, reached under the seat, and pulled out the pistol. He powered down his window and listened. He heard her voice, but it was coming from the phone not the night air.

"I cut north. Oh, no, I screwed up. There are two of them."

Donovan was about to accelerate to go around the block when he heard a gunshot come from between the buildings just to his left. He grabbed the phone and the gun and jumped out of the Porsche. He began running down sidewalks and as he turned a corner, he saw Erica's bag lying on the ground. He scooped it up and kept going. He looked at the phone, the counter was running, the call was still connected. From both the phone and to his right he heard a muffled scream.

He ran toward the sound, but before he reached the corner of the building, two men came the other way, they each had an arm under Erica's, half carrying, half dragging her. A strip of duct tape had been pressed over her mouth. Donovan stopped and raised the pistol. "Let her go!"

The second the words came out, he knew he'd made a mistake.

Buck's words echoes in his mind. *If you decide to point your gun, the time for talking is over.* The man on Donovan's left raised his free hand, a pistol clearly visible. Donovan squeezed the trigger just as the man fired. The sound of both gunshots was deafening as it echoed through the apartment complex. The man went limp and hit the sidewalk hard as he collapsed into Erica. She untangled herself from him, shoving the other man just as he, too, raised his gun and fired at Donovan. This time Donovan heard the hot sizzle of the bullet whiz past his head. Off balance, the remaining man struggled to aim his weapon. Donovan was about to fire again when Erica picked up the first man's weapon and shot the final assailant twice, once in the chest and once in the head. Erica ripped the tape off her mouth, fished in the pockets of the first man who'd gone down, and extracted both her gun and his wallet.

"Let's go," she said.

Donovan took one look back at the two men lying on the ground and with no remorse whatsoever, took Erica by the arm running with her back through the buildings to the Porsche, still idling in the street.

Donovan jumped behind the wheel, his thigh burning from the exertion. He pushed in the clutch, found first gear, and without turning on the headlights, sped into the night. Street by street Erica led him to a back way out of the development and onto a major road that fed into Highway 133 south that would take them through the canyon to Laguna Beach.

"The first shot I heard, you or them?"

"Me. I'd just put my key in the lock when the first guy showed up. I ran, but the second guy was on me before I could get off a good shot."

"You redeemed yourself," Donovan said. "Are you okay?"

"I'm fine. I watched you stand there all calm like, guns blazing, while you came to my rescue. Thank you."

Donovan wondered what she was really feeling. He wondered what he was feeling. They'd both just killed, and he felt nothing but relief. She seemed unaffected as well. He wondered if the shock and sorrow would come later, or if he were already so damaged that killing a man wouldn't even register above all the other stresses in his life.

"Who is he?" Donovan asked as Erica found the dome light and started going through the wallet she'd lifted.

"I don't know. All that's in this is cash and a key card. Did they look like any of the guys in the photos the FBI showed you, the ones from Hawaii?"

"They looked the absolute opposite. The crew from Hawaii were a little on the scruffy, unkempt side. The guys back there were wearing slacks and sport coats."

"They weren't messing around. They came right for me. It was hard to miss their intent. My question is why were they trying to kidnap me? Why not just kill me?"

"They wanted to interrogate you."

Erica looked behind them. "I hope we're not going very far. A red Porsche 911 is going to be easy to spot—you've got to think someone saw us leave the scene."

"We'll be fine. We're headed back to Laguna Beach, but first we need to get rid of these guns."

"Give yours to me," Erica held out her hand. She pulled a t-shirt from her bag, ejected the round from the cylinder, dropped the clip, and then broke down the rest of the pistol. She carefully wiped down each component then repeated the process on her gun as well as the one she'd taken from the scene. "Can your gun be traced back to you?"

"No."

"I hate to be without weapons right now, but you're right, we need to unload these."

"Where'd you learn to shoot?"

"I'm the only child of a man who'd hoped for a son."

He swung in behind an auto-body shop and Erica jumped out and buried the parts of the pistols in two different dumpsters.

Donovan pulled back out and they cruised into downtown Laguna Beach, finally swinging onto the Pacific Coast Highway, heading south.

Donovan's phone rang. It was a number he didn't recognize. He motioned for Erica not to say a word.

He answered as neutral as he could. "Nash here."

"Robert," the raspy voice began. "I wanted to give you a heads up about a new video that's going to go viral in about thirty minutes. Meredith would have really liked this one, so will you. I can't wait to see the public's reaction. You can find this one on YouTube under *bear's revenge*."

"Why try to kill me before you post another video? Seems rather counterproductive."

"It's not your time, Robert. You've grown paranoid. I told you, I don't want you to die just yet, I want you to suffer."

"I'm talking about your thugs twenty minutes ago."

"It wasn't me, but if you stop and think about it, you've developed quite a few new enemies in the last thirty-six hours. People are calling for your head. It's just like old times, isn't it? Good-bye, Robert, and be safe."

Donovan hung up the phone and looked at Erica. "That was Garrick. They're getting ready to post another video."

"Oh, God, it is so terrifying to think that you were on the phone with him. What did he say when you asked him why he tried to kill us?"

"He said it wasn't him. According to him, it's not my time. He wants me alive for the time being, and I believe him." Donovan started the car. "He doesn't know about you, and we need to keep it that way."

"Well, that narrows it down. If it's not him, then it's either your wife, the CIA, or Mossad."

"It's not Lauren, but we can't rule out the other two options, which makes this a far different game than if we were only hiding from Garrick. Take the battery out of your phone. We'll get you another one tomorrow. We also need to get this car back where I found it. It's not far."

Donovan pulled into the driveway and raised the garage door. He backed in and positioned the Porsche exactly where it had been. They took turns wiping down anything they might have touched.

Erica grabbed her bag and surveyed the small collection of automobiles. "Do you live here?"

"No, this is a friend's place. Follow me." Donovan shut the garage door. He called out for William as he headed for the study, but there was no answer.

"Jesus," Erica whispered as she took in the opulent surroundings.

Donovan made sure she followed him into the study where he found a note on the desk. William had gone to the hotel for the night, but he expected a call no matter how late it was. Donovan touched the mouse and the thirty-two-inch monitor sprang to life. He made a mental note to ask William a computer question as he quickly typed in the web address that Garrick had given him.

The image jumped badly and was out of focus, but Donovan could hear the distinct sound of someone breathing heavily. The focus sharpened, and he could see a heavyset man in his underwear running away from the camera. The scene was heavily forested. Periodically, the man would snap his neck around to gauge his distance from the person chasing him, and each time he did, the camera would get closer. The chase went on for maybe fifty yards before the man tripped and fell to his knees. He pitched forward, his shoulder slamming heavily into a tree trunk. Momentarily stunned, he shook his head and wobbled to his feet, his chest was heaving, steam rising from his overheated body. He took two steps toward the camera as if to attack, and the smooth, black barrel of a hunting rifle rose into the field of view. The image froze and another website address appeared. Donovan quickly typed and hit enter.

After the redirect, he clicked to start the next video. The cornered man charged the camera just as the rifle roared and bucked, the bullet opened up the flesh just below the man's left clavicle. There was a plume of misted blood, as the impact spun the man around, dropping him to his knees. The second shot was at nearly point-blank range and was aimed just above his ear. Donovan flinched as the man's lifeless body fell to the ground.

Wearing surgical gloves, two hands came into view, and an incision was made across the man's stomach. The image of the intestines spilling out onto the ground was sickening, and moments later the blade had removed a round organ about the size of a plum. It was carefully placed in a plastic bag.

"It's his gallbladder," Erica said.

The camera zoomed away from the body to a wider view, and two men wearing masks and gloves each grabbed a leg. As they turned to drag the corpse, Donovan saw that Eco-Watch was printed in bold letters across the back of their blue jackets. The dead man was dragged a short distance before he was rolled down an embankment where he came to a stop next to three other naked bodies. Every one of the men had been disemboweled. The screen faded out leaving one simple statement.

> IT'S ESTIMATED THAT POACHERS SUCH AS THESE ACCOUNT FOR 50,000 BLACK BEAR DEATHS EACH YEAR FOR THE ASIAN MARKETS. ECO-WATCH WILL RELENTLESSLY HUNT THESE CRIMINALS UNTIL THE FORESTS ARE ONCE AGAIN SAFE FOR ALL OF NATURE'S CREATURES.

"Did we just see that?" Erica said. "Oh, my God, that was awful."

"Yeah," Donovan noticed the number of views was already climbing. "Now he's making threats on my behalf."

Donovan's phone rang, and he saw it was Lauren. He let it go to voice mail, he'd catch up with her later. When the phone continued to ring, Donovan switched it to silent mode.

Erica pointed to the wet bar in the corner situated amongst the bookshelves. "I don't know about you, but I need a drink. What can I get you?"

"Crown Royal on the rocks." Donovan watched as Erica shed her jacket and boots and set them near the leather sofa. She released the elastic band from her ponytail and then ran her fingers through her blond hair. In her stocking feet she padded to the bar and began rummaging around until she found two glasses. As she filled them with ice, he saw that her hands were shaking. She found the bottle she was looking for and poured them both four fingers of Canadian whisky. She brought Donovan his drink and held up her own for a toast.

"What are we drinking to?" Donovan asked.

"I've finally decided not to shoot you." Erica touched her glass to his then took a drink, her eyes never leaving his.

"That's good to hear." Donovan looked away and sipped at his, but instead of savoring the smooth burn, he realized for the first time how truly beautiful Erica was, and he also understood it had been a long time since he'd been alone with such a desirable woman. He took another pull from the whisky, larger this time.

Erica reached out and put her hand on the side of his face, stood on her tiptoes, and kissed him lightly on the lips. "Thank you for saving my life."

Donovan took in her closeness as she kissed him again. He kissed back, feeling her warm breath against his skin.

She pulled away, cocked her head to one side, and studied him as she ran her fingers along his jaw line. "You've had work done. It's very good. Who did the surgery?"

Donovan was caught completely off guard, and he stepped back from her and turned away. His facial reconstruction had been done over twenty years earlier by a renowned doctor in Switzerland, who, like all Swiss, specialized in discretion. The multiple surgeries were the actual physical transformation from being Robert Huntington to becoming Donovan Nash. The doctor had been dead for years now, and as part of the agreement, Donovan had retained all of the medical files. No one had ever called him on it before. He knew she was asking out of professional curiosity, but he couldn't afford to be drawn into this conversation.

"I'm sorry," she said.

"It was a long time ago." Donovan shrugged, but deep down he found he was relieved. From the urgency of their kiss and the emotion of what they'd been through, he doubted they would have stopped. He was also aware that it was his hidden past and the lies that destroyed the moment, not any particular restraint on his part. "I was in an accident. I don't like to talk about it."

"I didn't mean to cross any boundaries."

"You didn't. You surprised me on a couple of different levels, that's all. I don't like to think about what happened." Donovan lowered his voice as he carefully worded the lie that would hopefully explain his reaction to her question. "Someone close to me died."

"I'm so sorry," Erica started to say something but stopped, then turned and went to the bar. She freshened his drink. "Peace offering?"

"Sure, thanks."

She spotted the remote control and turned on the large flatscreen television, switched it to CNN, and muted the sound. She moved around the desk and sat down, taking a big sip from her glass. "I was never sure if anyone at the clinic ever discovered I'd made copies. I never told a soul until tonight, and thirty minutes later someone shows up and tries to kidnap me. The only explanation is that your source triggered something. How exactly did you get that file on me? Someone knows about me because you went digging."

Donovan had already reached the same conclusion. If Garrick was the one who destroyed the clinic, and he knew Erica was alive, he'd simply kill her as he'd done with the other employees. If Lauren's information had been leaked, either it was from her source, which was CIA, or Mossad had somehow intercepted it and tried to snatch Erica.

"Are you listening to me?" Erica snapped. "Who else knows I left the clinic before the murders?"

"I'm not entirely certain."

Erica took another pull from her drink and closed her eyes.

Donovan wordlessly watched the television until he was convinced that at least for the moment, Eco-Watch wasn't the lead story on television. "I really should go make those calls now. I need to call my business partner and my wife."

Eyes still closed, Erica nodded.

He walked away and dialed William's cell phone. The elder statesman answered immediately.

"I hope I didn't wake you." Donovan said.

"No, I was waiting to hear from you, and then Peggy called and told me about the latest video. I trust you're up to speed?"

"Yeah, I got another call."

"Where are you? Did you find the girl?"

"I'm back at John's house. She's with me, and there were—complications. Do you remember Garrick Pearce?"

"Dear God, I thought he was rotting in a prison somewhere in South America where he belonged."

"He's out, and he has his vision back. There's also a woman, she might be the one the FBI and Interpol are trying to identify. Her name is Nikolett Kovarik."

"I'll see what I can dig up on her."

"While you're digging, can you find out if there are any open cases involving Erica Covington? The complications we ran into tonight may have been courtesy of Langley."

"That's not good. You think the CIA used you and Lauren to find this woman?"

"That's what I want to know."

"I'll make a few discreet inquiries," William said. "I found a wire transfer that took place shortly after the *Triton* sailed from Hawaii. I followed the thread and it looks like whoever killed John and Beverly extorted ten million dollars in the process."

"Can the money be traced?"

"No chance," William replied. "It's already bounced through half a dozen offshore accounts."

"Ten million is a lot of money to wage a personal war." Donovan sighed. "Does John own any guns?"

"Credenza, lower right-hand drawer, there's a gun safe, the code is 8-7-6-2."

"Thanks," Donovan replied.

"Get some rest," William said. "Be careful, and I'll be over first thing in the morning. There's work to be done."

"See you in the morning."

Donovan glanced across the room. Erica was leaning back in the soft leather desk chair with her feet up, and her eyes closed. Her hair had partially spilled over her forehead, and her cocktail was cradled in both hands resting on her stomach. He could see the glass slowly rise and fall with each breath as she slept. She looked both disheveled and angelic—a mix of chaos and flawlessness. He grabbed a blanket from the sofa, slipped the drink from her hands, and covered her.

He quietly opened the drawer of the credenza, punched in the code and picked up the heavy, forty-five-caliber Colt. He checked the magazine and chamber, happy that it was fully loaded. Gun in hand, he grabbed his drink and went up the stairs and into one of the guest rooms. He closed the door, sat in a chair, and spent a few minutes finishing his drink, collecting himself before he dialed Lauren.

CHAPTER THIRTEEN

Lauren held Abigail's hand as her energetic three-year-old pulled, then jumped up and down with excitement at the prospect of joining her friends at preschool. It was only a few hours, three times a week, but Lauren thought the structure was important, and her daughter was absorbing the French language at an astonishing rate.

"Give Mommy and Aunt Stephanie a kiss good-bye," Lauren said, kneeling to her daughter's level.

Abigail spun around, her blond locks bouncing wildly. She held Lauren's face in her little hands and planted a kiss on Lauren's cheek, and then on Stephanie's. Lauren always hated these separations.

Abigail pulled away, smiled, and waved. "Au revoir, Maman!"

Lauren returned the wave, her heart breaking a little at how much her daughter looked like her father. Lauren wasn't happy with Donovan, or at least she was unhappy with the events taking place in her husband's life. She'd called him when he was on his way to meet with Erica Covington. He'd said he'd call her back and hadn't. She'd called again when William had texted her about the newest video and still she hadn't heard anything. Part of her was worried and another part was just plain damn mad. Donovan always seemed to push her away when he was in crisis. The issue was at the core of their problems, and he was doing it again.

"Where shall we go?" Stephanie asked. "I don't think I can eat after seeing that video, but I'd love some good old-fashioned American coffee. How about that place we saw yesterday, it's not far. The Café Columbus? Maybe we can find a nice quiet table outside."

Lauren had been there many times, it would work nicely, and

Henri approved of the layout. Lauren had almost quit noticing her bodyguards. Giselle stayed at the school keeping an eye on Abigail. Henri and Philippe were somewhere, roving, watching.

It was early for the lunch crowd, and the café was nearly empty. Much to Stephanie's delight, they were able to find a corner table outside on the patio. It was just the two of them and they both ordered coffee.

"Donovan's fine," Stephanie said once they were alone. "He'll call when he can. There's the time difference, plus he's jumping time zones like crazy. There's got to be all kinds of fallout from this thing. Plus, he's surrounded by Buck and Michael and the FBI."

"Donovan ditched everyone to go meet with Erica. For all I know, she was a trap."

"He's fine. If it was a trap, he had a way out."

"How can you always be so confident when it comes to Donovan? Granted, he's done some remarkable things, but he's only human."

"I know he failed you. He knows it too, he has no defense for how badly he ignored and marginalized you. You have every right to feel hurt and betrayed, and I understand exactly why you left him. I get it. Donovan has enough demons for a roomful of people, and it was almost inevitable that his emotional house of cards was going to fall apart, but don't let his current failure cloud your entire vision."

"You know him as a friend," Lauren said, choosing her words carefully. "That allows for considerable more leeway in terms of his behavior. Donovan's job description in my universe is husband—not friend. I'm well aware of Donovan's baggage and how troubled he can be, and how the level of internal turmoil can vary from day to day. I know about Meredith, what she meant to him, it's one of the things that makes him human, makes me love him. But until Donovan can trust me enough to be honest, and to feel safe in coming to me with any or all of his troubles, as he seems to have been able to do with her, then we'll be at this impasse. I have no interest in being his wife if he chooses to treat me as if my place is on the sidelines. It's as simple as that."

"I know." Stephanie nodded her head in reluctant agreement. "You're right. I hope he figures it out."

Lauren's phone rang and Stephanie looked at her expectantly. She pulled it from her jacket pocket and saw that the call was from Donovan. "It's him, would you please excuse me for a moment?"

"I have to go to the restroom anyway." Stephanie got up from the table and disappeared into the restaurant.

"Hello," Lauren answered.

"Sorry it's taken me so long to call back, but it's been nothing but chaos here."

"Where are you?"

"I'm back at John's house, it's late here. Where are you?"

"I'm at a café with Stephanie. We just dropped Abigail off at preschool."

"She loves that place," Donovan's tone softened. "It's all she talks about when we Skype."

"Did you meet with her?" Lauren abruptly changed the subject. "Did she have anything useful to tell you?"

"Yeah, I know who's doing all of this to us."

Lauren didn't miss the fact that Donovan used the word us. She wondered if it referred to their marriage, or Eco-Watch.

"Can you tell me on an open line?"

"You've heard of him. He's British and was involved with her before I was—always held a grudge."

Lauren instantly knew he was talking about Garrick Pearce. A recent documentary of Meredith Barnes had covered Meredith's years before she met Robert Huntington. The film focused on Garrick, her former boyfriend turned militant environmentalist and the rift that developed when Meredith started dating Robert. From what Lauren remembered, Garrick was portrayed as volatile and impulsive. But he was supposed to be in a South American prison.

"Do you know who I'm talking about?"

"Yes, I thought he was somewhere south?"

"So did I, but he's not, and his stay in a German clinic restored his sight. You can't breathe a word about this to anyone but Stephanie. She'll remember him. Something else happened tonight that I don't understand."

Lauren recognized his tone of voice and braced herself. When Donovan said he didn't understand something, it usually meant he knew exactly what had happened and wasn't happy.

"Go on."

"After our meeting, I dropped her off and there were two men waiting. They tried to kidnap her."

"They failed?"

"Yes."

"Do you think the attempted kidnapping was connected to what's happening to Eco-Watch?"

"No."

"That's not good."

"I think your search sparked some concern. It's either Langley or Tel Aviv."

"Oh, God." Lauren suddenly wondered if she'd been compromised. "Where is she now?"

"I promised her a safe haven for her information."

"Of course, you did." The words jumped out before Lauren could stop them. She felt the unexpected pang of jealousy reach out and blindside her. Donovan always saw the good in people, and while he wasn't easily played, he could be naïve at times.

"What are you implying?"

"Nothing," Lauren backpedaled. "Forget I said that. What else did you learn?"

"While he was at the clinic, he was in the company of a Hungarian woman. I'll text you her name. She could be of interest."

Lauren heard her phone beep, alerting her to another call. A quick look told her it was Fredrick. "I'll see what I can do. I need to go. Let's talk later."

"I think we should—"

Lauren cut Donovan off midsentence and switched over to Fredrick. "Hello."

"We have a problem. You're being watched, and I don't think your security team has picked up on it yet. The gray Peugeot sedan parked down the street. It's been close since you left the apartment. We want to grab these guys. I have a team around the corner. All I need from you is a distraction that will get your bodyguards out of the mix."

"Get ready." Lauren said, then severed the call. From behind her sunglasses she located the car. It was the first she'd seen of it, but she trusted Fredrick and his team. She spotted Henri and then Philippe as they scouted the approaches to the patio. She needed to make her move while Stephanie was still inside the café.

Lauren stood up abruptly, a move that would be noticed by her bodyguards. Acting as if she were reacting to something from inside the café, Lauren bolted through the front door. She located the corridor that led to the restrooms, hurried past the customers and staff, and as soon as she was outside the door to the ladies' room she screamed as loud as she could for Stephanie.

The door flew open and Stephanie stood there, her eyes wide with terror.

"Oh, thank God!" Lauren threw her arms around her friend as Henri drew closer. Lauren whispered in Stephanie's ear, "Play along."

"I'm okay!" Stephanie nodded then clutched at Lauren as if she were truly terrified.

"What happened?" Henri moved into the narrow corridor, pistol drawn. Philippe moved past them and took up a defensive position guarding the hallway that led to the rear of the restaurant.

"I thought I heard something loud from inside, and then I thought I heard Stephanie scream. All I could think was that someone was trying to hurt her."

"I remember a sound too, but it wasn't me," Stephanie replied. "The next thing I heard was you."

"Where did this sound come from?" Henri demanded.

Stephanie shrugged and gestured toward the door to the ladies' room. "I was in there. It could have come from anywhere."

"I'll check out back." Philippe led with his pistol, eased down the corridor, and pushed through a door that led outside.

Henri got on his phone and called the school. He spoke briefly with Giselle and made sure Abigail was safe.

Philippe came back in and declared the alleyway clear of threats.

"Let's go out that way," Henri said. "We'll work our way toward the school and see if we're being followed. It was probably nothing, but let's not take any chances."

Lauren nodded her approval, and as they came out the door and joined the avenue, she glanced to where the Peugeot had been parked and found nothing but an empty space along the curb.

CHAPTER FOURTEEN

Donovan awoke the instant he heard someone call his name. He looked around and found that for the second night in a row he'd fallen asleep fully dressed, but at least this time he was lying on a bed instead of sitting in a chair. He swung his feet to the floor and rubbed his eyes.

Moments later, the door inched open and Erica stuck her head inside. "Oh, good, you're finally up."

"Yeah." Donovan mumbled and picked up his phone, wanting to forget about Lauren and their short conversation last night. He moved the forty-five to the side and realized he'd slept far later than he'd intended, and that his phone was still set to silent mode. He quickly thumbed through the unanswered calls and new texts and he recognized all but one. He opened it and found a single row of numbers and letters:

50410586N127581276W

"I've been up for a little while." Erica picked up the Colt. "I watched television and searched the web. There's no mention of what happened last night, nothing. How can that be? How could the media not cover a double shooting? Where did you get the forty-five?"

The string of numbers was perplexing, and he didn't recognize who'd sent him the text. Still groggy from sleep and distracted by Erica's insistence on talking, it took him longer to grasp the message than it should have. "Damn it!" He checked the time of the message and saw he'd received it shortly after he'd watched the newest video, right about the time he started ignoring his phone.

He jumped up, flew past Erica, and ran down the stairs toward the study.

"What are you doing?" Erica followed and stationed herself behind him to peer over his shoulder. "You didn't answer my question, where did you get the gun?"

"I borrowed it from the man who owns the house. Listen, a series of numbers and letters was left on my phone. I think Garrick sent it last night." Donovan Googled the word *coordinates* and clicked on the website he wanted. He split up the single line and retyped them as latitude and longitude, then pressed enter. A globe came into view and spun to show the Northern Hemisphere. It began to zoom in, borders appeared, and Donovan felt a rush of excitement as the exact spot on the globe was pinpointed. The location was on the north end of Vancouver Island, British Columbia. The area was heavily forested with swaths of open fields from clear-cutting, the exposed ground like a raw wound where the trees had been cut and hauled away. A few mining roads twisted like ribbons through the hills, there were no towns close, just a vast wilderness. Donovan zoomed in, but the image became distorted. Frustrated with the lack of clarity, he pulled up a different website. He typed in a password and began to sift through raw satellite images. NASA provided the access and Eco-Watch used the information for geophysical modeling. When he located Vancouver Island, he once again zoomed in on the coordinates. This time he was able to draw down until he had a crisp image of the exposed mining road closest to the coordinates.

"What are you looking for?" Erica asked.

"Tracks in the dirt." Donovan used the tip of a pen to show her what he was seeing. "This image was taken over a month ago. Look at the indentations in the soil. These wide tracks are most certainly from the heavy logging trucks, but they look old and washed out. These narrower tracks look altogether different."

"A car or a small truck?"

"The tires are too narrow." Donovan traced the length of road with the pen. "They begin here and end over here, multiple times.

I think we're looking at an improvised landing strip. Someone has been flying in and out, which is my guess as to how the poachers operate. These clear-cut areas would be a great place to bait the bears into the open."

"Is that how Garrick got there?"

Donovan turned his head and found her much closer than he expected and she was no less beautiful in the morning than she'd been last night. "I have no idea, but it's how we're getting there."

"And why would we do that?"

"Because that's where a pit full of dead poachers can be found."

"Are you kidding?" She leaned over him. "There's nothing out there besides that one little logging road. Plus, how are we getting into Canada? My passport is no doubt flagged; I'd never make it out of the airport. Just call the FBI, give them the coordinates, they'll call the Mounties and it's done."

"We need to get there first," Donovan took a closer look at the road and surrounding terrain. He judged the landing strip to be no more than two thousand feet long and about ten feet wide.

When he pulled up the aviation weather information for Vancouver Island, his hopes sunk. The entire area was covered by low clouds. He read the real-time reports from Port Hardy, the nearest airport, and found that the ceiling was below four hundred feet and the visibility less than a mile in fog and light rain. He read the forecast, which called for a clearing trend to begin in ten to twelve hours, followed by another front moving in that promised more low ceilings and marginal visibility. He clicked on the satellite image and could see the distinct striations in the swirling mass of moisture over the Pacific Northwest. Off the west coast of Vancouver Island was the gap in the clouds the forecast models described. He put the image into motion and glanced at his watch. He wouldn't get there as fast as he'd like, but he could conceivably be there when the weather cleared in twelve hours.

They both heard a door open and shut somewhere in the house and Donovan took the pistol from Erica and held it low. He relaxed when he heard William call out to ask if anyone was home.

"We're in here!" Donovan turned to Erica and spoke quietly. "William is in the loop about everything that happened last night except the part where we killed two people. Not a word."

Erica nodded.

When Donovan introduced Erica, William was gracious as always. After pleasantries, Donovan brought William up to speed and showed him where the coordinates led.

"Have you spoken to Michael?" William asked. "Do we know how soon the Gulfstream can fly?"

"I haven't, but maybe we need to forgo the Eco-Watch jet for this one."

"I think you're right." William said as he slid his phone from his pocket.

"Who are you calling?" Donovan asked.

"There are several options. Leave it to me. How soon do you want to leave and where do you want to land?"

"I keep telling you," Erica said, "customs will run my name, and the police will be waiting for me anywhere we land."

"Who said we're stopping at customs?" Donovan replied. "See if we can make our departure for noon. Erica and I have an errand to run. Set everything up to arrive at Bellingham, Washington."

"Got it," William said with a nod. "In some of John's papers, I found that he owns a Gulfstream IV as well as the Falcon 900 that Beverly used to get to Hawaii. He leases both of them back to the firm. Shall I see if the Gulfstream is free to run you up there, or do you want to charter?"

"How about you call Gulfstream and see what they can do for us? Have them book something for us so we can leave Eco-Watch entirely out of the equation."

"I like that."

"I almost forgot," Donovan said. "Something I've been meaning to ask you. Was John's computer on when we arrived yesterday, or did you use a password?"

"No, it was up and running, why?"

"Did you find that odd? That John would leave for Australia and leave his computer on."

"I assumed Beverly uses the office and in her haste to leave she left it on."

"Did you check the browser history?"

"It had been deleted."

"So someone erased the history, but left it on?" Donovan was beginning to get a bad feeling. "Does that strike anyone else as strange?"

"You think someone was here?" William asked. "Then erased the history?"

"Check the print queue," Erica offered. "See if anything's listed there that shouldn't be."

"I don't know what that means," Donovan said and moved his hands off the keyboard as Erica leaned in and maneuvered the mouse until she found what she was looking for.

"There you go," she said. "It's a log of everything that's been printed. There's the date and time."

Donovan scrolled down and instantly knew that someone had been in the house using the computer. He began clicking on each document, sending it to the printer. Donovan pulled out the first sheet, and after studying it briefly, realized he was looking at a contact list. The next four pages were more of the same. On the fifth page were his name, address, and phone numbers, along with his date of birth as well as Lauren and Abigail's. Three pages later came all of William's information as well as Stephanie's.

"Garrick was here. He accessed Beverly's address book. It's how he knew about Lauren and Abigail." Donovan handed the last sheet to William. "He also knows about you and Stephanie."

The whir of the printer announced that there were more pages coming, and as the next sheet hit the tray, Donovan felt a lurch in the pit of his stomach. They were photographs. Like most people, Beverly and John kept all of their photographs stored on their computer's hard drive. There were wedding pictures of Donovan and

Lauren, followed by images of Stephanie and William. The last image that landed in the tray was a recent photo of Lauren and Abigail taken in Europe. Abigail was wearing a new dress she'd told him all about, there was no mistaking the glass structure in the background. The photo was taken in Paris in front of the Louvre.

Donovan turned to William. "Garrick knows where they are."

CHAPTER FIFTEEN

"I don't want to know how you extracted the information," Lauren said to Fredrick. He'd called to update her on the two men they'd picked up earlier and persuaded to talk. "Besides, what makes you think any of it's true?"

"Despite your aversion to whatever methods we may have used, I promise they were effective. These guys aren't trained operatives, they're thugs. The men today had photos of you, Abigail, and Stephanie. In the car we found a Taser, rope, and rohypnol."

"The date-rape drug?" Lauren felt an involuntary shiver at the thought of being abducted. "They were going to kidnap us?"

"We also found a video camera."

Lauren knew exactly what the two men were trying to accomplish. Her revulsion turned into anger. This was Garrick Pearce's doing. He intended to send a video to Donovan—payback for what Garrick thought Donovan had done to Meredith. It was both simple and brutal. Lauren would never again underestimate the threat that Garrick Peace represented.

"We're not sure of anything at this point," Fredrick replied. "It could have been a kidnapping-for-ransom scheme, or a straight-up murder, captured on video to send a message."

"What does that mean?" Lauren asked.

"We've eliminated the immediate threat, but I have real concerns about your friends from Mossad. They should have detected this threat at the same time we did. Has there been any fallout at your end about the diversion you created today?"

"None. Henri is worried though."

"He should be. I want you to give some thought to leaving Paris. There's a safe house in England you could use while we sort this out."

"I'll think about it," Lauren already knew that if she left Paris it wouldn't be to a CIA safe house in England. She'd vanish where no one could find her. She remembered all too clearly what Donovan had said to her about the two men waiting for Erica Covington. As Lauren compared the two scenarios, something seemed off. Erica wasn't tied to Robert Huntington or Meredith Barnes. If anything, Erica was nothing more than a loose end in Garrick Pearce's bigger plan. Someone to kill, not kidnap. Donovan had inferred that Garrick hadn't been the one who tried to grab Erica, which if true, meant that there was another group involved, and it could very well be Mossad in connection with the German clinic. In Lauren's mind, when you don't know who to trust, you trust no one.

"I'll keep you posted as things develop," Fredrick said. "You do the same."

"Sure." Lauren ended the call and looked at Stephanie. "The guys Fredrick picked up were going to kidnap us. They had drugs, rope, and a video camera. Donovan told me who's behind this. I want to know everything you remember about Garrick Pearce."

"Oh shit," Stephanie stiffened as she heard the name.

"He's not in prison anymore. According to Donovan, the clinic in Germany is where he had his eyesight restored, where he met Erica Covington. You knew him, right?"

"Oh, yeah, I knew him. Meredith was involved with him for a year or so. He was tall, handsome, and charismatic. English, from up north of London, Luton, I believe, came from some money, had made a small name for himself as a documentary filmmaker. I think he and Meredith met during the taping of one of her television shows. They had an on-again off-again relationship. When Robert came along the relationship was at a low point. Everyone could see the end coming except Garrick."

"So he was a decent guy once?"

"I don't know about that. I remember at that time I was still shooting pictures for a living, and Meredith got me an exclusive shoot with *National Geographic*. A behind-the-scene look at Meredith Barnes on location in London. Garrick was there, hovering and generally being a jerk. Meredith was the picture of class and poise, and Garrick was volatile, like an unstable explosive that might go off with the slightest nudge."

"How many times were you actually in the same room with him?"

"Maybe half a dozen, mostly media events, a few parties. Once Meredith and Donovan were together, they eventually left Los Angeles and moved up to Monterey, California. That's when Garrick unraveled. Once, I was with some people at a club in Hollywood and Garrick was there. He came over, said hello. Polite at first, but all of a sudden, he became agitated, gesturing loudly, and then talking quietly, as if everything he said was classified. He started asking me if I wanted to win a Pulitzer, that he was going to commit the greatest protest on behalf of the environment the world had ever seen and did I want to be there to photograph the event? I tried to pin him down, but he was elusive. He told me that if I agreed, I'd have to be sequestered with the others until the protest. I told him no."

"He accepted that?"

"Not at first. He kept ranting. When I finally tried to walk away, he grabbed me. I guess he'd attracted attention because the second he touched me, there were two bouncers on him, and they dragged him out. I never saw him again, though Donovan told me later that he paid Garrick a visit to warn him in person that if he ever touched me again, he'd pay dearly. Donovan's threats are never subtle, so I can only imagine what was said."

"Didn't Meredith publicly disavow him?" Lauren asked. "When did that happen?"

"Garrick formed the One Earth Society, a direct reference to her best-selling book, and promised to pick up with violent action where her nonviolent tactics left off. His past ties with her lent him credibility and his visibility grew. At first the One Earth Society did jobs like setting fire to new subdivisions being built on virgin land or attacking Hummer dealerships to protest the gas-guzzling SUVs. They broke into a lab funded by a cosmetics company and rescued animals that were the subjects of tests, setting the place on fire as they fled. Media was on site for that one, masked men running from a burning building holding an assortment of puppies and monkeys. I heard he raised a lot of money from that job, and that's when Meredith stepped in and condemned his methods and actions, disavowing any and all connections with the OES, and publically denouncing Garrick and his group as nothing more than overgrown vandals. Garrick's flow of financial support dried up overnight."

"I vaguely remember that," Lauren said.

"So Garrick did what all belittled men do. He tried to commit some grand act of retribution, as if he could create virtue for himself where there was none. He tried to kidnap the CEO of Zenith Labs, the world's fifth largest pharmaceutical company. His effort failed and most of the members of OES were arrested. Garrick fled the country. I once heard him say that for a revolution to succeed, it needed violence, the more shocking the violence the more immediate the results. Garrick probably learned a great deal about brutality in a Brazilian prison. We've seen on the videos what he's capable of now, which makes him far more dangerous than he ever was before. Garrick is one of the angriest men I've ever met."

"He may not be our only problem," Lauren said. "Donovan also told me that someone tried to kidnap Erica Covington. When I asked him if he thought Garrick was behind it, he said no."

"Why would Garrick kidnap the girl? Wouldn't he just want her dead because she worked at the clinic?"

"That's what I thought, but remember what Aaron told us, how Mossad was very interested in a certain woman who may or may not be an assassin?"

Stephanie nodded.

"According to Donovan, Erica knows exactly who this woman is. She was at the clinic with Garrick, Donovan texted me her name. She goes by Nikolett Kovarik. I think Mossad wants Erica because she's a de facto witness to what took place at the clinic."

"How could Mossad know about her? How could they have moved on her as fast as they did?" Stephanie asked. "I mean, the CIA just learned there might be a survivor yesterday."

"Maybe Mossad had the CIA's help." Lauren felt her frustration rise. "I don't know anything right now except I don't trust anyone. I want to be free of all of them; Mossad, the CIA, everyone."

"How do we do that?"

"Let's give it some thought. We have to figure out how to get out of France with both Mossad and the CIA watching us."

"We also need to avoid Garrick's people," Stephanie added.

"Garrick's team got caught, and it might take some time for backup to arrive." Lauren's analytical mind was racing through a dozen scenarios she'd put in place the moment she'd arrived in Paris. "I'm going to make some phone calls, but we're leaving here as soon as possible."

"On what pretense?"

"I don't know, anything, we'll go shopping with Abigail, but once we leave we're not coming back."

"What about luggage?"

"Take what you can't live without and leave the rest," Lauren said. "You have a British passport, right?"

"I have two. I have a British passport under my married name. Once I got divorced, I kept it; it's still valid for another year. I also have a United States diplomatic passport issued through Uncle William and the State Department. It has my maiden name."

"Perfect. We'll use the British one. If people are looking for us, I bet they'll look for Stephanie VanGelder not Stephanie Osborn."

"What about you?"

"I have three different sets of identities," Lauren said. "Donovan saw to that a long time ago. Once I make some calls, we'll be able to figure out the rest of our plan, but I think sooner is better than later."

Stephanie leaned over, gave Lauren a hug, and whispered. "I hope one of those phone calls is to Donovan."

Lauren returned the hug, but didn't say a word. Her husband was the last person who needed to know what she was about to do.

CHAPTER SIXTEEN

William shook his head in frustration. "How could I have missed the fact that Garrick was here?"

"Garrick's smart and he had all the security codes and passwords from Beverly. If it hadn't been for Erica, we'd have never known," Donovan said. "This stays between the three of us. Garrick doesn't know about Erica or the fact that we know about him."

"You need to warn Lauren," William said.

"She already knows it's Garrick. She's in good hands. Erica and I need to leave. I gather you're going to stay here."

"That's my plan, unless you need me in Canada," William said as he initiated a call from his considerable list of stored numbers.

"No. In fact, I need your eyes and ears on the investigation here. My disappearing is going to make some people unhappy."

"That's an understatement," William said then turned away as his call was answered. He identified himself as William VanGelder, chairman of the board of Eco-Watch.

"That's it?" Erica said. "We're going to hop on a private jet and go to Bellingham? What do you have in mind then? Sneak into Canada, hunt for this mass grave, and not tell anyone, then what? How is that going to help us find Garrick?"

Donovan chose to ignore her instead of trying to explain before he was sure of anything. He decided to print out the weather and the image of the logging road and selected each page he wanted. When they were done, he turned to Erica. "I'm going to jump in the shower. We have a long day ahead, and I'll explain everything, I promise. Right now, though, I want to be out of here in forty-five minutes."

Donovan showered, packed, and was waiting in the kitchen for Erica. He decided he had enough time for a quick phone call. "Michael, it's Donovan, I was hoping you had an update on our airplane?"

"The good news is it's a pretty straightforward fix. The compression strut needs to be replaced, so at this very moment we're waiting for the parts we need. They were overnighted from the factory, so we should be airworthy by late this afternoon."

"Good work."

"I've seen the latest video. Are the FBI any closer to finding out who these people are?"

"The FBI has been scarce since yesterday. I think they're happier when we're not demanding their attention. Buck has things in Alaska under control, and according to Peggy, we're pretty well contained, at least for the moment."

"If anything changes at this end, I'll let you know. Maybe we could meet for dinner tonight?"

"I'll get back with you on that." Donovan turned as Erica entered the room. "I need to go. Talk to you later."

"I'm ready," Erica said as she brushed past him and walked toward the garage.

Donovan snatched his briefcase from the kitchen counter and followed.

"This one." Erica pointed to the gray BMW X5. "It'll be the least conspicuous."

"Donovan," William called out, "I just heard back from Gulfstream. They'll have an airplane at Signature Flight Support within the hour to take the two of you to Bellingham. The flight is being charged back as a demonstration flight for a local company. No mention of Eco-Watch, no names at all."

"Thank you," Donovan shook William's hand. "I'll leave the keys to this thing with Signature. Keep everything under control. I won't be reachable, but I'll be in touch."

"Be careful," William said and then handed one of his cards to

Erica. "Keep him out of trouble, and call me if you need help."

Donovan slid behind the wheel, and they pulled out of the garage, leaving Laguna Beach behind. The midmorning traffic was light and they made good time through the canyon. Erica had taken a shower, but she'd been forced to put on the same clothes.

"You're not a very restful sleeper," Erica said.

"What do you mean?"

"I woke up in the middle of the night. I was a little freaked out about everything that had happened. Anyway, it's a big house, but I heard you cry out. I finally found you, but by the time I did, you'd quieted down. Still, you tossed and turned like you were being tortured or something."

"I do remember having some bad dreams," Donovan said with a shrug.

"Make the next right turn." Erica pointed. "Let's drive past the crime scene first, and then we'll swing around to the apartment."

"Okay, but let's keep our eyes open for anyone watching us."

"Slow down." Erica leaned forward, looked past Donovan. Confused, she looked around until she spotted a street sign. "I don't understand. We left the bodies down there between those buildings, where those two sidewalks intersect. Shouldn't there be something there? Crime-scene tape, something?"

Donovan continued to drive, and they pulled around the corner where he eased into a parking lot and found a space. "Where's your apartment from here?"

"It's behind that building right there." Erica pointed off to the left.

Donovan reached into his briefcase, pulled out the pistol, and faced Erica. "Let's go. I want to walk past where we shot those guys. Then we'll check out your apartment."

They strolled down the sidewalk trying to act nonchalant. Donovan saw what could only be a bloodstain on the concrete. He glanced around for any sign of the spent brass that he and Erica had left at the scene. There was nothing. Even the grass looked undisturbed. As they continued to walk past, there were no signs of a crime scene.

"How is this possible?" Erica whispered.

"We need to get out of here. I'm starting to think there were more than two of them last night. Someone cleaned this up before the police showed."

"Oh, no," Erica said as they rounded a corner.

"What is it?"

"Jill's car is parked in the lot. I sublease the apartment from her. She stays at her boyfriend's, but she still has things here." Erica had her keys out and quickly opened the outside door that led into the building.

Donovan followed her down a carpeted hallway. She hurried to a door that read 105. When she turned the key in the deadbolt, the door swung inward. Donovan reached out and grasped her by the upper arm to keep her from charging into the apartment. With the other hand, he gripped the pistol and moved past her into the living room. One glance told him the place had been ransacked. Every drawer, every book, every cushion was lying on the floor. He motioned Erica to follow him quietly. With her behind him, they cleared the kitchen, the bathroom, and Jill's room. Each room had been searched. Donovan pushed open the door that led to Erica's room and on the floor amid all of the papers, books, and boxes, were two bodies. Both facedown, blood leaking from the base of their skulls.

"Oh, God." Erica pushed past Donovan, dropping to her knees next to Jill, putting two fingers on her neck checking for a pulse. She repeated the process with the young man, slumping when she realized they were both gone. "They're cold. They've been dead for hours. I just talked with Jill yesterday. She didn't say anything about coming over."

"I'm so sorry," Donovan offered.

Erica stood and faced Donovan. Tears streaked from pleading eyes as she leaned into him, sobbing, pounding his chest in absolute helplessness. "Those men were looking for me. They found Jill and David instead. How? They're both dead because of me. How is that even possible?"

CHAPTER SEVENTEEN

Lauren casually flipped through an elegant display of summer dresses. Abigail was nearby, playing with a new doll Stephanie had bought her. The three of them were at Le Bon Marché, one of the upscale boutique malls in Paris. She'd placed a series of calls to solidify her plans to escape Paris and leave both Mossad and the CIA behind.

A glance at her watch told her pieces of her escape plan were still being brought together and she had to continue to be patient. Once everything started, she and Stephanie needed to keep on a precise schedule to reach the rendezvous point that would get them out of the city.

Lauren's main concern was her three bodyguards. Henri, Philippe, and Giselle were roaming the floor. She easily found Henri, the tallest and with a shaved head. He was poised over by a rack of shoes that broke up his outline but gave him a sweeping view of the shopping area. As always, he had his earpiece firmly in place and could instantly connect to Philippe and Giselle who were out of sight but close.

Lauren glanced at her watch. They still had twenty-five minutes before all of the components would be in position for them to make their move. "Do you need to go to the little girl's room?" Lauren asked Abigail.

"Oui!" Abigail slid off the chair, carefully clutching her newest doll. Lauren took Abigail's hand and they walked down an aisle toward the ladies' room, finding Henri just ahead. She smiled. An instant later Henri's head snapped backward, and he dropped to the floor as if both legs had failed. Lauren, firmly holding Abigail's hand, dashed toward the downed man. She'd almost reached him when Philippe materialized from nowhere and scooped up Abigail, quietly but firmly ordering Lauren to go through the curtain that led into the shoe department's back room. Philippe spoke into his radio, telling Giselle that they were under fire and that Henri was down. He ordered her to collect Stephanie and to bring the car around to the rue de Babylone exit.

"Let me take her." Lauren reached out and took a shocked Abigail from Philippe. "Where's Stephanie?"

"She's with Giselle." Philippe, his weapon drawn, motioned Lauren to take the hallway to their right. "We need to get to the service elevator. It's this way."

"Did you see who did it?"

"I think there are two of them, a man and a woman, and they moved fast. They had a perfect shot at you and took out Henri instead. Silenced weapon, head shot. Henri was gone before he hit the ground."

"Mommy! Where are we going?"

"We need to do what Philippe tells us. Okay? It's like when we play hide-and-seek."

Abigail nodded, but the apprehension in her eyes told Lauren her daughter knew this wasn't a game. Voices behind them in the corridor injected a new wave of fear into the equation, and Lauren urged herself to run faster. They rounded a corner, and to the left, Lauren saw an elevator. She got there first, pressed the down button three times, and then when nothing happened, she instantly began looking for stairs. A weak chime sounded, announcing that the car had arrived. The doors began to open slowly. Lauren, with her hand over Abigail's head, lunged inside only to nearly trip over a body lying on the floor. Lauren spun around so Abigail couldn't see Fredrick's sightless corpse. Lauren fought her revulsion and pushed the button for the ground floor as more shots rang out. Bullets struck metal and drywall, tiny fragments stinging Lauren's face and arms. Philippe fired three quick rounds, backed into the elevator and fired down the hall until the doors eased closed and the elevator began to descend.

"Who's he?" Philippe said as he dropped the empty clip from his Glock, shoved it in his pocket, and rammed a fresh one into place.

"I don't know," Lauren lied. Abigail was clutching Lauren as hard as her three-year-old arms could squeeze. Lauren looked down and saw blood pooling beneath Philippe's leg. "You're hit."

"A little." Philippe nodded and then spoke rapidly. "Once the door opens, let me clear the hallway and then we're out and to the left. There should be an exit onto rue de Babylone. Giselle and Stephanie are already in the car headed our way."

Lauren nodded, relieved that Stephanie was safe, but the relief was short lived as the elevator bottomed out, hesitated, and the doors began to open. Philippe led with his pistol, pointed it first one way and then another. Somewhere in the distance Lauren could hear the distinctive French emergency sirens. The hallway was clear and to their left was a door that led into the retail section and, hopefully, the exit. Philippe took the lead as shoppers alarmed by the earlier gunshots moved toward the large glass doors. Philippe kept his gun low along his leg and motioned Lauren to blend into the crowd. Lauren couldn't help but see the trail of blood Philippe was leaving as they shuffled to the doors. She kept Abigail's head down and barely dared to breathe as they drew closer to freedom.

The small crowd slowed at the restriction of the doors themselves, but Lauren pushed past them, then down a small flight of stairs and out onto the sunlight. The moment she looked up, she saw Giselle flash the lights on the Jaguar. The next moment she saw a familiar face round the corner of the building. Young, pretty, with spiky black hair, and holding a gun. Now Lauren knew who she was running from. The woman in the picture Aaron had shown her—Nikolett Kovarik—the assassin.

Lauren ducked and moved away, trying to cross the street and put traffic between her and Nikolett. Philippe too saw the woman and raised his weapon to fire just as a slug zipped past Lauren and caught Philippe in the midsection. Nikolett hadn't fired; the bullet had come from behind them, across the street. The cluster of people still coming through the door screamed and parted, fleeing the blast of gunfire. Lauren searched for the second shooter, realizing they were pinned down.

Lauren crouched next to Philippe who'd gone white with shock. She picked up his Glock, her desire to protect Abigail far outweighing any hesitation. Desperately, Lauren scanned for Nikolett's accomplice until she spotted a man coming toward her. Lauren saw the gray Jaguar coming fast. Lauren fired at the man, causing him to hesitate long enough for the Jaguar's front grill to hit squarely into him. His gun tumbled away as his body tossed into the air and slammed into a parked delivery van. Giselle expertly backed away, fired three shots toward Nikolett, pinning her behind a parked car.

"Lauren!" Stephanie screamed as she pushed open the rear door of the Jaguar. The sirens told Lauren the police were close. As she bolted for the Jaguar, a volley of gunshots peppered the front of the car. Lauren reached the car and through the open door handed Abigail to Stephanie. Once Abigail was safe, Lauren turned and fired. Nikolett was using a parked car as cover, Lauren's first shot exploded the windshield. She squeezed the trigger and walked each round closer to the assassin. Nikolett hadn't expected return fire from Lauren and dove frantically between two parked cars. The moment Nikolett took cover, Lauren lunged into the backseat of the Jaguar.

"Go!" Stephanie screamed, but the car remained where it was.

Lauren spotted the blood spatter. Giselle had been hit. Without hesitation, Lauren jumped out, fired three more shots in the direction of their pursuer, pushed Giselle out of the way, and slid behind the wheel. Lauren backed up the Jaguar, spun the wheel, put it in drive, and rocketed down a side street. At the first intersection she turned left to find chaos. People were spilling out of Le Bon Marché. She leaned on her horn and parted the angry crowd. When she reached rue de Sèvres, the traffic light was red. Lauren had a window between cars and shot through the intersection, giving them a clear lane down the rue Saint-Placide. In her rearview mirror, Lauren saw a black Mercedes do the same exact thing and her momentary hope for escape vanished. Philippe's Glock was wedged beneath her thigh and the leather seat. She spotted Giselle's weapon on the floor of the passenger's side—well out of reach.

Lauren steered around a car, barely missing a parked truck. With each opening in the traffic, she went faster. She reached for her cell phone and dialed a number she'd committed to memory. A man answered, but she could hardly hear him, with the intense background noise.

"Please tell me you're close," she said. "We'll never make it to the primary extraction point. We're headed to the emergency location."

"Understand. We'll be at the emergency egress point in seven minutes. We're hearing some radio chatter that you're not getting out clean. Confirm your situation and position."

"We're almost there, but we have company. This could get ugly."

"Copy, we'll be on site as fast as possible."

Lauren disconnected the call.

"She's still behind us!" Stephanie said as she snuck a look.

Lauren saw the Mercedes in the mirror. She could see that Abigail had buried her face into Stephanie's shoulder and was screaming uncontrollably. Weaving in and out of slower traffic, ignoring the angry cursing and flashed gestures, each maneuver did nothing to put distance between her and the Mercedes. Nikolett was closing fast.

Lauren blew through a red light, jumped up over the curb, narrowly missing a light pole and two pedestrians. Amid a cacophony of blaring horns she made the right turn onto rue de Rennes. Their destination finally came into view—the fifty-six story Montparnasse Tower.

The Mercedes negotiated the corner Lauren had cut and was

again catching up to them. She maneuvered the Jaguar wildly through a rotary, cut off a bus, and made a hard turn onto rue du Départ. The skyscraper was only a block away. Up ahead a light turned red, she swerved to the right to avoid a car, glanced off a retaining wall, and then wedged the Jaguar up a flight of steps that led up from street level to the main door of the Montparnasse Tower.

"Run for the doors!" Lauren yelled as Stephanie and Abigail bolted for the lobby. She stepped out of the car, turned, and waited. Bystanders had started to move closer until they saw a bloody woman holding a pistol climb from the car, then they scattered.

A private security guard rushed from the building, saw that Lauren was armed, hesitated and drew his weapon.

"Do you speak English?" Lauren shouted, pointing her gun safely at the ground.

"Yes, I speak English. Please put down your gun."

"I'm being chased by an assassin. She's in a black Mercedes. Please help me!"

Lauren saw Stephanie and Abigail reach the doors and make it inside the building. She turned at the squeal of tires just as Nikolett leapt from the Mercedes and fired her pistol. The shot was wide, but startled the security guard. He spoke frantically into his radio, motioning Lauren to run to the doors as he returned fire. Lauren raised Philippe's Glock and fired once, it was her last bullet. Unarmed, she ran for the doors as more gunfire erupted.

Gasping for breath, Lauren, pushed through the first set of doors, stashed the gun in her purse, and pulled out her Defense Intelligence Agency credentials. She yanked the second door open, and to her left, she saw the express elevators to the top floor. Stephanie and Abigail must already be on their way up. Lauren turned to see two security guards running across the polished tile floor toward her. She held her credentials out at arm's length. "Federal investigator! Your colleague is taking fire outside! He needs backup!"

The sound of gunfire confirmed her story, and the men turned their attention toward the main door. Lauren ran to the elevator and frantically pushed the button. She jumped as the main glass doors behind her exploded inward from a volley of bullets and both security guards went down on the tiled floor. Lauren turned and stood helpless as Nikolett stepped into the lobby. Their eyes met and the assassin started toward her.

Nikolett came at Lauren with no fear. Behind Lauren the elevator pinged. Seconds later, the doors opened, and a man Lauren had never met pulled her into the elevator, placed himself between her and Nikolett, and opened fire as Nikolett ducked behind a pillar in the lobby. Dozens of slugs peppered the marble façade, and as the elevator doors closed, he squeezed off a final volley of retreating gunfire to keep Nikolett from returning fire.

"Who in the hell are you?" Lauren asked, every nerve ending in her body shaking from adrenaline.

"Dr. McKenna, I'm Reggie. I'm former SAS and a friend of Buck's. We spoke on the phone."

Lauren nodded the moment she recognized his cockney accent.

"Are you hurt?" Reggie asked as he inserted a fresh magazine into his weapon.

Lauren shook her head as the elevator climbed the last few flights before easing to a halt.

The doors opened and Reggie hit the emergency stop button inside the elevator, then he stepped out, ignoring the bell.

"Three flights of stairs to go," Reggie said. "Follow me."

Lauren climbed the remaining three floors and burst outside onto the observation deck. It was flat and oval and painted with a faded white circle. Sitting in the center was an idling Sikorsky S-76 helicopter. Abigail, still in Stephanie's arms, was in the back, her hands pressed over her ears.

As Lauren climbed inside, strong arms reached out to help. Within moments the door slammed shut, and the Sikorsky lifted off and banked north. Reggie helped Lauren get seated and buckled in next to Stephanie. Abigail moved to her mother's lap, and Lauren held her tight.

"Honey, are you hurt?" Lauren asked. The only response was a silent shake of her head.

"Are you armed?" Reggie asked Lauren.

"In my bag."

Reggie retrieved Lauren's Glock then expertly disassembled the weapon. "We'll dump this out over the English Channel."

"Tell Buck thank you," Lauren said.

Reggie pushed a button on a satellite phone and handed it to her. "Tell him yourself."

"Hello," Lauren said. She and Buck had talked at length the night before about the best way for them to get out of Paris.

"I'm glad you're safe," Buck replied without ceremony. "We're on a secure line. Tell me everything that happened."

Lauren covered one ear and held the phone tight against the other. She quickly explained events, leaving out none of the details. When she finished, the line was silent to the point she'd thought she'd lost the connection. "Are you still there?"

"Yeah, I'm just trying to piece this together. Can you describe this woman?"

"Mid-thirties, she's on the slender side and attractive. She has jet-black, short, spiky hair and is good with a gun."

"Would you recognize her again if you saw her?"

"Absolutely."

"You're about forty-five minutes out from London. Can you tell me what your plans are from there? I'm really hesitant to drop you off when we don't seem to know who the players are in all of this."

"I'm good, Buck, I promise. We'll be in London for about ten minutes, and then we'll be gone. I promise I'll be in touch, and thanks for your help, your guys saved the day."

"That's what we do," Buck replied. "Tell me where you're headed, or at least take Reggie with you. He's a good guy."

"Thanks, but no thanks." Lauren stroked Abigail's hair, wondering what kind of trauma had been inflicted on her daughter today. "I don't want anyone to know where we're going, especially after what just happened. I'd also prefer that Donovan hear about today's events from me. Can you promise me that much?"

"Not that I want to be the one to explain why his wife and daughter were in a firefight in Paris, but at the moment I can't tell your husband anything," Buck replied. "He's disappeared, and no one knows where he went."

Lauren processed the possibilities. "If you talk to him, don't tell him we've spoken. I'll fill him in on everything later."

"You're putting me in a really bad position here."

"Good-bye, Buck." Lauren handed the phone back to Reggie.

"The pilot needs a destination, ma'am?" Reggie said as he stowed the phone in his jumpsuit.

"Farnborough Airport, southwest of central London. Land at the TAG aviation facility. We have a jet standing by."

Reggie relayed the information to the cockpit and then smiled at Abigail and presented her with a cherry-red lollipop. Abigail took it from him without even a glance at her mother for permission. Lauren knew her daughter had been terrified. They all had, and if a lollipop made it better, then bless Reggie for his foresight. She'd try and call Donovan once they were safely on the jet, though if he'd gone underground, it was because he'd ditched everyone to go after Garrick. It also meant that he'd more than likely taken that Erica woman with him.

CHAPTER EIGHTEEN

Donovan had no words of comfort. Erica was right. Something they'd done had led the assassins to this apartment, and there was nothing he could say to ease her torment. He knew from experience that the initial shock would be intense, but short lived. His concern was to make sure she didn't lose it altogether. He needed her to stay with him. If the police or the FBI got to her, then he'd lose any advantage he had over Garrick. Later, her real grief would begin, the guilt-fueled despair that he knew all too well. When the entire universe would place the blame squarely at her feet, and she'd know in her heart it was hers.

He felt Erica's frame shudder and felt his own sadness try to push to the surface. His wasn't the same as hers, some of it was old, some was new, but it was his and it was always hovering. He pushed it down and began to look around the room. The killers had done a professional job. Everything that had been searched went on the floor. Once everything was on the floor, they'd finished. "We can't stay here much longer."

She nodded and sniffed.

He pulled away from her, stepped around the bodies, picked up a box of tissues, and handed them to her. "If you want, I can do this."

"It'll go quicker if we both work," Erica replied, her voice raw from the tears.

Together they filled a medium-size duffel bag. She was silent, but fresh tears trickled down her face as she worked. She cleared out her bathroom last, and while she was in there Donovan heard a few sobs escape. When she emerged she was wearing different clothes. She slung the duffel over her shoulder and nodded that she was ready.

"Are you sure you have everything?"

"Yeah, I should be good."

"What about your mail?"

"There is none. No credit cards, no bills, no mail."

Donovan picked up the duffel bag and followed her out of the apartment. He closed the door and when he looked up, Erica was already halfway to the stairs. He hurried to catch her, and once they burst out into the fresh air they took a direct route back to the BMW. He breathed a small sigh of relief as they drove away from her apartment complex.

"This is awful," Erica said, using a tissue to wipe her nose. "How long do you think it'll be until they're found?"

"Not long," Donovan replied. "Assuming they both have jobs, someone will start looking for them soon."

"I keep thinking about what you said last night. That it could be someone besides Garrick that tried to kidnap me. From what I've seen today, I think you're right. Garrick isn't even in California, and he isn't cleaning up after himself. He and his people are leaving bodies strewn everywhere. Whoever did this was organized and methodical—professional. For God's sake, they erased an entire crime scene. I saw how Jill and David were killed, I know enough about medical trauma to recognize a small-caliber bullet wound to the back of the head. Has Garrick showed anyone that kind of mercy?"

Donovan remained silent. She was getting angry, which was good. He hoped she'd get the first wave out of her system before they reached the airport.

"Let me see if I have this straight. There are two sets of bad guys here, right? There are the ones we're hunting, Garrick, and his little band of savage tree-hugging eco-terrorists. Right?"

"Yes," Donovan said.

"Then there's a different group hunting only me—an unknown group of professional killers, possibly sanctioned by the government who used the medical services of my former employer."

"I know it doesn't seem like it, but we have the advantage."

Erica turned her head and leveled a murderous glare at Donovan. "This all goes back to you somehow. You started digging, and now people are trying to kill me. I shot a man yesterday. My friend and her boyfriend have been murdered, and somehow from all of that, you seem to think we have some kind of tactical advantage? I don't know who you are, or where you come from, but from what I've seen so far, this is a goddamned disaster."

Erica took a breath to say something, and then all of the wind seemed to rush from her body. Her lips quivered and tears flooded her eyes. She tried one more time to speak, but all that escaped was a low, guttural sound, so wounded, so vulnerable.

For the rest of the drive, Erica turned away from him and quietly cried. He pulled into the parking lot of Signature Flight Support, switched off the ignition, and turned to face her. "When you initially called Eco-Watch, how many people did you give your name to?"

Erica looked up at Donovan as she thought about what he'd just asked. "Two. The man I talked with initially and then again when I spoke to Peggy, your administrative assistant."

"What phone did you call from?"

"My cell. Don't worry, it's not in my name."

"That's only part of the problem," Donovan said as he put the pieces together. "I think someone has bugged Eco-Watch's phones. You gave your number and your first name."

"Oh, my God, are you saying someone traced the call I made to Eco-Watch?"

"I don't think they could do that, but with the number, if they assumed you were in Southern California, they could have triangulated your later calls. Which is how they found you, or found me, we can only guess at this point. You told me they waited until you put your key in the lock before they tried to grab you. They knew the vicinity, not the exact address."

"They came back and waited?" Erica said shaking her head in disbelief.

Donovan nodded and dialed his phone. "Buck, it's Donovan. Listen, I think we have a problem at headquarters. I think someone has tapped into the phones and is recording our calls. Is this anything you know about?"

"It's nothing I authorized. I'll make some calls and get the place swept for any kind of electronic surveillance."

"I want it done fast and discreet."

"Anything else?"

"That's it for now. Call me the second you know anything." Donovan ended the call, then slid his pistol into his briefcase, along with Erica's phone.

"There's got to be another element to this," Erica said. "How could they react so fast to my call to Eco-Watch? All I left was a first name and a phone number. I mean, who has that kind of manpower besides a government?"

Donovan had asked himself the same question, and the answer he kept coming up with was Mossad. The CIA, if they were involved, would have used less lethal tactics. Or would they? Donovan had to admit that both entities were distinct possibilities.

"I'm right, aren't I?" Erica said. "I'm being hunted by a government, most likely Mossad."

Donovan nodded and then stepped out of the BMW. He walked around and opened her door. "At least for now, we're both off the grid. No one can find us, and maybe my people will have some answers."

They walked into the VIP lounge. She'd quit crying, but there was no hiding the fact she was upset. She stuck close to Donovan as he told the flight desk who he was. They paged his flight crew, who retrieved their luggage and escorted them to the waiting airplane. Donovan wasn't surprised that the charter arranged through

Gulfstream was in fact a Gulfstream 650, the newest model in the storied Gulfstream family.

As they reached the top of the stairs, he allowed Erica to go ahead of him and select a seat. He stopped in the galley, introduced himself to the flight attendant, and explained that they'd like to be left alone. If they needed anything, he'd let her know. Donovan sat across the aisle from Erica. The interior of the Gulfstream was as plush as any he'd ever seen. A sophisticated mix of fabrics, leather, and exotic woods blended with state-of-the-art electronics and a full-blown in-flight entertainment system. It was a stark contrast to the wire bundles and aluminum equipment racks of the *da Vinci*, but despite the creature comforts in the cabin, as always, he wished he were up front flying. Donovan was rarely a passenger and admittedly not a good one, but he tried to relax as the G-650 lifted off and climbed out over the ocean. As Donovan looked out at the sprawling city, he couldn't help but whisper a good-bye to all of the memories he and Meredith had left behind.

Erica had curled up in her seat. From her slow, rhythmic breathing, Donovan guessed that she'd fallen asleep, the perfect defense mechanism for what she'd been through. They'd been aloft for nearly an hour and a half before Erica stirred. She shifted positions and fell back into a sound sleep. Donovan wondered about her state of mind when she woke up. Would she have found the resolve to continue what they'd started? Or would the horrific events have immobilized her?

He slipped the pictures of Meredith from his briefcase and started with the one he'd taken from the bridge of the *Kaiyo Maru #7*. He stared at her face, her eyes, and her smile. The smile he'd loved, the one he'd seen first thing in the morning when he'd leaned over to kiss her good morning, the one that would vanish forever when she was murdered. He glanced at Erica and it registered that in the vulnerability of sleep, she and Meredith shared some of the same radiance, some of the same subtle and not so subtle energies.

Donovan forced himself to study the overexposed background. Was a timeline being established by each picture? The first photo had been found on the *Triton*, and Meredith had been in her early teens. She was standing on the deck of a boat. As memories came flooding in, Donovan was startled by their clarity. Could this be a game of geography to Garrick? Was he baiting Donovan to figure it out while forcing him to relive the past?

He remembered Meredith telling him about a fishing trip her dad had taken her on when they were on a family vacation. She said the water was choppy and some of the passengers became seasick. She hated the trip. When a fish was boated, the deckhands clubbed them to death before throwing them into buckets. Meredith had cried for each of the dead fish. The picture aboard the *Triton* had been taken on a family trip to Hawaii.

The second photo was taken later, when Meredith was in college. He'd been so busy looking at her that he'd failed to take in the entire picture. Where was she? What was she doing? The photo was taken in bright sunlight, and many of the details were washed out. He squinted and held the photo at different focal points until a vague shape that he thought was a simple cloud on a white background began to look like something else, like a mountain, like a big mountain.

Between sophomore and junior year, she'd taken a summer job in Washington State. The mountain could easily be Mount Baker or Mount Rainer. She worked with the Department of Fisheries to help count migrating salmon. She said it was boring work, and sad as the salmon spawned and died. The stench of dead fish permeated the entire river, and this in turn drew the bears. The bears were the link, and if Donovan was right, the coordinates would take him to a photo that would tell him where Garrick planned to strike next.

When Erica moved in her seat trying to get comfortable, Donovan slipped Meredith's pictures in his briefcase. When he looked over at Erica her eyes were open and she was watching him.

"How are you feeling?" he asked.

"Better," Erica replied, her voice thick with sleep. She stretched both arms and let out a groan, then brushed her hair away from her eyes. "Where are we?"

"We're almost there. We're just about to start our descent."

Erica stood and smoothed the wrinkles in her clothes. "I'm going to the restroom, I'll be back."

"You want anything to drink?" Donovan asked.

"Coffee, black for me, and I'm hungry. Did you eat?"

"No." Donovan motioned for the flight attendant and politely asked her if they had time for coffee and something to eat before they landed. She assured them they did and several minutes later she arrived with two cups of coffee, a small cheese and cracker tray, as well as a selection of finger sandwiches. Erica joined him just as the flight attendant finished setting everything out. Donovan noticed that Erica had fixed her hair and reapplied some of her eye makeup. It wasn't much, but the transformation was enough to hide the fact that she'd cried herself to sleep. She took her cup with both hands, sipped, and closed her eyes.

Donovan pulled his briefcase from the floor and began to rifle deep inside.

"What are you doing?" Erica cocked her head at the open briefcase.

"Getting some things we'll need when we land," Donovan replied and found the discreet zipper sewn into a compartment of his briefcase. The slot held a thin wallet. Donovan slid his own wallet from his trouser pocket and replaced it with the new one. He zipped everything up and put the briefcase on the floor.

"What's all that about?" Erica asked.

"I have a different identity," Donovan said. "I don't want there to be any trace that you or I were ever up here. We're going to have to rent a car, spend some money, and I don't want to leave a paper trail."

"We'll draw all kinds of the wrong attention if you try to take me through customs. Why don't you just go by yourself? Take the ferry, charter a plane, do whatever you need to do all nice and legal. I'll wait for you."

"We have to stay together," Donovan replied.

"Back in California, before we left the house, you looked at the weather," Erica said. "What did you see?"

Donovan checked the time on his watch. "In eight to ten hours from now, there'll be a window of good weather that should allow us to find a plane and fly up to the coordinates and back again."

"So we just hang around and wait for the weather to clear?"

"Why? What do you have in mind?"

"A boat," Erica said with a shrug. "We borrow one we like from the marina; some of these owners only use them a few weeks each summer. It's easy to tell which is which. We steal one, motor into Canada, and then you can find a plane and fly us where you want to go."

"I'm not a big fan of boats," Donovan said. "Too slow, I was thinking we borrow an airplane. Same theory, only faster."

"You're a professional pilot, right?"

Donovan nodded.

"How does a professional pilot plead ignorance when the authorities find you in a stolen airplane, in the wrong country, and you somehow forgot about customs?"

"Good point. Okay, how would this exercise of yours work?"

"We need to get from Bellingham to Anacortes, Washington. It's a little town on Fidalgo Island that marks the first of the San Juan archipelago."

Donovan was familiar with Anacortes and Fidalgo Island. Huntington Oil had a refinery on Fidalgo. What she was proposing made sense.

"There's lots of transient boat traffic and one large public marina. I know a nice place for dinner, and then we take a walk down the pier until I find the right boat. We pick our time and borrow it."

"What about security?"

"There's none to speak of. At first glance we're a couple getting ready to go on a cruise. We blend in perfectly."

"And you know how to do all the boat stuff?"

"Absolutely, I grew up around them. I learned to sail before I could drive. When I came back from Germany, I came to the San Juans and lived on a boat with a friend. We cruised all up and down these waters. We find a boat I'm familiar with and we'll be fine."

"How far is it from Anacortes to Vancouver Island?"

"Probably fifty miles. At six or seven knots, it'll take us maybe seven hours, eight depending on where we make landfall. In fact, by the time we get there, the window of good weather should have arrived and we're already in Canada. We're not flying across borders without a clearance."

"What are the chances of this boat still being there when we want to return?"

"Eighty-twenty, our favor. If it's not, we find another boat."

On an intellectual level Donovan liked Erica's plan. She seemed to know what she was doing, and it made more sense than waiting for the weather to clear and then trying to steal a plane and fly both ways. He looked at her, lowered his head, and said, "I'm not sure about the being at sea part."

"Why's that?"

"Something happened," Donovan said. "The boat sank."

"Oh, well, that'll do it. I promise we won't sink, and if we do, I'll be there to save you."

"If we go into the water up here, we have about ten minutes of useful ability."

"Oh yeah, you're absolutely right, the cold water is a killer. I didn't say I had all day to save you, only that I would. You'd do the same for me. Hell, you saved me last night, I owe you one."

Donovan felt his apprehension rise at the thought of being on a boat, but the plan made sense, and maybe, most importantly, he could keep her with him. The second Erica got scared and decided to turn herself in, or try to make a deal with the authorities, everything would be in jeopardy. The FBI would move in on Garrick before Donovan could, which would be a disaster. In addition, the people who'd killed Jill and David would know exactly where to find Erica, and they would no doubt find a way to finish the job.

As the Gulfstream broke out of the low clouds, Donovan's attention was drawn to the gray water of the Puget Sound. There were whitecaps and foamy streaks formed by the gusty winds. It looked like the North Atlantic, Donovan felt his stomach churn at the thought of being out on the water in these conditions.

The wheels touched down and the jet smoothly taxied to the ramp of Bellingham Jet Center and pulled to a stop. Donovan and Erica gathered their things, thanked the crew, and hurried to the lounge. The crew followed with their luggage. Within minutes, Donovan, using a Florida driver's license and credit cards issued under the name of Thomas Westmiller, rented a black Jeep Cherokee. They pulled out of the parking lot just as it started to rain and followed the signs for I-5 South.

"We're going to need some different clothes," Donovan said as he sped up the windshield wipers. "We'll be in the forest when we get to Vancouver Island. I packed for Hawaii."

"When we get off the interstate, we drive past a sporting goods place. We can pick up some things there."

Donovan looked at his watch. It was only a little before three in the afternoon, but with the dark-gray skies, it felt like it was eight o'clock in the evening.

"What is it you know that I don't?" Erica turned in her seat to face Donovan. "We're going to a lot of trouble to reach a crime scene that will tell us what, exactly?"

"I don't know. That's why we're going."

"But you're in the loop. The FBI will tell you what they found."

"It's not in the United States. We can't be sure the Canadians will be so quick to share."

"For Christ's sake, they're Canadians not North Koreans. Now quit jerking me around and tell me the truth. We're in this together. At this point we're both criminals, so either we trust each other completely, or this is a flawed partnership and we cut our losses, go our separate ways."

"I can't tell you everything because I don't know everything. But we stay together no matter what."

Erica leaned forward, her expression deadly serious. "You're not a very good liar. Turn off the bullshit. You've already confessed you hate being out on the ocean, so tell me why the hell we're sneaking to a crime scene in a boat."

Donovan couldn't miss the anger flash in her eyes. She was serious and wanted answers. Without Erica, the boat option was out, and he'd be forced to steal an airplane or run the risk of taking the ferry. The ferry meant cameras, and the weather was too dicey for a small plane. Besides, the worse the weather, the more eyebrows would be raised by a single-engine airplane taking off. If he wanted to be at the coordinates by morning, he needed Erica. Splitting up also put him at risk of her running to the FBI to make a deal, to use them to try to avenge her dead friends.

"Your exit is up ahead."

Moments later he pulled the Cherokee into the parking lot of Holiday Sporting Goods and switched off the engine.

"I'm still waiting. Quit stalling so you can run different damage-control scenarios. Knock it off and tell me the truth."

Donovan exhaled as if defeated. "Garrick made this personal. He's been leaving pictures at the scene of each atrocity. I think they're clues to where he's headed next. If the FBI gets to him before I do, then the justice system takes over. Garrick needs to answer to my justice, not anyone else's."

"And you know about these pictures, how?"

"I'm the only one who's seen them all. I think I figured it out. If we can get to the coordinates first, we'll find the picture and have a head start to where he's headed next."

"I want to see them."

"I left them with William," Donovan lied. "He's having them analyzed."

"But you have no intention of sharing these photos with anyone else."

"None whatsoever. I'm not helping the FBI or anyone else find him. He's a monster, and at the end of the day, I have no interest in an arrest, or a trial, or any of the other democratic trappings of justice. I want him dead."

"What about Nikolett?"

"She needs to die as well."

"What if they kill you first?"

"Then it falls on you to kill them. Neither one of us can go on with our lives until these people are dead."

"Is that really how you see it, no middle ground?"

"None at all. Even if they're captured, you and I aren't safe. It's like cutting the heads off the Hydra, nothing short of their deaths will set you and me free."

Erica put her hand inside his, their fingers entwined and she looked him in the eyes. "Then I promise to finish the job if you can't."

Donovan kissed the back of her hand. "Thank you." Then he opened the door and stepped out into the drizzle. Once Erica joined him they hurried inside.

The aisles were narrow and the shelves stacked high. The store smelled like canvas and leather. With Erica behind him, Donovan worked his way to the far side of the floor where clothes hung on circular racks. He found a rain suit, heavy-duty hunting pants, a coat, two flannel shirts, and heavy socks. Several aisles over, Erica, too, was collecting an assortment of purchases. Donovan found a dressing room and went inside to try on the clothes.

He'd slipped out of his pants and stripped down to his underwear. He was taking a pair of trousers off a hanger when Erica opened the door and slipped into the room.

"There's only one dressing room, and I didn't want to stand out there alone." She sat on the bench and pulled off her boots, then stood and dropped her jeans into a puddle on the floor. Then she stood and unfolded the waterproof slacks she'd selected.

Donovan didn't say a word, neither did he make an effort to camouflage the fact that he was watching.

She ignored him, pulled her top over her head, and placed it on one of the hooks. She was about to try on the pants when she glanced in the mirror and stopped. She reached to lightly grip his arm, then turned his wrist up to the light to see the wound. "This is from a knife. Is this from that same night?"

Donovan nodded and turned his back to her. She pressed herself closer, reached around and watched in their reflection as she touched the massive scar on his thigh. She traced her finger the entire length, before bringing her hand up and circling the bullet wound in his shoulder. That's when he turned around to face her. He leaned in, found her lips with his. The kiss was deep, urgent. She ran her hands through Donovan's hair and across his back. He dropped his hand to the small of her back and pulled her into him as she lowered her arm and slid her fingers along his skin just inside the waist of his boxers.

When Donovan broke their kiss and opened his eyes, all he saw was lust and a need that startled him. They pulled at each other's clothes. Donovan pressed her up against the wall of the small cubicle and they began to make love.

Afterward, Erica was the first to disengage. She kissed him and then pulled away.

"We need to go," she said. Avoiding eye contact, she quickly dressed, collected the clothes she'd picked out, and let herself out of the dressing room.

Donovan had experienced a wide range of emotions in the last twenty-four hours and couldn't ignore the tiniest feeling he'd just been maneuvered. Though the one element that took him completely by surprise was the sense that he'd experienced something essential—something he didn't even know was missing.

CHAPTER NINETEEN

"Just ahead." Erica nodded toward the boat to their left. "The *Irish Wake*. It's perfect, a thirty-six foot Selene exactly like my friend owned. By the amount of dirt that's accumulated, I'd say it's been sitting here for a while. It's certainly not in daily use. By the look of all the antennas up top, it has a full complement of electronics, plus all the lines are shipshape, and the knots are tied perfectly. Whoever owns this boat cares about the details. They just don't get a chance to go out all that often."

The vessel was smaller than Donovan had hoped. It was pitch-dark out. The earlier wind and rain had all but blown over, and now it was almost dead calm. But he had no idea what the ocean would be like beyond the harbor. They continued out to the end of the pier and then turned and walked back. Erica had her arm locked around his and they walked slowly, as if a couple out for an after dinner stroll. As they approached *Irish Wake* they walked along-side and boarded amidships.

"Is it unlocked?" Donovan whispered.

Erica gripped the stainless steel latch and eased it aft until the latch clicked. She slid the door open and stepped down into the salon. Donovan watched as she located the keys stashed in a drawer beneath the chart table. She crouched in front of a circuit panel and began selecting switches. Once the batteries were supplying power to the systems, she checked the instrument panel.

"The fuel tanks are full. Go get the rest of our things. I'll have the boat ready to go by the time you move the car."

Donovan ducked out of the salon, stepped back onto the pier, and headed back to the parking lot. They'd elected to leave the majority of their luggage in the rental car, reducing their load to a duffel bag and a daypack. Whatever happened, they'd have to come back and retrieve the car. When he returned to the *Irish Wake*, he tossed their belongings in the salon, then returned to the Cherokee.

They'd discussed their options and decided that instead of leaving the rental car in the parking lot of the marina where they'd stolen a boat, they'd move it to the lot of a nearby fitness center. Donovan backed the SUV into an unobtrusive slot between two buildings, parked the Cherokee, stepped out, and locked the car.

He stopped for a moment and looked at the March Point refinery complex situated across the bay. When he was at the helm of Huntington Oil, years ago, he'd been here several times. Donovan marveled at the improvements that had been made to the waterfront. A mill that at one time had churned out paper and noxious fumes was completely gone. Where it once stood the ground was graded flat and it looked like some basic utilities had been installed underground in preparation for the next phase. He shook off the visit to his former life, turned away, and began the short walk back to the marina.

As he neared the slip, he could hear the soft rumble of a diesel engine and the subtle gurgle of water being pumped overboard. He made his way to the starboard side and saw the soft glow from the instrument panel illuminating Erica's face. She was seated in the captain's chair, head down, studying a chart.

At hearing him return, she turned and smiled. "We're ready. I've cast off every line except the one on the stern. Can you get it and we'll be on our way?"

Donovan went back out, climbed onto the dock, and found the remaining line fixed tightly to the cleat. He undid the line, tossed the rope aboard, and boarded the trawler. He stood in the night air as Erica slipped the boat into gear and eased away from the dock. He heard the brief whine of the bow thruster as she used it to swing them around so they could maneuver down the row of boats toward the exit. With little noise and seemingly no effort, they glided free of the marina and Donovan secured the fenders.

"All set," he said as he entered the salon and stood next to her. They were just clearing the breakwater. She'd switched on the running lights. Straight ahead was the deep-water terminal that off-loaded the crude oil from the tankers. Huge pipes pumped the cargo from the ships to holding tanks at the refinery. Donovan felt a pang of nostalgia for his parents and the family business begun by his great-grandfather. He watched Erica switch the radio to an automated weather forecast, and they both listened intently to what they already knew. One front was moving through and another was on the way. Nothing had changed.

Donovan leaned over the chart table, located their position, and brought the chart over to Erica. "How exactly are we going to do this? Show me what you have in mind. Once we get to Vancouver Island, is there a specific place for us to go ashore, or do we make it up as we go?"

"You're not a very good passenger, are you?"

"Yachting is like flying, the safest, most effective crews talk and plan."

"You didn't answer my question."

"No, I suck as a passenger. I suck even more committing felonies while operating completely in the dark."

"Would you relax? I've never seen you when you didn't believe you were in complete control and I'm rather enjoying the spectacle." Erica moved the map under the light. "We're right here between Guemes and Fidalgo islands. We're going to go west between Blakely and Decatur Islands and then maneuver just north of Lopez, south of Orcas Island. From there we'll cruise north of San Juan Island itself, cross into Canadian territory, and head for a little marina I know of just outside Sidney."

Donovan estimated the distances involved. "How long is it going to take us?"

"The tide and currents are working against us, so it'll be right at seven hours."

"What about fuel? Will we have enough to get there and get back without having to refuel?"

"We've got five hundred gallons onboard. We're burning less than three gallons per hour, so I figure we've got a range of about a thousand miles."

Donovan surveyed the galley and salon, then turned his attention back to the instrumentation. Erica had a moving map generated by GPS, radar, sonar, and enough radio equipment to make him feel like he was aboard a jet airplane. In the dim light it was easy to imagine that the entire world was just the two of them.

"I love it out here." Erica took a deep breath. "Smell the salt air mixed with the fir and pine trees. The Puget Sound and the waters north of here are so beautiful. In the summer you can see orcas, humpback whales, dolphins, seals, and a million seabirds. I still remember on clear days being able to see the Cascade Mountains to the east and the Olympic Mountains to the west. One day I'd love to live here full time and just cruise in my boat. Sometimes I think I must have been a mariner in a past life."

Donovan couldn't imagine anything more awful than a life at sea.

"How are you doing?" Erica looked up at him.

Donovan had been so caught up in the conversation that he hadn't noticed that they'd moved out into open water. The waves weren't large, but the boat was rising and falling. The knot in his stomach was there, but it wasn't debilitating.

"With what?" he replied.

"I was referring to you being out here on the water." Erica cocked her head to one side. "Why, is there something else on your mind?"

"Not at all," Donovan turned his attention back to the chart.

Erica went up on her tiptoes and kissed him, then pulled away without breaking eye contact. "About earlier, I can't explain why. Part of me is appalled. I mean you're married. I couldn't help but notice from the pictures I saw in Laguna that you have a beautiful wife and daughter. I told myself after Germany, I'd never do that again."

"And the other part?"

"The other part of me wants you regardless of your situation.

I mean, we may die tomorrow or the day after that. I get that now. So please don't start talking about what we should or shouldn't do or what anything means. I don't want to deal with anything except the here and now."

"Okay."

"Tell me about your wife."

"We're separated."

"For real? Or are you making that up?"

"It's the truth. She left me and took our daughter with her."

"Your daughter is so cute. How old is she? What's her name?"

"Her name is Abigail and she's three going on four. And I can already tell she's going to be a handful one day."

"I was like that once." Erica smiled at some distant memory. "It only gets worse."

"I've noticed."

"Cute. Why did your wife leave you?"

"I work too much. She felt neglected." Donovan didn't mind her asking the questions, but, as always, he went on heightened alert for fear of saying something that would threaten to unravel the tightly woven web of lies and deceit surrounding his past. "You know, it's rarely one thing."

"Do you love her?"

"Yes."

"I appreciate your honesty. How long ago did she leave?"

"Seven months ago."

"Did she leave you before or after the terrorist tried to kill you?"

"Just after. In fact, she left me right after I came out of surgery."

"That's a little harsh."

"It had been a long time in coming, and to be honest, I deserved it. The stress leading up to that day was enormous. Not just for me, but for her as well. Stopping the terrorists and being injured was the catalyst, not the cause."

"You were pretty heroic that day."

"Not really. The FBI agent I was with did all the hard work. I landed the plane—I'm a pilot, that's what we do."

"I remember those images on television. The plane was pretty much destroyed."

"In my defense, by the time we reached the airport, there wasn't much of a plane left to land."

"Still, for her to leave you while you were still in the hospital, she had to be pretty upset with you, or it could have been a response to the stress event. I've seen it before, kind of like post-traumatic stress disorder. She removed herself from a setting that was too unbearable to contemplate losing. It makes no sense, but it happens, especially to people who are unaware of the triggers."

"My wife is one of the smartest and most analytical people I've ever met. She has a Ph.D from MIT. She works as an analyst for the Defense Intelligence Agency. I doubt that her leaving me was a spur-of-the-moment decision based on a whim, or anything triggered by a sudden event. She's nothing if not deliberate, so I'm pretty sure that she'd been thinking about it for quite some time, and my behavior that day set it all into motion."

"That says quite a bit."

"About her?"

"No, about you." Erica reached out, entwined her fingers with his, raised his hand to her lips, and kissed the back of his hand. "I know how you got the other scars. How did you get this one?"

"That one came from the same guy."

"It's not a knife wound."

"It's from a screwdriver. Why all the questions, and what is it you think you've learned?"

"I think you're stronger than I thought you were and that you're far more honest and forthright than most men. I'm your rebound, aren't I? Figures you would find a woman who does things impulsively. I'm the exact opposite of your wife."

It was the element that he found the most compelling about Erica. Lauren was many things, but she wasn't spontaneous or whimsical and never would be.

"It's okay. You're my rebound of sorts, and you're not anything like he was. You have a backbone. I like that in a man. Now, can you take over while I make some coffee? It's going to be a long night for me, but I suggest you try to get some sleep."

Erica pointed out the dark spot between the distant lights that he was to navigate toward, kissed him on the lips, and then disappeared down into the forward stateroom. Donovan moved over, sat in the chair, and felt the warmth she'd left behind. The vessel was on autopilot, but Donovan gripped the wheel anyway. All alone, he felt his fingers tighten and his breathing begin to accelerate. He battled his fear as it rose and fell in the moment, as if each swell were a distinct obstacle to try to live through. The uneasy sensation of being exposed to the ocean was familiar, but his thoughts of Erica and the comfort she generated—that feeling was completely foreign.

CHAPTER TWENTY

Lauren felt the jet come to a stop. All she could think about was a hot bath and cool sheets. The flight attendant opened the door and a female customs inspector joined them in the cabin. Lauren handed her their passports and general declaration cards and hoped this would be over quickly. Even though there'd been a brief fuel stop in Goose Bay, Labrador, they'd spent nearly twelve hours aboard since they departed London. Thankfully the flight attendant had given Lauren a clean blouse to wear so she could dispose of the one stained with blood.

The official studied the paperwork, but when she saw Stephanie's diplomatic passport, she skimmed over the rest and thanked them for their patience.

"Your car is pulling up to the plane now," the captain said. "The local time is ten thirty. Have a good rest of your evening."

"No one knows we're here, how can we have a car?" Lauren said to Stephanie, her concern evident.

When Lauren saw William VanGelder stepping out of the back-seat, her heart sunk. She thought she'd have a chance for some meaningful sleep before she had to face William.

"It's Uncle William," Stephanie said. "I wonder how he knew we were landing."

"He's William," Lauren replied, as she wondered about that as well. If he'd found them, who else knew they were in Southern California?

Lauren let Stephanie go first. She and her uncle embraced at the foot of the airstair. Lauren trailed behind, having to contain Abigail when she saw the man she knew as Grandpa. Abigail squealed with unrestrained joy as William swept her into a gigantic hug.

Once Lauren and William locked eyes, whatever anger and imagined recrimination she thought she might find after all these months was absent. His eyes were warm and welcoming and he shifted Abigail to one arm and used the other to draw Lauren close enough to kiss her on the cheek.

"Welcome home," William said. "You've been missed."

"It's good to see you too." Lauren replied, touched by William's words.

"I understand you have no luggage, so I suggest we get in the car," William said, showing no intention of releasing Abigail. "It's probably not wise to stand out here in the open like this. Get in."

They all slipped into the rear club seating of the limo. The driver whisked them off the ramp and through the gate, and soon they were rolling south on the freeway.

"Where are we going?" Lauren asked. "And how did you know we were arriving?"

"I got a courtesy call from a friend in Ottawa. I unofficially flagged Stephanie's diplomatic passport after rumors began to float out of Paris about a shootout and escape. He passed along that you were in Goose Bay headed to Los Angeles and gave me the tail number of the aircraft. The rest was easy." William opened a compartment at his elbow and pulled out a box of juice and a straw for Abigail. He helped her insert the straw, and she happily took the drink. "As to where we're going, I thought it best to rent a house in Laguna Beach near John and Beverly's. The memorial service is day after tomorrow, and I'm still tied up with matters of their estate. I took the liberty of arranging clothes and toiletries for the three of you, to tide you over until you get some rest and can go shopping for yourselves."

"William, that's all well and good, and we appreciate everything you've done but—" Lauren hesitated as she shot a worrisome glance at Abigail. "You do understand there are people who might try and find us?"

"Steps have already been taken," William replied. "I've spoken at length with Buck. He's rented us a house on the recommendation of someone familiar with protection requirements. He also rounded up a security team from his acquaintances in the military. You'll not be disturbed."

"Where's Donovan?" Lauren asked point-blank.

"Honestly, I have no idea," William matched her tone.

"Is he with Erica Covington?"

"Yes. They're hunting Garrick."

"Does Donovan know about Paris?" Lauren asked.

"If he does, it's only from the media."

"Michael?"

"Same."

"I have no idea what's being said on television." Lauren sat back and put her hand to her forehead, feeling her exhaustion. "Do we know about the people in my protection detail?"

"I'm sorry, they all died," William said.

They were on the Pacific Coast Highway, and Lauren turned and stared out the window at the darkness she knew was the Pacific Ocean. She felt immensely sad and silently thanked Henri, Philippe, Giselle, and Fredrick. They'd died keeping her, Abigail, and Stephanie safe. She wished she could stop everything and weep for them. They'd become her friends, but that would have to come later.

"How much trouble are we in?" Stephanie asked.

"It's containable. The French authorities are furious, of course, assassins chasing American agents and diplomats with Israeli bodyguards, border incursions by foreign helicopters. The list goes on and on, but they're focused on the shooters and no footage of the two of you has been released to the media. The CIA is in a quiet uproar over the death of one of their own. They're calling for your head, but they've quieted down for now."

"How much of that is your doing?" Lauren asked.

"I made some calls," William replied. "The woman assassin has been positively identified as Nikolett Kovarik, but we already knew that. She's tied in with Garrick, though we're not sure how or when their alliance began. She escaped Paris, but not before she killed an innocent bystander whose car she used to flee the scene. There was no shortage of witnesses who attested to the fact that Nikolett was clearly the predator. Bottom line: both you and Stephanie are wanted for questioning by Paris authorities. So for the time being, I wouldn't hurry back to France."

"Can you pass along to the CIA that Fredrick died trying to protect us? His actions the day before tipped us off that something was wrong. That saved our lives."

"I can do that, but at some point you're going to have to be debriefed by Langley."

"They can wait. Any idea where Nikolett is now?" Lauren asked.

"None, but I can promise you, she's not in France. She's too smart to hang around. Besides her target isn't in Europe anymore."

"How much time did I buy?" Lauren asked.

"By doing what you did, you probably have a twenty-four-hour window before she catches up with you."

"I won't make it easy for her. I don't plan to stay in one place."

"What do you mean? The best place is here in Laguna Beach surrounded by Buck's handpicked team."

Lauren leaned forward toward William as if to emphasize how serious she was.

"I was surrounded by Aaron's handpicked team, as well as a CIA operative, and Nikolett made quick work of them. From here on out, I'm the one in charge of my security."

CHAPTER TWENTY-ONE

Through the early morning fog, Donovan spotted the indistinct images of the other ships tied to mooring balls. Erica had the *Irish Wake* barely moving, using the radar to ease her way into the harbor. When he pointed to an empty mooring buoy, Erica nodded that she saw it as well. They'd discussed the maneuver, and Donovan was on the bow with the boat hook.

Erica followed Donovan's hand signals and swung the bow twenty degrees starboard, shifted into forward for ten seconds, then eased it back into neutral to bring the boat to a gentle stop.

Donovan reached out with the hook, snared the steel ring on the buoy, and hauled it up to deck level. Dashing from the cockpit, Erica threaded two lines through the heavy iron ring and then eased it back over the side. The *Irish Wake* came to a gentle stop as the lines gathered up the tension. She checked that everything was securely tied off on either side of the bow before returning to the bridge to shut down the engine.

Cloaked in fog, they'd easily sailed into Canadian waters and were now less than two miles from the Sidney, British Columbia, airport. As predicted, a small, slow-moving boat had drawn no attention from anyone. Erica had explained that where they were wasn't the most popular or the busiest harbor, which suited their needs perfectly. Using the ship's nautical charts, Donovan had calculated that from the airport, they needed a plane capable of flying two hundred miles northwest and then back again.

"Help me launch the dingy," Erica whispered. "You take this side. I'll take the other."

Donovan began removing the straps from the inflatable runabout while Erica climbed up and began to release the lines that secured the davit. Once everything was free, she hooked the davit to the harness, and with the electric winch, hoisted the smaller boat out of its cradle, swung it out over the railing, and lowered it into the water next to the hull. Donovan leaned over and released the winch cable, grabbed a bowline, and eased the dingy astern to the swim platform.

Donovan had loaded the backpack with a few essentials. The pistol he'd taken from John's house, as well as the extra ammo, binoculars, dry socks for the two of them as well as the rain gear, plus an assortment of energy bars and bottled water. The final item was a dark-blue baseball cap which he pulled low.

"Let's go." Erica joined him and took the line from his hand.

Donovan carefully stepped into the dingy and sat down. Erica yanked twice on the starter rope, and the small outboard sputtered to life. She spun them around and headed toward the fog-shrouded shore.

Erica found the marina and pulled the dingy up to a section of the dock reserved for the boats moored in the harbor. She maneuvered them in close, cut the engine, jumped out onto the dock, and tied the dingy to a cleat. Donovan stepped onto the immovable dock and immediately felt a sense of relief wash over him. Only when the stress and tension were lessening did he realize how much fear had built up in his body. He shook it off, found his land legs, and together they walked toward shore.

"It's early. We might be the only ones around," Erica whispered.

"Which way is the main parking lot?"

"Up this path to the left. Do you have any idea how to steal a car?"

"Yeah, it's a small town, you find the one with the keys inside."

On their third try they found an unlocked twenty-year-old Ford pickup with the keys stashed in the overhead sun visor. Once a light blue, the truck's rundown appearance made it impossible to tell if it had been there a month or an hour. All Donovan cared about was that it ran. The engine turned over and started on the second try. When the radio blared to life, Erica cranked the knob to a lower level. Donovan put the Ford into gear, switched on the windshield wipers and headlights, and drove out of the parking lot. The first street they approached looked like it would take them south toward Sidney and the Victoria airport.

They didn't have to go far before Donovan turned the truck onto a road that fed into the airport property. They followed the road as it curved around the perimeter fence off the end of runway two-seven. In the distance, Donovan saw a collection of hangars, both large and small. The ramp held a few scattered airplanes. As they slowly cruised past the different buildings, Donovan spotted a parking lot down a side road. He made the turn, pulled into the small lot, and shut off the engine.

"This weather doesn't look like it's getting much better. Are you sure it's going to clear up enough to fly?" Erica asked. "Or should we be thinking about driving?"

"The edge of the system shouldn't be far away. The coordinates are at least a seven-hour drive each way, maybe more, plus we're on an island in a stolen vehicle. We can't afford that much exposure."

"How do you think Garrick got up there?"

"I've been thinking about that. Garrick must have found someone who knew all of the details about the transportation part of the operation. I'm thinking Garrick and his men flew in on a bush plane, one that was expected. Otherwise, there's no way Garrick gets the upper hand with armed poachers."

"Listen," Erica said as she turned up the volume on the radio.

"Recapping today's top story out of Vancouver. Police have released more information about the five people found murdered downtown. It's unknown yet exactly when the murders took place, but witnesses at the scene said the smell coming from the apartment was what prompted a call to the police. The identities of the four men and one woman have yet to be confirmed. The five were found shot in an upscale loft in the Yaletown section of downtown.

There have been no official reports of suspects or that any arrests have been made. Detectives on the scene did acknowledge that they couldn't rule out a connection to this crime and a recently released video of black bear poachers being murdered for their alleged crimes against the environment by the global organization Eco-Watch. One unnamed source from the Ministry of Environment was quoted as saying that they're still looking for the location in the video, and that evidence at the Yaletown murder scene may aid in that search. We'll have more on this story at the top of the hour. Now stay tuned for today's financial news."

"Garrick murdered those people, didn't he?" Erica said as she turned the volume down.

"Yeah, it sounds like they've been dead for a while. They're probably the ones who knew where the poachers were and how to get to them. Garrick or someone working for him killed them."

"Are we too late? Do you think the authorities have the same coordinates we do?"

"I don't know, but we don't have any choice but to find out."

"What if the place is crawling with police?"

"Then we turn around and get the hell out of there."

"A judicious retreat might work, but first things first, how do we steal an airplane?"

"Hand me the binoculars." Donovan spotted some activity and wanted a closer look. He held out his hand as Erica reached into the duffel bag.

Donovan adjusted the focus as he surveyed a hangar that was about a hundred yards away. The doors had just opened, and two men on a tug were getting ready to pull an airplane from the hangar. As Donovan inspected the equipment, he could tell it was a maintenance bay, various airplanes inside were in different stages of disassembly. The airplane they were about to wheel out was a Cessna 185, a rugged, high-winged tail dragger favored by many a bush pilot. Donovan estimated he had logged nearly five hundred hours in the 185 during his time in Africa. The Cessna would be perfect.

The linemen pulled the red-and-white Cessna away from the hangar and parked it at the edge of the ramp. A mechanic ambled out and checked all the cowling fasteners. Then he did a slow careful walk-around before hauling himself up into the cockpit and starting the engine.

As Donovan waited, the mechanic finished his run-up and shut down the Cessna. He climbed out, gave it one last walk around, then clipboard in hand, headed back toward the hangar. Next to the hangar sat several fuel trucks, Donovan memorized the operator's information painted on the side.

"Erica, give me your disposable phone. We need to make a call." The moment the phone powered up, Donovan dialed the number.

"Good morning, Victoria Aerocentre. How can I help you?"

"Good morning," Donovan said smoothly. "Is this operations?"

"I'll connect you, one moment."

"Operations. This is Brandy."

"Hello, Brandy, I hope you can help me. My boss's Cessna is in for maintenance, and it's scheduled to be finished this morning. He plans to fly later today, and wanted me to check on it for him, a Cessna 185, foxtrot-tango-papa-mike."

"Sure, let me check."

Donovan kept up a steady scan of their surroundings while he waited.

"Hello, sir," Brandy came back on the line. "It looks like they've just finished running the airplane. Once they complete the paperwork, it should be ready to go."

"Oh, perfect," Donovan replied. "Can you make sure they top off both wing tanks and add that to the bill?"

"Will do."

Donovan ended the call, powered the phone down, and turned to Erica. "One problem solved. Once they fuel the plane, we need to be ready to make our move."

Erica pointed to the north. "I'm starting to see some blue sky."

Donovan studied the horizon and through the patchy ground fog, he could see the sharply defined edge of the higher overcast, which meant as soon as the Cessna was fueled the weather may have moved far enough southeastward. He heard the heavy fuel truck growling through its gears before he saw it, but moments later the red-and-white Esso truck motored into view and eased to a stop in front of the Cessna.

"I guess I should ask if you can fly that thing?"

Donovan turned and gave her a look of disbelief, slightly annoyed that she'd bothered to even ask the question. He didn't think she was really concerned, more like nervous chatter. She didn't like giving up control any more than he did. "Keep in mind we've gone to a lot of trouble to get here. Do you really think I'd jeopardize everything by screwing up the part I do for a living?"

"I know, it's just that I thought the plane we'd steal would somehow be—bigger."

"It'll be fine." Donovan watched as the linemen pumped fuel into both wings and then reeled in the hose, climbed into the truck, and drove off the way he'd come.

"See that dumpster over there by the fence?" Donovan waited until Erica turned, saw what he was looking at, and nodded. "The only security camera I've seen is on the building behind us, and none seem to be pointed in this direction. We're using the dumpster to go up and over the fence. Then we walk out to the plane. No running, just act like you belong."

"What makes you think the keys are in the airplane? Airplanes have keys like cars and boats, right?"

"It's actually easier to hotwire a Cessna than a car. It'll take me less than thirty seconds. Do you have anything sharp I could use to strip insulation?"

Erica nodded, dug in her bag, and came up with some nail clippers. "Would this work?"

"Perfect."

"Here, I almost forgot." She pulled out a handful of thin latex gloves. "Put these on. I found them on the boat. In fact, before we go, let's take a moment and wipe everything down. I don't want to go to jail for stealing a crappy old truck."

Donovan pulled the gloves on, tested his dexterity, and then nodded that he was good.

Erica unfolded two cloth napkins she'd taken from the boat, and they quickly wiped the truck clean of fingerprints.

"Ready? Once this starts we're going to move fast," Donovan said.

She leaned in and kissed him, her lips lingering momentarily before she pulled away. She took her knitted beret and slid it on, then tucked her ponytail inside. She put on her sunglasses and turned to face Donovan. "Let's do this."

Donovan pulled his cap lower, slid on his sunglasses as well, and stepped out of the truck.

CHAPTER TWENTY-TWO

Donovan went over the fence, then pushed free from the strands of barbed wire at the top, and landed harder than he expected. The force of impact resonated up through his bad leg and jarred his spine. Erica landed catlike from the top of the fence. He picked his bag off the ground, lowered his head, and they walked exposed across the ramp toward the Cessna, something he'd done thousands of times, but never with the intention of stealing.

He opened the cockpit door. Erica crawled in first; Donovan followed, then closed and latched the door. He tossed his bag in the back, slid his seat forward, and took a moment to scan the ramp and make sure they hadn't drawn anyone's attention. Everything seemed normal.

The controls and switches were identical to the 185s he'd flown before, but the radios in this airplane had been updated. He was relieved to see a GPS receiver. One last sweep of the switches and he was ready. Fourteen thousand hours of flight time gave him the confidence to understand what he faced, and more than one narrow escape gave him the wisdom to know he needed to stay sharp in an airplane he hadn't flown in over fifteen years.

"Can we go?" Erica broke the silence. "Or do you need a little more time to do whatever it is you're doing?"

Donovan ignored her, though he did appreciate that as her stress levels went up, so did her sarcasm, always a helpful mechanism against freezing up and becoming useless. He wondered if it was from her medical training. He probed under the panel until he felt the small bundle of wires that led to the ignition. One swift yank and they were free. He leaned down, and using the clippers, stripped the plastic insulation off the ends of the wires. He switched on the battery, pushed the mixture all the way in, double-checked the fuel, and then touched the ignition wires to ground.

The propeller jerked to life and spun until the three-hundred-horsepower engine purred to life. Donovan twisted the leads securely together as the engine oil pressure climbed into the green. He flipped switches, adjusted the trim, set the flaps for takeoff, and picked up the microphone. He made one more quick check of the instruments then cleared his throat and prepared to alter his voice. All the transmissions on radio frequencies were recorded, and he preferred to remain unidentified.

"Victoria ground, this is Cessna foxtrot-tango-papa-mike. We're parked at Aerocentre, taxi for takeoff, VFR eastbound, over."

"Roger, foxtrot-tango-papa-mike, turn left out of Aerocentre, taxi to and hold short of runway three-one. Altimeter 1004, calm winds."

"Papa-mike, we copy, hold short of runway three-one." Donovan slid the microphone back in its holder, released the brakes, and the lightly loaded airplane only needed a nudge of the throttle to begin moving forward.

Donovan checked the flight instruments as they rolled to the hold short point for runway three-one. Each transmission from the tower, and Donovan expected the worst, that they'd been spotted and would be ordered to return to the ramp, or worse, airport security vehicles would surround them with guns drawn.

Donovan switched the frequency on the radio, turned to Erica. "You ready?"

She nodded.

"Victoria Tower. Foxtrot-tango-papa-mike, ready for takeoff, runway three-one, request eastbound departure."

"Foxtrot-tango-papa-mike. Wind calm, cleared for takeoff runway three-one, right turnout after departure approved."

Donovan acknowledged the clearance, advanced the throttle, and swung the single-engine Cessna out onto the runway. He double-checked the flaps and trim settings, and satisfied all was good, he pushed the prop control to the stops and then eased the throttle forward. They surged forward and the Cessna quickly accelerated down the runway. Donovan's toes lightly danced on the rudder pedals to keep the airplane on the centerline as the tail came up and then he eased back on the controls and the airplane lifted from the concrete. The 185 clawed skyward and out of eight hundred feet he began a turn.

As he climbed, Donovan was relieved to see the backside of the weather front had slid a little more to the south. As far as he could see to the northwest, the horizon was free of clouds. Behind them was nothing but low clouds, fog, and rain. He leveled the airplane at fifteen hundred feet, announced to Victoria tower that he was departing the area, and then turned to the GPS and began to enter Garrick's coordinates into the navigation system. Once the calculations were complete, Donovan put it up on the primary display. They were one hundred ninety-two miles southeast. At their present speed they would be overhead in one hour and twenty-two minutes.

Donovan looked outside. To the east, beyond Puget Sound, the snow-capped Cascade Mountains pushed up through the overcast into the sunshine. Vancouver Island was fifty or so miles wide and to the west was nothing but thousands of miles of open ocean. He reached around and found one of the navigation charts he'd taken from the *Irish Wake*. He opened it and smoothed it out on his leg. It gave him basic topographical information. Donovan eased the Cessna into a gentle bank and lined the airplane up to track their course.

"How far away are we?" Erica asked.

"One hundred eighty-nine miles." Donovan pointed to the display.

"Have you given any thought to this being a trap?" Erica asked. "One where Garrick is waiting for you, that this is where he intends to kill you and, by default, me as well."

"It's crossed my mind, but I don't think so. It's not the grand finale that someone like Garrick would go for. He's using these hints to maneuver and manipulate me."

"That part of his plan seems to be working pretty well."

"He's also trying to split me off from the authorities while pushing my buttons. I think he hopes I'll be reckless."

"He seems like a genius to me."

"That's exactly what we want him to think." Donovan shot Erica a rare smile. "He's already made his critical mistake. He just doesn't understand it yet."

"What's that?"

"He thinks he's this anonymous voice on the phone, but, thanks to you, I know exactly who I'm dealing with. And maybe his biggest mistake of all is that he has no idea you're still alive."

CHAPTER TWENTY-THREE

Donovan circled the coordinates, making a steep turn three thousand feet above the terrain. Below them were tree-covered hills, lakes, creeks, and a logging road that led from one clear-cut area of timber to another.

"I don't see anyone down there at all," Erica said after she lowered the binoculars. "In fact, I don't see a single sign that anyone was ever here."

Wordlessly, Donovan eased off on the throttle and slowed the Cessna to start his descent. He'd spotted the relatively open stretch of road and it matched the NASA image he'd printed. To the east of the road was a field of stumps where a thriving forest had once been. He widened out and began a low approach. With flaps down, he slowed the single-engine Cessna, descended until they were only fifty feet above the road, and gave the surface a good look as they flew over. Donovan saw tire marks and the surface looked firm enough to support the plane. It was certainly flat enough and long enough. Donovan poured the power to the engine, climbed up and away from the road, and swung around for the actual landing.

"Make sure you're strapped in tight, this could get a little rough. I need to land and leave enough runway in front of us to take off again." As Donovan explained his plan, he swung the Cessna on final approach and slowed to sixty knots. Flying at half the approach speed of the Gulfstream, Donovan felt like they were hanging in the sky.

He made tiny, yet meticulous, corrections using rudder and aileron to keep the 185 lined up straight. He guessed he only had four feet on either side of the main landing gear before the road fell off into a ditch. As they neared the ground, he came off the throttle, and the main gear lightly touched the surface.

Donovan touched the brakes, and the airplane bounced and swayed as it slowed on the makeshift strip. Donovan used the brakes to bring the airplane to a dead stop. The propeller spun down and it was quiet. He opened the door and breathed in the pine-filled air. It had warmed up, so he peeled off his jacket, found his gun, and slid it under his belt. He jumped out of the cockpit to the ground, tested the soil under his feet, and found a firm mixture of gravel and wet clay. The Cessna had handled it well, tires sitting up nicely, not sunk into ruts.

"Is there a problem?" Erica asked.

Donovan looked at how much road remained in front of the 185. "No, I think we're good. We should be able to fly out of here without any problems."

While Erica stretched away her stiffness, Donovan took in the area. Three hundred yards behind them, crows were raucously calling out to each other from the tops of the Douglas firs, shattering the quiet alpine morning. More crows arrived and joined the fray. Donovan wondered what had gotten their attention. Was it their arrival or was it something else?

"Let's grab our gear. I want to know what those crows are doing," Donovan said as he transferred the gun from under his belt into his right hand and slung the backpack over his shoulder. According to the last coordinates from the Cessna's GPS they were about a quarter of a mile from where they needed to be.

"I'm ready," Erica said as she secured her shoulder bag.

"We'll stay on the road as long as we can." Donovan fell in beside her as they started walking.

"Ugh, do you smell that?" Erica said, as she recoiled from the odor.

Donovan, too, was hit by the same putrid smell. A sickly sweet rancid odor that was so thick he couldn't get a full breath. He inwardly cursed Garrick, the stench reminded him of what he'd found on the *Kaiyo Maru #7*.

"Oh, my God, that's awful," Erica leaned over, resting her

hands on her knees. "I've observed an autopsy or two, but this is magnitudes worse."

Donovan tested the wind and then looked up at the trees for confirmation. "There's not much wind, but it's coming from the northwest. If we cut across that cleared area, closer to where the crows are, I think we'll find what we came for."

Erica tied a bandana around her mouth and nose. Donovan did the same, and they set off over the uneven terrain. They encountered moss-covered rocks, standing water, and underbrush with needle-sharp prongs that tore at their flesh. Halfway across the clearing, they came to a faint trail that ran toward a stand of trees. The crows circled in a frenzy. Donovan headed down the path, and they walked underneath the tremendous green canopy of the rain forest. Weaving among the trees, ferns, and fallen limbs, they continued.

"I remember this from the video," Erica said, her voice muffled by the bandana. "I think this could be where we saw the man running."

Twenty more feet and Donovan came to a muddy stretch and pointed. "Look, boot prints."

"And footprints. We're in the right place."

"A bear print," Donovan said as he knelt, placing his hand inside the massive indention. "a big one."

"Donovan, stop!" Erica hissed. "On the trail, dead ahead, there's a black bear."

Donovan spotted the adult bear in the dappled shadows about fifty yards in front of them. Slowly, he placed his left hand under his right and brought his weapon up to eye level. "Stay behind me and whatever you do, don't run."

"Oh, God, we need to get out of here." Erica pulled at the back of his shirt as she tried to move away, but Donovan held his ground.

"No, we've come too far." Donovan took a step forward. "Go away, bear! Get out of here!"

The bear reacted by rising up on its hind legs, and Donovan

felt Erica dig in while still clutching his shirt.

"Get! Go away, bear!" Donovan powered forward, Erica reluctantly following.

The bear dropped down on all fours and exhaled, a huff that couldn't be mistaken for anything other than what it was—a warning.

"Go on! Get out of here!" Donovan walked faster and squared his shoulders. "I said, go!"

The bear lowered its head and without any prelude charged them. Erica screamed as the bear stayed low, its broad chest whipping the vegetation as it pounded closer, mounds of dirt thrown upward by huge paws.

The bear covered half the distance in seconds. Donovan planted his feet and fired three of the heavy rounds that passed only feet over its head. The bear snorted loudly, dug its front paws into the soft ground, and stopped, the fur rippling on its back with the sudden maneuver. Donovan leveled his weapon and aimed it between the gigantic dark eyes staring at him from twenty feet away.

"Go!" Donovan yelled. "Go on!"

The bear pawed the ground and then swung its broad head back and forth. Donovan kept the sights trained on the bear and squeezed off one more round that threw up dirt inches in front of the bear's nose. The bear turned and ambled off a few yards, stopped, eyed them again, and then turned and vanished in the undergrowth.

"You are a goddamned crazy man!" Erica said, still clutching his shirt as she tried unsuccessfully to yank him around so she could face him. Undeterred, she sidestepped until she could make eye contact. "What were you thinking? That bear could have killed both of us!"

"He didn't want to kill us, he wanted us to go away."

"We should have done what the bear wanted. How can you be so calm? What's wrong with you?"

"Nothing's wrong with me—I'm carrying a gun. It wasn't like the bear was going to win." Donovan shrugged, knowing from his years of flying that the worse the situation became, the calmer he felt. "Now let's keep going before that bear comes back spoiling for another fight."

"Can you hear that?" Erica said.

Donovan listened and finally heard a buzzing sound.

"Insects—lots of them." Erica looked around the forest. "We're close."

Donovan moved as fast as he dared. He kept his head moving back and forth and occasionally behind, watching for predators. As they drew closer to the sound, the path opened up into a clearing exposing the shallow pit containing the bodies of the four men. Donovan looked away as clouds of flies rose, swarming overhead. The bodies weren't in the same small pile as on the video. The bears and other scavengers had ravaged them, scattering them about, huge chunks of flesh and appendages were missing. Donovan felt his throat close off, his stomach lurch. His eyes were watering and he needed to flee this grisly place. Silently, he cursed Garrick for killing these men, blaming Eco-Watch, and then making Donovan travel here to see it firsthand. He glanced at Erica, wondering if he could even speak when over her shoulder he spotted a plastic bag fixed to a tree.

He went to the tree, where a closer inspection revealed a simple plastic bag tacked to the bark. Inside, a picture of Meredith. Donovan instantly identified the backdrop as Alaska. Meredith was standing in front of the Trans-Alaska pipeline after a rupture had spilled 280,000 gallons of crude onto the tundra. He snapped the bag and picture off the tree and turned it over to see if anything was written in the back. To his surprise, he found Meredith's flowing script: *The earth always pays for the mistakes of man.*

"I recognize her," Erica said, standing beside him. "That's Meredith Barnes."

"It's Garrick's message." Donovan handed the plastic envelope to her. "We need to get to the plane."

Scanning for bears, they hurried back to the plane, climbed in, and Donovan quickly went through the start procedures as before.

He adjusted the trim, set the flaps, and made one last visual sweep of the panel. Once he was ready, he stood on the brakes and pushed the throttle all the way to the stops. The airframe shuddered and bucked against the forces as Donovan held the controls all the way back to keep the propeller from digging into the ground. When he released the brakes, the Cessna lurched forward. Donovan jockeyed the controls to keep them straight, the main tires plowing through some sand, losing a fraction of their momentum. Donovan's eyes jumped back and forth between their airspeed and the trees dead ahead. He not only needed to get the Cessna into the air, he needed to clear the one-hundred-foot firs—it was going to be closer than he thought. Donovan eased back a touch on the controls and felt the wings strain to lift the airframe off the ground.

He was running out of space as he coaxed the Cessna into the air. Their speed surged as they broke free from the dirt, and Donovan pulled back as much as he dared, his eyes glued to the airspeed indicator. If he flew too slow, they'd stall and the two of them would die a quick death as the Cessna lost lift and slammed nose first into the ground below. Dancing on the aerodynamic precipice, they roared toward the tops of trees, and in an instant they flashed past. Donovan expected the sound of branches hitting aluminum, but the 185 clawed skyward. He banked the plane southeast, reduced the power on the roaring engine, and raised the remaining flaps. He took a quick glance at Erica who sat wide-eyed, still gripping the armrests.

"That was close," she said as she turned to meet his gaze. "I mean, that was really close. We about crashed, didn't we?"

"Not even close." Donovan slipped on his sunglasses, pulled his hat low, and shot her a mischievous grin. "We probably could have plowed through the top five feet of those trees and kept flying. The branches are pretty small at the top."

Erica leaned over, kissed him on the cheek, and then hesitated as her attention snapped into focus over his shoulder. "Oh, shit."

Donovan jerked his head around and found the helicopter, above and slightly behind them. He recognized it as a Eurocopter, overall white with red-and-yellow stripes that merged into a solid blue tail. Up near the rotor mast he spotted an emblem, a bison head ringed by oak leaves topped with a crown.

"Who are they?" Erica sunk down in her seat.

"Royal Canadian Mounted Police. Stay down, find your hat and glasses and put them on, tuck your hair up underneath like before," Donovan said as he cinched up his seat belt.

"What are you doing?"

"We need to lose this guy." Donovan's eyes swept the terrain below, then the distant horizon. "Make sure your seat belt is good and tight."

Erica had just finished pulling on her beret, making her blond hair invisible. She pulled hard on her seat belt and turned toward Donovan. "How are we possibly going to shake this guy?"

Without warning, Donovan threw the Cessna into a ninety-degree bank to the left and forced the nose almost straight down. The airplane built up speed quickly and Donovan nudged the airspeed up to the red line. He flattened out the descent and leveled the wings. He kept descending until they roared below the tops of the hills. At the entry into the first valley, they were at treetop level, going flat-out as Donovan hugged the contour of the terrain. Another valley opened up ahead and Donovan waited until the last second before making a hard turn to the east. He dropped the Cessna down low, flying just above a logging road, and allowed the speed to inch above the red line.

"I don't see them," Erica yelled above the noise of the engine and the slipstream. Donovan looked for himself and found nothing but empty sky, but he understood it was only a temporary reprieve. The RCMP radio frequencies would be already buzzing as assets out ahead of them swung into action.

CHAPTER TWENTY-FOUR

Lauren woke to a silent house and she struggled for a moment to collect her bearings. She was in Laguna Beach, the house Buck had arranged. She glanced at the clock and discovered it was late morning. She threw on a pair of sweatpants and a hooded sweatshirt from William's stock of clothes, grabbed the folded sheets of paper she'd been working on the night before, and in stocking feet went to check on her daughter. Abigail might sleep for another couple hours. She'd been excited last night to see Grandpa William, and, thankfully, the combination of travel and playing with William had worn her out. The door to Stephanie's room was closed, so she was probably still asleep.

Lauren went to the great room and through the expansive picture windows took in the Pacific Ocean.

"Good morning," William called from the kitchen. "Coffee?"

Lauren turned to see William, he in his suit, standing with another man she didn't recognize. The stranger was probably late-twenties, longish blond hair, unshaven. Definitely not FBI, maybe CIA. Curious, she joined them.

"Who are you?"

"I'm security, Dr. McKenna, my name is Marcus."

"Are you a friend of Buck's?"

"No, ma'am, I never had the privilege of serving with Lt. Buckley, but it would have been an honor. I hear from my former commanding officer that he's done some amazing things."

"Buck set all this up," William said. "There's a small team of people watching out for our safety."

"Have you been briefed on Nikolett Kovarik and what she managed to do in Paris?"

"Yes, ma'am." Marcus's eyes shot from Lauren to William and then back to Lauren. "I promise, Dr. McKenna. She won't get past us."

"How many are in your detail?" Lauren asked.

"There are five of us, ma'am. We're running twenty-four-hour surveillance from multiple vantage points. The cliff out back goes straight down eighty feet all the way to the beach, there're motion detectors and infrared cameras. There's no way anyone gets in that way. We're on a cul-de-sac on a quiet street. Only one way in or out. You're safe, ma'am."

Lauren could hear Henri telling her the same thing not three days ago. Then she pictured him collapsing in the department store, Philippe shot multiple times before he succumbed, and Giselle coming to their rescue in the car only to take a bullet to the neck. "I hope so, Marcus, for all our sakes." Lauren found some orange juice, poured a glass, then headed to the deck for the fresh morning air.

"I'm sorry," Marcus said. "I need to ask you to stay inside the house and try not to loiter in front of any open windows."

Instead of the inviting table and chairs in the sun, Lauren settled for the kitchen table. She switched on her phone. As soon as it powered up, she heard the beeping that meant she had multiple messages.

First, she glanced at her e-mails, finding nothing of significance, and then she listened to her voice mail. The first was from Aaron calling from Paris, imploring her to make contact. The second was also Aaron, more or less demanding her to call. The third was her boss, Calvin Reynolds, at the Defense Intelligence Agency asking her to please check in with him, informing her that the CIA was anxious to speak with her. Once she was caught up, she shut her phone down again. All the calls were ones she'd expected. She'd hoped there would be at least one from Donovan, but that wasn't the case. He was still off the grid.

"Mind if I join you?" William asked, holding a plateful of bagels.

"Please," Lauren jumped up, pulled out a chair for William, and then helped him set out plates and pour coffee. Once they were seated, she studied his familiar face and decided that in the preceding eight months since she'd seen him, he'd seemed to grow older. He still had his piercing intelligent eyes and wonderful smile, but the lines on his face seemed etched deeper, his skin tired and drawn. She wondered if he was thinking the same about her, because she knew it was a fact.

"How do you feel?" William asked. "Did you get any sleep?"

"A little, my body is still out of whack and probably will be for a couple of days. Is there anything new going on? Has anyone heard from Donovan?"

"No, Donovan is still underground." William took a sip of coffee. "A couple of things were reported this morning. I'm still in the loop with the FBI, and they called with news out of Vancouver. The authorities believe they found the British Columbia connection to the poachers."

"Any survivors?" Lauren had begun to assume that any people Garrick touched were murdered.

"No." William shook his head. "The FBI didn't have any details, but they suspect the group was involved in the procurement and smuggling of the gallbladders once they arrived in Vancouver."

"So we can assume that Donovan is someplace in British Columbia? He went to find where the video was made." Lauren shot a questioning look at William. "Garrick is leaving pictures of Meredith. They're clues, aren't they? Donovan figured out what they mean and now he thinks he has to get there before the authorities."

"Something like that. The plan has its merits."

"Let's move on, you said there were a couple of things reported this morning. What happened besides Vancouver?"

"The Orange County sheriff's office found two bodies in an apartment not far from here in Laguna Hills. A young couple found in a ransacked apartment, killed by carefully placed shots to the back of the head."

"A professional hit?"

"That's what the FBI thinks," William replied. "The woman was a medical professional."

"Connections to Erica?"

"The FBI doesn't know about Erica, so until I get a name of the victim, I can't run a background check to find out."

"There's something else, isn't there?" Lauren asked. "You have that look."

"I had a long conversation with Buck this morning. He passed on that at Donovan's insistence he made some inquiries, and it's been discovered that the phones at Eco-Watch headquarters are being monitored."

"Oh, perfect. Any idea by whom?" Lauren asked.

"According to Buck, the phone tap is a professional job, domestic, and not all that high tech, something you'd see from any mid-level private investigative service."

"How long has someone been listening?"

"Buck didn't know."

"Maybe that's the link I haven't been able to figure out. I've been trying to understand who tried to kill Donovan and Erica here in Orange County. In fact, I can't understand who knew Erica was even alive, aside from myself and the CIA."

"Donovan didn't think it was Garrick."

"And I believe him—Garrick wants Donovan to suffer, not die. Help me break this down. If the gunmen Donovan encountered here in California weren't part of Garrick's little nightmare, then who were they? CIA?"

"Doubtful."

"I agree. Erica made contact with Eco-Watch, so her incoming number would have been logged, if the phones are bugged it would lead back to Orange County. Erica surfaces for the first time since the massacre at the German clinic, and someone tries to kill her. I have to think the information from CIA ended up in the hands of someone who wanted her dead."

"That sounds like Garrick," William replied.

"For the sake of argument, let's say Donovan is right, this wasn't Garrick's work. Who does that leave?"

"Mossad."

"The people connected to the clinic where she worked."

William's phone rang and he swept it to his ear. "Yes, that's fine. Let him in and tell him we're in the kitchen."

"Who is it? I'm not showered or dressed for company."

"Don't worry, it's family." William stood.

Lauren looked over William's shoulder and was horrified to find the last person she expected to see, or even wanted to see. She'd run this scenario in her head a hundred times and it never turned out well.

"Hello, Lauren."

"Hello, Michael." Lauren stood face to face with the man she knew was her biggest detractor. He was Donovan's best friend and the number-two man at Eco-Watch. Michael was usually relaxed and casual, more likely to smile and laugh than do what he was doing right now—which was to stare at her with no discernible emotion whatsoever. He looked like he'd lost some weight and he looked good, same blond-haired, overgrown surfer out of Southern California.

"William, could you give us a moment?" Michael said, breaking the silence.

"Of course," William replied.

Michael gestured for Lauren to take a seat. Once she did, he sat as well. "What brings you to Laguna Beach?"

Lauren hated chitchat. She wanted to pull the pin on this grenade and see what was left afterward. "Someone tried to kill me in Paris. The three of us fled Europe and came here."

"Three?"

"Abigail and Stephanie VanGelder, William's niece, you remember her, but, of course, your first concern was finding out if I'm with another man. Am I right? Never mind the part where someone tried to kill me."

"Donovan was right," Michael said. "You don't make anything easy, do you?"

Lauren recoiled at the words, even though she knew there was an element of truth to them. "What else does Donovan say? The two of you have had months to dissect what a bitch I am. Come on, let's hear it."

"I'll be honest, at first there was a lot of anger and harsh words. You leaving was hard on everyone, not just Donovan. He was beat up, both mentally and physically. I ran Eco-Watch while he recovered. Susan and I took turns making sure he was eating, going to physical therapy, not drinking. Yeah, to be honest, I was furious."

"Was?"

"I finally realized one day that the only one who was still angry with you—was me." Michael lowered his head. "I hated you for leaving my friend in his hour of need, until I finally listened to what Donovan had been telling me for months. He didn't blame you, he admitted it was his fault and the timing was his doing as well. He took full responsibility, told me he'd hurt you and that I shouldn't be angry with you. He said that if I wanted to be mad at anyone to be mad at him for screwing everything up."

Lauren processed what she was hearing. Nothing she hadn't heard directly from Donovan. He'd never tried to blame her or deflect his own culpability for the implosion of their relationship.

"Is it true?" Michael asked. "Is this all his fault?"

"It takes two. I'm not blameless, but I think you should take him at his word."

"Then I owe you an apology."

"Thank you, Michael." Lauren cherished this small repair in the devastation she and Donovan had wrought. "I really appreciate you coming here. I've missed you and Susan and the boys."

"We've missed you as well. Are you here because you're coming home?"

"No." Lauren shook her head and watched the smile drop from Michael's face.

"That seems a little absolute," Michael replied. "How can you be so emphatic when you haven't even seen him yet? Why come at all?"

Lauren absorbed the isolation of the situation, as if Donovan and his friends wanted her in their lives, but only on their terms. "I'm here because Eco-Watch is under attack. People are trying to kill my family. My entire security team was murdered in Paris. I came to the nearest safe haven I could think of, which was here with Abigail's father. As it turns out, he's not here, is he? And no one seems to know where he ran off to, only that he's with another woman. So, no, I'm not coming home."

CHAPTER TWENTY-FIVE

For the last hour and a half, Donovan had flown in and out of the valleys, slowly working his way toward the Strait of Georgia, staying as low as possible to avoid radar. Once over the water, he weaved through the islands that dotted the area, hoping to create nothing more than an intermittent target.

"Look!" Erica pointed off to the right and waited until Donovan spotted the threat.

The UH-60 was nearly on top of them and easily closed the gap as they banked in above and slightly behind the Cessna. Just one glimpse of the black-and-gold markings told him it was the United States Border Patrol. Dead ahead was Haro Strait, which would feed them into U.S. airspace near the San Juan Islands. A light mist had started to fall, and the ceiling was dropping along with the visibility. They'd finally caught up to the backside of the weather front they'd left behind hours ago, and the conditions were deteriorating quickly. Donovan was forced to inch closer to the water to keep his outside visual reference.

Donovan handed Erica the *Irish Wake's* nautical charts. "Help me find the best way through these islands. With the weather getting worse, we might have a chance to lose them if we treat it like a maze. The more twists and turns the better. A dead end and we crash."

"Where are we?" Erica said as she took the charts from Donovan.

"South of Spieden Island."

She studied the nautical chart for a moment then turned to him. "Where do we want to end up?"

"There's an airport outside Burlington, or even Arlington. All

I want is to lose these guys long enough to land and get away. We need to be careful, there's a Naval Air Station near the north end of Whidbey Island and there are Navy installations all the way down Puget Sound to Seattle. I think someone might get nervous enough to start shooting if we pushed it too far in that direction."

"Okay. Just ahead is the south side of Shaw Island. Tell me what you think about this." Erica held up the map so Donovan could see what she had in mind as she traced a zigzag course through the islands.

Donovan glanced from the ocean racing past, to the chart, and back again. Erica had devised a serpentine route through the dozens of islands that would make it difficult for the Border Patrol to stay with them. "Those places on the east side of Lopez Island—you have us going over land twice. We may not have the ceiling. If we end up in the clouds we're finished—the running will be over."

"Trust me." Erica put her hand on his arm. "I've stood on both of these places. It's flat, all of five feet above sea level. We'll be fine, but the sudden terrain might cause the helicopter pilots to back off a bit."

"Is this Shaw Island off to my left?"

"Yeah. Get ready for the first turn. Trust me. I'll talk you through this as we go. Just do what I say. There will be a hard ninety-degree turn to the left then straight for five miles then a hard right turn."

Donovan glanced back at the helicopter. He knew the guys flying it were good, but it was like playing football in lousy weather. The advantage goes to the player who knows the route he's running.

"Get ready. Turn now!"

Donovan threw the Cessna into a forty-five-degree bank that forced the helicopter to climb to get out of the way. The sudden maneuver caught them by surprise, and the UH-60 lost ground.

"We can't see it yet," Erica said without looking up from the chart. "Canoe Island is just ahead. Pass left of it and get ready to make a right turn on my mark."

Out of the mist, the island materialized and then just as quickly vanished into the fog behind them. Donovan was down to fifty feet. He estimated that visibility was less than half a mile.

"Twenty degrees to the right," Erica said as she looked up from the paper chart in her hand. "We need to keep the Lopez Island shoreline in sight. You're going to see a beach, then a point. That point is where you need to make a hard ninety-degree turn until we get past Shoal Bay. Then we're going to make it interesting."

Donovan loved the certainty in her voice. He could hardly see the island that rose from the water and towered above them. His airspeed was pegged at redline when the point shot past and Erica called out for him to turn.

"Perfect," Erica said as she searched for their next landmark. Just as quickly, she called out, "Donovan! Look out!"

Donovan saw the churning water below them, a ship's wake. He snapped the Cessna to the right a fraction of a second before the massive Washington State Ferry appeared out of the fog like a green-and-white monolith. He continued the turn to the right, and as the ferry flashed past, he could see people standing on the fantail and a wooden plaque near the bridge that read *Hyak*. Donovan twisted in his seat and watched as the chopper matched his move, narrowly missing the ship.

"We turned too far!" Erica yelled. "There're trees dead ahead!"

Donovan set his jaw and cranked the Cessna in a steep turn back to the left, carefully holding his altitude so as not to put a wingtip into the waves. He guessed they'd just missed the rocks on the peninsula by a matter of feet.

"Oh, Jesus." Erica put her hand up to her heart. "Fly a one-seventy heading. Be careful, there's a marina out here and some houses dead ahead, but the terrain isn't very high."

In the gloom, Donovan saw the marina slide past, far smaller than the one in Anacortes, but it got him thinking. He saw the scattered houses ahead on the sand spit and easily dodged them as they raced south.

"Okay," Erica said, "turn right ten degrees and be careful, there are a couple of big rocks out here. We're going over Spencer Spit, it's a little piece of sandy beach that juts out and almost touches that island. There's a log cabin on the beach. Use it as a reference point."

Donovan rolled to the new heading and marveled as the strip of land appeared off the nose, a solitary cabin made for a perfect navigation tool. To his left and right the terrain reached up into the overcast. It was like flying indoors at 175 miles per hour, navigating from room to room careful not to touch the walls, floor, or ceiling.

"We're in Lopez Sound. Stay on this heading. We'll come up on two big rocks, which is the point where we go left and thread ourselves through another narrow area."

"Where is he now?" Donovan asked.

Erica turned around and scanned behind them. "He's lost ground; he's maybe a quarter mile back."

"Once we leave Lopez Island, where do we go?"

"After Lopez, it's open water all the way to Fidalgo Island and Anacortes, which is where we started. Oh, and once we're out over Rosario Strait, heads-up, there will be major ship traffic."

Donovan processed what Erica had just said and pulled on his memory of the area. Not only what he'd seen yesterday, but what he remembered from twenty-five years ago. "Erica, look at the map, the southern part of Fidalgo Island where it almost touches Whidbey Island. A place called Deception Pass. How far?"

"Seven miles once we leave Lopez Island behind. There's your rock! Turn left." Erica pointed and held on as Donovan banked the Cessna steeply.

Donovan saw trees to his left and a gap on his right. He corrected slightly to avoid a huge glass-enclosed house, and they roared above the beach and out over open water. A glance behind them confirmed the helicopter was trailing about a quarter mile. Donovan pushed for more power, but the throttle was already against the stops. The engine instruments were past redlines and he didn't care. He only needed the engine to hold together for another eleven minutes and then, one way or another, all of this would be over.

"With our latex gloves, there's nothing we need to wipe down inside this plane, is there?" Donovan asked. "The moment we're down, we're running. Make sure we don't leave anything behind that can be used to identify us."

Erica reached back and pulled up her bag as well as their duffel bag. She made sure everything was fastened and cinched. Then she loosened her seat belt, and made a thorough search for anything they'd left on the floor or under the seat of the plane. Once she was satisfied, she secured her harness.

Donovan kept the airplane just feet above the waves, as he scanned ahead. The steep cliffs and treacherous winds of Deception Pass were somewhere dead ahead in the mist. He asked to see the chart, and then he placed his finger on the spot he had in mind, explaining to Erica what he had planned. When he finished, she nodded a wide-eyed understanding before pulling her seat belt even tighter.

"Take a one-one-seven-degree heading," Erica said. "We'll see Deception Island first. From there it's less than a mile to the bridge."

"There it is," Donovan said as the island appeared out of the mist and rain. He swung to the north, and the two separate spans of the Deception Pass Bridge emerged out of the mist.

"The gap on the left is really narrow, maybe one-hundred-fifty-feet across at water level." Erica was focused on her chart. "The span on the right is wider, it's four hundred feet across. Beneath is Pass Island."

Donovan banked toward the left, toward the narrowest gap. As the rocks and the mass of steel girders towered above them, Donovan considered the fact that he only had three wingspans of space to shoot the gap.

"Is he following?" Donovan didn't dare risk a look behind them.

"Yes."

"Let me know the second we lose sight of him." Donovan's muscles tensed as they shot past a narrow bay to his left and then roared under the bridge, racing toward the eastern tip of Pass Island.

"I've lost him!"

Donovan immediately yanked the throttle all the way to idle to bleed off as much speed as he could for the turn. He cranked the Cessna into a steep bank to the right. Above him, five-hundred-foot cliffs kept them confined within the narrow gorge. He kept turning until the wings were almost ninety degrees to the water. G-forces drove him down into his seat, and he added pressure to the tortured controls to keep the airplane from being pulled into the water. Pass Island seemed to hover just off the right wing, dangerously close to rocks, steel, and the icy-cold water. Donovan pivoted the Cessna in a tight, one-hundred-eighty-degree turn. He used the massive steel girders above him as a reference point. They flashed beneath the longer of the two spans and headed back the way they'd just come. Donovan slammed full power to the engine, and in an instant, they were west of the bridge. He made another turn and aimed for the narrow cove dead ahead. If his calculations were correct, the Border Patrol should just now be emerging on the east side of the bridge—searching an empty sky.

There was a narrow gap in the rocks at the end of the cove. Donovan banked to thread the Cessna through the trees, and then they shot out over Bowman Bay. He swept left to avoid a wooden pier and a pleasure boat. He had no choice but to haul back on the controls and climb away from the water, hugging the rocks on a narrow peninsula, then immediately dove back down to wave-top height on the other side. Just off the right wing, logs and kelp mixed with the house-size boulders marked the steep cliffs of Fidalgo Island. He put as much distance between them and the bridge as he could, until finally, he climbed up and over the vertical cliff and leveled off just above the trees.

Donovan kept the Cessna fifty feet above a road that would lead them into Anacortes. He couldn't see it, but he knew that Mt.

Erie towered just off the right wing and rose over a thousand feet above them.

"I don't see them," Erica called out as she kept searching for any sign of the helicopter. "I think we lost them."

"It won't take them long to figure out what we did." Donovan held the Cessna steady.

Erica's gaze was still glued behind them. "Nothing."

They shot over the first subdivisions, and Donovan throttled back to slow the airplane. He saw the familiar shoreline and brought the engine all the way to idle. When he had the speed, he began to lower the flaps. Just beyond the first marina was the strip of open land where the paper mill had once been. Donovan settled in his seat, the open land he'd noticed yesterday looked far smaller than when he was standing next to it on the ground.

Erica stole a glance forward and then looked at Donovan and whispered, "Holy shit." Then she turned back to watch for their pursuers.

Donovan slowed the Cessna as much as he dared. They passed over a boatyard, the masts of the sailboats reaching up dangerously into their flight path. When they crossed over a parking lot, Donovan saw people look up and point. They flew over a fence, a collection of construction trailers, and the moment the wheels were over dirt, Donovan flared the Cessna and the main tires kissed the ground.

The landing area was rougher than it looked, and Erica let out a small scream as the 185 lurched and bounced. Donovan stood on the brakes, the noise deafening as the entire airframe shook. The chain-link fence at the end of the lot was coming up fast.

Donovan knew they weren't going to stop before they reached the fence. His thigh burned in protest as he used all his strength on the brake pedals. He made a decision; he released the brake pressure from the left side and held his breath as the Cessna instantly pivoted to the right. The left main gear strut hit the ditch first and took the brunt of the impact. Like a fifteen-foot scythe, the wing tip sliced into the fence, ripping it to shreds as the entire left side of the plane slammed into the water-filled culvert creating a huge geyser. The Cessna's left side windows shattered and snapped inward, spewing water and debris into the cabin as they came to a halt. Still spinning, the propeller threw huge clods of mud into the sky before the bent props finally ground to a halt.

As fast as he could, Donovan cut the fuel to the engine, turned off the battery switch, threw off his harness, and reached over to release Erica's harness. "Go!"

Erica threw open her door, grabbed their things, and with Donovan right behind her, climbed out of the wrecked airplane. The smell of gasoline from the Cessna's ruptured fuel tanks filled the air.

They both jumped into the ditch. Donovan took the duffel from her and pulled her by the arm up the embankment. They climbed over what remained of the fence and began to run. Off to his left, people began to erupt from an office building and move toward them.

"Run! It's going to blow!" Donovan yelled, and waved them away. Immediately, their would-be rescuers turned and fled back into the building.

Breathing heavily, Donovan rounded the corner. The rented Cherokee was dead ahead. He pulled out the keys, pushed the button that unlocked the doors, and he and Erica jumped inside. He started the engine, threw it into drive, and sped away. A quick glance in the rearview mirror told him they weren't being followed—yet.

"We have to get off this island! One roadblock and it's over."

"We can't make a mad dash for the bridge. We need to drive normal, blend in with traffic. We bought ourselves some time. Hopefully, it'll take a few minutes for the authorities to respond."

"You're bleeding," Erica said, pointing at his hand.

He felt the pain in his left shoulder for the first time and reached with his right hand to probe for the source of the blood. He winced and pulled his bloody fingers away. "There's something stuck in there. I'm not dying, it'll have to wait."

"Look back at the harbor," Erica said.

Donovan glanced in the mirror to find a plume of dirty black smoke, emanating from where they'd left the Cessna. The Border Patrol helicopter orbited, now joined by a red-and-white Coast Guard HH-65.

"How did you know it was going to burn? You saved those people."

"I didn't," Donovan said. "I didn't want a bunch of people to get a good look at us. I yelled the first thing I thought of that would make them scatter."

"Do you know where you're going?"

"Yeah. Up ahead, we make a left turn and take Highway 20 off the island. Once we're over the bridge, we can go anywhere we want."

"Uh-oh." Erica pointed up ahead.

Donovan spotted the patrol car going the opposite direction, toward town and moving fast, every light flashing. Using all of his patience and self-control, Donovan kept the Cherokee at the speed limit. They breezed through two green lights until he could see the twin concrete arches that marked the bridge off the island. No roadblocks yet. As they drew closer, on the opposite span, two police cruisers appeared, lights flashing, but they weren't going very fast.

"Oh, shit," Erica said as the two patrol cars slowed and pulled into the median.

Donovan was already in the slow lane. There was a truck ahead of them, a Volvo station wagon in the inside lane, and a quarter mile behind was a panel van. "Quick, take off your hat, I doubt if they're looking for a couple."

They passed both troopers at 55 mph and started across the bridge. In his rearview mirror Donovan saw the highway patrol cruisers swing out onto the pavement to block traffic.

"We were the last car off the island. Holy shit! I can't believe we pulled that off," Erica said as they headed east.

"We're not free yet. Look at the map, see if there's a way to get to Seattle other than on the interstate."

Erica found the rental car map under the visor. "Yeah, there is. Just up here on the right is a turnoff. It looks like if we follow it to Route Nine, it'll eventually take us south into Seattle."

"Perfect. Now I need you to do one more thing. Find your phone."

While Erica dug in her bag, Donovan reflected on her actions today, her fearless navigation, and her complete trust in his abilities. He couldn't help but feel a swelling of admiration at how poised she'd been.

"What? Why are you looking at me that way?" Erica asked, phone in hand.

"Thanks for all the help back there."

Erica leaned over and gave him a quick kiss. "We're a team. Now, who am I calling?"

"Michael Ross, he's the one flying us to Alaska."

CHAPTER TWENTY-SIX

Lauren heard the familiar sound of the landing gear being lowered. The earlier conversation she and Michael had been having in California had been interrupted by a call from Erica Covington. Donovan was driving, but Erica relayed that they needed the *da Vinci* to pick them up in Seattle and fly them to Anchorage. Michael had called Gulfstream, and they'd recommended an experienced local freelance pilot, Scott West, to act as Michael's copilot. On impulse, Lauren had insisted on going.

She closed the laptop she'd been buried in for the last hour and a half. There was nothing new out of Paris where the authorities were still searching for a dark-haired woman in connection with the department store shooting spree. Lauren read more about the killings in Vancouver. The police there were asking the public for information, and the Asian Pacific Community was outraged over the lack of progress in what some were calling a hate crime.

The most interesting news story was the one she'd just been reading. Breaking news out of Anacortes, Washington: a small, single-engine Cessna, the kind favored by bush pilots, had been stolen from Victoria International Airport in British Columbia, and after evading authorities, crash landed near downtown Anacortes. Lauren made a quick map check and discovered that Anacortes was a two-hour drive north of Seattle. The report had gone on to say that two people had fled the scene of the crash after warning witnesses of the danger of an explosion. The airplane did burn, which will hamper the investigation. Lauren had clicked through the photographs of the burnt and mangled airplane. There was absolutely nothing to connect Donovan to the story, but she knew in her heart this was her husband's doing. Whatever Garrick's ultimate goal, he was leaving nothing but chaos in his wake.

The view out the window of the *da Vinci* beyond the wingtip was opaque nothingness. This was the first time Lauren had been in the newest incarnation of the *Spirit of da Vinci;* it still smelled new. The added length from upgrading to the G500 from the older GIV, had been utilized to create a small VIP seating area forward of all of the science stations.

When they broke out of the clouds, Lauren spotted Lake Union, the Space Needle, and then downtown itself. She always thought the entire city looked washed clean from all the rain.

Michael touched down smoothly, and once they slowed, he swung off the runway and taxied toward the ramp. Lauren checked her watch. It was three and a half hours since Donovan had called.

They pivoted into a parking spot, and Michael shut down the engines, jumped out of the cockpit, and opened the door. Lauren made no effort to get up. She knew this was a quick turn. A flight plan had already been filed, fuel would be loaded, and the food Michael had ordered would arrive. They'd be on their way to Alaska inside thirty minutes. When Lauren heard footsteps coming up the airstair, she braced herself for it to be Donovan. Instead, Erica Covington appeared.

"Oh, hello." Erica seemed startled when she realized there was someone on the plane.

Donovan came up the stairs and stopped behind Erica, who stepped to the side so that he could go in front of her. Donovan leaned down and kissed Lauren on the cheek. "Michael just told me you were here. Erica, this is my wife, Lauren."

"Hello," Lauren said, not at all expecting such a casual attitude from Donovan and certainly not expecting Erica Covington to be much more beautiful than her picture.

Donovan turned to Erica. "There's a spot in the back where two of the chairs fold down into a bed. Let's take this show back there. I want to do this before we take off."

Lauren found herself sitting alone in the small VIP section as

Donovan went aft with Erica to where they could make a bed. She flung off her seat belt and followed.

"Help Erica with the shades," Donovan told Lauren as he aligned two of the science station chairs and lowered their backs creating a narrow bunk. Not sure what was happening, Lauren nodded and lowered the shades on the trademark Gulfstream oval windows.

When it was clear no one could see inside, Erica helped Donovan with his jacket and shirt, revealing his blood-streaked arm.

"You're hurt!" Lauren blurted out the obvious before she could stop herself. "What happened?"

"It feels like a piece of Plexiglas," Erica said as she gingerly probed the wound.

Lauren looked at Donovan's naked torso for the first time since he'd been hurt. Her eyes darted from the reddish scar on his wrist to the round bullet hole near his clavicle. She also noticed Erica didn't so much as glance at the wounds. Lauren felt a white-hot flush of jealousy. Erica had seen them before.

"Sit here," Erica told Donovan as she maneuvered the overhead swiveling light. She turned to Lauren. "Donovan said there was a first-aid kit onboard. Could you get it for me? And a flashlight would be helpful."

Lauren nodded and turned away, infuriated to be reduced to fetching supplies. When Lauren returned, Erica unzipped the bag, found everything she would need, and spread it out in sequence. She snapped on latex gloves, took the flashlight, and examined the wound. "Once I pull this out, depending how deep it is, it's going to bleed quite a bit. Your shirt is already ruined so we'll use it to soak up the excess while I flush out the wound and suture it closed. Lauren, can you hold the shirt under here like this?"

Lauren did as instructed, not prepared for the effect the nearness to Donovan was having on her. She felt the familiar attraction to a man she'd shared a bed with for years, but there was also a foreignness she didn't know how to process.

"We're ready to roll. What the hell is going on back here?" Michael peered over Lauren's shoulder.

Donovan lifted his head in Michael's direction. "I'd appreciate it if we didn't start moving quite yet."

"Ten minutes," Erica said, forceps poised in her gloved hand. She faced Donovan. "This might hurt. Are you ready?"

Donovan nodded and kept his eyes fixed on Erica.

Michael turned away and walked toward the cockpit. "Someone come and tell me when we can go."

Lauren wasn't squeamish, so when Erica pulled out the Plexiglas shard she didn't flinch. The blood oozed down Donovan's arm into the shirt. He simply closed his eyes as Erica probed the wound for any other debris. Satisfied, she applied antiseptic and expertly sutured the wound shut. Once she was finished, she applied gauze and securely taped it to his arm.

Once the bleeding stopped, Lauren carried the blood-soaked shirt forward, found a plastic bag in the galley, and took it back to collect all of the other trash.

"You should probably destroy those pants as well," Lauren said. "There's blood all down the side of them."

"Erica, if you're done being my doctor, would you mind giving my wife and me some privacy? You can tell Michael he's free to depart."

"Of course," Erica quickly zipped up the first-aid kit and took it forward.

"Can you get my bag?" Donovan asked Lauren as he massaged his aching thigh.

Lauren unzipped his overnight bag and found a pair of folded khakis. She handed them over and helped steady her husband as he stood and changed clothes. The scar on his leg was bright red and larger than she ever imagined. She turned away, feeling a jab of guilt for leaving him with such severe wounds. She rummaged around and found him an undershirt and a button-down shirt. She helped him dress, then he asked her to help him arrange the chairs back the way they were.

Then Donovan sat and strapped himself in, motioning for Lauren to do the same. Lauren heard the airstair close and moments later the engines began their familiar hum, and they began taxiing out to the runway.

"Why are you here?" Donovan asked bluntly. "Where's Abigail?"

"She's fine. She didn't want to come. She's sick of airplanes and she wanted to stay in Laguna Beach with Stephanie and William. Buck assembled a small army of bodyguards to protect them, so I came alone."

"Did you tell Abigail you were coming to see me?"

"No, I think that would have been confusing."

"Yeah, probably," Donovan replied as he thought of how much he missed his little girl. They sat in silence as the engines spooled up and the *da Vinci* rolled down the runway. The Gulfstream lifted off, quickly enveloped in the heavy, gray clouds.

"I have a question for you," she said. "I saw the story out of Anacortes, the Cessna. Was that you?"

"Yes," Donovan replied. "That's how I hurt my arm. Now, finish answering my question. Why are you here?"

"I'm here because an assassin, Nikolett Kovarik, tried to kill me in Paris. Thanks to my bodyguards, the CIA, and Buck, we escaped, but my entire security detail was killed. I didn't know where else to go." Lauren took a measured breath, switching into DIA analyst mode, which allowed her to recount details in a completely unemotional manner. The horror of those few minutes still threatened to unravel her emotionally. "Garrick's primary focus is you, but he seems to want me dead, I'm assuming to pay you back for the death of Meredith. He's using Nikolett to hunt me down. Right now I'd prefer to be a moving target, somewhere away from Abigail."

"Abigail was with you? How much did she see?"

"Everything. I've never heard her scream like that before. She was terrified."

Donovan closed his eyes as if trying to fight through the horrifying images of his little girl being caught in the middle of a firefight. "How is she doing?"

"I don't know. After Paris, we spent twelve hours on a jet, traveling from London to Orange County. She woke up just as I was leaving, but she was happy to not have to get on another plane and thrilled to be with William. Maybe what she needs most right now is a protective male figure. I have no idea. Let's just hope she'll be okay."

Donovan nodded his agreement. "When all of this is over, maybe I can spend some time with her."

"I think that would be a good idea."

"I'm happy you and Abigail are safe."

"Why are we going to Alaska? What did the next picture tell you?"

"It was a picture of Meredith taken after the Alaskan pipeline ruptured."

"So you think he's targeting the pipeline?"

"I don't know yet; I've been a little busy. But the pipeline is vulnerable, I'm just not sure what statement he's trying to make."

"Busy? Sleeping with Erica?"

"That discussion isn't pertinent," Donovan said. "For the moment, let's focus on more important matters, like stopping Garrick."

Lauren had her answer.

"Back up a minute. You think Nikolett is still looking for you?"

"I can only assume it's part of Garrick's twisted little game of retribution."

"We know for the moment that she can't find you," Donovan said. "What if we leak that information?"

"Why?"

"We bring Nikolett to Alaska to find you, and she'll lead us to Garrick."

"I get that, but exactly what are you thinking?"

"We use the media. If the press doesn't already know this airplane is headed to Anchorage, we tell them ourselves. Trust me, they'll be there waiting when we land."

"Aren't you trying to sneak up on Garrick? Blasting into

Anchorage with the Eco-Watch jet into a throng of reporters isn't exactly subtle."

"When we arrive, you'll be the only one who gets off the plane. The main thing is to get your picture on television. That should get Garrick riled up and also get Nikolett on her way to Anchorage."

"I think that could work." Lauren nodded her approval. "Are you headed for the pipeline?"

"No. You are. The best way to keep an eye on the pipeline is in the *da Vinci*. With the new equipment, the color infrared-camera technology, and the synthetic-aperture radar, we can produce and record real-time full-motion video. It's all the latest generation software and hardware."

"I'm familiar with all the systems."

"The *da Vinci* can traverse the entire eight hundred miles of the pipeline every two hours. We'll spot Garrick without him even knowing. We'll have the helicopter from the *Pacific Titan* on alert and ready to move."

"What if Garrick gets caught before you can get to him?" Lauren said. "He'll tell the world who you really are. What then?"

"I don't think Garrick has any intentions of going back to prison. He'll either fight to the death or run, but he won't be captured."

"Who else is coming with me to run all the equipment back here?"

"No one. I was hoping you could manage all of it yourself. We've automated a great deal of the control functions. We can set it up to route all of the data to one central command station. Michael can bring you up to speed, plus you already know your way around the back of an Eco-Watch Gulfstream."

Lauren knew she'd go on the mission, that was a given, she was the logical choice and she knew how to operate the equipment. Over the last few years, thanks to being married to the director of Eco-Watch, she'd had unofficial access to the design elements and installation.

"I'm going to call Buck. I need to brief him about the press and let him know our plans for tomorrow. And, Lauren," Donovan said as she got up and stood in the aisle, "I'm glad you're here."

Lauren smiled, nodded, then turned away and her smile vanished. She fully understood that she was on a plane with her estranged husband and his new lover. The moment Donovan didn't deny that he'd slept with Erica, then took the subject off the table, she knew it had already happened. God, he'd only known the woman for two days. Lauren walked into the forward VIP section past Erica who sat with her head back and eyes closed. She was about to enter the cockpit when she heard Erica call her name.

"Dr. McKenna," Erica said gently, "I hope I'm not disturbing you."

"No," Lauren replied as she stopped and turned. "I was going up front to talk to Michael. What can I help you with?"

"Can we talk?" Erica gestured to the empty seat across the aisle. "Please."

Lauren sat and waited. If this woman had something to say to her, there was no reason to make it easy.

"I can tell you don't like me very much, and if the roles were reversed, I wouldn't like me much either. I've spent a few days with Donovan, under the most trying of circumstances and while it's no big secret he's been through hell, I think you should know that your husband still loves you very much."

"Not that it's any of your business, but that's never been the problem."

"My only intention here was to tell you woman to woman, that your husband is still in love with you. I'm not a threat."

"Did he tell you that before or after you screwed him? And just for the record, I never thought you were a threat to anything but his life," Lauren replied with a smile. She couldn't believe that this young woman had the gall to sleep with her husband and then offer him back as some sort of gift.

"I think we're set," Donovan made himself heard as he came up the aisle. "Buck and I have a plan in place for when we arrive in

Anchorage."

"Let's hear it," Lauren said, angry after her exchange with Erica.

Donovan explained that Lauren would deplane immediately after landing and go with Buck. He and Erica would remain hidden aboard the *da Vinci* and leave only after the press had departed and their exit could go unobserved. When he and Erica finally slipped away from the airport, they would be free to continue their hunt for Garrick, who would have no idea they were in Alaska.

Lauren listened, and while her rational brain understood that her scientific capabilities were in demand, her emotions couldn't ignore the message: *other than that, her presence here wasn't required—or even welcomed.*

CHAPTER TWENTY-SEVEN

The *da Vinci* touched down at Ted Stevens International Airport in Anchorage at a little past six in the evening. It was overcast and raining. The *da Vinci* taxied to the general aviation ramp and came to a stop. Donovan listened as Michael shut down both of the engines. The air-stair door was lowered, and Buck was the first one into the cabin. He said a quick hello to Michael and Lauren, then made his way aft to where Donovan and Erica waited.

"I'll make this quick," Buck said. "There are three media trucks outside taping our arrival. We're at Signature Flight Support. None of the ground crew will be allowed aboard the airplane. They're going to put the airplane into a hangar once Lauren and I leave. Not long after that, Michael and Scott will leave as well. At the rear of the hangar is a door that leads to a small parking lot. It's between two buildings so no one should spot you. Here are the keys to a blue Ford Explorer as well as keys to your rooms at the Hotel Captain Cook downtown. We're all on the nineteenth floor of tower three. You're in the Crow's Nest suites, numbers four and five. I have men posted throughout the hotel so we're as safe as we can be."

"Before you go, what's Lauren's room number?"

"She's in suite number two, I'm in suite one."

Donovan nodded his thanks just as Michael shut down the auxiliary power unit and all of the lights went out. Buck grabbed Lauren's suitcase, hurried back up the aisle, and went down the steps. With all the shades pulled, the only light came from the cockpit windows.

Donovan watched as Michael finished the postflight checklist

and gathered his luggage from the front closet. Donovan thanked
Scott for filling in on such short notice. Michael stepped in and
asked if Scott had all of his belongings, then asked the freelance
pilot if he would go outside to monitor the ground crew.

"You sure you know what you're doing?" Michael asked, making direct eye contact with Donovan. "I mean, about all of this?"

As usual, Michael was mixing business and personal aspects to
pose a question that probed at several levels. Donovan knew his
friend well enough to know that anything he asked came from a
good place. "Yeah, I'm sure."

"Okay, see you later." When Michael departed the airplane, he
closed the door leaving Donovan and Erica alone. The interior was
dark and deathly quiet.

"I can't tell you how happy I am that everyone is finally gone."
Erica loosened her hair from its ponytail. "That was a little intense."

"What part?"

"Well, that last exchange with Michael was all about us, and
his lack of approval. Right?" Donovan shrugged his agreement,
and she continued, "Then that earlier chat with your wife was
more than a little stressful."

"In what way?" Donovan said as a loud bang sounded from the
front of the plane.

"What was that?"

"They're hooking up the tow bar, getting ready to push us into
the hangar." As if on cue the *da Vinci* began to move. "What did
Lauren say to you?"

"She accused me of screwing you."

"What did you tell her?"

"I should have told her the truth, that it was a spur-of-the-moment post-traumatic stress response and to deal with it," Erica
replied. "But I didn't. How's your arm feel?"

"What *did* you say to her?"

"I should look at your dressing while we have some time. I
didn't respond to her accusation. All I said to her was that you still

loved her." Erica rose from her seat and straddled Donovan, wrapped her arms around his neck and kissed him gently on the lips as she began to unbutton his shirt. "You sit still, I'll do the work."

Donovan felt the *da Vinci* rock to a stop inside the hangar. He listened as the line crew put chocks under the wheels and then unhooked the tug.

Erica opened his shirt and carefully eased the fabric over his shoulder.

"How are you going to see my arm?" Donovan said as the hangar doors slammed shut, leaving it almost completely dark inside the *da Vinci*.

"I'll check it afterward."

"We're not doing this right now."

"We've got some time to kill. Sit back and relax." Erica pulled her sweater over her head, her hair tumbling down onto her shoulders. She reached around to unfasten her bra, but Donovan put his hands over hers to stop her.

"What's wrong?" Erica leaned closer and brushed his lips with hers.

"You like to initiate sex when you can control what happens, like it's your prize and no one else's."

Erica exhaled, pushed away from him, found her sweater, and stood in the aisle, getting dressed.

Donovan buttoned his shirt and stood. "You don't get told no very often, do you?"

"I get it, the proximity to your wife and all," Erica said as she put her hair back into a ponytail. "Either that or you're the most arrogant man I've ever met."

"I'll take that as a no." Donovan went forward to the cockpit and scanned the hangar, carefully looking at each of the other planes for any sign of activity. After several minutes, he decided they were alone. He threw the handle on the air-stair. It unfolded and slowly extended to the ground. Wordlessly, Erica set their luggage near the door. Donovan grabbed their overnighters and carried them down to the hangar floor. The Gulfstream was parked in the corner. The door Buck told him to use was directly behind the tail.

Erica was standing in the doorway, and as Donovan slid past, he said, "I'm going to take the luggage out to the rental car. I'll be back in a minute for the rest of our things, then we'll close up the plane." Without waiting for a reply, he walked the short distance to the door that led outside. He stood there for a moment, squinting against the sudden brightness. He unlocked the Explorer, tossed their bags into the backseat, and then closed the door. A reflection in the window glass told him there was a woman standing behind him. Before Donovan could turn around, he took a powerful blow to his right kidney that dropped him to one knee. A kick in the back drove him into the cold metal of the Explorer and toppled him over onto his side. He looked up into a gun barrel that was pointed at his forehead. Beyond the muzzle was an attractive woman in blue jeans, boots, and a photographer's vest. She had long, reddish hair, and when she removed her sunglasses, he found dark lethal eyes and a superior grin. Even with the wig, he knew it was Nikolett Kovarik.

"Hello, Robert. Garrick sends his regards."

Donovan could taste blood in his mouth and he spat on the pavement as his greeting.

"I read about your adventures in British Columbia and Washington. You came close to being caught, didn't you? That would have been embarrassing. Who are you traveling with?"

"No one," Donovan said.

"Don't lie to me, Robert. You just put two bags in the backseat. One has a pink ribbon on the handle."

"How did you find me?" Donovan tried to stall. He knew the longer he was gone, the more impatient Erica would become until she burst out of the door. The moment Nikolett turned away, Donovan would make his play.

"You do know it's relatively easy to track an airplane's movements if you know the registration number. I saw that the plane stopped in Seattle, which is in the general vicinity of where you've been. I've been here for a while, watched your security guy move cars around, and when you didn't get off the plane with your wife, I knew where you'd be eventually. Now get up." Nikolett gestured with the barrel of her gun. "Garrick doesn't want me to kill you, but I have significant latitude in how much pain I can inflict."

Donovan had no doubt that she was dangerous with or without her pistol. He rose to his feet and fought off the unsteady feeling in his legs from the attack. She stepped aside to allow Donovan a clear path to the door into the hangar.

"I'm right behind you. Do anything stupid, I'll put a bullet in your good leg."

As Donovan hobbled to the door, the entire right side of his torso felt battered. He pulled it open, hoping Erica would see Nikolett and react, instead of blindly arriving at her own murder. The darkness made vision impossible for a few seconds. As his eyes adjusted, he heard Erica moving to his right, and his expectations plummeted.

"Where have you been?" Erica called out. "I was about to come and find you."

Without hesitation Donovan planted his left foot to make his move, but with martial arts precision, Nikolett delivered a vicious blow to his ribs that rendered him speechless. As hard as he tried, he couldn't find any air in his lungs as he crumpled to the hangar floor.

"Donovan!" Erica called out as she ran closer.

When Erica was ten paces away, she spotted Nikolett. Donovan could do nothing but watch as she abruptly stopped, unsure what to do.

"Don't move," Nikolett aggressively closed the distance, leading with the barrel of her pistol and freezing Erica until the muzzle was three feet away from Erica's forehead. Nikolett studied Erica's face until the recognition registered, and then in a blur of motion, she threw a single jab to Erica's throat. The blow stunned Erica, dropping her to both knees, a look of painful resignation on her face. Nikolett threw two more punches and crumpled Erica onto her back.

Erica raised herself up on one elbow, leaned over, and emptied the contents of her stomach onto the hangar floor. Donovan winced as she gagged and choked in the process, her groans of agony echoing through the rafters.

"That will pass, as will the inability to talk. Focus on breathing," Nikolett said. She turned to Donovan. "I'm suddenly starting to understand a great many things. Erica somehow survived the business at the clinic, found you, and is the new object of your affection. You and your wife are separated. It's why she and your daughter were living in Paris. Have you told Erica who you are?"

"She doesn't need to know," Donovan said.

"Oh, but I think she does." Nikolett turned to Erica. "I'd like to introduce you to the world famous billionaire, Robert Huntington, the man who killed Meredith Barnes."

Donovan's eyes found Erica's, her face clouded with confusion as she processed what she'd heard.

Erica spoke first, her voice raspy and forced. "Is it true?"

"Yes."

"Does your wife know?"

"It's why she left me."

"I won't," Erica replied, her eyes wide and unblinking.

Donovan was caught off guard by the intensity of Erica's words. Was she acting? Was it for Nikolett's benefit or an admission about how she really felt?

"Oh, you're leaving him." Nikolett pulled a snap-tie from one of the many pockets in her vest, pointed the gun at Erica's face, and ordered her to roll over and put her hands behind her back. Erica complied, and the tie was looped around her wrists and pulled snug. "The fact that you're alive is an oversight on my part. I assumed that the young blond your Viktor was with at the time he died was you. I was wrong. Obviously, you'd already been replaced. It was not a big loss. When I seduced the doctor, I found him to be a piggish, selfish lover."

"You bitch," Erica gurgled.

"The people who tried to kill us in California," Donovan asked. "Was that you?"

"No. You've obviously made many enemies in the last few days," Nikolett replied. "Your turn, roll over."

On his stomach, with Nikolett's knee planted in the small of his back, Donovan made eye contact with Erica and found nothing but resignation mixed with fear.

"Up!" Nikolett ordered and forced Donovan to his knees, then finally to his feet by pulling on the snap-tie fastened securely around his wrists. With the gun pressed into his back, she marched him up the stairs of the *da Vinci* and prodded him to the rear of the plane where she sat him down at one of the science stations. Using two more snap-ties she secured him to the chair.

"Someone will come along eventually." Nikolett stepped away from him. "Until then, imagine what we're doing to Erica."

The moment Nikolett left, Donovan struggled against his restraints until his wrists were raw. His phone began ringing, but there was no way to answer. As hard as he'd tried, he couldn't get free. His only hope was someone would finally come into the hangar.

He was still trying to process what Erica had said to him. Either she'd thrown up a smokescreen to get Nikolett to forget about Lauren, or she'd meant the words she'd said. She was convincing enough that he didn't know what she'd intended. The more urgent problem was that Erica was there while Buck had given them the hotel and room number where Lauren was staying. He had no doubt that Nikolett was adept at extracting information. At the thought of either Lauren or Erica being hurt, the blind anger at his helplessness gave way to another massive effort to pull free, ending in pain and the warm trickle of blood oozing down his hands.

Donovan thought he heard the sound of a door being opened in the hangar. He controlled his breathing and listened.

"Donovan!" a voice called out.

Michael's voice, Donovan felt an immense relief wash over him as he yelled as loud as he could. "In here! Michael, I'm in the airplane!" His shouts were rewarded by the unmistakable sound of footsteps hurrying up the air-stair. Michael and someone else he'd never seen rushed to the back of the plane. Michael opened a compartment, pulled out a small tool kit, then knelt to get at Donovan's wrists. The other man opened his windbreaker, drew his weapon, and moved to the door of the *da Vinci*.

"Who's your friend?"

"Jason. Buck hired him. He's ex-Special Forces."

"How long since we landed?" Donovan asked.

"Almost two hours. What in the hell happened?" Michael asked as he snipped the restraints from Donovan's wrists.

"Nikolett, the woman who tried to kill Lauren in Paris, she was here. She kidnapped Erica." Donovan pulled out his cell phone, ignored his bloody fingers, and dialed Lauren's cell.

"Where are you?" Lauren said as she answered. "Michael's looking for you."

"He just found me. Nikolett was here. She took Erica. Find Buck and tell him you're in danger."

"I'm with Buck now. Hang on. I'm handing him the phone."

"Donovan, where are you? Are Michael and Jason with you?"

"They're here, so was Nikolett. She took Erica, so she probably knows where you are."

"We're on the move now!" Buck shot back. "We'll call you later with a rendezvous point. Tell Jason backup is en route, but for the time being get the hell out of there."

"What did they say?" Michael asked.

"Jason!" Donovan called out. "I just spoke with Buck. He says backup is on the way, but that we're supposed to get out of here!"

"Roger, sir. That means we need to move. Now! How bad are your injuries? Can you walk?"

"I'm fine." Donovan winced as he stood and hobbled toward the door.

Jason motioned him to wait. "Stay here until I reach the door and check the parking lot. Buck tells me you might be armed."

On the floor next to one of the VIP seats, was Donovan's brief-case, as well as Erica's shoulder bag. Donovan crouched and re-trieved the pistol. "I am now."

"If we're threatened, we shoot until the threat no longer ex-ists."

"You have a gun?" Michael looked at Donovan as if seeing him for the first time. "Since when do you carry a gun? We're Eco-Watch, we save stuff, we don't shoot people."

"We do both now." Donovan watched as Jason opened the door and surveyed the parking lot. Judging it safe, he motioned for the two of them to leave the safety of the Gulfstream. Donovan let Michael go first. He grabbed Erica's bag and his briefcase and fol-lowed. Michael quickly shut and locked the *da Vinci's* door. Then the two of them hurried toward Jason.

"I'll get in the SUV and pull around to create a barricade," Jason said. "Once I'm in position, you both get in on this side. I want the two of you in the seats behind me. Strap in, and stay low, because we're leaving here like we're on fire."

CHAPTER TWENTY-EIGHT

"Where's Dr. McKenna?" Donovan asked as another SUV swung in behind them.

"She's in transit to the same location." Jason half turned as he spoke. "They're five minutes ahead of us. The SUV behind us is our backup. They'll escort us all the way to the safe house."

"I feel like I just sat down in the middle of a movie and I have no clue what's going on," Michael said. "Tell me exactly why you were in Seattle. How did you get there? How did you get hurt and who in the hell is Erica and why was she kidnapped?"

"It's complicated," Donovan said to buy himself some time to think. He knew Michael wasn't going to rest until he had answers, and the moment they were at the safe house, Buck and Lauren would be asking the exact same questions. He needed a story that would stand up to everyone's scrutiny.

"I'm up for complicated," Michael said. "I'm a pretty bright guy—try me."

"Erica reached out to us through headquarters while we were in Orange County. Turns out she has information about who is behind everything that's been happening. Lauren ran some things past her contacts in the CIA, Erica seemed legitimate, and the evidence we needed was in Seattle."

"Not very complicated so far. How did you get to Seattle?"

"A brand-new G650, compliments of Gulfstream. The *da Vinci* was still down for maintenance."

"What's the evidence she had? Who are these people?"

"They're some sort of splinter group from an old organization called the One Earth Society." Donovan continued the lie. "Erica knew of another former member who lived in Seattle, someone who was farther up the food chain than she was. Erica contacted him, and he was willing to speak with us, but by the time we got to him he was gone, vanished."

"How did you get hurt?"

"We were in a sketchy part of Seattle. There was a thug with a bad temper."

"Why was Erica kidnapped and not you?"

"Trust me, I've been thinking about that for the last two hours. The only reason I can come up with is to continue to make me take the blame for the atrocities they're committing."

"Are they going to kill her or ransom her?" Michael asked.

"I don't know."

"Do you care about her?"

"Yes."

"What does Lauren think about Erica being in the picture?"

"Why, what did Lauren say?"

"Nothing directly, but she's upset. I can only assume that means she thinks you and Erica are involved. Are you?"

"I honestly don't know how to answer that question."

Michael studied his friend for a moment. "You just did."

Donovan was about to try to explain when his phone rang. The number was blocked. He paused a moment, collected himself against who he suspected was calling, then answered.

"Nash."

"Hello, Robert. I see you've been rescued. I hope my friend wasn't too hard on you. She can play a little rough at times. Interesting turn of events today, wouldn't you say."

"What do you want?"

"As usual, you're no doubt surrounded by friends you have to lie to everyday. Don't worry, that burden will be lifted soon enough. I do have to say, Robert, Erica was quite the surprise, and how long have you known her? When exactly did you discover it was me pulling your strings?"

Donovan could tell that Garrick was outside. He could hear the faint ebb and flow of the wind in the background. "What do you want?"

"Erica's beautiful, isn't she? It's tragic really, now you've lost another woman you care about, a loved one under your safekeeping has been kidnapped. No bodyguards to intervene, just your arrogance and stupidity. Meredith and Costa Rica all over again, only this time there will be no ransom, no negotiations, just the fact that after I learn everything she knows—I'm going to kill her."

Donovan remained as passive as he could despite the avalanche of rage he felt for the man on the other end of the line. In a hushed voice he replied. "If you do, I'll hunt you down with every last molecule of my being. You'd better think long and hard about that reality."

"You don't scare me, Robert. You never did. Once I destroy Eco-Watch, as well as your family name, I'll reduce you to a man who has to hide from his own shadow. You'll be living in your own private hell, just as I did. You won't have any fight left in you, I promise."

The sound of the wind abruptly ended, and Donovan knew that Garrick was gone.

"Him?" Michael asked.

"Yeah, they have Erica."

"Any ransom demands?"

"No, nothing but taunts and threats. He's a vicious bastard."

"We'll deal with him."

"Thanks, Michael," Donovan said.

"We're here," Jason announced.

Donovan looked outside as the SUV turned down a long, tree-bordered driveway that emptied into a paved area that led to a three-car garage. Two SUVs were already sitting outside, evidence that the other half of the entourage had arrived. The house was a large two-story cedar structure with a giant wraparound porch, and based on the brick chimneys, there were at least two fireplaces. Donovan couldn't see any other homes, but he did spot two armed men stationed outside.

"Let's move it, men," Buck called to them from the front door. "I've got a medic standing by to dress those wounds."

Michael and Donovan followed Jason out of the vehicle down the sidewalk.

"Who owns this place?" Michael asked.

"A friend," Jason replied as they walked into the cavernous living room.

"This way," Buck said, and led the way.

Donovan followed and the hallway opened up into a warm, very homey kitchen. There was a vaulted ceiling, lots of wood and granite, very rustic. Across the room, Lauren sat on one of the bar stools that separated the eating area from the kitchen. One of Buck's men was waiting, with an impressive first-aid kit open on the table.

"Can we give Mr. Nash some privacy?" He said to those in the room.

"She can stay. She's my wife," Donovan said, though it appeared Lauren didn't intend to get up. Jason, Michael, and Buck filtered out until it was just the three of them.

"I'm a doctor. We don't use last names when we're on the job. Just call me Pete. Can you please remove your shirt and describe to me what happened."

Donovan placed his briefcase as well as Erica's bag on one of the kitchen stools, took off his shirt, and then very gingerly peeled his undershirt over his head. The pain in his lower back was making it difficult to move, so he was forced to stop and try to free his arms one at a time. He felt a pair of helping hands and when the fabric finally pulled free, he realized Lauren had provided the assist. The expression on her face told him the bruise on his back wasn't pretty.

"How did this happen?" Pete asked as he took a closer look.

"The attack was from behind. I was hit in the kidney first and then it was followed up by a kick in the back. That was when I hit my head on the side of a car. I also took a shot to the ribs."

"Does this hurt?" Pete asked as he touched the bruised area.

The speed at which Donovan twisted away gave him his answer. "What happened here? These stitches are new."

"Oh, that's nothing. I've been a little accident-prone lately," Donovan said as he dismissed the wound to his upper arm.

"Judging from all the other scars, you've always been a little accident-prone."

"Since I was a kid." Donovan shrugged it off.

"Have you urinated since all of this happened?"

"No," Donovan replied. "Is there a bigger problem than just a bruise and some tenderness?"

"Hard to say." Pete stood and examined the minor bump on Donovan's forehead, checked his pupils, peripheral vision, then used a magnifying instrument to check both retinas. Pete took Donovan by the forearms and examined the abrasions on his wrists.

"Snap-ties," Donovan said. "They're stronger than they look."

"There's a reason people use them. Can you move all of your fingers? Rotate your wrists. Good. Now I need you to hold still while I examine your ribs. This might hurt."

Donovan did as he was asked. As Lauren watched, Donovan couldn't help but notice her arms crossed defensively in front of her, an expression of disapproval on her face.

Pete asked Donovan to sit down and he proceeded to clean, disinfect, and dress the abrasions and cuts. When he was finished, he handed Donovan two unmarked bottles of pills. "Buck already informed me you don't have any drug allergies, so here are some antibiotics. One tablet four times a day. Take them until they're gone. The other pills are Vicodin, take them every four hours as needed for pain, watch the liquor consumption, the two don't mix. If you discover more than a trace of blood in your urine, I need to be informed immediately."

"Thank you, Pete," Lauren said.

As Pete gathered his things, Donovan threw on his shirt and had it buttoned halfway when Buck strode into the room followed by Michael.

"I know you're tired, but I need to debrief you." Buck motioned for Donovan to sit. "This won't take long. First, how many of them were there?"

"I'll stand," Donovan said, not wanting this meeting to last very long. "Only Nikolett Kovarik. She ambushed me in the parking lot."

"You never saw her coming?"

"Not until it was too late to do anything. We were trying to fool the press, not a trained operative. She forced me at gunpoint back into the hangar where she subdued Erica and bound our hands behind our backs."

"Did you try and get her to talk?" Buck continued. "Did she say anything at all?"

"She said she'd been tracking the Eco-Watch jet online since it left Seattle and she was waiting for us when we landed. When she saw you meet Lauren and no one else got off the plane, she remembered seeing you shuffle cars around. That's where she waited."

"Damn it!" Buck shook his head as if accepting the blame. "I can promise you she didn't follow Lauren. The only reason she's in Anchorage is because the others are here as well. Why did she take Erica?"

"I think she believed she was making it personal." Donovan replied. "They killed John and Beverly Stratton. They tried to kill Lauren. For all we know they'll try to kill everyone I care about."

"That's not going to happen." Buck folded his hands together, his words solemn, more fact than wish. "You told me on the phone you suspected the pipeline was a target. Why?"

"One of the environmental debates right now is drilling for oil in the Alaska National Wildlife Refuge. If something happened to the pipeline, the political and environmental fallout would ensure no drilling would ever take place inside ANWR. Erica recalled talk of sabotaging the pipeline. If these people manage to blame Eco-Watch in the process, it would be a fatal blow to the organization."

"This is why we need to alert everyone in Alaska who can help us stop these people," Michael said, scanning the others' faces, trying to gather support.

"It would create utter chaos," Buck said. "Every armed citizen who cares about this state would be out in force to guard the pipeline. We'd scare them off, and they'd vanish. We'd lose them for sure."

"Until their next eco-crime and then the cycle starts again," Lauren added. "They can't be very alarmed at this point. We haven't come close to touching these people. It's the three of us against them. Erica is probably telling them the same thing."

"Logistically, if the pipeline is in fact the target, the mountains are where they have the best chance of getting in and getting back out. With all the latest equipment in the *da Vinci*, we can watch them without them knowing and have the Eco-Watch helicopter ready to move the moment we spot something suspicious."

"I see what you're thinking and from a tactical point of view it's not bad," Buck said. "I maintain that we play our hunch, but if we discover a threat, we alert the authorities."

"Agreed," Donovan said though he had no intention of being a spectator, or stepping aside. "We need people and machines in place at first light."

"That makes it a short night," Buck replied.

"I'll see everyone in the morning," Lauren said, then turned to Donovan. "Can we find somewhere private to talk?"

"There are two bedrooms and a bathroom in the basement," Buck told them, "Your luggage is already downstairs."

Lauren found the door to the basement. Donovan grabbed his briefcase and Erica's bag and followed. Once downstairs, they switched on the lights, moved past a pool table and down a hallway where they found a door that led to one of the guest bedrooms. Lauren closed the door behind them and leaned up against it as if trying to hold the world at bay.

Donovan sat on the bed and waited. He wanted Lauren to start this conversation. She obviously had something to say, and whatever it was, would set the tone.

"I heard everything you said upstairs. Buck bought it, I'm not so sure about Michael."

"Michael and I spoke in the car coming here, he's good." Donovan said.

"What else happened?"

"Nikolett told Erica who I am," Donovan said in a hushed voice.

"She's probably not going to be able to do much with that information before Garrick kills her."

"Unless she uses the one bargaining chip she has left. I've not seen them, but Erica claims to have taken copies of all the files from the clinic before she left. She holds information on nearly two dozen people who have had their appearance changed. Most of them are probably Mossad operatives."

"Do you have any idea where the files are?"

"No."

"What else did she say?" Lauren began to pace, eager for more information.

"Nikolett did jump to one wrong conclusion. It occurred to her that because you were in Paris, you and I must be separated. Therefore, Erica must be my new romantic interest."

"You already alluded to that. That's not much of a leap," Lauren said without malice.

"Erica ran with it."

Lauren stopped pacing and turned to face Donovan. "Are you telling me Erica led Nikolett to believe that her death would hurt you more than mine?"

"I think she knew she was going to die anyway." Donovan nodded.

"Is it how she really feels about you?"

Donovan had no ready answer. "Garrick called."

"When?"

"On my way here. Just his usual rhetoric, but he did confirm that he had Erica. He made some comparisons to Meredith in Costa Rica. Laughed that someone I cared about was going to die."

Lauren stopped pacing and sat down next to her husband. "I'm sorry about Erica. I know how much you like to protect the people you care about. That's one of the things I love most about you. How are you doing with all of this?"

"I can't process anything right now except stopping Garrick and Nikolett." Donovan took Lauren's hand and squeezed affectionately. "I'm glad you're here though."

"I'm glad I'm here too." Lauren glanced to where Donovan's soft-sided briefcase lay on its side, the contents exposed. "When did you start carrying a gun?"

"Since I came home from the hospital," Donovan replied. "Let's not talk about all of that tonight, okay? We have to get up early, tomorrow promises to be a long day."

"I understand about the gun," Lauren said. "The safe, normal life we once led seems like a distant memory. In Paris, my people were dying, and Nikolett just kept coming. She was relentless. I grabbed a pistol and fired at her, I just kept pulling the trigger. I was so angry and frightened, I wanted her dead."

"It's okay," Donovan wrapped his arms around Lauren and pulled her close. He had no words for his wife. He'd killed a man in California, and if everything went as he hoped, he'd soon add Garrick and Nikolett to that list. He felt no remorse or uncertainty, they deserved to die.

"What have we become?" Lauren whispered.

Donovan found her lips with his and what started as a tentative embrace quickly became a powerful force. Breathing heavily, Lauren wrapped her arms around him and pulled him back on the bed. Donovan moved on top of her and saw that she was half lying on his briefcase. He swept it off the bed while Lauren arched her back and pulled Erica's bag out from under her. She had it by the straps and was about to fling it away when she stopped.

"Wait!" Lauren gasped as she wriggled her other arm free.

"What are you doing?" Donovan said as he raised himself up.

Lauren rolled onto her side and used both hands on the strap, kneading the fabric with her fingers. She held the inch-wide strap up to the light and then examined the stitching. "There's something in here. I can feel it, and the thread here is newer than the adjoining stitches."

"She never let that out of her sight." Donovan slid off the bed and found his suitcase and the small knife he carried. He opened the sharpest blade and handed it to Lauren.

Lauren carefully opened up half a dozen stitches, separated the fill, and removed a small jump drive.

"The files?" Donovan said as he retrieved his laptop.

While the computer booted up, Lauren began going through the contents of Erica's bag.

"What else is in there?" Donovan asked.

"There's a wallet, a hat, tissues, birth control pills, a small makeup bag, tampons, and a gun." Lauren held it up for him to see.

Donovan took the subcompact pistol from Lauren. It was a large-caliber Beretta, yet it almost disappeared in his hand. It only had a three-inch barrel, but up close would be lethal.

"Charming," Lauren said. "I guess everyone carries a gun these days."

"The computer's up." Donovan set the gun aside and opened the menu, Lauren inserted the jump drive into the USB port, and they both waited. The prompt finally appeared, Donovan clicked to open the drive, and a page of individual files spread across the screen. Each line of text was written in German, followed by a seven-digit number. Donovan shrugged and clicked on the first one only to discover that the file required a password.

"I was afraid of that. For all we know, there could be twenty-three different passwords."

"Wait," Donovan quickly counted the files and came up with the same number. "Erica said there were seventeen men and five women who wanted her dead. That's twenty-two. What's the other file?"

"No clue."

"Do you think someone you trust at the DIA or the CIA could break the code?"

"I'm sure someone could, but not tonight." Lauren stood. "I

have to think about what it is we think we have. I'm not so sure we should let anyone see what's inside right now. I'm in big trouble with Langley for my part in getting one of their agents killed in Paris. Add that to the fact that I'm obstructing an open investigation by not reporting my information about Erica Covington."

Donovan ejected the jump drive and handed it to Lauren. "You hold onto it, you're the spy."

Lauren put it in her purse. "This spy is going to take a shower."

Donovan nodded and began to stow his laptop when he looked up and noticed Lauren standing in the doorway.

"Well," Lauren asked, "are you joining me or not?"

CHAPTER TWENTY-NINE

It was a few minutes before five in the morning when the *da Vinci* climbed out of Anchorage and made a sweeping turn to the east. Michael set a course toward the small town of Valdez, the terminus of the Alaska pipeline. Lauren gazed out the window, but all she could see below were clouds. An early season cold front, rain mixed with snow, had enveloped Prince William Sound. High winds dominated the entire area. The only land she could spot were the snow-covered peaks surrounding the Harding Icefield, each jagged peak rising up into the first light of the day. Lauren wished she were of a mind to drink in the sheer beauty of the moment, but she couldn't. Last night had been a mixture of the familiar and the unfamiliar.

She'd helped Donovan undress, studied each of his new wounds up close, felt his familiar embrace, but his body felt different, leaner and harder, as if he'd become tougher to survive his new reality. Quick work with a shower cap kept most of the water from his stitches. After the shower, they didn't talk, they simply fell into bed and made love with an urgency she had never experienced with him before. Afterward, she'd lain in his arms, and for the first time since she could remember, he slept quietly, without his demons. She and Donovan had always had a great physical connection, but something was different. Finally, she'd drifted off despite a cyclone of thoughts swirling in her head.

They were still entwined when she awoke. She'd slipped out of bed, taken a shower, dressed, gathered her things, and left him there. She had Erica's bag along with her own, the jump drive safely tucked into her purse.

"Lauren," Michael's voice came over her headset. "We're coming up on Valdez. Confirm all surveillance systems are up and functioning."

"Stand by," Lauren replied as she checked the panel and made sure each independent system was in the green. The synthetic-aperture radar dominated the twenty-eight inch-high-definition monitor in front of her, giving her the ability to dial in on objects as they flew eight miles overhead. The resolution was good enough for her to read a license plate off a moving vehicle despite the weather. She also had at her fingertips the newly developed full-spectrum infrared imaging system that gave her day or night capability to lock in and follow multiple targets. She also had a high-definition color or black-and-white camera that could be overlaid and blended with the other systems to give her a real time, day or night, rain or shine, picture of the world below. With the few strokes of the keyboard, she transferred each image to the twenty-eight-inch monitor.

If she saw anything, a click of the mouse would zoom in and track the object until it could be identified. To test that all the moving parts were functional, she located a moving heat source nearly eight miles away. She zoomed in, locked the computer to track the object, then brought the high-resolution video camera to bear. As the software fine-tuned the object, she recognized a bald eagle, a fish in its talons. Satisfied, she reset the range to forty miles and locked in on the pipeline. She switched the image to display white-hot, meaning the oil, which was far warmer than the surrounding ground, glowing like a white-hot cylinder snaking north from Valdez. Lauren wasn't worried about the half of the eight-hundred-mile-long pipeline that was buried underground. If Garrick wanted to rupture the pipeline, he'd want to do it above ground. Images of the oil covering the Alaskan wilderness would make the kind of statement he was after.

"Everything's up and running back here," Lauren reported. "I'm going to get a cup of coffee before we start. Anyone else want some?"

"Stay put, I'm coming back there," Michael replied.

Lauren had a small repeater of the *da Vinci's* primary flight display. She could see that they were level at thirty-nine thousand feet, about to cross over Valdez and turn north. She squinted out the window again, noting nothing but clouds below them. To the east, however, the brilliant morning sun silhouetted the sixteen-plus-thousand-foot-high Wrangel Mountains. But the sun washed out her display screen, and despite the scenery, she reluctantly powered down the window shade just as Michael came back with coffee.

"Here you go." Michael handed her a cup. "I don't know about you, but I'm not sure anyone got much sleep last night."

Lauren chose to ignore Michael's comment; she could tell he was digging. "How far north do you want to follow the pipeline?"

"From a tactical standpoint, a small plane or a helicopter would give them the most flexibility to attack the pipeline and also give them the best chance of escape. My thinking is we travel fast, go all the way north to Fairbanks, then turn back, like a swimmer doing laps. Buck and Donovan will move toward Valdez in the Eco-Watch helicopter. Hopefully, with all of our assets, we'll find what we're looking for."

"I have another question, nonmission related." Lauren couldn't help but bring up the question that plagued her since last night.

"Sure."

"You, more than anyone else, know what a solitary creature Donovan can be. Does he seem more content without the daily pressure of being married and having a family to worry about?"

"Come on, Lauren." Michael shook his head in dismay. "First of all, there's no way he doesn't worry. You know that as well as anyone. His concern for you and Abigail is off the charts. Secondly, in the years I've known him, I think I can count on one hand the number of times I'd say he was truly content—and they all involve either you or Abigail. So, to answer your question, no."

"But he seemed less stressed yesterday than I've seen him in a long time."

"You didn't take many psychology classes at MIT, did you? Just math and stuff? One of the benefits of having been married for twenty-five years is that I have a vague working knowledge of how the female brain works. Have you somehow churned yourself up into a froth thinking that his perceived contentment is due to factors that you can't combat?"

Lauren realized that Michael had managed to cut to the center of her concern. She regretted her question. Now she wanted the conversation to end.

"The reason he may or may not seem as stressed at the moment is simply because you're here. You're the source of any perceived contentment. There's no other explanation."

"Thank you, Michael. I wish I could believe that were the case."

"So do I," Michael replied. "You know, sometimes you need to get out of your own way and quit overprocessing everything."

"Easier said than done."

"I should probably get back up front. How's everything looking so far?"

Lauren turned and studied the monitor. Her trained eye took a few seconds to scan each display for anything out of the ordinary. "All normal so far. I'm also monitoring several radio frequencies. Who knows, we might get lucky and hear something."

Michael turned to go, then stopped. "The workload in the cockpit is pretty light. If you need a break, let me know, and I can come back and keep an eye on things."

"Thanks." Lauren nodded. She didn't know what to think. Had she made a mistake last night? Should she have slept in the other bedroom instead of confusing the issue? Did the things that Michael said mean anything—or everything? She was still debating the questions when a radio transmission caught her attention. She sat up straight and adjusted the volume.

"*Vigilant*, this is Valdez Traffic, come in please."

Lauren listened for a response from the *Vigilant*, but there was nothing. She double-checked the audio panel. Everything was in order.

"*Vigilant*, this is Valdez Traffic. How do you read?"

Again Lauren waited for a reply, but there was only dead air.

"Valdez Traffic calling vessel *North Star*. How do you read?"

A long twenty seconds passed, and there was no reply from the second vessel.

"Valdez Traffic calling vessel *Guardian*. How do you read?"

Lauren was perplexed. Out of three ships, not a single one was answering the radio calls. Another voice came on the frequency, and she knew she wasn't the only one with rising concerns.

"This is Coast Guard Station Valdez calling vessel *Vigilant*, how do you read?"

Lauren swiveled in her chair to a separate keyboard and began typing. The first data that came up on the secondary screen was for the tugboat *Vigilant*. She was a ten-year-old, one-hundred-forty-foot long, steel-hulled ship out of Valdez. Her primary task was listed as a towing vessel. She typed in *Guardian* and a similar vessel popped up on her screen. They were both owned by the same shipping company.

"Coast Guard Station Valdez calling vessel *North Star*. How do you read?"

Lauren typed in *North Star* and when the image appeared on her screen her apprehension rose. The *North Star* was a nine-hundred-and-twenty-foot-long supertanker, one of seven Constellation-class tankers built by Avondale Shipyard in Louisiana; all ships in the class were named after prominent celestial bodies. The *North Star* was owned and operated by Constellation Marine, a subsidiary of Huntington Oil. Lauren looked under capacities; the *North Star* carried a million barrels of Alaskan crude, which equated to forty-two million gallons. How could a vessel like that not respond to a radio call?

"Vessel *North Star*, this is Coast Guard Anchorage calling. We've lost your AIS beacon. Please respond any channel."

Lauren knew that AIS stood for Automatic Information System, basically a transponder that sent out the vessel's name, type, position, course, and speed to other ships as well as land-based operators.

Lauren keyed the microphone. "Michael, I think we need to

turn around."

"What do you have?"

"I'm listening to radio chatter in Prince William Sound. The Coast Guard is trying to make radio contact with two tugs and a supertanker, but no one is answering."

"There are three different ships not answering?" Michael asked.

"That's what it sounds like."

"I know that these days, two tugs escort each tanker out of Prince William Sound, one of the changes they made after the *Exxon Valdez* spill. Are we sure we're not out of range? We're almost two hundred miles north of Valdez. The ships could be another fifty or sixty miles south. That's a long way for VHF."

"It's not that we're not receiving them—no one can make contact. Even the Coast Guard sector command center in Anchorage gave it a try," Lauren explained. "How long would it take us to be over Prince William Sound?"

"Thirty, forty minutes at the most, but it means abandoning the pipeline mission over a few lost communications."

"I know, but I think we should investigate."

"I'm coming back. Why don't we contact the Coast Guard on the satellite phone, offer our assistance? Maybe they have this under control. In the meantime, I'm going to stick to our original plan."

Lauren typed in the Coast Guard Station for Valdez and pulled up a phone number. She was dialing when Michael came hurrying down the aisle. "I'm ringing the Coast Guard now. You want to talk or should I?"

"You talk. I'll keep an eye on the screen."

Lauren nodded as the phone picked up.

"Coast Guard Station Valdez. Lieutenant Brody speaking."

"Lieutenant Brody, this is Dr. Lauren McKenna. I'm aboard an Eco-Watch Gulfstream two hundred miles north of your position. We've been monitoring the situation involving the loss of communications with the tanker *North Star*. May we be of assistance?"

"I can't comment on any ongoing operations."

"I understand, just so you're aware, we're a research aircraft with surveillance equipment including infrared sensors and synthetic-aperture radar. We can be overhead in less than an hour and stream real-time video to your operations center."

"Uh, stand by, Dr. McKenna."

"What's going on?" Michael asked. "What are they saying?"

"He's checking with someone."

"Dr. McKenna, thank you for holding. Due to the current situation surrounding Eco-Watch, we ask that you remain well clear of Prince William Sound airspace. Failure to do so will result in you being intercepted and escorted to Elmendorf Air Force Base in Anchorage."

Lauren disconnected the call without responding and looked up at Michael. "We basically just got told to go screw ourselves."

"So your response was to hang up on them?"

"If anyone asks, we lost the connection. I never actually heard him say that any interference would result in us being intercepted and escorted to Elmendorf Air Force Base."

"Clever, but now I'm starting to agree that something's up," Michael said. "Have you heard anything more on the open radio frequencies?"

"Just the same. No answer from any of the three ships."

"Can you put what you're hearing on speaker?"

Lauren flipped a switch and the scratchy VHF transmissions filled the cabin.

"This is Coast Guard 45009, underway out of Valdez Harbor."

"Roger Coast Guard 45009. Visibility in the sound is one mile or less with intermittent rain mixed with snow. Wind out of the south at ten to fifteen knots. Swells reported at three to six feet."

"Roger, our ETA on site is one four five two."

"Okay. A Coast Guard response boat just left Valdez to go find out what happened to those ships. They'll be there in fifty-two minutes. Call Donovan and tell him what's going on. I have a bad feeling there's a tanker loose in Prince William Sound. I'm turning us around. We can be there before the Coast Guard."

"What about the Air Force?"

"Don't worry," Michael shot her a crooked grin. "They'll never see this old Navy pilot coming."

CHAPTER THIRTY

Donovan pressed the satellite phone tightly against his ear to seal out the rotor noise.

"It's Lauren, can you hear me? Where are you?"

"I'm in the helicopter. We just made it through Portage Pass near Whittier. The weather sucks. We're down on the deck, headed east. What's going on?"

"We've turned around and we're heading toward Prince William Sound. I've been monitoring Coast Guard communications, and as it stands now, they can't seem to find three ships. Two tugs and the ship they were escorting. Donovan, it's a fully laden tanker, the Huntington Oil ship *North Star.*"

"Oh, no. It's not the pipeline—I was wrong. Do you have any idea where the tanker is now?"

"The AIS transponders are all off-line. I don't think anyone really knows. They scrambled a Coast Guard surface vessel from Valdez to go investigate. It'll take them almost an hour to arrive at the last known position."

"Contact the Coast Guard. Offer them our services."

"I already did. They turned us away and warned us to stay away from Prince William Sound or we'd be escorted to Elmendorf. We're suspected criminals it seems."

"What did Michael say about that?"

"Michael's flying this thing as fast as it will go. He said something about the Air Force never seeing this old Navy pilot coming."

"Gotta love him. Find that ship."

"Will do," Lauren replied.

Donovan disconnected the call and readjusted his headset. All the Huntington Oil Constellation class ships were double hulled. He knew the specifications since he and Meredith had talked at length about the need for safety years before the first ship put to sea. She'd pushed for ten feet of space between the outer and inner hulls and she'd been right. A year later, the *Exxon Valdez* had gone aground spilling ten million gallons of crude oil into Prince William Sound. The *North Star* held forty-two million gallons of oil, and if Garrick managed to rupture the hull, the resulting eco-disaster would quadruple the *Exxon Valdez* spill. He had no doubt Garrick was in control of that ship and had every intention of creating a disaster that would dwarf the *Exxon* fiasco, and the blame would be squarely on Huntington Oil.

"Who was that? Anything going on?" Buck asked over the intercom.

"I need everyone to listen closely," Donovan said. In the front seat, next to Buck was longtime Eco-Watch pilot Janie Kinkaid. Janie was in her mid-thirties, a pear-shaped brunette from Australia. When Donovan and Michael first met her, she'd been a charter pilot in Queensland. During an Eco-Watch mission, she'd impressed Michael with her flying skills.

With four older brothers, Janie developed a wicked sense of humor and a rough-and-tumble attitude toward life. Michael and Donovan later came to understand Janie had grown up around aviation and spent her entire life flying helicopters. They also learned firsthand that her drinking skills could put just about any man under the table. After that weeklong deployment, they'd stayed in touch, and when Eco-Watch expanded with a second ship in the Pacific, Janie had easily beat out all the other candidates. Michael was the first to tell anyone that her flying abilities were as good as anyone he'd ever seen.

Seated next to Donovan was Jason, Buck's ex-Special Forces recruit from Anchorage. Everyone but Donovan was dressed in fatigues and bulletproof vests, and Buck and Jason carried multiple weapons. Donovan had a radio and was armed with a single Glock. Considering the news he was about to impart, he felt a little underequipped. "That was the crew aboard the *da Vinci*. Seems the Coast Guard has lost contact with three ships, two escort tugs and a supertanker. It's possible that the terrorists have taken control of a fully loaded supertanker. At this point, no one knows where the tanker is, but the *da Vinci* is headed south as fast as possible, and once on scene, should be able to quickly pinpoint the tanker's location."

"What tanker is it?" Buck asked.

"Lauren says it's a Constellation-class ship," Donovan replied. "The *North Star*, why do you ask?"

"East Africa, years ago, when Somali pirates began hijacking tankers coming out of the gulf, my SEAL team trained how to regain control of such a ship. The Constellation class was one of several we used in our training scenarios. Janie, there's a helipad port side amidships, more of a place to drop and go as opposed to an actual landing pad. For all we know, they'll be shooting at us. Can you put down quickly and get out?"

"No problem," Janie said with a nod. "Just don't be shy about shooting back every now and then, if you know what I mean."

"Will do. Once you drop us off, retreat and hover somewhere safe, out of rifle range, and stand by for an extraction. How much loiter time would you estimate you have?"

"Depends when we find them. Prince William Sound is a big place, but regardless, we'll have forty-five minutes, maybe an hour of fuel remaining, mind you, that's back to Anchorage. There are other, closer options. I promise not to get anyone wet."

"That should work. Once we're down, we'll make our way to the bridge. Jason, let me remind you that this could end up being all hand-to-hand combat. Be careful where you shoot, nothing much good happens when you mix gunfire and a loaded supertanker."

"There may be other complications," Donovan said. "When the *da Vinci* offered to assist the Coast Guard in finding the ship, they were warned to stay out of Prince William Sound airspace or they'd be escorted to Elmendorf."

"Michael just ignored them, right?" Buck asked.

"Yeah, he's good at that, but my point is, if we swoop in on anyone in an Eco-Watch helicopter, we may run into opposition. That doesn't mean that the ship has been hijacked, it means they read a newspaper."

"Good point," Buck replied. "But any tanker out of the shipping lane is in distress. Most vessels don't allow guns on board, but these guys will most definitely be armed. It won't take long for us to figure out who the bad guys are, and we'll react accordingly."

"What about the ship's crew?" Jason asked. "How many?"

"All together, they'll be twenty-five to thirty officers and crew. Most of them will probably be locked below somewhere, if they're still alive. There could also be officers held hostage on the bridge."

"Security at the Valdez oil terminal is pretty tight," Jason said. "I'm thinking the bad guys had to have boarded later, by small boat, so there couldn't be all that many of them on board."

"That's how I'd do it, especially in this weather. A small boat could easily go unobserved in these seas," Buck said. "It wouldn't take but a few men to overpower an unarmed tanker crew. I'm thinking there could be as few as five, as many as ten. We saw from surveillance cameras in Hawaii that there were probably four or five guys that boarded the Japanese fishing vessel. From what I could see, they may have had military training, but certainly not at the elite level. These guys are criminals, thugs, and should be treated as such. The two of us should be more than enough to take them down."

"Three of us." Donovan corrected him.

"No way you're setting foot on that ship." Buck turned to face Donovan. "The group who has sworn to destroy you are aboard this tanker. They're armed, and when we show up, they're going to feel trapped and desperate. Jason and I spent years training for this very thing, it's not a hobby. The only place you need to be is out of the line of fire."

Donovan started to argue, but Buck cut him off.

"I won't accept any other scenario. I see how gingerly you've been moving today. You got your ass kicked yesterday. The answer is no. Any more resistance, and I abort this mission and resign. Your choice."

Donovan knew that Buck was right. He'd hired Buck to make the tough decisions regarding security, and he'd just made the call. Donovan needed to step back. He hated to admit it, but the two former Special Forces soldiers spoke a language and had a lethal confidence that Donovan didn't possess. Being left out made sense, and if his calculations were correct, Garrick would fight to the death rather than surrender to live the rest of his life in jail. The decision left a bitter taste in Donovan's mouth, but if at the end of the day, Garrick and Nikolett were dead, then that's all that mattered.

"It's why you hired me," Buck said, softening his tone.

"I know." Donovan nodded his agreement. "It's just not my style to sit and watch."

"I'm well aware how difficult this is for you, but this is my area of expertise. I promise we'll get them."

Donovan sat back as Buck continued planning with Jason about making their way to the bridge of the *North Star*. If Garrick was aboard the ship, then Nikolett was probably with him as well. Had they taken Erica with them, or was she already dead? The thought of her death sent a jolt of sadness through his body. He wasn't in love with her. He didn't really know her, but maybe that was the worst part. She was smart, capable, beautiful, spontaneous, and perhaps what he already missed was not the loss of what was, but the loss of what could have been. The potential had seemed enticing and now it was most likely gone forever.

CHAPTER THIRTY-ONE

Lauren sat with her eyes locked on the monitor. Whatever she'd momentarily seen was gone. It was a brief, ghostly, infrared blur, then it vanished. She dared not blink for fear of missing it again. She looked at the television camera and found nothing but ice below them and clouds and mountains ahead. The synthetic-aperture radar suggested that the momentary heat source could have flashed due to a brief alley through the mountains ahead that led all the way to Prince William Sound. It could have been anything, a small boat, a low-flying bush plane, or helicopter.

Michael had canceled their clearance with air traffic control the second they were below eighteen thousand feet. They were now at twelve thousand feet between Valdez and the Yale Glacier. The *da Vinci* rocked from the turbulence generated by the nearby high terrain, and Lauren tightened her seat belt. Michael's plan was to drop below the highest peaks and weave their way to Prince William Sound below Elmendorf's radar. Ahead of them stretched an ice field that seemed to go forever.

The range of her radar had been decreased by their loss in altitude and also by the terrain that blocked the line of sight to the northern portion of the sound. The poor weather made for very little boat traffic in the sound. The only targets she'd picked up so far were the heat signature from the Coast Guard ship speeding south. Beyond were the heat signatures of a half dozen ships and she'd locked onto the two she assumed were the escort tugs. One was burning. The flames clearly visible on her monitor, leaping from what was left of the bridge. The other generated very little heat and seemed to be adrift. There was no sign of the *North Star*.

Lauren checked the time. A little less than forty minutes had passed since they'd turned around. She did the math. Even at the tanker's maximum speed of seventeen knots, it couldn't have traveled more than thirteen or fourteen miles. Unless Garrick had already somehow scuttled it, in which case, all they were looking for was a forty-two-million-gallon oil slick.

She'd added Air Force tactical frequencies to the others she'd been monitoring and heard no alarming chatter out of Elmendorf, but the Coast Guard frequency had been busy. There'd been several transmissions between Coast Guard Command Center Anchorage and the Coast Guard cutters *Long Island* and *Mustang*. They'd both been ordered to investigate. They were one-hundred-ten-foot Island-class cutters, no capability for a helicopter, but each had a top speed of nearly thirty knots. She hadn't been able to ascertain either ship's actual position, and nothing that size was showing up on her equipment. She'd also heard some communications about an Alaskan State Police helicopter departing Anchorage. Again, she had no firm grasp of the timelines involved, but people were alarmed, and in turn, making things happen.

"In less than five minutes, we'll be out of the mountains, and you'll have a better view." Michael reported from the cockpit.

"Michael, can you take us down Unakwik Inlet? I saw a momentary flash of something generating heat down there. We should check it out." Lauren immediately felt Michael roll the *da Vinci* into a steep turn to the right. She checked the moving map display; they were now headed directly toward the Meares Glacier. It would require another sharp turn where the glacier ended and Prince William Sound began, but it would allow them to fly the length of Unakwik Inlet.

Lauren kept her attention focused on the screen. Dead ahead was the precipice where the Meares Glacier met the sea. It was little over a mile wide at its terminus and three hundred feet tall. Lauren was in awe of the magnitude of the glacier. Below, in the turquoise-colored water were thousand of chunks of ice that had calved from the face. Some were no larger than a basketball, others the size of a house. Michael banked the *da Vinci* to the left until they were flying down the center of the inlet. The fjord was fifteen miles long and two miles wide. Michael was flying just below the ragged edges of the overcast, but his vision was in no way encumbered since the *da Vinci* was equipped with all the latest enhanced-vision systems. Michael could fly the Gulfstream as if it were a sunny day.

A small heat source blinked into view dead ahead. It was blocked by the surrounding terrain, so Lauren only had a small indistinct picture. As they ate up the miles, the shape began forming on her screen. Seconds later, she could make out what looked like an angled edge, followed by a massive bow wave and a huge anchor. The *North Star* was angling toward the entrance into Unakwik Inlet.

"Michael, do you see it?" Lauren zoomed in on the bridge, knowing that the high-resolution camera captured everything. She panned back and forth and then backed off and had just enough time to shoot the entire deck before the *da Vinci* ripped past the ship. Lauren was pressed into her seat as Michael pulled at least two Gs bringing the Gulfstream back around for another look. Lauren hit redial on the satellite phone as she played back the frames she'd just taken. Six stories above the deck, the bridge superstructure towered above the ship. The detail was remarkable. She could see the windshield wipers moving back and forth, the spinning radar antenna, and each individual section of railing. In one of the dozens of windows that stretched the entire one-hundred-fifty-foot width of the *North Star,* Lauren stopped the video. Standing close to the glass, holding a pair of binoculars was a familiar face. Nikolett Kovarik.

Michael was leveling out the wings of the *da Vinci* and coming up behind the supertanker. Lauren switched her screen back to real time just as Donovan answered the phone.

"Did you find it?" Donovan asked.

"The *North Star* is steaming full speed toward Unakwik Inlet."

CHAPTER THIRTY-TWO

"Janie! Unakwik Inlet. How far?" Donovan snapped.

Janie glanced down to the chart on her knee and immediately banked the helicopter to the north. "We'll be there in fifteen minutes."

"We're fifteen minutes away," Donovan told Lauren. "How much time do we have?"

"They're doing sixteen knots. They'll reach the very end of the inlet in fifty-six minutes," Lauren replied. "I saw Nikolett on the bridge—they're aboard."

"Full speed? I can't believe they'd do this—the devastation will be catastrophic. Alert the Coast Guard, tell them everything, and then call me back."

Donovan severed the connection, still reeling from the enormity of what Garrick had accomplished. "That was Lauren. They've found the *North Star,* and it's steaming toward Unakwik Inlet. She confirmed that Nikolett Kovarik is on the bridge, so we can dispense with any pleasantries or hesitation about boarding the vessel."

"Once we're on the deck, it's roughly four hundred feet from the helipad to the first external gangway that leads up to the bridge," Buck explained. "Jason, you're going to take the outside route, no chance of getting lost. I'm going to take the inside route."

"Guys, I know I'm just driving this thing, but can I throw something out there?" Janie offered. "We've got some lines stowed in the back. I land on ships all the time. If there's a flat spot you like, I'll hover over it, and you can rappel down far closer to the bridge than four hundred feet. The top of the bridge might even be an option, and they'd never see it coming."

"That's brilliant, Janie," Buck said. "It's your call. Jason, get the lines ready."

When Donovan's phone rang again, he answered immediately.

"We've got problems," Lauren said. "The Coast Guard ordered us to leave the area. They've closed Prince William Sound. Every vessel has been ordered to stay in port or anchor at the nearest suitable refuge and await further instructions. I'm pretty sure fighters are being scrambled as we speak as are state law enforcement personnel. In the Coast Guard's eyes this is a full-blown terrorist attack, and we're in the middle of it. Maybe even the cause."

"Does anyone have the slightest chance of reaching the *North Star* before we do?"

"No," Lauren replied. "There's a Special Emergency Response Team being scrambled via helicopter out of Anchorage, I don't have an ETA, and I don't see them yet on my equipment."

"Okay. If fighters show up, do what they ask. Your flight data recorders will prove your innocence. How far out are we?"

"Seven minutes."

"Keep talking," Donovan urged. Buck pointed out front, and Donovan leaned over to catch his first glimpse of the *North Star*. Through a momentary snow squall, the distinctive blue hull with all white above decks distinguished it as one of the Constellation-class tankers. It looked impossible for a huge ship to be in such a narrow channel, but the tanker plowed through six-foot waves like they weren't there.

Buck leaned in toward Janie and pointed toward the tanker. "See that very top platform, the one with the radar antenna spinning on top?"

"Yeah, sure." Janie nodded. "Is that where you want off?"

"If I made it so that the antenna wasn't turning, could you hover while we go down a line to the platform? It would save precious minutes."

"No worries. How about if I come in low and behind, use the exhaust stack of the ship to block any view of us. When we're right on them, I'll climb fast and put you right next to the platform. They might hear us, but they won't know where we are."

"If you can do that, you'll be my hero. We'll be out fast, you break it off, and get out of automatic weapons range and wait. You're our ride off if we can't stop the damn thing."

"Will do."

"Hand me one of those lines," Buck said, reaching back to Jason.

From his seat behind Buck, Donovan spotted the platform that Buck had pointed out. The tallest point on the *North Star* was a three-legged raised platform with two radar antennas spinning on top. The entire structure rose ten or twelve feet above and slightly aft of the main bridge and the platform itself was large enough to accommodate both Buck and Jason. From this angle, Donovan could see that there was a stairway that led down from the platform, to a hatch that looked as if it would connect to the bridge. The obstacles were the two spinning radar arrays. Buck made a knot every three feet or so in the line to assist with the descent. Donovan could smell the diesel exhaust from the ship as they dropped down to wave-top level.

Buck and Jason tied off the lines to the seat belt harness. They worked quickly with the certain knowledge that in minutes they'd be out the door onto the ship.

"You ready?" Janie asked, as the stern of the tanker loomed large. They were tucked in close; no one from the bridge could possibly see them. "When I climb, I'm going to offset to the left of the platform so you'll both be going out the doors on the right side of the helicopter."

"Okay to open the doors?" Buck said and waited until Janie gave him a nod.

Donovan felt the icy blast of cold air rush into the cabin. He did his best to ignore the churning sea that boiled out from behind the massive vessel. Instead, he watched as Buck removed his head-phones and put in his tactical earbuds. He put one foot out into the slipstream to brace himself on the flight step. Jason followed suit from the rear door. They both had their weapons ready.

Buck gave Janie a nod.

Janie pulled hard on the collective, and the 407 clawed upward, just missed the flagpole on the fantail, and streaked upward toward the platform. She matched the exact speed of the ship while guid-ing the helicopter into position with the right skid only feet from the spinning radar array. Janie held the helicopter rock steady. Buck leveled his twelve-gauge shotgun and fired four quick shells into the motor assemblies. The antennas quickly ground to a stop, and once they were no longer spinning, what remained was a platform large enough for two men.

Buck and Jason swung off the skids and rappeled down to the platform. Once they were clear, Janie banked the helicopter hard to the left and fell away from the ship in a plunge toward the water that made Donovan reach out and brace himself. She leveled out just above the waves and sped to a position well off the starboard amidships. She climbed up to two hundred feet and hovered. Janie handed Donovan a handheld tactical radio so he could listen in on Buck and Jason's transmissions. He, in turn, relayed what was hap-pening to Lauren on the *da Vinci*.

"We've reached the bridge, negative resistance. Everyone's gone," Buck reported. "All the controls have been sabotaged, every-thing's been gutted, nothing's responding."

"We've got new problems," Lauren said in a rush. "There's a helicopter inbound at your ten o'clock position and less than a mile. Popped up out of nowhere and is heading for the ship. I've identi-fied it as a commercial version of the Huey, a 212, white with gray stripes, the registration number is taped over, and I don't see any other markings. There are two pilots and at least one more in the back. The side doors are open and it looks as if they have machine guns. I've got people coming out of a hatch onto the main deck of the *North Star*. I count seven of them, and it looks like they're in a hurry. They're headed for the helipad."

"Buck," Donovan relayed, "armed chopper inbound. Bad guys are on the deck headed for the helipad."

"Damn it! I see them," Buck replied. "They're standing on a million barrels of oil. We can't shoot them. And we'll never catch them."

"Forget about them. Can you stop the ship?" Donovan asked.

"Not from the bridge. Jason and I are headed down to the engine room. Maybe we can get control from there. Keep me posted."

"Buck. Get down!" Donovan yelled as an automatic weapon aboard the helicopter began to fire at the tanker. He and Janie sat helpless as bullets raked the bridge, peppering the entire glass enclosure.

Janie banked the nimble 407 to a point in space where they were out of the line of fire, but still had a view of the deck.

"Buck, are you still there?" Donovan transmitted.

"I'm here. Jason's down. He's beyond help. Keep your distance. I'm headed down to the engine room."

"The other helicopter has touched down," Lauren reported. "I can see faces. One of them is Erica."

Donovan pulled out a set of binoculars, panned and focused, until he had a view of the helicopter now on the deck, its rotor still turning. Garrick was climbing aboard, Nikolett a few feet behind him. Donovan located Erica, her hands bound behind her back. From behind, a man prodded her with a machine gun to move faster. Donovan watched with intensity as Erica glanced up in the direction of the *da Vinci*, then turned and looked over her shoulder, as if staring directly at him. An instant later, she stopped and snapped her head back into the face of the man trailing her. He reeled from the blow. Erica kicked him in the crotch, turned, and sprinted for the edge of the deck. Just before she jumped off the ship, a plume of red mist billowed from her back. Off balance, Erica twisted sideways as she went over the side. They were hovering on the opposite side of the ship, but Donovan found Nikolett, arm raised and a pistol in her hand. She looked directly toward the helicopter and gave him a mock salute before turning away.

Just before the big 212 lifted off the deck, Buck burst out of a hatch and unleashed a burst of machine gun fire at the open door of the departing helicopter. He ducked back inside as his fire was returned, the slugs ripping all around his position. The helicopter lifted off the *North Star*, lowered its nose, and quickly accelerated away.

"Janie!" Donovan yelled. "Erica's in the water! Get us down there now!"

Janie nodded as she dipped the nose and banked left to cut around the stern of the ship.

"Donovan," Lauren said calmly, "I'm locked onto Erica's heat signature. She's alive, and she made it back to the surface. She's trying to kick and stay afloat."

"Where!" Donovan began looking at the wake behind the ship. The chance of spotting a person in the churned-up water and rough seas was remote at best. Lauren was their only chance.

"Tell Janie to turn twenty degrees to the left. The target will be fifty yards straight ahead."

"Twenty degrees left, fifty yards." Donovan repeated and Janie immediately turned the chopper and brought it down to ten feet above the waves.

"Keep going," Lauren urged. "She went under, but I still have her position marked. Get ready."

"We're almost on top of her!" Donovan relayed to Janie.

"Ten feet," Lauren reported.

Donovan opened the door. He spotted her as she broke the surface, gasping for air, kicking and trying to take another breath before the next wave forced her under. Without thinking, Donovan held onto the rope Jason had left behind and climbed out onto the left skid. Janie flew by feel, looking back over her shoulder and jockeying the helicopter up and down in rhythm with the rolling waves. She timed the next wave perfectly, and Donovan reached out and clutched Erica by the collar of her sweater, the water crimson from her blood. He pulled her close and managed to heave her out of the water until he had her under both arms. Her skin had gone shock white, drained, and nearly lifeless. Pure adrenaline propelled him as he ignored the ocean, the waves, and his own pain, and lifted until he was sitting on the edge of the door with Erica's hip resting on the skid. One last backbreaking heave and he rolled her halfway into the helicopter. Janie did the rest by climbing and banking the 407, letting gravity help tumble them both onto the floor of the chopper. Donovan turned Erica on her back and checked her pulse. He couldn't find one. She'd stopped breathing. He tipped her head sideways to clear the water from her mouth and then began CPR.

"Donovan!" Janie yelled over the slipstream. "Buck needs you! We're heading back to the ship."

"Why!" Donovan yelled back.

"He's in the engine room and he can't control them. He can only shut them down and he says that won't stop the ship. You need to get to the bow of the tanker and manually drop the anchors."

"Do it!" Donovan said as he kept working on Erica. He compressed her sternum with both hands and counted out the repetitions, silently urging her to live. He glanced outside. They were less than thirty seconds until touchdown, and he could feel desperation rise at the thought of abandoning her. He leaned in to give her mouth-to-mouth when she suddenly groaned and vomited up seawater. Without hesitation Donovan yanked the first-aid kit out of its housing and ripped it open. He found scissors that he used to slice the snap-tie that held her hands. He cut open her sweater and found the gunshot wound as well as dozens of smaller lesions that appeared to be burns, evidence of Nikolett's interrogation.

Donovan found the source of the blood. She'd been hit in the flesh just under her left arm. The bullet had only grazed her, but it had made a nasty furrow in her skin. He tore open a handful of dressings and pressed them to the wound to try to stop the bleed-

ing. She gasped for air, and Donovan used the last remaining seconds to open a roll of elastic bandage to wrap around her wounds
to help maintain the pressure. He could feel the helicopter settle
into a hover as Erica's eyes fluttered open. He leaned down and
kissed her gently on the lips.

"I knew you'd come," she mouthed, her voice far too weak to
overcome the noise of the chopper.

"You promised me once you'd do the same for me if I ended
up in the ocean." Donovan felt the skids touch the deck. "Janie!
Leave me here! Get her to Anchorage."

Erica managed a weak smile.

The moment the skids touched, Donovan squeezed Erica's
hand, grabbed the tactical radio, and stepped out onto the deck of
the *North Star*. He closed the door, ducked under the blades, and
ran until he reached an elevated gangway that stretched the length
of the ship. It was built above the oil manifold piping on the main
deck and gave him a clear path to the bow. Behind him, Janie lifted
off the pad and sped away.

Donovan began to run. The wind and rain peppered his skin.
He ignored the elements, the burning pain in his back and thigh,
and kept going. He had no idea how to drop the anchors. All he
knew was he had to get it done. As he ran, he felt a slight aberration
from below his feet, then another one, stronger this time. Donovan
felt the ship shudder, and he slid to a halt, wrapped his left hand
around one of the metal stanchions along the handrail. A glance
told him the water ahead of the ship wasn't deep blue—they'd
reached the shallows.

"Buck, we're going to hit! Brace yourself!" Donovan said into
his walkie-talkie. He heard a distorted reply. Then the radio flew
from his hand as his legs whipped out from under him with his
arms pulling against the railing as the massive ship ran aground.
The sickening, shrieking sound of tortured steel being ripped apart
filled the morning air. The shock waves from the failing metal vi-
brated and resonated through the entire ship.

When the screeching of twisting metal faded, Donovan felt the deceleration forces release his body. The only sound came from the roaring twin engines still trying to propel them forward. Moments later, one engine quit, followed by the other. The sudden silence seemed eerie. Donovan released his grip from the railing, giving silent thanks he hadn't gone over the side of the twenty-foot-high elevated gangway. His radio was nowhere to be seen.

He pulled himself to his feet, moving aft to the nearest stairwell. He hurried down to the main deck and once there, maneuvered through the maze of pipes until he was leaning over a railing amidships. Below him he saw dark-blue water of the sound, but as he looked forward, he could see where the pristine blue water suddenly gave way to a shallow shelf that ran all the way to shore. Groans from the still-creaking metal rose from under the hull, continuing to resonate through the ship. The water near the bow was churned brown, and for one sickening moment, Donovan thought the ship was leaking oil. Closer inspection told him the brown stain was mud and debris boiling up from below the ship. He hoped the ten-foot barrier in the double hull had done its job.

Donovan felt his legs quiver, recognizing the effect of the massive amounts of adrenaline pumping through his system. Stepping away from the railing, he began to run toward the distant stairs that would take him to the bridge. His bad leg ached unmercifully, and his lungs burned as he topped the six flights of stairs. His attention was riveted upward as a blue-and-white helicopter roared overhead. Gun barrels protruding from open doors, the Alaska State Troopers were in full tactical mode. The helicopter hovered as armed men in full battle dress rappeled down to the deck. Just as quickly, the helicopter lifted off again, circling. From the railing, Donovan heaved his Glock over the side of the ship, making sure it cleared the hull and plunged into the ocean.

Breathing heavily, he pushed through the hatch into the bridge and found Jason's body, the bullet wound in his neck clearly evident. All the way across the length of the bridge, piles of shattered glass littered the carpet. Donovan hurried to the main control console, where panels had been pried open, wire bundles ripped out and severed. Frantically, he searched for the picture he was sure Garrick had left behind.

He couldn't help but think how Eco-Watch had been outmaneuvered. Garrick had really done a number on him today. Erica, the tanker, and now Donovan Nash, Eco-Watch's chief operations officer, was moments from being discovered onboard the bridge of a hijacked Huntington Oil supertanker that had just run aground. Donovan was still searching when the deafening noise of a helicopter filled the bridge. He looked up as the helicopter rose above the line of windows and hovered there. He saw a trooper with an automatic weapon aimed at his chest. A voice over the loudspeaker ordered him to put his hands behind his head. Donovan had run out of time. He had no choice but to raise his hands in surrender.

CHAPTER THIRTY-THREE

"Michael." Lauren eased into the cockpit as they taxied the *da Vinci* toward the small armada of official cars, both civilian and military, awaiting their arrival. "I've got the disc from today's flight. I don't know who's waiting for us, but I'm going to find the highest rank-ing official and get in his face and see if my Defense Intelligence Agency credentials will make anything good happen. I can't believe the military ordered us out of the airspace. You don't think they would have really shot us down, do you?"

"They weren't happy; no use calling the Air Force's bluff. How long were you able to track the helicopter?" Michael asked.

"Not long, I saw the tanker run aground, and by the time I went back to search for the chopper, they were gone."

"I radioed Janie. As soon as she drops Erica at the hospital, she knows to come here and get ready to go back out."

Michael eased the *da Vinci* to a stop, set the brakes, and shut down both engines.

"Let's see what's waiting for us." Lauren lowered the airstair and stood in the doorway. A woman, appearing to be in her mid-forties, ended a phone call, spoke to those around her as if issuing orders, then strode toward the plane. When she came to the steps, she stopped and peered up into the Gulfstream.

"Please, come aboard," Lauren called out.

The woman climbed the steps. Trailing her were two men. One took up a position at the foot of the stairs, the other followed the woman.

"I'm Special Agent Kathleen Martinson, FBI. How many peo-ple are aboard this plane?"

"Myself and two pilots," Lauren replied. "I'm Dr. Lauren McKenna, Defense Intelligence Agency."

"I know who you are. My man needs to make a quick sweep. Then we can talk."

"Of course." Lauren stepped aside to allow the agent access to the cabin. The search was brief, and when he finished, he joined his fellow agent at the bottom of the stairs.

"Have we met before?" Lauren asked.

"No. I only know you by reputation and what's in your FBI file, though we have several acquaintances in common, one being the director of the FBI."

"Agent Martinson, I've got something to show you. Please follow me." Lauren offered Agent Martinson a seat in front of the HD monitor she'd been sitting at all morning. "Before you say anything or make any uninformed decisions, you need the truth of what took place today. I saw all of this as it was happening, and you need to see it as well."

"Dr. McKenna, please spare me the preamble. You have my undivided attention. I'm well aware of your reputation and qualifications as well as this airplane's capability. Now, what is it I'm about to see?"

"These images were taken this morning."

"Before we begin," Martinson said. "Why exactly were Eco-Watch's assets out seemingly patrolling the pipeline as well as Prince William Sound?"

"Operating on a hunch by Eco-Watch's chief of operations, Mr. Donovan Nash."

"A hunch developed from what source?"

"An informant who believed that the pipeline might be a target," Lauren said.

"Continue," Agent Martinson said.

"The individuals aboard the Eco-Watch helicopter, besides the pilot, are Mr. Howard Buckley, Eco-Watch chief of security, Mr. Jason Mahoney, a private security consultant, and, of course, Mr. Nash."

"I'm aware of Mr. Nash. His reputation precedes him." Martinson turned to face Lauren. "I can also assure you that your husband has the respect of some of the powers that be, but not all of them. I've heard the term 'loose cannon' used to describe him. Would that be accurate?"

"Would it?" Lauren answered the question with a question, curious where this was going.

"I understand while he was in Hawaii he leaped from a helicopter onto a runaway ship. Does that sound like your husband?"

"Did he save the ship?" Lauren fired back, angry that this was the first she'd heard of this event, and that she was forced to play defense in blind support of her husband.

"Yes, he did."

"So he was effective. How does that make him a loose cannon?"

"Point taken. How effective was he today?"

"Please, just watch." Lauren had no intention of discussing Donovan with the FBI, or anyone else for that matter. Lauren switched on the monitor and initiated playback starting the moment the *North Star* was spotted.

"No audio?"

"Video only," Lauren replied. She and Donovan had been talking via satellite phone, which was a separate system. Thankfully, there was no direct interface between the data recording.

"We'd been up north toward Fairbanks when I intercepted Coast Guard communications indicating problems locating a tanker as well as its escort vessels."

"Yes. I already know about your initial conversation with the Coast Guard in Valdez. Did you know you were ordered to vacate the airspace above Prince William Sound?"

"Really? I remember that initial call being cut off." Lauren's feigned puzzlement was the best she had, and Martinson seemed to have bought the lie, at least for the moment.

"Continue."

Lauren hit play, and the two of them watched the entire video in silence.

"What did your men find when they boarded the ship?" Martinson asked.

"The bridge controls had been disabled, so there was no way to alter the course of the ship. One man went below in an effort to shut them down. Mr. Nash went back aboard to get to the bow and manually try to drop the anchors. The ship ran aground before either man could make a difference."

"Anything else to this story you'd care to pass along?"

"That's all there is. We were ordered to leave the area by the military. You know what happened next."

"Who was the woman that went into the water?"

"Her name is Erica. She was assisting us and disappeared last night."

"Did you report her disappearance?" Martinson swiveled in her chair to face Lauren.

"To my knowledge, there wasn't any evidence of a crime. I understood that she simply didn't show up for a meeting."

"Was she your informant?"

"I'm not at liberty to discuss Eco-Watch's internal matters," Lauren replied. "You'll have to take that up with Mr. Nash."

"All of this state-of-the-art equipment at your fingertips, how is it you weren't able to get any clear images of all the people who did this?"

"As you can see, the aircraft was trying to stay below the ceiling and within the constraints of the terrain." Lauren smoothly switched into her DIA persona. "It's like gathering intelligence from a satellite. You can only see what's in the current field of view, nothing more. I was able to get a partial view of some of the people; the man filming the events had his face blocked completely by his camera. The helicopter itself was in clear view. Hopefully, you can track them down that way."

"I'm more interested in the witness. The woman who went overboard, is she alive?"

"She was flown to a local hospital. I don't know anything more than that." Lauren didn't want to stop to process all the possible implications of her husband, who hated helicopters nearly as much as he hated the ocean, doing what he did to save Erica.

"If she's still alive, maybe she can tell us more about what happened. Can you go back to when the perpetrators boarded the helicopter?"

Lauren backed up the file until she found the correct point in time.

"Can you slow it down?"

Lauren adjusted the advance rate and leaned in closer, curious what the FBI agent had seen.

"Right there, freeze it!"

Lauren saw what had caught the FBI agent's attention. The momentary volley of fire from Buck had been on target. Three bullets perforated the thin aluminum skin aft of the door and someone inside the cabin fell over sideways as if struck, which prompted a burst of return gunfire, empty brass spilling onto the deck.

"I think your man may have hit one of the hijackers. We'll alert every hospital in southern Alaska. Maybe we'll get lucky," Martinson said. "Dr. McKenna, you've accomplished what you set out to do. It's clear, at least for the moment, that Eco-Watch is not directly involved with what took place today. I'll need a copy of that recording."

"What exactly did take place today?" Lauren made no move to extract the requested disc. "How did these people steal a supertanker?"

"The Coast Guard is still piecing this together, but apparently they gained access to the tanker by way of a small boat or by boarding the assist tugs in Valdez Harbor. Once they were in the shipping lanes, beyond radar, they destroyed both escort vessels. The damage I saw to the tugs indicates they used high explosives, possibly shoulder-fired antitank missiles to effectively eliminate both ships. It happened fast, took place without a single distress call being made. By the time anyone knew something was wrong, the tanker was well on its way to Unakwik Inlet."

"Is the *North Star* leaking any oil?"

"Not yet. Containment areas are being set up as we speak," Martinson replied. "Now, if you'll give me the copy you promised, I'll be on my way."

Lauren handed over the disc. "What about the Eco-Watch personnel still aboard the *North Star?*"

"They're being held for debriefing. I'll release them as soon as it's clear they are in no way involved. Dr. McKenna, I also expect you and your crew to remain available for any follow-up interviews that may be necessary."

"Agent Martinson," one of the FBI agents called out from the front of the plane. "There's a story breaking on CNN you need to see."

Martinson turned to Lauren. "Can all of this fancy equipment pull up CNN?"

"Up front." Lauren led the way and called Michael to join them. Lauren switched the television on and tuned it to CNN. They were greeted by the grainy image of an oil tanker shot by someone aboard the *North Star.*

Martinson's phone rang and she answered immediately, listened, and replied. "How soon can you arrange transport? I see. Keep me updated."

"They're going to replay this footage from the top," Lauren said and increased the volume.

"This just in from Prince William Sound, Alaska. CNN just received exclusive footage of what appears to be another act of terrorism at the hands of the scientific research organization, Eco-Watch. Early this morning, the Huntington Oil tanker *North Star* was hijacked and ultimately run aground. The clip we're about to show you is completely unedited."

The screen showed a shaky shot of the sky. The muffled sound of the wind could be heard in the background until the noise of an approaching jet dominated the audio. As the aircraft flew past at low altitude, the camera zoomed in until it was clear that it was an Eco-Watch Gulfstream. The jet was then seen to make a steep bank to come back around. The shot stabilized and panned across the expanse of glass that marked the bridge of the *North Star*. Moments later the entire front section of glass exploded inward by withering automatic gunfire. The next image was of the Eco-Watch helicopter hovering off the starboard side of the ship.

"Jesus Christ," Michael said aloud.

The news anchor once again filled the screen. "Latest reports from the scene confirm the supertanker *North Star* has run aground on a reef just east of Olsen Island in Prince William Sound. We hope to have a live feed from the scene shortly. It was in 1989 that the tanker Exxon Valdez ran aground not far from this very location, spilling nearly eleven million gallons of oil."

Lauren felt sick to her stomach and muted the television. Anyone who saw this clip would have no choice but to come to the conclusion that Eco-Watch had hijacked an oil tanker and caused it to run aground. She suddenly felt like a sitting target. Outside she heard the beating rotors from an approaching helicopter.

Martinson looked out her window, then back to Lauren. "It's the Eco-Watch helicopter. I need to ask a favor."

Lauren sensed the urgency in her request. "What can I do?"

"I can't say anything at this point, but my transportation is delayed. Can we use your helicopter? I need to get out to that ship with two of my crime-scene people and we need to go now."

"Of course, Eco-Watch is happy to assist," Lauren turned to Michael. "Tell Janie we're going back out to the tanker as soon as possible."

"Once she refuels, she'll be ready to go."

"After everything that's happened today," Martinson said, "I'd advise all of Eco-Watch's assets to leave the state of Alaska immediately. I'm not sure you, or your assets, can be protected from what is going to be a very angry public."

"I agree," Michael said to Lauren. "Go out there and get Donovan and Buck off that ship. I'm dead serious. There's nothing more they can do that the Coast Guard, the State Police, and Huntington Oil can't. Don't let them make the *North Star* their problem. We all need to get the hell out of here while we still can."

CHAPTER THIRTY-FOUR

The screech of twisting, stressed steel rose up from deep inside the *North Star*. Donovan, his hands bound behind his back, was sitting on the floor leaning against a wall in an interior room on the main deck level of the tanker. Buck had been brought in a few minutes ago and was seated across the room from him. They'd both given their statements to the Alaskan State Police and now a state trooper had been positioned to watch over them. In the last hour, several helicopters had arrived and dropped off more men. Through the open hatchway, Donovan had seen that the newest arrivals were civilians.

"I felt that vibration in the seat of my pants," Buck said. "Overstressed steel just can't be good."

A trooper stuck his head into the room. "Lieutenant says cut 'em loose and get 'em up to the bridge."

With their escort bringing up the rear, Donovan and Buck climbed up six flights of stairs to the bridge. They saw that Jason's body had been covered. From where Donovan stood he could see at least two men working under the massive console on the wiring that Garrick had shredded. Looking toward the bow, a Coast Guard's HH-60 was on the pad, rotors idling. When he looked aft, Donovan saw a flurry of vessels, three were Coast Guard ships, two, one-hundred-ten-foot Island-class cutters, and a larger, one-hundred-fifty-four-foot Sentinel-class ship. All were positioned outside of larger vessels that were offloading containment booming, a floating barrier that was used to contain oil spills. They were cordoning off the ship in case the inner hull ruptured.

Three men huddled over a chart table, each man holding a

walkie-talkie. One was a Coast Guard officer, the other two civilians.

"His rank is captain," Buck told Donovan. "He'll be the one in charge of the vessel."

"Mr. Nash, Mr. Buckley," I'm Captain Hughes, United States Coast Guard. This is Larry Davis, he's with Alyeska, and Tim Gunnison, he's in charge of SERVS, the Ship Escort/Response Vessel System."

"Who finally decided we weren't a threat?" Buck asked.

"My understanding is the State Police got a call from the FBI," Hughes replied. "The Alaskan State Police are heading up the criminal aspect until the FBI arrives. We're trying to assess the ship itself."

Donovan was familiar with both Alyeska and SERVS. Alyeska was the group formed by all the oil companies to oversee the construction and continued operation of the Alaskan pipeline system. SERVS answered to Alyeska and was directly in charge of getting the oil safely out of Valdez and into the open ocean. They were also directed with the task of responding to and containing any type of spill. Though each man was old enough to have had dealings with Huntington Oil when he was CEO. Donovan didn't recognize them.

"I understand we all lost some men today. You have my condolences," Donovan said to Gunnison who looked every bit of sixty years old, his weathered skin marked by the lines and wrinkles of a man who lived and worked in the harsh Alaskan elements.

"It's a sad day for sure." Gunnison shook his head. "Troopers found twenty-four of the *North Star's* crew locked in the mess hall. They'd all been killed. The bastards shot everyone onboard and killed every crewman aboard both escort tugs when they sank them. It's been a goddamned bloodbath."

The news of the dead crew saddened Donovan. He hadn't been connected with Huntington Oil for over two decades, but still, the dead men were part of a company he still cared about deeply. Donovan could see all of this was especially hard on the man from

Alyeska. Davis stood rigid, hands balled into fists, jaw muscles working beneath his skin, and eyes narrowed into hate-filled slits. He, too, looked as if he was pushing sixty, completely bald and carrying a large gut, but despite being long out of shape, he still carried himself with the demeanor of a man who was used to getting what he wanted.

"They'll pay," Buck said.

Donovan was about to ask about the blueprints laid out on the chart table when a series of lights on the control console flickered to life accompanied by a shrill warning bell. One of the men working on the console silenced the warning and then began flipping switches and cycling through different screens on one of the monitors

"What was that?" Donovan asked.

"Unless I'm wrong," Buck spoke first, "that was a warning that water has breached the outer hull."

"Correct," Captain Hughes replied. "You sound like you're familiar with ships?"

"Yes, sir, U.S. Navy SEAL, retired."

"Glad to have your expertise on board."

"When we first got here, our number-one priority was to reestablish the power to the vessel monitoring-and-control system. Seems we've accomplished part of that task," Gunnison said. "We already know the outer hull is ruptured. It's the inner hull we're concerned about as well as the settling of the ship itself. I'm sure you've heard the sounds coming from below."

Buck had leaned forward to study the blueprints. He traced the drawing with his finger and then rifled through the charts underneath until he found the one he was looking for, pulled it free, and laid it on top of the stack. When he spun it around to get the view he wanted, his expression turned from curious to understanding and then to alarm. He went to the nearest window and looked outside. "What's the tidal swing here?"

"There's roughly a fourteen-foot difference between high and low tide. Why?" Hughes's brow furrowed as he spoke.

"Have you considered what effects the outgoing tide is having on the hull?"

Before any of the men could process the implications of what Buck had asked, the distinct groan of bending steel once again rose from the bowels of the ship and resonated through the entire structure.

"How much of the hull is firmly aground?" Buck asked.

"Roughly a hundred and eighty feet," Gunnison replied.

"According to the marine chart of this reef, the first one hundred eighty feet of this ship are aground, no floatation whatsoever." Buck placed his fingertips on the edge of the table to illustrate his point. "The remaining eight hundred feet of ship is afloat in two hundred forty feet of water. As the tide goes out, the stern of the ship tilts downward. If you look at the blueprints, the fulcrum point where the ship and the edge of the reef come together is between two major supports. I think the sounds we're hearing is the buckling of steel from that stress. We all know what happens if you bend a piece of metal back and forth enough times—it'll break into two."

"So you're saying that next low tide, twelve hours from now, this ship could rupture?" Davis asked.

"That depends," Buck said. "We're at low tide right now, so as the tide turns and starts coming in, the situation may stabilize briefly. This is all just a theory, but if it were up to me, I'd get divers down there to examine the hull, see where it's buckling and how bad. Then talk to your marine architects. They'll give you what you're looking for. All I'm doing is guessing."

"I already have divers getting into position. I've also got two more tugs on the way from Valdez as well as all the spill-response vessels and equipment we own," Gunnison said. "Two of my other tugs are headed south to escort an empty tanker that was inbound to Valdez. It's the Huntington *Orion*, sister ship to the *North Star*. We'll have it standing by to take on all the oil from this ship."

"How long does it take to pump a million barrels of oil?" Buck asked.

"Anywhere from sixteen to eighteen hours."

"Does all the oil have to be pumped out to get the ship free?" Donovan asked. "What if you pumped off a third of the weight, or only the oil in the forward tanks? Could that buy you time to get the ship floating again before another low tide?"

"Again, a question for the engineers and architects," Buck said. "Though, I would suggest that if you've got a sister ship to this one within helicopter range, get some of the crew flown from the *Orion* to the *North Star*, at least enough to help run this ship."

"I'm on it," Davis replied and began talking into his radio.

"How far out is the *Orion*?" Donovan asked. "And how long would it take to get her in position?"

"She's still south of the Hinchinbrook entrance, which is every bit of sixty nautical miles, so we're talking six or seven hours," Gunnison replied. "That's just to get here, add another couple of hours to get it into position and get everything hooked up, so we're talking eight hours, minimum. There's still the problem of rewiring the damage to the bridge, though hopefully we'll have those issues resolved by then."

"If I looked at the schematics correctly," Buck said, "there are twelve separate compartments filled with oil. A tear in the inner and outer hulls would compromise no more than four of those containers. How much oil are we talking about if we look at the immediate threat?"

"Three hundred thousand barrels or about fifty thousand barrels more than the *Exxon Valdez* spill. At that point, we also have a ship with a ruptured hull that puts the other seven hundred thousand barrels at risk." Davis turned his attention out the front of the ship as the Coast Guard helicopter lifted from the deck, pivoted ninety degrees, and departed to the south.

Davis rejoined the group. "I just spoke with Captain Joseph Flemming, the master of the *Orion*, he's assembling a small crew to transfer to the *North Star* and assist. The Coast Guard helicopter is on their way out to get them. Plus, I've just learned we've got another helicopter inbound, it seems Eco-Watch is bringing out the FBI."

Donovan broke away from the group and walked to the section of blown-out windows to look for his helicopter. As he stepped around the glass from the shattered windows, he spotted what looked like a photograph buried face down under a pile of crazed glass. He fought the impulse to reach down and pick it up as Buck and the others were looking directly at him. He had no choice but to wait.

CHAPTER THIRTY-FIVE

Lauren couldn't believe how much had changed since she and Michael had departed the inlet in the *da Vinci* a little less than three hours earlier. The ceiling had lifted a bit, though the weather was still blustery with intermittent rain and snow showers. Amid the whitecaps she spotted three Coast Guard ships, which Janie told her were cordoning off the area to any unauthorized vessels. The entire vicinity had been designated a no-fly zone to restrict air traffic. News helicopters from Anchorage had been moved back five miles. The last thing the salvage operation or the Coast Guard wanted was crowded airspace and a horde of spectators. Lauren knew their arrival was being broadcast live, courtesy of the long lenses mounted on the helicopters. She could only hope that their presence would be depicted in a positive light.

Floating containment booms encircled the *North Star*. Lauren counted two massive tugboats, plus three other support vessels poised to react to an oil spill. Inside the boom, a service ship was connected to the tanker by multiple hoses, making her wonder if they'd already began pumping oil off the tanker. Lauren watched as Janie swung around the superstructure and then brought the helicopter in until its skids kissed the metal in the exact center of the landing pad.

"Nice landing," Martinson said.

"Piece of cake when the ship's standing still," Janie replied, giving Lauren and the others the signal they could open the doors.

Lauren turned to Janie. "My plan is to get Donovan and Buck off this ship and head back to Anchorage."

"The Coast Guard said I can wait here until the next inbound chopper arrives, then I have to leave. I can loiter in the area for a little while, but then I might have to go to Valdez and refuel."

"Do whatever you need to do, but let's try and cooperate with the authorities," Lauren said, happy to be leaving the chopper. Even though Janie had tried to clean it up, Erica's bloodstains were still visible in the aft cabin. Lauren still hadn't taken the time to analyze her emotions at the sight of Donovan coming to her rescue the way he did. She cleared her head and stepped off the helicopter onto the deck of the *North Star*, as did the three other passengers. Besides Agent Martinson were Agents Boswell and Williams, both forensic-evidence specialists sent to collect and document as much of the crime scene as they could. Martinson looked around until she spotted what she was looking for, and then pointed toward several shell casings lying against the deck edging. Agent Boswell, mindful of the rotor wash, bagged the evidence, and then the four of them were escorted from under the spinning blades by a Coast Guard seaman.

"Follow me," the seaman said above the noise of the helicopter. "I do need to point out that the situation onboard is highly unstable. If the abandon ship order is given, you are to meet me at the starboard lifeboat station. See the enclosed orange lifeboat up there with the small round portholes? That's ours. It'll keep us alive in any kind of sea state—just don't be late."

Lauren took in the view from deck level. The lifeboat seemed tiny against the enormity of the ship. The size of the *North Star* was almost overwhelming, and she knew the bulk of the one-thousand-foot-long supertanker lay underwater. Looking aft, six stories up from the deck were the row of windows that marked the bridge. Another level higher was the small radar stanchion where Buck and Jason had boarded. The small entourage fell in behind the Coast Guard crewman and headed for the bridge.

"I understand there are victims in two different locations?" Martinson asked the crewman.

"Yes, the mess hall and the bridge."

Martinson turned to Boswell. "You start in the mess hall. I

want lots of pictures. We'll go to the bridge and join you as soon as we can."

As they reached the bridge superstructure, Boswell peeled off. Lauren, Agent Martinson, and Agent Williams began the trek up the stairs. They walked onto the bridge directly into the middle of what looked like an intense discussion. Lauren spotted her husband standing next to Buck and a Coast Guard officer. Two other men were squared off, the heavier man was jabbing his finger onto the chart table as if to make his point.

"Gentleman, I'm FBI Special Agent Martinson." She held up her credentials and instantly silenced the room. "Captain Hughes, I'm well aware that this is your ship, but this is a crime scene, specifically an FBI crime scene, and I'll need you to move this meeting somewhere else so my technician can process the scene."

"Agent Martinson, I'm Tim Gunnison, I'm with SERVS, and for the moment I'm in charge of this situation, and with all due respect, there's a bigger crime in progress here." Gunnison held out a stack of 8 x 10 color photos. "These are pictures my divers took of the ruptured hull of this tanker. We have a full-blown crisis on our hands and every warning light and bell is located on this bridge. We need to know the second things start to go from bad to worse."

"Thank you, Mr. Gunnison," Agent Martinson replied, then turned to the man across from him. "Then you must be the Alyeska representative?"

"Yes, ma'am, Larry Davis, and I'm going to have to insist we remain on the bridge as well as the technicians trying to repair the damage done to the electronics. We could lose this entire ship and a million barrels of oil if we don't stay on top of this."

"All I want is for you gentleman to take your pictures and charts, and walk twenty feet over there to a place where there isn't blood on the carpet and continue doing your jobs. Now, which one of you is Mr. Buckley?"

"I am," Buck said.

"Mr. Buckley, I understand you witnessed this man's death?"

"That's correct."

"I'll expect a full statement."

"Of course."

Martinson turned to Donovan. "Then you must be Mr. Nash. I need a word with you, in private. Now."

Lauren gave him a subtle nod that he should go.

"You too, Dr. McKenna, both of you, follow me. Mr. Buckley, don't leave the bridge."

Martinson led the way up one flight of stairs and out onto the roof of the bridge. Above them were the disabled radar antennas. Lauren could see dozens of holes where Buck's shotgun had disabled the motors. From this vantage point, Martinson stood silent, taking in the entire scene, the radar platform, SERVS ships, the containment booms, the Coast Guard vessels, and the enormous tanker itself. Donovan turned up his collar to fight off the brisk wind and light rain that was still falling.

Martinson turned and faced them. "Everything I've seen and heard today feels like it's almost the truth, but not quite. I think the two of you know far more than you're telling me, and it's time for the real story."

"I can't think of anything I've missed." Lauren offered.

"Mr. Nash. You didn't have a hunch. You were tipped off about this weren't you? Whoever did this enticed you into action so they could film you and use it against you. You were badly outmaneuvered here today, and your organization took a serious hit—but that's your problem, not mine. What I want, right now, is the entire truth or both of you and the rest of your little group will be facing serious obstruction charges. The director's words, not mine. Now, who are these people and why are they doing this?"

Martinson's satellite phone rang, and she stepped away while she answered the call.

"What in the hell is happening?" Donovan said as the FBI agent walked out of earshot. "What film? What don't I know?"

"The terrorists filmed aspects of what happened today," Lauren said. "They spliced it together to make it appear as if Eco-Watch attacked then hijacked the tanker and released it to CNN. I turned over a copy of the recordings from the *da Vinci*. The images aren't good enough for the FBI to identify Garrick, but Nikolett and some of the other men are clearly visible."

"So we're running out of time."

"Buck fired some shots at them as they were boarding the helicopter. Looks like he might have hit someone. If that person shows up at a hospital or a morgue, it might shorten the time we have to find Garrick ourselves. In addition, the FBI is going to put someone on Erica, monitor her because she's an eyewitness. First thing they're going to want to know is who she is, and for me, that poses a huge problem. I'm supposed to have alerted the CIA if I knew of her whereabouts—and I didn't."

"Damn it!" Donovan said.

"She's off the phone," Lauren said evenly, but the anger that flared in her eyes couldn't be missed. "If at all possible, let me do the talking. I know what lies I've already told."

"I'm running out of patience," Martinson said. "The woman who was shot and flown to Anchorage has now disappeared. She received treatment for a superficial gunshot wound, not deemed serious. She also had two cracked ribs, presumably from the twenty-five-foot fall she took from the deck of this ship. After all of that, she managed to sneak out of the hospital. My agent at the hospital tells me that all of the information she gave admissions was false. Did she have help from you two? Tell me who she is and where she's headed.

"Erica?" Lauren shrugged. "I have no idea. As I explained earlier, she was a volunteer."

"We've identified the woman who shot her. She's one of the assassins who tried to kill you in Paris."

"These people are nothing if not thorough," Lauren continued. "They kill everyone who isn't inside their inner circle. That's why we know nothing about them, no descriptions, and no names. Nothing. These people are ghosts."

"So you really have no idea who's doing this to you?"

"Not a clue," Lauren said, hating all the lies and half-truths. She was in Alaska, separated from her daughter, exposed to assassins, lying to federal agents about the woman her husband had slept with—hating every moment of what she'd become. The cost of living in Donovan's world just kept getting higher and higher.

"Special Agent Martinson!" A Coast Guardsman called from the top of the stairway. "Ma'am, you have a priority phone call on the bridge. Mr. Nash, the chopper that's inbound from the *Orion* is twenty minutes out—we're going to need your helicopter clear of the pad by then."

"We'll pick this up later," Martinson said over her shoulder as she headed for the bridge.

"Wait," Donovan stopped Lauren from following Martinson. "We need to talk."

"Why?" Lauren yanked her arm away. "So we can coordinate the rest of the lies we're going to tell? Maybe sometime you can fill me in on you leaping from a helicopter to an abandoned ship. Did that involve a woman as well?"

"It's about Captain Flemming. I know him. He was on the advisory board that oversaw the design of the Constellation class ships. We worked together for months. I can't afford to run into him. He could recognize my voice. We need to go with Janie."

"The deceptions to protect the lies just keep coming, don't they? You get to lie from here on out. I'm done." As Lauren headed back to the bridge, she felt as if she were being squeezed in a vise, and everyone around her was taking turns tightening the screws.

CHAPTER THIRTY-SIX

Everyone was clustered around the chart table studying a set of photographs when Lauren and Donovan entered the bridge.

"The pictures the divers took aren't definitive," Davis said to Gunnison. "One set of architects insist the hull shouldn't rupture at low tide. Another group of marine engineers says, yes, it will. They're telling us to hurry up and offload as much of the forward oil as we can and then to pull the tanker off at high tide. They say we'll have a spill, but a smaller one and we can maintain full containment."

"Maybe," Gunnison replied. "What if pulling the ship off the reef puts us in danger of capsizing the ship and leaking all of its oil?"

"This is a nightmare." Davis rubbed the whisker stubble on his face. "The risk of either one of us being wrong is the kiss of death for Prince William Sound and the oil business. Lawyers are already on jets—it's a goddamn mess. No one wants to stick their neck out—they're the only two solutions we have and they both suck."

"You're wrong," Lauren said as all eyes turned toward her. "There's another solution."

"I'd like you to meet my wife," Donovan said. "Dr. Lauren McKenna."

"With all due respect, Dr. McKenna," Gunnison replied. "We have a combined eighty years of marine experience and there are no other options."

"Hang on a minute," Buck said as he stopped studying the photographs. "Dr. McKenna has a Ph.D. from MIT and she consults for the Defense Intelligence Agency. I can promise you she's the smartest person in this room. I, for one, want to hear what she has to say."

"Go on, then." Gunnison replied.

"We create a higher tide and float the ship off the reef, gently. More or less."

"Ma'am, only the good Lord can do that," Gunnison said.

"At the north end of Unakwik Inlet is the Meares Glacier. If we can coax a large enough section of the ice to calve into the bay, we'll in effect create a controlled tsunami that will lift the hull free and sweep the ship out into deeper water."

"How would we do that exactly?" Davis asked. "Blow up the glacier?"

"Yes," Lauren replied. "We'd do a little math first, and use some precision detonation, but yeah, in the end, we'd blow up enough of the glacier to make our wave."

Everyone except Donovan and Buck paused and looked at each other, as if waiting for someone to say she was crazy. No one did.

"Has something like this ever been done before?" Davis asked.

"Of course not, not intentionally anyway," Lauren replied. "Show me a chart that covers this area of Prince William Sound."

Buck selected the correct chart and laid it on top of the schematics of the ship.

"Right here, Miners Lake," Lauren pointed. "It's all of, what, twelve miles away? This was the epicenter of the 1964 Alaskan earthquake that was measured at 9.2 on the Richter scale, the second strongest in recorded history. I can promise you that there was a hell of a wave that day, it killed people in Oregon and California. That inherent instability in the surrounding ground works in our favor. The Meares Glacier, which is up here, thanks to its proximity to the fault line, is riddled with fissures and crevices. Getting the explosives in the right position should be easy. If any of you have ever seen an explosion in an open-pit mine, they place precision charges into the ground, and then when it's detonated the blast drops a measured slice of the mountain into rubble. Same principle, except what we're doing is displacing water, which in turn has no place to go in the narrow fjord except out to sea, which is where we want it to go."

"Can you create a big enough wave?" Donovan asked, as he slowly moved toward the pile of glass where the photograph lay. He kept his eyes out the window as if he were picturing the wave Lauren was describing.

"I flew over the glacier earlier this morning. It's what, maybe two fifty, three hundred feet tall at the face?"

"Yeah, that's about right," Captain Hughes replied.

"Big chunks calve off all the time," Lauren continued. "We know from history that the 1958 Lituya Bay tsunami in Southeast Alaska created a seventeen-hundred-foot wave after forty million cubic yards of earth slid into the water. We don't want that big of a wave. We want one roughly twenty-five times smaller. At its edge, the Meares Glacier drops off into one hundred and eighty feet of water, that's plenty of depth to get the kind of displacement needed."

"The biggest risk comes if the wave isn't big enough and it moves the ship without lifting it up," Buck said. "You'll push it along the reef and, without a doubt, rupture the inner hull."

"Then, gentlemen," Lauren said, "I suggest you make a big enough wave so that doesn't happen."

"We'd like you to oversee this operation, if we decide to do it, that is," Gunnison said.

While all eyes were on Lauren, Donovan reached down, picked up the photograph, palmed it, and smoothly slipped it into his jacket pocket. When he looked up again, he was relieved to find that his move had gone unnoticed.

"I'm more of a theoretical scientist." Lauren held up her hands as if to slow Gunnison down. "You need real-world experts to make this happen. I might suggest, though, that you start the process immediately; you can always decide later whether or not to push the button."

"I agree," Gunnison said emphatically. "I'm calling the CEO of Selkirk Mining. He should have the experts we need, as well as the explosives. Dr. McKenna, if it wouldn't be too much trouble, could you theorize where this wave is going once it's floated this ship off the reef? I think some folks are going to want to know the answer to that question."

"Sure," Lauren replied. "But I'm going to need a bigger map."

As people hurried off in different directions, Donovan went to his wife and whispered in her ear, "You're a genius. I'll send Janie back for you and Buck, but I need to get off this ship, get back to Anchorage, and start running damage control for Eco-Watch."

"Do whatever you need to do," Lauren said. When she turned, anger flashed in her eyes.

Donovan resisted trying to reason with her. She was furious with him and anything he said was only going to make things worse. There was no fixing anything at this point. He was a hostage to his past, and that past had once again dictated his actions. Donovan glanced around the bridge. Buck was here, so Lauren was safe. Everyone was occupied for the moment, and he used the opportunity to quietly slip away.

CHAPTER THIRTY-SEVEN

The Bell 407 lifted off the *North Star* just as the Coast Guard HH-60 with Captain Flemming arrived on the scene. Janie flew low and fast toward Anchorage. Donovan picked up one of the charts, pretending to study its features as he slipped the photograph from his pocket and used the chart to hide it from Janie. The image was faded and washed out; it showed Meredith standing just outside the door of a Gulfstream. She was wearing an evening dress, her hair was up, and she was waving. He recognized the airplane as one of the fleet of Huntington Oil corporate jets. There was nothing in the background that gave him the slightest hint to when or where the picture had been taken. He turned it over. Whatever had been written had been smudged to the point where he couldn't make it out. Donovan had no idea what message Garrick had intended. He took another long look, and the only thing he noticed the second time was the faint image of someone in the left seat, waving good-bye as well. Closer inspection and he recognized himself, but then he often flew Meredith and himself to different functions so this could have been any one of dozens of trips they made together. He slipped the photo back into his pocket and closed his eyes to think. When he opened them, he discovered they were descending to land.

"Mr. Nash," Janie said when she noticed he was awake. "I'm going to refuel to be ready to fly back out, unless you have other instructions for me."

"Take a break, you've earned it, but stay close," Donovan replied. "At some point Lauren and Buck will need to be flown off the ship."

Janie hovered briefly and then eased the helicopter down next to a hangar; inside Donovan spotted the *da Vinci*. He waited for her to shut down the helicopter.

"Janie, what you did today was remarkable in every sense of the word. I may not know much about helicopters, but I know a good pilot when I see one, and you're one of the best. I'll fly with you anytime. Thank you."

"I appreciate that, sir, I'm just glad to have helped."

Donovan popped the door and stepped out of the 407 onto the concrete ramp. He gave Janie a quick salute and then walked to the *da Vinci*, happy to see that an external power cart had been connected to the airplane. He unlocked the main cabin door and stood to the side as the stairs extended. He ducked under the wing, briefly checked the electrical panel on the power cart, and then pushed a button that started the unit. The hum of electricity was matched by a green light.

He climbed the steps, stopped at the top, and turned back to face the ramp as Meredith had in the latest photo. He tried to imagine where they were and why the fond farewell. Her hair, the dress. He pulled out the picture and the answer hit him. There, on her left hand was the engagement ring. They'd been with William. They'd flown out to Washington, D.C., to tell him in person they were engaged. It was William they were waving good-bye to. Garrick had eliminated the date and time on the photo to make Donovan once again relive his time with Meredith. The warning that came with the realization nearly made Donovan sick to his stomach. He powered up his phone and waited impatiently.

He was just about to make the call when his phone rang. William—exactly who he needed to reach.

"Hello, Robert," Garrick said.

Donovan's entire body went rigid. There was only one way Garrick could be calling from William's phone. "Leave him alone. I'll do whatever you want."

"What I want is for you to come to me. Just you. If you call the police, William dies. I'll also leave behind a jump drive I've assembled that explains Robert Huntington's entire life story. I was very careful not to leave out anything. Don't come in the Eco-Watch jet, that'll draw too much attention. You've got six hours."

Donovan had no idea if Stephanie and Abigail were prisoners as well and he didn't dare ask. "I may have to catch a commercial flight which will take me more than six hours."

"I'd get a little more creative than that, Robert. Charter a plane, steal one. I don't really care, but you only have six hours. I'm a busy man."

"Where are you?"

"Call once you arrive in Los Angeles, and I'll tell you."

"How do I know he's still alive?"

"You don't. You're on the clock. Good-bye, Robert."

Donovan immediately dialed Stephanie. She picked up on the first ring.

"Oh, Donovan, thank God it's you."

Donovan thought she sounded out of breath or scared. "I'm here. What's happening? Is Abigail with you? Are you somewhere safe?"

"We're both safe, I think. We were in town when William called. He said he'd just gotten a warning from Erica that Garrick was on his way to Southern California. He told me to run, get Abigail somewhere safe, and not to talk to anyone but you or Lauren. We were on the phone when I heard shouting and what sounded like gunshots, and then the phone went dead."

"How long ago?" Donovan closed his eyes and tried not to imagine the worst.

"Twenty minutes. Abigail and I were at a frozen yogurt place she loves."

"You take care of Abigail. Don't tell anyone where you are. I'm on my way to Los Angeles. Tell Abigail her mom and dad love her dearly and we'll see her soon."

"Please help Uncle William."

"You know I'll do everything in my power. I promise."

Donovan ended the call and was nearly overwhelmed with a

mixture of grief and rage. William was being held hostage and his daughter and Stephanie had missed being captured only by Erica's warning. From the bottom of the stairs, he heard an unfamiliar female voice call out and ask if anyone was aboard. He hurried into the baggage compartment and found Erica's satchel and the small pistol inside. He checked that there was a bullet in the chamber and then walked quietly to the main cabin door and peeked around the corner. At the bottom of the airstair was an attractive woman who looked vaguely familiar. She wasn't particularly tall, maybe five foot five, but she was compact and very well put together with blond hair, big eyes, and brilliant smile. Dressed stylishly, she looked up and smiled up at him.

"Excuse me, do you work for Eco-Watch?"

"Who wants to know?" Donovan replied, unsure where he'd seen her before and how she'd wandered unescorted into the hangar.

"My name is Amanda Sullivan, I'm with Global Media Partners. I'd like to ask you some questions."

Hearing her name brought it all together. She was a well-known journalist, an investigative reporter with a Pulitzer for her coverage in Haiti after the devastating earthquake. Global Media Partners was one of the largest communications conglomerates in the world. Print, television, radio, GMP was everywhere. "Ms. Sullivan, how did you get past security?"

"We just landed, and I noticed the Eco-Watch aircraft as we taxied by. I thought I'd walk over and see if anyone was aboard, and here you are. Now, if I may, what is your position within Eco-Watch?"

"No comment," Donovan replied automatically. As a rule he avoided the media as much as possible. Then he had another thought. "Ms. Sullivan, you said you just landed, may I ask from where?"

"New York."

"What kind of an airplane?"

"It's a Falcon 900. Why do you ask?"

"Are you here to cover the story about the tanker in Prince William Sound?"

"Of course, have you been out there? What can you tell me?"

"Ms. Sullivan, please, come aboard. We need to talk." Donovan stashed the pistol out of sight in his jacket pocket.

Donovan escorted Amanda into the nerve center of the *da Vinci*, where he powered up the mainframe computer to view the footage Lauren had captured from today's events. It took a moment for the system to boot up, but from the expression on her face, he knew he had her complete attention.

"You still haven't told me who you are."

Donovan took out his wallet and handed her a business card. As she read the name her eyes flared for just a moment and then quickly narrowed, as if calculating how much the stakes had just gone up. "Mr. Nash, you're a very private and elusive man. How do I know it's really you?"

Donovan slipped out his driver's license.

"It's a pleasure to meet you." Amanda smiled as she returned his ID.

"Here's what I want," Donovan said as he slid his license back into his wallet. "I'm prepared to give you an exclusive interview about recent events, as well as access to the footage shot today of the *North Star* hijacking. Not the fabricated footage I understand is being shown on CNN, but actual high-resolution images taken by the state-of-the art systems aboard this aircraft. I won't agree to being photographed or recorded. This interview will be the old-fashioned kind where I talk and you take notes. That's my one and only offer. Oh, and the interview can last no longer than four and a half hours."

"That's an odd set of conditions, Mr. Nash. What is it you want from me?"

"Conduct the interview as you fly me to Los Angeles in your Falcon."

Amanda didn't as much as flinch. "It's possible, but I'll need to see the tape. If I think you have something of value, I'll call my office in New York."

Donovan expected as much. He switched on the monitor, selected the file from the menu, and hit play. The first image filling the screen was that of the *North Star* as the *da Vinci* streaked overhead. Amanda watched in silence, and Donovan waited for the final scene, the one that was going to get him to Los Angeles. Lauren had managed to capture the *North Star* as the ship ran aground. Even with no sound, the sight of the blue water beneath the ship suddenly becoming a brown reef and then the visual of the tanker steaming straight into it was journalistic gold. The high-resolution image captured the individual shock waves rippling through the steel of the hull as the *North Star* dug into the reef. Metal and water exploded into the air as the impact obliterated the outer hull. The sight of a solitary man racing toward the bow added scale to the enormity of the event.

Wordlessly, Amanda began dialing her phone, and as she did, Donovan pushed the button that would make her a copy of the file.

While he waited, he used his phone to listen to his voice mail in hopes that there was one from Erica. What he heard was his life falling apart around him. Peggy had called to report that CNN had called, as had most of the other major news outlets. There was also news that Congressman Brandt out of Oregon had appeared on a political talk show and gone on record suggesting all contracts with Eco-Watch be halted until the Justice Department could conduct a full investigation. There were three messages from members of Eco-Watch's board of trustees wanting to talk, as well as two major foundations, significant financial supporters. Donovan decided they could all screw themselves. Eco-Watch was circling the drain, and he wasn't sure he could stop the inevitable. In the face of losing William, nothing else really mattered. When he reached the last message without any word from Erica, all he felt was more fear.

CHAPTER THIRTY-EIGHT

"Where's Donovan?" Buck asked Lauren.

"He's headed back to Anchorage to try and minimize the fallout for Eco-Watch."

Buck started to swear, caught himself, and just shook his head in frustration. "Really? He heads back to the one place where there are probably people trying to kill him, and he went unescorted in an Eco-Watch helicopter?"

"There's nothing for him to do here. You and I can both contribute to this situation, so he left. He's a big boy, and it's not your problem."

"He is my problem," Buck replied.

"Look, I'm sorry you signed on in the middle of all this chaos between Donovan and me. We had a fight, I wanted him off the ship, and now he's gone." Her anger flared, and even though her words held a modicum of truth, Lauren hated every syllable of the latest lie she'd just told. Once again, Donovan was off doing whatever he wanted, and she was left trying to make excuses for him to maintain the deception. "He's probably with Michael, brainstorming with William on how best to contain the damage these people have inflicted."

"I'm just going to have to get used to Mr. Nash doing what he does."

"I couldn't." Lauren turned to distance herself from Buck. She hated the lies, especially when they were to Buck, a man who had once saved her life. She tried to take her mind off of Donovan. If he was doing any brainstorming, he was figuring out how to get to Erica.

Agent Martinson had gone below to assist her agents with the crime scene and when Lauren heard voices behind her, she turned to find Gunnison escorting a tall, thin man onto the bridge.

"Dr. McKenna, this is Captain Joseph Flemming from the *Orion*. I was just bringing him up to date on the plan."

"Doctor," Flemming took the hand that Lauren offered and they shook. "I've got to tell you, this is a hell of a thing you dreamed up."

"It's only one option," Lauren replied. She found Flemming's kind eyes and his smooth Texas accent charming. She turned to Gunnison as Davis and Hughes joined the conversation. "What's the latest status of the ship?"

"Creating a tsunami is now our only option. Our divers were able to get some photos of the inner hull. There are creases beginning to form. The architects say it's going to fail at the next low tide." Gunnison paused as he was handed a sheet of paper and he quickly scanned the text. "Final okay just came down from the governor. In Washington, the president just issued an executive order and the Pentagon has mobilized military assets to be at our disposal. They'll be working in conjunction with the Coast Guard to evacuate the people in all of the affected areas. We have mining experts as well as a team from the U.S. Geological Survey on the glacier right now to begin examining the ice. Their people are generating computer models to predict the aftermath of the wave. We've also linked up with the architectural team who designed the ship to help us understand how the wave will impact the compromised structural aspects of the *North Star*. It's a complicated job."

Captain Flemming drew himself up to his full six foot six, removed his watch cap, and ran his hand over the gray stubble on his scalp. "Dr. McKenna, let me see if I understand this. You're confident that these folks can create a tsunami to lift this crippled tanker free of the reef and push it out into the sound, in the belief that action will prevent an oil spill."

"In broad strokes, yes, that's the plan. It's simple physics, really."

"Hell of a thing." Flemming put his cap back on. "Okay, what is it you want from me?"

"I understand you were on the committee that helped Huntington Oil design this ship."

"You're very well informed, but that was years ago. We can all thank the late Meredith Barnes for the ten feet of space between the hulls, may she rest in peace. I can tell you, if we spill any oil today, it would have broken both their hearts."

"Both?" Lauren asked.

"Meredith Barnes and Robert Huntington. I've never seen two people more passionate about their respective jobs and the responsibility they held."

Lauren was instantly sorry she'd gone fishing for Flemming's impression of a younger Robert Huntington. She especially didn't need to hear how well he worked with Meredith. "We need you to help us figure out how this ship is going to react once it's free. Hopefully, you'll have the *North Star's* own engines to assist, as well as two supertugs tethered to the ship. Once the tanker is free from the reef, we want it to stay inside the oil containment area, not flung out into the sound, just in case it is leaking oil. Now, what will it take to accomplish that?"

"A goddamned miracle," Flemming bellowed. "The way I see it, you're going to need a forty- to fifty-foot rise in water to get a clean lift. This tsunami you're talking about is going to come charging down the inlet at about five hundred miles per hour. I don't have an advanced degree, but I know a little bit about mass and acceleration, and you're going to have a shitload of both. What's to stop this wave from capsizing the ship or shearing off the entire upper decks?"

"Fair questions to be sure. You're correct, the energy is traveling through the water at five hundred miles per hour, but most of the impulse will pass beneath the ship in deep water and be gone. At the reef, the ocean floor rises up from a steady one hundred seventy fathoms, to one forty, and then gradually continues to rise until it reaches the tanker. That's where the wave will form and it's *that* upward energy we're interested in controlling. By my calculations, this ship is going to be pushed up and off the reef and spun clockwise by the current due to the variations of the seafloor approaching the reef. Left to its own devices, the *North Star* will travel a little over five nautical miles before the kinetic energy has been expended. Now if we factor in the two tugs and full power from the tanker's engines, how much can we reduce that distance?"

"Half, maybe a little less if we're lucky. The tugs and the tanker will be traveling with the same wave. That's a great deal of mass to decelerate," Flemming said as he leaned over and once again studied the chart. "What's to stop it from spinning the other way, in which case we'll be slammed into the island?"

"I can promise you that won't happen, Olsen Island isn't in play," Lauren replied. "The ship will be rotating clockwise."

"Physics again?" Flemming arched an eyebrow.

"Yes. The initial upswell is hard to predict, as is the damage to the ship. It'll be a small miracle if the hull isn't leaking some oil, which in my mind makes it essential that the tanker is kept inside the containment area no matter what."

"That said, if it were me, I'd run the containment booms two miles south and hope for the best," Flemming replied.

One of the electrical engineers brought over from the *Orion* stuck his head out from underneath the console. "Captain Flemming, I've spliced everything back together, run the diagnostics, and it tells me you have bridge control of both engines and full rudder authority. The bow thrusters are destroyed, but everything else should work."

"Good work. Let's start 'em both up right now and make sure we have power." Flemming turned back to face Gunnison. "I'm told that all vessels except the two tugs will be moved out into the sound. They'll ride out the tsunami in the open water away from any islands."

"Yes, sir. We want to minimize the number of ships in the *North Star*'s immediate vicinity."

Lauren motioned for Buck to join her. "Captain, I'd like to introduce Howard Buckley, former Navy SEAL and Eco-Watch chief of security. He's going to explain how all of this can go wrong, and hopefully, what we can do to prevent that from happening."

"Captain." Buck shook Flemming's hand. "I gather you're going to be at the helm when we do this."

"That's my job."

"What do you have in mind for a crew?"

"I'll need a minimum of three. My engineer, and two lookouts on either side of the ship. I want everyone else off the *North Star*."

"Very good. You can select your own men, or if you're asking for volunteers, I'd happily join you. Now that Dr. McKenna has explained the science, let's talk about the intangibles. When the wave arrives, we'll know by the receding water levels off the bow as the sea draws back. My recommendation at this point is to be at idle power. It is possible that the receding water will simply finish the job the tide was doing and snap the ship in half. Captain, if that happens, then your job will be to use your engines to do all you can to keep what's left of the ship within the containment area. The tug captains have already received this briefing. All of you will be in constant radio contact with each other. Our fervent hope is that the wave does what Dr. McKenna thinks it will do and simply lift the tanker up and off the reef and slide it out into deeper water. At that point, you and the tugs swing into action and get this thing stopped."

"Where are you going to be, Dr. McKenna?" Flemming asked.

"I'd like to be on the bridge, but I have a feeling Mr. Buckley will overrule that."

"Dr. McKenna will be monitoring the situation from the Eco-Watch helicopter," Buck replied. "Her talents can best be utilized by her seeing the big picture."

"I need to make a call to the head office," Flemming said. "Timewise, how soon are we making this happen?"

Gunnison looked at Flemming, unblinking. "As soon as possible because this ship is coming apart as we speak."

CHAPTER THIRTY-NINE

Donovan waited as Amanda flipped back through the pages of notes she'd already taken. They were coming up on the four-hour mark of the interview, and Donovan felt drained. Before they'd departed Anchorage, he'd watched Garrick's video on CNN, which only strengthened his resolve to open up to Amanda. During the first hour and a half of the flight, they'd gone through the *da Vinci* video step-by-step, and now they were nearing the end of the one-on-one interview. Donovan felt pretty good about how it had gone so far. Amanda was smart, knowledgeable, and she possessed a remarkable ability to keep all the plates spinning while she dissected each element, unerringly returning to the next plate until she was completely satisfied. Part of the time she was a relentless interrogator, other times she backed off, relaxed, and acted like a close friend, a confidante. Donovan had been grilled many times, in many venues, and he'd always held his own, as he had so far today. Though compared to the others, he wouldn't wish four hours of Amanda Sullivan on anyone.

"So, Mr. Nash, let's go back to the point where Erica contacted Eco-Watch. I'd like to delve a little deeper into how a phone tip led her to join forces with Eco-Watch. The entire world is going to watch her being shot in the back as she flings herself off the ship— it's a powerful moment. Tell me more about her."

"No. I need to protect her identity from those who would do her harm," Donovan replied. "She helped us on grounds that she remains anonymous."

"Fair enough. Was she able to help you identify the people who were behind the elaborate efforts to destroy Eco-Watch?"

"She helped us get closer."

"Can you tell me what you felt at the moment she was shot as she leaped from the ship?"

"Only that I needed to try and save her." Donovan was relieved to be back on firm ground where he could tell the truth.

"Which you did, heroically, I might add. What was she like, as a person?"

"Hard to say, really," Donovan had been waiting for the question. Amanda was in best friend mode right now. "She was smart, but I think her overriding state of fear kept any of us from really getting to know her. It's ironic that despite her fear she did one of the bravest things I've ever seen when she jumped from that ship."

"The way I see it, she put her trust in you, and she was right to do so," Amanda said. "Now, when you say us, who do you mean exactly?"

"My wife, members of my staff. We all admired her immensely, but she was so guarded. I don't think we ever got to see the real person underneath, only that she put us in a position to avert a possible ecological catastrophe. If our work with Alyeska, the Coast Guard, the FBI, and the state of Alaska results in saving the *North Star*, then we all have Erica to thank."

"So you truly believe that the timely presence of the Eco-Watch jet and the boarding by your security forces via helicopter were what caused the hijackers to abandon the *North Star*."

"I do. Obviously, their intention was to cause an oil spill. Farther into Unakwik Inlet is a stretch of very shallow water. I believe that's where they were headed. If we hadn't shown up, I'm convinced they would have stayed aboard to make sure that's where the ship ran aground. Had they stayed the course, the hull would certainly have been ripped apart."

"Do you have anything else to add?"

"I think we've covered everything," Donovan replied.

"Okay." Amanda snapped her notebook shut and leaned back. "That's it. I thank you."

Donovan felt the tension begin to leave his body. They should touchdown in Santa Ana in less than fifteen minutes. "How soon is all this going to run?"

"We'll do a little editing, and I'll supply the voice-over to the video as soon as I can get to our Los Angeles studio. Once I'm finished, it will air on all of our broadcast outlets worldwide immediately, as well as our online platforms. As far as the print versions, some aspect of the interview will hit the bigger newspapers tomorrow, but I'm thinking maybe I'll hold on to the bulk of what we talked about and add the summation of the *North Star* hijacking to the story. Maybe even run it as a serialized exposé."

"Going for a second Pulitzer?"

Amanda replied with a smile, "I do have one more question that's totally off the record."

"You can always ask," Donovan said.

"You're a man with a jet at his disposal. We were sitting in it in Alaska. Why did you need my airplane to get to Los Angeles?"

"I run a nonprofit scientific research organization, so it's not like it's my personal jet. Plus, the crew was exhausted, well past the duty time limitations laid out for everyone's safety. With the current climate surrounding Eco-Watch, my security chief didn't want me to fly on the commercial airlines. I was in the process of waiting for a charter to be found when you showed up."

"Why the urgency to get to Los Angeles?"

"Not really urgent, there's an informal meeting tomorrow with the Eco-Watch board of directors. Most of the members are in town for the Strattons's memorial service, so we thought it best to convene and discuss recent events, and perhaps reach a consensus on further operations."

"As in shut Eco-Watch down?" Amanda's voice registered surprise at the thought.

"I'm sure that's one of the possibilities," Donovan replied. "We took some hits today and we may never recover."

"That would be a shame."

"Yes, it would. Eco-Watch is worth saving." Donovan made a grim face that almost touched on sadness, nodded, and then turned to look out the window. As he took in the sight of Los Angeles, his thoughts couldn't be further from Eco-Watch. All he could think about out there in the ocean of humanity of Southern California was Garrick. As things stood, he had no idea if William was still alive.

CHAPTER FORTY

"Okay, I can talk freely now." Lauren was up on top of the *North Star*'s superstructure where she and Donovan and FBI agent Martinson had had their earlier chat. It gave her privacy as well as excellent satellite reception for the phone she'd borrowed. Spencer, an old friend from her days at MIT, had called and urgently wanted to speak with her. "Where are you?"

"I'm on the glacier. We're about to depart and move to the holding area."

"How's it going?" Lauren could tell from his tone that he was worried. Spencer was a brilliant geologist, but at the end of the day he worked for the government, which also made him a bureaucrat, and risk was something to be avoided.

"I don't really know. I crunch data. I haven't tromped around on top of a glacier in a decade. I have a bad feeling about this. There are so many uncertainties, and everything was put together so fast."

"The timing sucks, but that's out of your control. No one has ever done this before. Think about it, you'll be the world's authority on shearing off the face of a glacier."

"No, I'll be the guy who sank the oil tanker in Prince William Sound. I do have a detailed geological survey of the Meares Glacier based on the fact that of all the glaciers in Alaska, this one is getting bigger, not smaller. It's also one of the most unstable. The underlying seismic activity is anyone's guess, but in the last eighteen months we've recorded half a dozen earthquake swarms emanating from the fault line that exists between the Aleutian plate and the

Pacific plate. The complexity of the deep crevasse structure is impossible to predict."

Lauren's geological knowledge was considerable. She knew as well as Spencer that there were vertical tubes called moulins that ran through all glaciers at these latitudes, they carried the meltwater through the glacier and typically ran all the way down to bedrock. "Spencer, you're overthinking the whole deal. Insert the explosives in the moulins in a way that stretches the width of the terminus, stand back, and detonate the explosives. Gravity does the rest; the seismic instability is a plus, I promise."

"We're using the moulins as planned, but their structural design bothers me. There was no way to drill a typical blast pattern in time, so we improvised. Using portable steam drills airlifted into place, we were able to bore enough shafts to connect four separate deep fissures. The blast should create one large section that will slide from the main glacier."

"That's genius, Spencer."

"I hope so. God knows we did the calculations a million times. We need thirty-five feet of the glacier to calve off the face. That gives us nearly one-point-eight million cubic yards of displacement. It's not the math that worries me, it's the intangibles."

"Think big, the last thing you want is a dud."

"I know it sounds easy, but this early in the season I'm worried the vents don't run deep enough, so the temptation I'm hearing from the demolition people is to err on the high side. We're using a hundred thirty-five thousand pounds of explosives—trust me, we won't have a dud. I'm worried the moulins intersect with deep creases we're not aware of, and we get expansion energy in directions we hadn't planned."

"Spencer, can you bring down enough of the glacier to create a fifty-foot wave surge at the tanker?"

"Absolutely."

Lauren saw Buck coming up the stairs, seemingly looking for her. "Bottom line it for me, Spencer. What's the worst scenario?"

"We could get a far larger wave than we wanted or a secondary wave that's every bit as big as the first."

"I think that's unlikely given the data I looked at from USGS as well as satellite imagery provided by NASA. Spencer, give me something beyond a gut feeling. What are the odds?"

"There's a fifteen to twenty percent chance of some calving beyond what we've projected."

"Can we both live with that? There's a hundred percent chance this tanker is going to break apart if we do nothing."

"We don't have a choice. I don't think we could stop this operation now if we wanted to. I have to go, they're waving us back into the choppers. I'll see you later."

Buck only had to gesture off to the port side of the ship to convey his message. She turned and saw the familiar blue-and-gold markings of the Eco-Watch helicopter as it approached. Their ride off the ship had arrived.

"It's time to go," Buck announced. "The *da Vinci* just left Anchorage. When they're in position, this is going to happen."

Lauren nodded. The bodies of the fallen had been transferred to a boat bound for a temporary morgue in Valdez. Special Agent Martinson and the FBI crime team as well as the State Police units had flown back to Anchorage hours ago. The core group of Aleyska and SERVS personnel were aboard the Sentinel-class Coast Guard Cutter *William Flores.* All the vessels out in the sound were positioned well outside the inlet with their bows pointed into the impending wave. Three HH-60 Coast Guard helicopters as well as air assets from the state of Alaska were maintaining a strict no-fly zone for five miles around the entire inlet. The growing numbers of media helicopters were issued strict orders to operate in an area that would give them a full view, but keep them out of the way.

A weapons expert from Elmendorf Air Force Base who was familiar with all of the *da Vinci's* latest equipment had been recruited to operate the complicated optics array. Also aboard in strictly an observational capacity was the governor of Alaska, as well as the head of the Department of Natural Resources. Two last minute additions included a member of the NOAA tsunami warning station who'd flown from Palmer, Alaska, and the CEO of Alyeska. Lauren hoped that after everything they'd done, the ship would come off the reef as planned.

Lauren fell in behind Buck as they entered the bridge. Captain Flemming's core group was in place. All three of the volunteers were men from the *Orion*. Flemming was at the helm, as was his chief engineer, who would handle the thirty-thousand-horsepower engines. Lookouts were stationed at both ends of the bridge to relay everything they saw back to Flemming. The captain was in radio contact with both tugs as well as the Coast Guard. One of the screens on the control panel was linked to the images the *da Vinci* would provide. As events unfolded, Flemming's view would be nearly omniscient.

"Doctor, I take it you're leaving?" Flemming asked as Lauren drew near.

"I'd stay if I could," Lauren said. "Buck and I will hover nearby providing you a play-by-play of the events. We'll check in once we're airborne."

"Very well. Thank you both for everything." Flemming shook hands with Buck and Lauren before returning to his post.

Lauren and Buck went down the stairs in silence. It struck Lauren how deserted the ship was. Besides she and Buck, there was only Captain Flemming and his crew of three. Once they were on the elevated catwalk walking toward the bow, Janie brought the Bell 407 overhead, made a steep turn that ended in a brief hover, then touched down gently on the helipad. Buck led the way down the last flight of steps, walked to the chopper, and opened the front passenger door for Lauren. Once she was in, he hopped into the back.

"Everyone strapped in and ready?" Janie asked over the intercom.

Lauren double-checked her harness and adjusted the volume on her headset. "I'm set."

"Ready back here," Buck replied.

"We've time for a quick briefing then. They've cleared the airspace for five miles around the tanker. No distractions or interference. It'll be just the *da Vinci* and us. Michael and I spoke earlier. We'll stay at five hundred feet or below. The rest of the airspace is his, so there's no chance of a collision. If you spot any other aircraft, they're not supposed to be here, and I need to know immediately. Dr. McKenna, once we're airborne, where would you like me to position the helicopter?"

"We need to stay near the ship. We'll have to watch the detonation via the *da Vinci's* cameras. Once the glacier calves, it will take three minutes for the wave to reach the *North Star*, far faster than we can fly. Our job is to offer an aerial point of view for Captain Flemming."

"Very good then. The *da Vinci* is ten minutes out; Michael and his crew won't need long to get into position. Let's set up a hover at five hundred feet and find the angle that suits you best."

"Michael and his crew?" Lauren asked. "Donovan's not flying this mission?"

"I guess not," Janie replied. "Michael seemed surprised when I asked him the same question. It seems no one has seen Mr. Nash since I dropped him in Anchorage."

Lauren was livid, she felt duped, and powerless. Donovan had left her to do his lying, and now he couldn't be bothered to show up for work. Had he found Erica? Were they watching this together on his laptop in some hotel?

Janie quickly keyed her microphone. "Eco-Watch zero four is lifting off tanker *North Star*. We'll be circling below five hundred feet, over."

Lauren opened her laptop, not surprised that her hands were shaking. She booted up the computer, using more force in her keystrokes than was necessary, but it was the only outlet for her rage she had at her disposal. Moments later, she was linked up via encrypted satellite feed so she could see exactly what the *da Vinci* was seeing. The synthetic-aperture radar image was already being transmitted. It showed the tanker with the helicopter just lifting off the deck. As Janie climbed, Lauren could see both tractor tugs idling a safe distance off the starboard side. A slack line was attached from one tug to the stern of the tanker. The other tug was connected to the bow. Each tug had over ten thousand horse power and was capable of delivering over two hundred thousand pounds of pull. Combined with the *North Star's* thirty thousand horsepower it was hoped that not only would the tugs be able to halt the rotation caused by the wave, but also a combined fifty thousand horsepower would bring the entire ship dead in the water within the two miles of containment booms that encircled the tanker.

The wind was still out of the south, as were the incoming seas. Both wind and waves were right into the *North Star's* stern, which was good. Any force that could slow down the tanker was welcome. Janie circled the ship, and Lauren made a quick radio check with Captain Flemming.

"I think I'd like to hover just off the starboard quarter of the bow," Lauren said. "If we point the helicopter north, up the inlet, we'll see the wave coming, and the ship and tugs will be in full view below us. Once the *North Star* starts to move, I'd like us to stay with the ship and remain in the same relative position."

"Will do," Janie pivoted the chopper until Lauren nodded her approval.

"Too bad we can't see the glacier from here," Buck said. "That'd be worth seeing."

"You can watch it here." Lauren positioned her laptop so all three of them could see what happened when the explosives went off. "How far out is the *da Vinci*?"

"They're inside the no-fly zone setting up at a thousand feet," Janie replied. "When they're ready, and all the cameras are rolling, they'll give the word."

Buck leaned over the seat to look at the computer screen. Janie's eyes darted from the instrument panel to the computer and then back again. Overhead, Lauren saw the *da Vinci* fly past them toward the glacier. She still couldn't believe that Donovan wasn't aboard. The radio chatter between the tugs and the tanker died out, as well as communication between the tanker and the Coast Guard ships. The detonation itself would be done via remote control from the back of the *da Vinci*.

"Eco-Watch zero one is in position, all telemetry up and running," Michael broadcast.

"Eco-Watch zero four in position," Janie added.

"This is Coast Guard cutter *William Flores*. All parties are safe and accounted for. The area is secure for detonation."

Lauren looked to the north. The glacier itself was obscured by the terrain, but the view from the *da Vinci* was crisp and clean. She could feel her pulse quicken as the next broadcast broke the silence on the frequency.

"Here we go then," Michael said. "In five, four, three, two, one—we have detonation."

On the computer screen, the first explosions threw up a geyser of snow and ice hundreds of feet into the air, followed by all two hundred fifty-two explosions in a carefully orchestrated sequence. Debris peppered the ocean in front of the glacier and thousands of small chunks of ice fell into the frigid water. A cloud of smoke and vaporized snow hung over the glacier and even above the beating blades of the helicopter, Lauren heard the massive explosion as it echoed off the surrounding hills.

"Wow!" Buck exclaimed.

Lauren frowned. She understood there would be a short delay after the charges went off, but so far nothing had happened.

All three of them stared at the computer screen waiting for the glacier to react in some way, but it sat motionless, as if it had shrugged off all of man's attempts to impose his will on the million-year-old river of ice. At first a small sinkhole formed, then it grew larger and a fissure opened.

"Oh, no," Lauren said as the crevice began to race the width of the glacier.

"What is it?" Buck asked.

"It's too much," Lauren said as the last of the friction gave way and gravity pulled a sixty-foot section of glacier into the ocean.

The resulting explosion of water hid the beginning of a wave that formed underwater. Below the surface, millions of square yards of water were instantly displaced by the ice, and the shockwave that formed began to race the only direction it could, south toward the *North Star*. Lauren keyed her microphone. "All hands, the wave is going to be twice the size we anticipated. I repeat, the wave is going to be almost a hundred feet high when it reaches the tanker."

"Oh, shit!" Janie yelled as she snapped her head around and then desperately tried to turn the helicopter.

Lauren caught the movement outside the same time Janie did. There was no time to avoid the hundreds of startled ducks frantically winging away from the deafening roar of the explosion.

Lauren winced as the birds slammed against the helicopter. Dozens of collisions peppered the fuselage, each as loud as a gunshot. With each hit, the Plexiglas spider-webbed, but held together. Bells erupted, and Lauren could feel the vibrations in the airframe change. Red lights flashed on the panel, and the dull roar from the turbine engine began winding down.

"We've lost the engine," Janie yelled. "We're going down. Brace for impact!"

CHAPTER FORTY-ONE

Putting Amanda Sullivan behind him, Donovan walked into Signature Flight Support at John Wayne Airport. He discovered the BMW X5 that he and Erica had borrowed still parked in the lot of the executive terminal. He'd immediately called William's phone and Garrick's damaged voice instructed him to go to the Stratton house, alone. After the short drive, Donovan pulled into John Stratton's garage and parked the BMW. He had no choice but to face Garrick one-on-one. As he slid out of the SUV, the weight of Erica's pistol in his hand was reassuring.

Donovan opened the door that led into the house and found a body lying facedown in the hallway. A pool of blood had formed around the head. One of William's bodyguards. In the instant his eyes had been drawn to the floor, Nikolett appeared behind him and pressed the barrel of a pistol against the skin of his neck.

"Drop the gun. Put your hands up and slowly walk toward the kitchen."

Donovan stepped around the corpse, and Nikolett prodded him down the hallway. As they walked through the opulent living room Donovan saw another body on the floor, William's other bodyguard. Garrick and Nikolett's entry must have been swift and brutal. Donovan remembered they'd been here once before and knew the layout of house. They probably had their own set of keys. William's bodyguards hadn't stood a chance.

"In the den. Garrick is waiting for you."

Donovan entered the den and found William sitting in a chair in the middle of the room. His wrists appeared to be tied behind his back, his face swollen and bloody. Standing over him was Garrick Pearce, the man Donovan had sworn to kill. Garrick looked gaunt, almost hollow. His eyes were unmoving orbs. He could blink, but as Erica had explained, he had to turn his head if he wanted to look at something. Donovan could see the scar tissue from acid burns on his face and neck and hands. Garrick looked twenty years older than he was.

"Robert, you made good time. William and I were just talking about old times."

"Takes a real man to hit someone tied in a chair, but then you always were kind of a pussy."

Garrick's expression didn't change. It couldn't, but his anger was obvious as he stepped forward and swung at Donovan's jaw.

Donovan turned his head, the blow grazing his cheek. In one swift motion he swung and nailed Garrick in the mouth and nose with his fist. Blood exploded from Garrick's face and he staggered away. Donovan's smile was short lived as Nikolett delivered a savage blow to his lower back, collapsing him to the carpet.

Garrick held tissues to his face and stared blankly at Donovan. "I'll give you that one. Now I'm going to ask you what I've been asking William. I've been going over his phone log. He had an incoming call from an unknown number just before we arrived. He then called Stephanie. Why? Where is she?"

"She's in Europe." Donovan tried to match the lie he thought William would have told. A small nod from his mentor told him he'd guessed correctly.

"Bullshit!" Garrick yelled. "Where is she?"

"Why are you doing this, Garrick? Why all the killing?"

"It's a war."

"You weren't at war with the clinic in Germany. They helped you regain your sight. Why kill them?"

"Tel Aviv wanted to shut the place down. We took the job as payment for services rendered. That was strictly business."

"What is it you think you've accomplished by spilling a million barrels of oil into Prince William Sound?" Donovan continued. "You and I both know Meredith would be horrified."

"Meredith would love what I've done. Commercial fishing boats are under siege all over the world, being recalled by their owners. Fishermen are dying from improvised explosive devices planted in their gill and drift nets. We've created a frenzy. Two ships from Japan's whaling fleet have already been attacked and sunk. Norway and Iceland have reported damaging attacks as well. Have you read about the vigilantes? All over the world people are hunting down and killing poachers. As for Alaska, when the ship finally does rupture, there will have been time for the entire world to catch up to the fact that Eco-Watch was responsible. The media will have had hours and hours to run the video I made for them. Have you seen it yet?"

"Yes."

"In the end, there will never be any drilling in ANWR, and for that, I'm so very happy. I think Meredith would be too. You, on the other hand, will probably be arrested, and good luck with all those Senate investigations and hearings. I hear they're a bitch, especially when they discover who you really are. Eco-Watch is on life support and the plug is about to be pulled."

"You're right. You've brought about the end to Eco-Watch. There's probably nothing I can do to stop that now, but the minute Eco-Watch is gone, the fear you've created will end. You'll have changed nothing, certainly nothing lasting, and that's why Meredith hated your tactics. Blood for headlines, and then, ultimately, failure."

"The beauty of my plan is that once Eco-Watch is gone, I'm going to tell the world who you are. The world will never forget Eco-Watch, because they'll never forget about the ruthless billionaire Robert Huntington who killed Meredith Barnes, and then faked his death to escape his crimes."

"You always believed that the end justifies the means. That's what Meredith hated about you, why she condemned you."

"She didn't hate me. You lured her away from me with your wealth, so you could kill her. Meredith hated you. I can tell you from experience that there's a certain clarity that forms when you're locked up. She experienced that in her final days when she was held prisoner. She saw you for who you really were."

"We were engaged," Donovan said. "You never knew that, did you? I'd asked her to marry me, and she said yes. I wasn't her murderer. I was going to spend the rest of my life with her."

"You're making that up," Garrick snapped. "There was no way she was ever going to marry you."

"The picture you left on the bridge of the *North Star* was taken when we told William we were engaged. You can see the ring."

"She didn't wear a ring. You weren't engaged. The media would have been all over that announcement."

"She didn't wear it in public for that very reason. She didn't want to pull the focus away from the Costa Rican summit, which was only six weeks away. We were going to wait until afterward to make our announcement."

"Where's the picture?"

"You stole them, didn't you?" Donovan slowly pulled the photo out of his wallet and handed it over. "We were in Washington. We'd just had dinner with William. If you look close, you can see the ring."

Garrick struggled with his damaged eyes, but when he angrily flipped the picture to the floor, Donovan knew he'd seen the diamond. "Garrick, I didn't kill her. I loved her. I still love her, and just like you, I try to honor her memory and all she stood for each and every day. We're not all that much different, you and I. Look, you have money now. Use it for things that would make Meredith proud of you. It'll never bring her back, but it keeps her memory alive. Live a life that's worthy of being linked to hers."

"We're nothing alike, I can assure you. Locked up in that hellhole of a prison, I examined every second of your existence with her. It's obvious you killed her. You betrayed her, left her to be held prisoner, and then allowed her to be executed. Where were you when all of that was happening?"

"I was there, searching for her."

"You were holed up in the most expensive hotel suite in San Jose. You never saw the brutality she no doubt suffered, and you certainly didn't see the expression on her face when they pulled the trigger. You didn't see the life slip from her eyes as she toppled over and bled on the floor."

"And neither did you."

"I've been where she was, in a prison with no hope. She and I are alike in that respect. You, on the other hand, have known nothing but luxury."

Donovan could see that Garrick was getting himself worked up; he was pacing back and forth, gesturing with the heavy, forty-five-caliber pistol. "I did everything I could. I had the money, I practically had to smuggle it into the country, but I had it, and was willing to pay. I'd have given it all away to save her life."

"That's what never made sense! You were Robert Huntington. You could do anything you wanted, and what you wanted was exactly what happened. Meredith died, and the world lost its greatest voice against industrialists like you, like John Stratton. Meredith hated you people and you killed her." Garrick stopped pacing, stretched out his arm, and placed the muzzle of the pistol to William's temple. "I'm going to show you how it feels to be helpless, for you to actually witness the pain of a loved one's last moment alive."

CHAPTER FORTY-TWO

"We've lost power!" Janie said as she battled the crippled helicopter.

"We have to make it to the ship!" Lauren yelled, terrified as the helicopter pivoted three hundred sixty degrees as it plunged downward. She saw water, sky, and then steel. If they ditched, it would put them directly in the path of the huge wave they'd created.

Janie used what little control she had and arrested their free fall only seconds before they hit the deck. The landing skids of the Bell crumpled from the force of the impact and absorbed much of the energy. The main rotor blades buckled and sliced into the deck, instantly exploding into pieces of deadly shrapnel. The fuselage whipped around, and Lauren saw they were hurtling toward the towering six-story-high superstructure of the *North Star*. As the steel wall filled the shattered windscreen, the battered body of the helicopter made one last partial rotation. The tail boom hit first. The passenger compartment slammed into the crumpled boom, tipped on its side, and came to a rest.

Hanging by her harness, Lauren was enveloped by the unmistakable smell of fuel. At first she thought they'd ripped a hole in the deck of the tanker until drops of jet fuel began to drip from above.

"Get out!" Buck yelled, dropping to the deck, then turning and ripping open the door next to Lauren. "Everyone out! Now!"

Lauren released her straps and fell into Buck's waiting arms. He quickly placed her on her feet and then repeated the process with Janie. Lauren could see blood on Janie's forehead, her eyes were closed, and she was cradling what was clearly a dislocated elbow. Then she heard the whoosh of the fuel igniting.

"We have to go up!" Lauren could see enough of the ocean to realized that the sea was pulling back from the reef; the wave was almost on them. With Buck carrying Janie, the three of them escaped the heat from the fire and found the first flight of stairs. Lauren led the way, taking the steps two at a time. She reached the first landing, turned, and tried to make it to the hatch that would allow them to reach safety inside the ship. She moved three steps before the rising heat from the furiously burning helicopter drove her backward.

"Go to the next level!" Buck urged.

When Lauren turned toward the bow of the *North Star,* she saw that the underwater shockwave had reached shallow water. The wave was beginning to build as the surge slowed, the water behind had nowhere to go but up. The water was already higher than the deck and growing. She felt the ship began to rise as tons of water surged beneath the hull. The bow rode up to meet the surge and then vanished under the onslaught of the monstrous wave. Lauren fought the urge to scream. The wall of water was going to strip them off the ship like insects.

CHAPTER FORTY-THREE

Nikolett's head snapped backward and a plume of bloody mist exploded from her shattered skull. Garrick flinched, his lack of peripheral vision forcing him to turn toward Nikolett as she collapsed. Garrick pivoted toward the door, raised his pistol, and fired two shots at a figure in the hallway. Without hesitation, Donovan lunged forward toward Garrick as the sound of the gunshots filled the room. Garrick spun back toward William and pressed the barrel of his pistol to William's temple. Donovan managed to reach out and slapped his hand on top of Garrick's forty-five just as Garrick pulled the trigger. The flesh between Donovan's thumb and forefinger pinched beneath the hammer, stopping it from striking the firing pin. Donovan crashed into Garrick as both men fought for control of the gun. With one hand still attached to the gun, Donovan used his free hand to hit Garrick as hard as he could in the face. Fresh blood spewed from Garrick's nose and mouth. He punched Garrick in the face twice more, but Garrick rolled away, and in the process the pistol ripped a chunk of flesh from Donovan's hand. Garrick fumbled to clear the hammer, and Donovan turned and dove toward Nikolett. He reached her corpse as Garrick aimed through bloody and swollen eyes and fired wide. Donovan picked up Nikolett's pistol, pointed it at Garrick, and pulled the trigger. The pistol bucked in his hand, and Donovan watched as a bloody hole formed in the center of Garrick's chest. Donovan kept firing until Garrick sank to the floor and his newly repaired eyes went sightless.

Leading with his gun, he kicked the forty-five out of Garrick's dead hand, stepped over Garrick's body, and went to the doorway. There was a figure lying on the floor.

Donovan sank to his knees and brushed the blond hair away from Erica's face. He saw an entry wound in her abdomen, the blood pooling beneath her. "Stay with me, Erica, don't leave me."

Erica moved her lips, and Donovan leaned down to listen. Her words hardly more than a whisper.

"I couldn't find you. Our promise to each other—finish job. Remember?"

"I remember," Donovan said as his eyes welled up with tears.

"Are they dead?"

"Yes, you saved us." Donovan found her hand and clutched it with his own, remembering her solemn promise that if something happened to him, she'd kill Nikolett and Garrick.

She winced as if in pain as she struggled to speak. "Are you really him?"

"Yes."

"You changed. I like you," Erica said, her voice fading as her breathing became more labored. "My bag—strap, files. Neptune Trident. In German."

Donovan heard her last breath slowly escape, her grip on his hand faded and then there was nothing but silence. His eyes filled with tears as he gently checked her motionless pupils and felt for a pulse that he knew wasn't there. He closed her eyelids, leaned down, and kissed her for the last time. He had no idea how she'd gotten from the hospital in Anchorage to this hallway, but he felt an overwhelming sense of gratitude mixed with a depth of loss that he couldn't begin to absorb. He wiped away his tears. She'd given him the password for the files. Her last act had been to give him the information he might need to protect himself. An open sob escaped from deep inside and he shook his head against the unbelievable anguish. He sat with her, collecting himself, then finally found the strength to get up and go to William.

Donovan removed the duct tape they'd used to secure his

hands, then took him in his arms to steady his old friend. He rubbed William's wrists to get the circulation to return and tried to judge William's condition.

"I'll be all right," William said, his voice shaky. "Who's in the doorway? Who shot Nikolett?"

"Erica," Donovan said. "She's dead."

William's head sunk at the news. "Garrick arrived only moments after her warning. I was able to call Stephanie and Abigail. Are they safe?"

"As far as I know. You need an ambulance. How bad did they hurt you?" Donovan remembered the burns on Erica's skin, proof of the violence Garrick and Nikolett could inflict.

"I'm fine," William managed to stand, still massaging his wrists. "We have work to do and we need to make sure we have our stories straight before we call the police."

"I agree." Donovan was thankful that William was up and thinking.

"First and foremost, we tell the police we don't know who these people are. For the rest of the story, we can pretty much stick with the truth. This guy had some kind of vendetta. If we let the facts speak for themselves, they should steer the police toward the connection between John's investments in the Brazilian plant that ended up blinding Garrick. The authorities need to believe that John was Garrick's target. Since Eco-Watch was also important to John, it became another target, as did I. From there I think the investigation will go in the direction we want it to go. Garrick's computer and briefcase are over there. They also have a car in the garage. We need to search it and make sure there's nothing that ties to Robert Huntington. We'll stash everything we find in John's safe and dispose of it later."

"William, you take care of Garrick's things in here. Garrick mentioned a jump drive, see if you can find one. I'll go check out their car. Once we're finished, we'll call 911. Then I have another call to make."

"Who?" William asked.

"Amanda Sullivan." Donovan pulled her business card from his pocket.

"The reporter? Why do you have her card?"

"I already gave her an interview. Now I'm giving her the final installment. The world needs to see what happened here."

Donovan found Garrick's rental car, and careful not to leave any fingerprints, he removed two pieces of luggage from the trunk and thoroughly searched them both. He found nothing of consequence. Confident that any of the incriminating evidence against him was in Garrick's briefcase and laptop, he replaced both items and rejoined William in the den.

"Everything is locked in the safe," William announced upon Donovan's return. "I found a jump drive in Garrick's pocket. I think we're good. It's time to call the police."

"Do it." Donovan nodded, walked away, and dialed Amanda's direct number.

"Mr. Nash," Amanda said as she answered her phone, "I didn't expect to hear from you so soon."

"I'm offering you another exclusive interview."

"I'm listening."

"The two people responsible for all of the eco-atrocities are dead. I also found Erica. Are you interested?"

"Where are you? And how much is this going to cost me?"

"Nothing. The same terms as before, an old-fashioned pencil-and-paper interview."

"With Erica as well as you?"

"Erica's dead."

"Can I have exclusive use of the additional footage being taken from your airplane in Alaska?"

"You already have it."

"I'm talking about the footage being shot right now."

"What footage?" Donovan asked.

"They're getting ready to try and refloat the tanker. Do we have a deal?"

"Yes, we're at the Stratton estate in Laguna Beach."

"Mr. Nash, I'm on my way—and you need to turn on a television."

Donovan grabbed the remote control, found CNN, and took a moment to orient himself. The grainy picture was the *North Star*, no doubt taken from a long lens mounted on a helicopter circling miles away. The image shook slightly due to the distance, but it was clear enough to see what was happening. The Eco-Watch helicopter was circling overhead. The view jumped to the glacier where plumes of snow and ice were flung into the sky. Moments later came the sound of an unseen explosion.

"What was that?" William asked.

"They just blew the glacier. Lauren came up with the idea to create a tsunami to free the tanker. I had no idea they'd do it so quickly."

"What's happening?" William asked. "It looks like there's something wrong with the helicopter."

"Oh, no," Donovan whispered. The helicopter began flying erratically, twisting and descending. Shocked, he could only watch as the Bell 407 lost altitude and crash landed on the deck of the ship where it skidded and spun until it buckled and crashed into the *North Star's* superstructure. From that distance he couldn't see much more than exploding rotor blades and parts flung from the twisted wreckage. The thick black smoke twisted upward, leaving no doubt that it was on fire.

"Oh, dear God!" William said. "The wave."

A mountain of water had begun to build in front of the ship. Donovan remembered Lauren's estimates that the wave would be around fifty feet high. The one that had formed was twice that, and as it topped out, it curled over and completely enveloped the *North Star*. When the wave crashed downward it exploded, sending millions of tons of seawater into the sky.

Donovan held his breath as both tugs and the tanker vanished beneath a mountain of water. He felt that he was being crushed, that he couldn't breathe. In his mind, Janie, and whoever was in the helicopter had just perished, and the only people he could imagine onboard would be Lauren and Buck. Donovan felt mortally wounded. His legs went weak and he staggered backward. William guided him to a chair. He was numb, in shock, he didn't know what to feel or think. Erica was dead, and now all that registered was the immeasurable fear that he'd just watched his wife die as well.

CHAPTER FORTY-FOUR

"Lauren!" Buck yelled above the roar of the wave as it raced toward them, completely engulfing the front half of ship as it did.

She turned and found that Buck had opened the hatch on one of the enclosed lifeboats. She only had seconds. Buck pushed Janie into the fully enclosed hull, reached out and took Lauren's hand just as she felt herself being pulled away as the bow rose skyward. Lauren kicked and pushed, praying that Buck wouldn't let go. If he did, in a matter of seconds, she'd be swept over the railing and off the stern of the ship to plummet sixty feet into the icy ocean. She reached out with her free hand and clutched the opening as Buck grabbed the back of her waterlogged coat, and they both tumbled inside the boat. Lauren lay on the floor next to Janie, coughing up water, knowing her shoulder was probably separated.

Buck slammed the hatch shut just as the sound of tearing steel rose above the roar of the water. Then he was thrown hard into the side as the forward davit ripped free, and the hull of the tiny boat slammed against the steel of the ship.

"Everyone hold on to something!" Buck threw himself on top of Janie and gathered Lauren in close.

Lauren clung to Buck, who in turn protected Janie. The noise was deafening as the full force of the wave hit, and Lauren felt the G forces press her against the floor as the lifeboat began to tumble wildly inside the hundred-foot wave.

The three of them were slammed repeatedly against the rigid hull of the boat. All Lauren could think about was the Coast Guard seaman who explained to her that the lifeboat could survive in any sea state. Her tortured shoulder felt like it was on fire as the boat rolled over and over in the rushing water. She wondered what it would feel like if the hull failed and they were flung into the ocean.

Caught in another onslaught of tumbling, Buck lost his leverage, letting Lauren slide away from him. Her legs whipped around, and she hit something hard with her head before Buck once again gathered her close. She felt the small boat shoot up and down, bobbing in the remainder of the wave until it slowly righted itself as the tsunami raced past.

Curled up on the floor of the lifeboat, Lauren felt something warm trickle down her scalp toward her ear. Then her entire torso began to shake from both the freezing cold and the adrenaline surging in her system. She touched her head and her fingers came away covered in blood. She lay next to Janie and could see that her heart was beating through a vein in her neck. Buck was conscious; he, too, was bloodied, but they were all still alive.

Buck tried to stand and immediately doubled over, holding his midsection. "That's not good," he said with a groan.

When Lauren tried to move, her shoulder responded with pain that nearly took her breath away. The portholes were well above where she lay. It seemed the worst was over. They were afloat. She could feel the hull beneath her rock and sway. Favoring her shoulder, and careful not to step on Janie, Lauren managed to get to her feet so she could see out of the porthole.

Not far away, she spotted one of the Coast Guard cutters racing toward them, its sharp bow plowing through the still heaving sea. She staggered to the other side and took in the scene. A quarter mile away was the *North Star*, water streaming off the massive ship, but it was afloat and looked to be in one piece. Hard to tell exactly where they'd ended up, but she could see they were still inside the containment booms. Lauren saw that the tugs had hauled in the slack from their lines. Churning froth from the tanker's own massive props told her that Captain Flemming was in the process of bringing his ship to a stop.

"What do you see?" Buck asked.

"There's a cutter bearing down on us. The tanker's floating in one piece. It might have worked after all," Lauren said as she moved down and sat next to him. "How are you doing?"

"Busted ribs," Buck groaned, "and my leg is messed up."

"The Coast Guard will be here shortly. Janie's out of it, but she's alive," Lauren said through chattering teeth.

"You're hypothermic. Take off your wet coat."

"I can't, my shoulder won't move."

"You're bleeding."

"We all are, but we're alive," Lauren used her good hand to reach out and cradle Buck's face. "I don't know how you managed to get me inside this boat, but you did. Thank you."

Buck took Lauren's hand into his and they entwined fingers. She heard the beating sound of a helicopter overhead, but neither of them made an effort to move. They sat, spent, wounded, safe in the closeness of the moment, a bond of survival that only people who'd been there could ever know. They waited in silence for the rescue swimmer to open the hatch from the outside.

CHAPTER FORTY-FIVE

"The *da Vinci*," Donovan said the words like an electric shock had passed through him. He raced to John's desk. His hands shook as he brought up the secure website and typed in the password that would allow him to tap into the real-time satellite feed being streamed from the *da Vinci*. William stood at his side as the system went through the protocols and finally displayed a small video image.

Donovan expanded it to full size and realized that they were looking through the spinning rotor blades of a Coast Guard Jayhawk helicopter hovering over a blaze-orange lifeboat. The top hatch was open and they were easing someone out into the basket. Janie. She had on a neck brace, an inflatable cast on her left arm and bandages on her head, but she was conscious and moving. She was hoisted up, and as soon as she was aboard, the basket was lowered again. A mane of auburn hair popped through the hatch, and an involuntary gasp escaped Donovan's chest. His eyes clouded with tears. Lauren was alive, though her shoulder was wrapped, pinning her right arm to her torso. As soon as she was away, the process was repeated. This time Buck emerged, his leg was in a cast, and through the high-resolution capability of the optics, Donovan could see he was in great pain.

The warble of multiple sirens grew closer and then stopped as the police arrived outside. Moments later, officers with their guns drawn charged into the room.

Escorted out of the den by the arriving police, Donovan was placed in the dining room, one of the few rooms downstairs that didn't contain a body. When the paramedics arrived, a quick check confirmed five dead. As a precaution, William was loaded on a stretcher, headed to the hospital for a full evaluation. A paramedic bandaged Donovan's bloody hand while a detective named Gonzales began taking Donovan's statement.

"Who's in charge here?" a man in a suit asked as he walked into the room.

"I'm Detective Gonzales, Orange County sheriff's office. Who are you?"

"I'm FBI Special Agent Christopher Hudson. This crime scene is now under federal jurisdiction. Detective, I'll need to ask you and your men to assemble outside," Hudson said. Then he spotted Donovan. "You get around."

"I could say the same about you. How come you're here?"

"I'm working with the task force we set up to find these people."

"Wait a minute," Gonzales held up his hands. "You can't walk into my crime scene and start shooting the shit with an eyewitness. I'm going to need to see a badge and verify this with my bosses."

"I understand," Hudson handed Gonzales his credentials. "We'll get all this squared away outside. Let's let my crime-scene people do their job."

"Can I have my phone?" Donovan asked. "Oh, and by the way, Amanda Sullivan is on her way over. I've promised her an in-depth interview."

Hudson turned to Gonzales. "Let's make Mr. Nash comfortable. He's not a federal suspect at this time, so I think we could return his phone."

"Hayes!" Gonzales called out to another detective. "FBI's taking over. Get all the men outside and someone bring me Nash's phone."

"You've seen what happened in there?" Donovan asked Hudson.

"Just briefly, I also managed to speak with Mr. VanGelder as they were putting him in an ambulance. He gave me the quick-and-dirty version of what happened. You're a lucky man."

"How'd you get here so fast?" Donovan asked.

"You met Agent Martinson in Alaska? She uncovered evidence that led us to believe the suspects chartered a jet out of Anchorage to come here. We've been trying to track their movements ever since. When the call came in for a possible shooting at the Stratton estate, I was already at John Wayne Airport. I'm just the first, there are a lot more agents on their way, I promise."

"What about the other hijackers who were aboard the *North Star*? Have you found them?"

"FBI agents in Anchorage found the abandoned helicopter they used to escape from the tanker. There were five bodies aboard. They'd all been shot. One was killed by multiple gunshots, probably from your chief of security as they departed the tanker. The others were shot at point-blank range. According to the footage taken by your plane, there were still two people unaccounted for, my guess is the two people lying dead in there cleaned house before they left Alaska."

"You're saying it's over? All the people are accounted for?"

"It's too soon to say for certain, but every person captured on film in Hawaii or video in Alaska is in a body bag." Hudson said. "I do have to ask. Why go for media coverage now? From what I saw in Hawaii, you were dead set against giving any kind of statement."

"I'm trying to save Eco-Watch from what those bastards did to us. They used the media, so I will too, and I have better sources as well as the luxury of the last word."

"The woman in the hall, she's the one you saved in Alaska."

"She saved William. Hell, she saved everyone." Donovan could feel his throat constrict and tears begin to form. "I'd be very grateful if one day you'd explain to me how she got all the way from an emergency room in Anchorage to that doorway, in time to kill a professional assassin."

"I can do that," Hudson answered.

"Thank you," Donovan said as Hayes opened an evidence bag and handed him the phone. Donovan turned it on. "Now, if you'll excuse me I need to make some calls."

"Take it outside, but don't leave the premises. Someone will take your statement, then you and I need to talk."

Donovan did as he was told. As he walked, he dialed Stephanie.

"Donovan, is it you?" Stephanie asked.

"It's me, it's over. William is okay. They took him to the hospital as a precaution, but he'll be fine."

"What about Garrick?"

"Dead."

"Did you kill him?"

"Yes."

"Are you okay?"

"Probably not," Donovan answered truthfully, though it had nothing to do with Garrick. He had pushed himself from paralyzing grief until he was now running on adrenaline and rage. Later, when both were spent, he would start paying the price for all that had happened in the last few days. In the background, he heard the unmistakable announcement that a commercial flight was boarding. "You're at an airport. Where are you taking my daughter?"

"Not on an unsecured line," Stephanie replied. "This was where I was headed when we last spoke. It's part of an escape plan Lauren and I had in place. We're boarding, I need to go."

"You don't have to run. It's over," Donovan said.

"I just spoke to Lauren. She called me from the back of a Coast Guard helicopter. I brought her up to speed on what was happening."

"So all she knows is that Garrick is holding William hostage, and I'm on my way to deal with the situation."

"I'm sorry, that's all I knew at the time. I have to respect her wishes."

Donovan closed his eyes and took a deep breath while he considered the implications. He'd wanted to be the one to explain the situation to Lauren, but that was no longer an option. He didn't blame Stephanie. He'd only wished it had gone differently. "How did she sound?"

"She's tired, hurt, and more than a little scared. Donovan, I'm sorry, but I have to go. I'll call you later."

Donovan heard the beep from his phone that alerted him to an incoming call. A quick check told him the number was blocked. "I have another call. I'm glad you were here, Stephanie."

"You'd be there for me."

Donovan jumped to the other call and immediately heard the muffled sound of a helicopter's rotor blades. "Lauren, is that you?"

"Can you hear me?" Lauren asked.

"I can hear you. I saw what happened. How bad is everyone hurt?"

"First things first. Stephanie told me that William had been taken hostage, that you were in Los Angeles. Is William okay?"

"He's fine. It's over," Donovan glanced around to make sure no one could hear him. "Garrick and Nikolett are dead. Call Stephanie and tell her not to leave."

"Are you crazy?" Lauren replied. "Are they all dead, every single last one? Can you guarantee me that all the people who attacked Eco-Watch are dead?"

Donovan felt himself deflate under Lauren's blistering tirade, made even worse by the fact that she was right. "No, there are no guarantees, but the risk is negligible."

"Not good enough."

"Look, Stephanie and Abigail and I can fly up to Anchorage in the morning. We can sort through all of this tomorrow."

"Donovan, I can't. I won't." Lauren paused as if searching for the right words. "Once again you deserted me, and I had to clean up your mess. Nothing's changed. I was almost killed today, I'm hurt, I'm upset, and I can't see you now or anytime soon."

Donovan lowered his head in defeat. She wasn't wrong and her anger wasn't misplaced. Arguing with her now would be pointless. A judicious retreat might at least keep things from getting worse. "I understand."

"Is Erica with you? Did you find her?"

"She was the one who warned William, allowing Stephanie and Abigail to escape. She showed up in Los Angeles on her own. She saved us."

"So she's there? That's just perfect. I don't know what kind of arrangement you made with her, but here's the one I'm making. Tell her I have her jump drive with the files she took from Germany. If she so much as breathes a word about your past, or in any other way jeopardizes my daughter's present or future well-being, I'll open the files and then turn them over to the agency that'll do her the most harm."

"She died saving William and me," Donovan said. He then severed the connection and any possibility that his white-hot rage would cause him to say something he'd regret. He didn't know what was causing him the most pain, the fact that Erica was gone, or the continued deterioration of his marriage. Everything he'd done had been an act of preservation, trying to save his wife and family, their future, as well as his past. Lauren had just done the same thing with her threat against Erica. How had he and Lauren become so far apart, when they really wanted the same things?

"Are you okay?" Hudson said as he approached. "We're ready to take your statement."

"I'll survive." Donovan replied with an empty shrug, though the temptation to give in to the staggering pain of Erica's death pulled at him hard.

"You know, I've read your file, I watched the video of you in Alaska, and that's the one thing I know for sure about you. More than anyone I've ever met, you always seem to find a way to survive."

EPILOGUE

Donovan parked the car. He'd long since switched off his cell phone, tired of it ringing. Two weeks had passed since the *North Star* had been refloated and the oil offloaded. Good weather allowed the tanker to be escorted to a dry dock facility in Portland, Oregon, where it would be repaired. All Donovan could seem to do was mourn Erica.

Amanda Sullivan had used her interviews with Donovan, as well as the exclusive footage he'd provided, to leverage herself into the voice of everything surrounding Garrick Pearce and his actions. With her journalist integrity and her exclusive access to Eco-Watch's video, she became Eco-Watch's biggest champion. Amanda had done an exceptional job keeping Donovan out of the limelight, instead, highlighting Eco-Watch, the organization. She produced a comprehensive exposé for television that aired on primetime's most prestigious and long-running news show. The installment was the most watched in the show's twenty-two-year history. The top-five news publications had featured Eco-Watch on the cover, as did nearly every other publication.

The effect had been immediate. Talk of Senate investigations evaporated as did the protests and threats. Any suspected wrong-doing on the part of Eco-Watch had been dispelled by Amanda's in-depth reporting and the visual evidence. Financial donations into Eco-Watch had tripled, and many of the foundations that had been longtime contributors had written letters of intent to continue their support. The media couldn't get enough of the man-made tsunami, which did exactly what it was designed to do; it swept the *North Star* off the reef. No oil was spilled. Because of the combined efforts of everyone involved, not a single life was lost as the wave pushed out into Prince William Sound and dissipated.

In going through Garrick's briefcase, Donovan found an envelope with a dozen more pictures of Meredith. Some were found in the public domain and had been easy to identify. In one she was holding a Geiger counter, an unidentified reactor-cooling tower serving as the backdrop. There was another of Meredith standing on a pier in the Japanese harbor of Shimonoseki, home to Japan's whaling fleet. One photo was easy for Donovan to identify: The headquarters of Newton-Boyce Industries located outside Denver, Colorado. The parent company of the mining operation that Garrick attacked in Brazil that led to his imprisonment. The remaining pictures told Donovan that Garrick may have had nine more targets in mind had he not been stopped.

In death, Garrick Pearce had become the face of extremism gone wrong. The public was outraged and condemned all who used violence against others in the name of the environment. Millions of dollars had been donated from people all over the world to assist the victims' families, and the vigilante attacks around the world slowly ceased. With Nikolett Kovarik dead, the FBI, CIA, as well as Interpol, had been able to close the books on dozens of her crimes. By tracing Garrick's movements since the Brazilian prison escape, many of the former prisoners had been recaptured and deported back to Brazil.

As promised, Hudson had forwarded the FBI's findings on Erica's movements from the hospital in Anchorage to the shootout in California. Donovan still couldn't fathom how she found the strength to do what she did. Despite her gunshot wound, injured ribs, and near drowning, once the doctor had stitched her up, she used the chaos of the emergency room to lift a woman's credit cards and cash, plus her driver's license. They were close in age, both were blond—it was enough. She called William to warn him, then using a public computer, she booked a round-trip ticket from Anchorage to Los Angeles. She found a cab, bought some clothes, changed, and went to the Anchorage airport and boarded the flight.

A flight attendant told authorities that Erica slept for the entire trip to Los Angeles. Once on the ground in California, she rented a car and drove straight to the Stratton house. The gun she used to kill Nikolett was one she'd taken from a dead bodyguard. Donovan knew the rest. Each time he thought of her journey, he relived her dedication to her promise and missed her even more.

Buck and Janie were both expected to recover fully from their injuries. Buck was in Virginia, resting at home. Donovan provided round-the-clock care so that he could rehab at the pace the former SEAL demanded. Janie had become an instant celebrity for her exceptional flying skills in the face of the monstrous wave. She'd gladly taken the first-class ticket Eco-Watch provided to recuperate from her concussion and broken elbow at home in Australia. William had fully recovered from his ordeal at the hands of Garrick and Nikolett. Donovan knew better than anyone the elder statesman was far tougher than he looked.

Lauren and Abigail were in Washington, staying at the house in Centreville; Lauren's only condition: that he *not* be there. From what William had passed on, her debriefing with the CIA and Department of Justice hadn't been going well. Lauren had made some powerful people very unhappy with her decision to withhold information regarding Erica Covington. There was also the death of the CIA agent in Paris as well her continued involvement with Mossad. Donovan had no problem grasping the fact that he was to blame for Lauren's current situation. As the hearings intensified, he'd finally swung into action, and using influential inside sources, he brokered a backroom deal with the CIA on Lauren's behalf. In return for a full pardon and reinstatement of all of her previous rights and privileges, Donovan provided the CIA with the password that Erica had given him, *Neptun Drezack*: German for Neptune Trident. Lauren in turn, handed over the files, and in that instant, her problems vanished.

Donovan gave a great deal of thought to what Garrick had told him about the people responsible for the attack on Erica and her friends in Southern California. It was Donovan's belief that

Mossad had learned Erica was alive and had taken steps to eliminate her. Donovan felt no remorse in the fact that he and Erica had killed two of the men sent to kidnap her. In his mind, turning over the files from the clinic served as payback for Mossad's actions.

He Skyped with Abigail almost every day and, thankfully, his daughter seemed to bounce back to normal. He and Lauren had yet to discuss all of the events that had transpired. They agreed there would come a day, but the fact they were still talking was enough for Donovan. In his mind it wasn't over until someone quit.

Eco-Watch had not only survived, it had flourished, which made it easy for Donovan to leave Michael in charge and take an indefinite leave of absence. He'd packed a bag, chartered a jet, and flown to Missoula, Montana, where he rented a car, drove south, and spent a few days surveying the area. He leased a comfortable, furnished, log cabin on the West Fork of the Bitterroot River. It was time to take a much-needed break. Once the paperwork on the cabin was complete, he'd flown to Seattle, rented another car, and returned to Anacortes to take care of one last detail.

He'd completed the arrangements several days ago, and as he sat in the car at the marina, he was flooded with memories of Erica. He'd driven past the sporting goods store, the restaurant where they'd had dinner. This was the last place he'd seen her truly happy, maybe the only time he'd ever seen her when she wasn't scared and on the run.

He glanced at his watch. It was time. He opened the car door and from the trunk, he retrieved a duffel bag and his overnight bag and started for the dock.

"You're not an easy man to find," a voice called out.

Donovan instantly recognized the voice, but couldn't believe his ears. He turned, and walking toward him was Stephanie Van-Gelder. He could see her smile, the happiness in her eyes as she neared. He set his things down and they hugged.

"I didn't know anyone was looking for me." Donovan said as his elation at seeing her became clouded with suspicion. "How did you find me? Or maybe the better question is why did you find me?"

"William and Lauren are both worried. Lauren finally filled me in on everything that happened from the time you met Erica in California, until the moment you hung up on her after killing Garrick."

"Lauren told you *her* version of everything, and how in the hell does Lauren know I'm here?"

"She knows the different names you have at your disposal, and from that, it was easy to follow the money trail from Montana to Seattle, and then here. I volunteered to fly out. She's worried about you and she's so sorry about what she said regarding Erica."

"I'm over it," Donovan shrugged. "That was a difficult day for everyone."

"I saw you, hell the entire world saw you save Erica from drowning. Hanging from a helicopter over the ocean, two things I happen to know you hate. From that act alone, I can only guess what she meant to you."

"I'm fine."

"You're like an older brother to me. I've known you long enough to know you're hurting. I'm here as someone who loves you and is worried about you. Why in the world are you at a marina? You hate boats."

"Erica didn't." Donovan said and gestured to the duffel bag. "I have her ashes. She didn't have any family, so I made all the arrangements. There's a boat waiting."

"Oh, Donovan, I didn't know. I'm sorry."

Donovan hadn't realized until he'd said Erica's name aloud how hard this was going to be. Of all the people in the world, perhaps Stephanie was exactly the person he needed right now. He didn't have to hide anything from her.

"Would you care for some company?" She asked, as if she'd sensed his sudden vulnerability.

"A friend might be nice."

"What's the plan?"

"We're going to Friday Harbor to pick up a priest. Then we're sailing out into Haro Strait for a small ceremony at sunset and spread her ashes into the sea. After that, we drop the priest back off at Friday Harbor, and as we cruise back here, we're going to have dinner. I'm going to crack the seal on a very expensive bottle of single cask whisky. After that I have no real plans."

"The crew knows all about this?"

"Yeah, they're a local husband and wife. He's the captain and she's the first mate and chef."

"Here we are," Donovan said as he pointed to a boat moored at the end of the dock.

"Really?" Stephanie said when she saw the size of the yacht. "It's huge."

"It's a long story, part of Erica's story." Donovan whispered. "She and I stole a boat from this very harbor the night we snuck into Canada. It was the night she told me that she was most at peace when she was sailing these waters. She loved the mix of the salt air and pine trees, the presence of all of the wildlife, from the whales to the smallest sea birds. She admitted that in another life she may have been a mariner. She said she hoped one day to spend all of her time up here. It was maybe the one and only time I ever saw her truly happy. Anyway, when I inquired about chartering, everything seemed small and unworthy, so in the end, I bought the biggest boat for sale in the area. It's a fifty-five-foot Nordhavn. I named it *Erica's Dream*, I wanted her sendoff to be perfect."

The captain and his wife greeted them, introductions were made and they cast off the boat and got underway. They followed the same route from the harbor as he and Erica had done that dark night. In the daylight there were other boats, gulls wheeling in the perfect blue sky. In the updraft created by the Cap Santé peak, he caught sight of a bald eagle riding the wind. Across the bay was the Huntington tanker, *Hercules*. She rode at anchor, waiting to offload her cargo of Alaskan crude oil. He and Stephanie climbed up to the flying bridge, sipping coffee, sitting together on the sofa. Donovan felt the familiar trepidation as the deck swayed beneath his feet in the mild swells, but somehow having sailed these waters with Erica it wasn't as acute as usual. He silently gave her the credit.

"You seem surprisingly positive. Are you really okay?" Stephanie asked.

"Not really," Donovan stopped and found her eyes with his own. "The hardest people to lose are the ones you feel like you could have saved. I should have been better prepared for someone like Garrick; too many died because I was complacent. I'm the only one who understands all the distant and sometimes deadly echoes from the past that can intersect and collide with the present. I should have been informed the minute Garrick escaped from prison and been in a position to deal with him. Instead, he killed a lot of innocent people and nearly destroyed everything I've built while I tried to catch up to him. Erica and a great many others died because of my shortsightedness."

"Garrick killed those people, not you, and in terms of Erica, how could you have known she was headed to California?"

"When I pulled her out of Prince William Sound, I could see the burns on her skin where she'd been tortured. I should have stopped to consider everything she would have told Garrick and what it could have meant."

"Weren't you trying to stop a runaway supertanker?"

"There's no excuse. She and I'd made a promise to each other that if something happened to one of us, the other would kill Garrick and Nikolett. At that point, she knew the truth about my past and understood why I didn't want Garrick captured. I stopped hunting Garrick when I stayed on the *North Star*, she didn't let anything stop her—she fulfilled her promise."

"She was a brave woman. I understand why you miss her, but the choices she made were hers. She, too, had a vested interest in seeing Garrick and Nikolett dead, same as you."

"I know, and I'm sure her reasons grew after being captured and shot. I keep thinking about the time she spent while she was being held. Being tortured, she no doubt told Garrick what he wanted to know. One of those questions was how to get to William. When she left the hospital, I wasn't there, and she couldn't reach me, but she could warn William. She knew what she'd been forced to tell Garrick, what he was planning, and where she could find him. It must have felt to her that she was the only one left to finish what we'd started. So, yes, I feel guilt over her death."

Stephanie leaned in and hugged him. "She sounds like an exceptional woman. It's her day and I'm happy to listen. Start at the beginning, I want to hear everything. How did you first meet her?"

Through misty eyes, Donovan smiled at the memory. "I was driving John's Porsche and had just broken every traffic rule ever written to get to her. When I pulled into a restaurant parking lot in Laguna Hills, she walked up, pointed a gun at me, and demanded to see my identification."

"I like her already," Stephanie said. "Then what happened?"

"I told her I had a gun, too, and to get in." Donovan smiled briefly at the memory. "I've only been in love with two women in my entire life. I wasn't in love with Erica, but I loved what she showed me. I was drawn to her almost from the start. She was smart, capable, her strength and resolve was extraordinary. She was a survivor. We had a lot in common, and in the end, she kept her promise to me. I can't stand the fact that she's gone. There are so many things that needed to be said."

"What would you say to her if she were here?"

"I'd thank her. She changed me with everything we went through. I was forced to trust her—something I don't always do very well, but it worked. Erica showed me what I was capable of, a single glimpse of a different pattern of behavior. Maybe I can take what I learned and use it with Lauren and Abigail. I may never be able to be anything other than who I am, but Erica gave me something to strive for, something that might make me a better husband and father, a better person. For that, I'll always be thankful."

"I wish I'd met her." Stephanie put her head on his shoulder. "I believe she's here, in spirit, and you just gave her about the most beautiful eulogy a person could ever receive."

CPSIA information can be obtained
at www.ICGtesting.com
Printed in the USA
LVOW10s0038160217
524411LV00002B/13/P